VEIL *of the*
DESERTERS

VEIL *of the* DESERTERS

Bloodsounder's Arc Book Two

JEFF SALYARDS

NIGHT SHADE BOOKS

NEW YORK

Night Shade books may be purchased in bulk at special discounts for sales promotion, corporate gifts, fund-raising, or educational purposes. Special editions can also be created to specifications. For details, contact the Special Sales Department, Night Shade Books, 307 West 36th Street, 11th Floor, New York, NY 10018 or info@skyhorsepublishing.com.
Night Shade Books™ is a trademark of Skyhorse Publishing, Inc.®, a Delaware corporation.

Visit our website at www.nightshadebooks.com.
10 9 8 7 6 5 4 3 2 1
Library of Congress Cataloging-in-Publication Data
Salyards, Jeff.
Veil of the deserters : Bloodsounder's arc book two / Jeff Salyards.
    pages cm -- (Bloodsounder's arc ; 2)
ISBN 978-1-59780-490-5 (hardback)
1. Scribes--Fiction. 2. Soldiers--Fiction. 3. Fantasy fiction. I. Title.
PS3619.A44266V35 2014
813.6--dc23

                    2014008785

Printed in the United States of America

To Jane, who always treated me as her own flesh and blood.

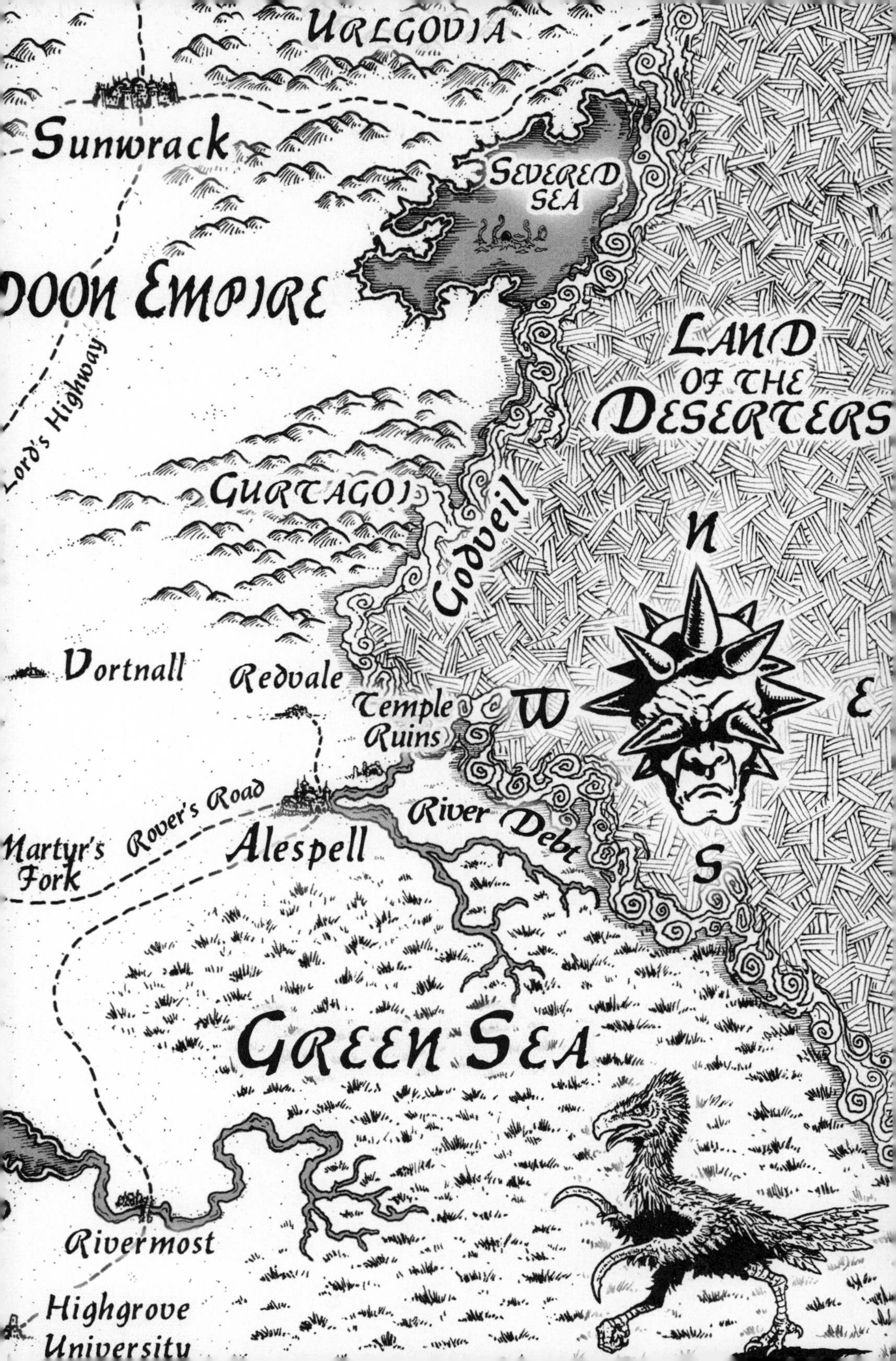

URLGOVIA

Sunwrack

DOON EMPIRE

SEVERED
SEA

LAND
OF THE
DESERTERS

Lord's Highway

GURTAGON

Godveil

Vortnall

Redvale

Temple
Ruins

W

N

E

S

Rover's Road

Martyr's
Fork

Alespell

River Debt

GREEN SEA

Rivermost

Highgrove
University

VEIL *of the*
DESERTERS

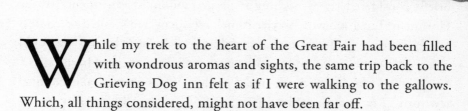

While my trek to the heart of the Great Fair had been filled with wondrous aromas and sights, the same trip back to the Grieving Dog inn felt as if I were walking to the gallows. Which, all things considered, might not have been far off.

Walking to the bazaar, I'd noticed the rich smells of breads and meats and cook fires burning; returning, only the strong reek of urine emanating from alleyways, hot and rancid; before, I'd been so buoyed by my new-found sense of freedom, I failed to notice just how powerful and heinous the stench was. So, too, I'd felt a lightness in my step as I left the Syldoon behind to go exploring; heading back to the Dog, it was now mud, horse and dog feces, and other sucking sludge I couldn't place, all trying to steal a shoe or spoil the hose. Odorous, odious quicksand.

Even the faces and voices took on a new cast. Where I'd seen and heard joy, mirth, and wonder on the streets on my way to the bazaar, I now saw irritation as someone felt at how light their purse had become, or disgust on a fiefholder's face at having to rub shoulders with his lessers, or the dull blankness the whores wore like masks as they moved among the throng halfheartedly trying to lure patrons to one establishment or the other, or the shrill shout of a mother scolding her disobedient children.

The journey both ways was identical—surely not much could have changed in so short a time—but my mood and perceptions couldn't have been more different. Amazing how one small thing could utterly transform one's perception of the world. The bruised face of the young Hornman in the crowd, the mutual recognition, him darting off, and the realization that urging Braylar to spare his life in the grass might prove to be everyone's undoing. It was enough to ruin a perfectly good day, and possibly ensure there weren't many more to follow, good or bad.

I forced one foot in front of the other, each heavier than the last, as I was filled with dread and my stomach rolled and heaved the closer I got. I was committed to returning to the Grieving Dog and telling the captain what I'd seen. He'd spin off into a rage, no doubt. And I would bear the brunt of it. Justifiably, as it happened. But the alternatives were less pleasant. I wasn't about to run to the baron or to try to flee Alespell. Seeing the captain wouldn't end well, but those routes only led to worse. I briefly considered saying nothing at all, pretending I hadn't identified the Hornman. But I knew if Braylar somehow discovered I failed to confess what I'd seen, as unlikely as that possibility might have been, that would surely only result in my body adding to the momentous stink in the alleys.

Still, as I closed in on the inn, I couldn't make myself take the final few turns. I moved off in the other direction, hoping the pressure on my chest might lighten, that my heart might stop beating like a frenzied bird in a cage. I decided to follow the crowd, at least for a little bit, to ride the jetty and surge wherever it took me, and forget all of this for a time, no matter how short. I wasn't ready to deliver the news of what I'd seen. Not yet. Moving, moving was the key.

After heading to the thoroughfare, it didn't take long for me to get my wish, as I was carried along almost immediately. I should have been hungry or thirsty—I hadn't even finished the ale and scallops I'd choked on earlier—but I couldn't really think of eating just then—my stomach felt rebellious and angry. I was perfectly content to follow the ever-shifting currents of humanity around me, barely paying attention to landmarks or the chipped enameled bars on the walls. Even without anything stronger than water in my belly, I would probably have trouble finding my way back to the Dog, but at that moment, I just didn't care.

I moved along like that, following the crowd, and when it threatened to thin as I reached side streets or residential neighborhoods, I turned until I found another press moving in a different direction. Even with so many having returned to their homesteads and farms, and the street stalls pulling their small leather and faded canvas awnings down, there was still an impressive number of people in attendance, so it wasn't difficult to find new groups to carry me somewhere, anywhere.

As I entered a plaza, I heard a cacophony of sounds—squeals of delight, and possibly fear (it was difficult to determine), as well as a great deal of murmuring, the kind where people turn to the person next to them and speak with animation, but still quietly, as if they are anxious as well as excited or in awe. A single voice shouting above the din with a practiced pitch of some kind. And there was periodically something else. An alien sound, something between a piercing screech and a roar that made your stomach clench and your breath catch, forcing all the other noise to stop momentarily before it slowly built up again.

The people had formed a fairly dense circle around the center of the plaza. Driven by something I couldn't quite name just then, I pushed my way forward in a fashion Mulldoos might have been proud of, though I lacked the bulk to separate people quickly, and earned curses and glares when people realized it was only a reedy lad trying to get closer. Though I had never heard sounds like those coming from the center of the plaza before, I somehow knew what was making them, and as I made out the top of a tall cage, I was positive I was right.

Though all the certainty in the world didn't prepare me for what I found.

Every time I'd heard a monster story as a child, I'd tried to imagine if the beast's eyes glowed like lanterns, if it was foul like dung or something worse, what kind of noise its claws would make scuffling across the wooden planks of the inn or in the dirt just behind me in the fields, and especially what kind of roar or outburst it made. Craning my neck to look over folks in front of me, I was about to glimpse my first monster in the flesh.

There was a large, extremely tall cage forming a rectangle, roughly sixty feet by ninety. In the far corner, an opening leading to a caged ramp up to a robust wagon, with bars for walls and a solid wooden roof, and no beasts of burden attached to pull it. There was another large, flatbed wagon a little further away, yoked to six oxen that were also decidedly nervous.

On one side of the cage, there was a gate, locked tight, and a short caged corridor leading to a smaller rectangular cage in the interior of the larger one. That's when I saw the creature, circling that small caged area in the middle, though it was presently unoccupied.

It was a massive bird, at least eight or nine feet tall, with mottled yellow and black feathers, a thick, muscular neck, and a head nearly as large as a horse's with that dense looking beak at the front.

Just as Lloi had described, it had no wings, but instead, thin feathered limbs ending in three talons, two very short, with a much longer curved talon between that was like a bone scythe blade. Its legs were muscular and stout as tree trunks, and led down to huge talons that kicked up dust as it paced around the cage, its small black eyes staring out at the crowd of onlookers.

The hawker was circling as well, though of course on the outside of the cage, a leather vest over his oiled chest, hair and forked beard equally oiled, nose and ears housing countless hoops and studs glinting in the setting sun, and a long goad in one hand. Two younger versions of himself, different only in that they had stubble rather than a full beard, and their pants were puffier, also moved around the edge of the crowd, one with a bucket of meat, the other with a bucket for collecting coins.

Though certainly not a Grass Dog, it appeared the hawker was trying to approximate one, and he called out, "This is a genuine ripper, my lords and ladies. The most dangerous predator on the Green Sea. I've witnessed it kill a horse in one blow, ripping its throat out in the entirety."

He waited as the crowd murmured their appreciation, then continued, "And here is the chance you've been waiting for. For a mere pittance, you can feed the beasts from the safety of the outside of the cage. But for those more stalwart among you," he gestured at the cage in the middle with his goad, "you can experience coming to grips with the ripper, to feel what it is to be prey in your final moments before being torn to shreds." Several in the crowd gasped, and he smiled, showing several silver teeth. "Fear not—though beast of prodigious strength and speed, no ripper can break the bars, nor jump them. You would be safe. And yet, you would have an experience unlike any other." He raised his voice still louder, "So, who among you will feed the beast, whose thirst for blood cannot be slaked." He looked at the ripper and then back to the crowd. "And who among you will brave the inner cage? You?" He pointed the goad at a terrified-looking girl. "Or you?" to a man a few rows back. "Or you, young sir?" He pointed at a farmer who had his girl pulled tight to his side.

After a brief hesitation, a boy ran up, dropping a coin in the bucket. The hawker's son stuck a piece of raw meat on the end of a long two-pronged fork, issued some instructions, though they must have only amounted to, "Don't stick your arm inside," and then moved aside as the boy walked slowly up to the cage, the meat held before him, though not high enough for me to see.

He stood several feet from the bars, the meat barely sticking in. The ripper, though, didn't need much encouragement. In two quick strides, it crossed the whole cage with surprising speed. The boy jumped back, dropping the fork as the crowd erupted in laughter, and the ripper cut it short, raising its beak and issuing another shriek sharp enough to still blood. The crowd again murmured, as the hawker encouraged the boy to stick the meat in again. "The bars protect you, boy! Master yourself and feed the beast!"

The boy stepped forward, as a few other boys hooted from the crowd. He stuck the meat through the bars and the ripper whirled around and snatched it from the tongs, nearly pulling the fork through as well.

The crowd cheered. Pale and shaken, the boy raised his arm, as if he had triumphed over some superior foe, or cheated death itself.

Then one of the boy's friends, clearly trying to show him up, marched up to the hawker's son with the buckets and asked, loudly enough for all to hear, "How much to go inside?"

It would have been more inspiring if his voice hadn't cracked, or if his eyes hadn't been obscured by disheveled hair, but still, a passable bit of bravado. I'm not sure when lads are more stupid—trying to impress their own sex or the other. Either way, the crowd gave appreciative applause, as if this were a scripted puppet theatre and not a boy willingly putting himself as close as possible to a dire threat.

The hawker clapped twice. "Very good, very good! This way, my boy, this way!" He led the lad to the cage corridor and unlocked the gate. The ripper didn't seem to be paying much attention to the idiot boy as the hawker handed him a long fork with a large chunk of bloody meat on the end. "Now mind, boy, once you're in there, stay well back from the bars."

The youth snatched the fork. "I'll mind whatever I plaguing have a mind to mind, old man. Don't tell me nothing."

Something rippled across the hawker's face so quickly I wasn't sure if it was simply the play of shadows or anger, but if the latter, the presence of a paying audience made it disappear in an instant. He bowed. "As you will, young sir. Still, my sons will be close by, never fear."

"Never do," the boy replied, taking a few steps down the caged corridor, the first two full of the same foolishness youth can summon without any exertion at all, but the third a bit more halting as the ripper looked at him from across the other side of the enclosure, as if curious. Or measuring. The boy saw that, felt that, and stalled.

The hawker called out, "To the center, boy, the center. Safer there. Move to the center, and feed it from there."

With the ripper looking directly at him, dark eyes tender as molten stones, and the reality perhaps sinking in a bit, the boy hurried along, no longer concerned with impressing anyone just then, the hawker's sons just behind him.

The ripper opened its huge beak, and I was expecting another baleful screech, but instead it only let out a long, slow hiss and continued tracking the boy as he moved. The youth stepped into the larger caged area in the middle and then stood there, staring back at this creature that surely seemed much more imposing and deadly real than it had when he was standing among other stupid boys in the crowd.

The hawker, now walking around the perimeter of the enclosure again, yelled, "The meat, boy. Step to the bars—close, but not too close—and stick it out there for the beast. Help him, Askill." The boy didn't respond, standing still in the cage, arms at his sides as if tied there, as the hawker's larger son stepped alongside and tried to show him how to proceed while the other watched the ripper watching them.

A few of the boy's friends called out from the crowd, though it was hard to tell if it was encouragement or derision. Likely some of both.

The boy looked back at the audience, now seeming even younger than his years, clearly wishing he'd held his tongue and maintained his place. But he stepped closer to the bars, careful to listen to Askill's advice though, and very slowly raised the fork and stuck it out a foot, the meat dangling on the end.

I was wondering what animal it once belonged to when the ripper raised its head, its small talons clicking against the much longer scythe claw at the end of those thin limbs, as it alternated staring directly at the boy, then to what he was holding just outside the bars, almost as if the creature was surveying and calculating, assessing the boy to determine how powerful it was. Or quick.

It took a few steps toward the center, eyes again locked with the boy's, who continued holding the fork out between two bars. And then, as if it had transfixed the boy and rooted him to the spot, it took three strides, so long and unexpected and blinding fast it was difficult to believe. One instant it was twenty paces from the cage in the middle, and the next, just outside the bars, its beak clamped down on the fork.

The ripper jerked its large head sideways, but instead of letting go of the fork as he'd probably been instructed, the boy held on and he was pulled into the bars, slamming into them with his shoulder. He finally released the handle, but it was too late—the ripper's thin arms snaked between the bars and small talons fastened on the boy's wrist. He screamed then, and the hawker's sons stepped forward with their goads, but couldn't move quickly enough. The ripper pulled the boy's arm through the bars, dropping the fork from its maw as the huge beak crushed down on the forearm between its talons.

Askill and his brother jabbed their goads into the ripper's side, but it knocked one free with the scythe talon on the other limb and ripped it free. Askill jumped back, as the ripper ignored the other brother's goad, biting down twice, snapping bones and rending flesh while its prey screamed. And then the boy fell back into the smaller hawker's son, knocking him and his goad back as blood pulsed out of the severed forearm.

The ripper jumped away from the cage out of the reach of any more goading, and then crunched the hand in its beak twice before swallowing it.

Where the crowd had mostly been watching in hushed tones, aside from a few boys who occasionally called out taunts, now noise erupted everywhere. Yelling, cries for the city watch, a final scream from the boy before he fell back in the dirt, staring at the blood pumping out of his stump, Askill yelling for his father, the other covering up the wound with his tunic and trying to staunch the flow as much as possible, looking around for help.

Seeing that foolish boy cradling his wrist, in shock that it no longer ended in his hand, which was now dissolving in a ripper's gullet, all I could think of was how Lloi had been mutilated and reduced herself. I wondered how her family had done it, and if she had looked at the small bloody nubs after, in shock that she no longer had real fingers, even though she probably knew the punishment was coming. Can you ever be prepared to have some part of you lopped off forever? Had she accepted her fate, or had she fought and had to be restrained by those she once considered kin? Given what I'd known of her, I suspected she fought hard and bloodied some folks of her own before the deed was done.

I wondered what she would have made about this captive ripper and the Anjurian and his boys who saw fit to wheel it from city to city, a dangerous attraction for those seeking cheap thrills. Would she have hated him, wished him harm? Probably not—she didn't even hate her own people who'd mistreated her so.

But that didn't stop me. The whole scene made me angry, and I had the impulse to shout at the keeper that he was a fraud and a villain, that it was him who deserved to lose a limb. He hadn't mutilated the boy himself, but he might as well have, and he certainly profited. For a mad moment, I wondered—if I could somehow open the cage, would the beast attack him, its captor and tormentor? Or would it simply run, or rip open some other innocent nearby?

It struck me then how stupid that impulse to yell at the keeper was, not only because it would accomplish nothing, because there was so much commotion no one could have even heard me, but even if they could over the roar, it would only draw attention to myself. And this realization was followed by just how stupid I was being in general.

Begging Braylar to spare the young Hornman in the grass? Stupid. Not returning to the Grieving Dog immediately once I recognized him at the Fair? Compounded stupidity. And maybe leaving Rivermost with the Syldoon was the most exceptionally stupid thing I'd ever done. But I'd done it. There it was. It might have been impossible to undo. So there was nothing left to do but head to the Dog and try to make the best of things.

I left the plaza, heart heavy, stomach fluttering, not looking back at the bloody scene behind me, and made my way back to the inn. My feet were moving slowly, even if I was finally headed in the right direction.

Finally standing before the front entrance to the Grieving Dog, I couldn't quite make myself take the final steps inside. I thought about circling the building once or twice to build up courage, but that seemed ridiculous. Still, I stood there, berating myself for not moving. It wasn't simply fear of reprisal—I doubted my mercy (misguided as it was turning out to be) would cause the captain to do more than give me a verbal lashing, and given his peculiar condition, I might even escape that. Temporarily, at least. After all, he'd been the one holding the crossbow in the Green Sea, not me. It was his decision to spare the Hornman, even if I'd been the one who somehow convinced him. He had to recognize some culpability. Well, maybe not. But either way, it wasn't even imagined wrath that gave me pause. It was the thought that my admission would likely cost me whatever small measure of esteem I'd attained by saving his life at the temple.

The fact that I was overwrought about potentially losing the limited respect of a man who was a scheming manipulator actually irked and emboldened me. I knocked the shit and muck off my boots as best I could, stepped through the front door, and walked up the stairs. I'd made my choice to alert Braylar—however it played out after that was how it played out. There was nothing to be gained by perseverating.

Heading down the hall, I saw Mulldoos and Vendurro standing outside the door to the common quarters. They were close together, foreheads almost touching, and Mulldoos's huge paw was wrapped around the back of Vendurro's neck, holding him there as he spoke quietly to the younger man. I couldn't make out the words, which was all for the best, as the scene was clearly intimate, and a display of affection that I would never have suspected from Mulldoos. I was about to turn around and leave them to it when Vendurro nodded twice, and Mulldoos gave the smaller Syldoon a hard clap on the back, then turned and noticed me there. Whatever tenderness was on display was immediately replaced by a scowl.

Mulldoos looked at Vendurro and said, "Tell Cap I'm on it." He started down the narrow hall, limping noticeably, clearly expecting me to make way, which I did without a word. He stopped next to me as I pressed up against a wall, and he moved in closer, and I couldn't help but remember Vendurro doing the same thing when we first met, only he was on horse, and yet Mulldoos on foot was somehow twice as terrifying. "Got a real talent for being where you ought not to, and not being where you should. This a scribbler thing, or is being a burning arrow in the ass just something particular to you?"

The words flew out of my mouth before I had a chance to consider them, "Well, I can't presume to speak for the entire chronicling profession, so I suppose it's just me. Or just you who thinks so." A wrinkle bridged his pale brows as some surprise crossed his face, and then an instant later Mulldoos elbowed me hard just below the sternum. I doubled over, grabbing onto his elbow to hold myself up, which also proved to be a mistake, as be backed up and I fell onto my hands and knees, gasping for breath that was nowhere to be found.

He leaned over and said, "Gless, dead. Lloi, deader. Hew, me, and Cap, injured plenty good. What you got going on right now, that thing filling you with a queer panic, making your eyes water, making you feel like whatever garlicky business you got in your stomach is about to come rushing back up, that ain't nothing at all." He patted the pommel of the big falchion on his hip. "Count yourself lucky, scribbler. Real lucky."

Mulldoos headed down the stairs as I knelt there holding my stomach, hugging myself. Clearly, he knew how to hit a man in just the right spot, because he was right about all of the symptoms, only he neglected to mention the vision going blurry as I nearly passed out before sputtering as I finally felt my lungs start working again.

I coughed a few times, and suddenly saw a hand in front of my face. For a moment, I feared Mulldoos had returned to deliver some more good luck, but I looked up and saw Vendurro there. He offered his hand again, which I gladly accepted, and he helped me to my feet.

"Seen him do that a time or ten. Been on the receiving end more than twice. No man takes you down harder than Mulldoos. Sharp elbows, he's got. Sharp."

I tried to straighten, felt my stomach muscles spasm, nearly retched, waited until it passed, then tried again. My ribs were on fire from one tip to the next, but Mulldoos had been right about that, too—no lasting damage. "Why. . . " I waited for some more breath to come back into my lungs, and Vendurro waited with me until I could breathe without sputtering. "What did I do. . . why is he so angry with me?"

Vendurro had a small smile, not nearly as big and toothy as I'd come to expect, but a smile nonetheless. "Oh, wouldn't say it's specific to you none. Well, no more than most things and people. The lieutenant, if he's not angry at one thing, he's angrier at something else. But just now, I'd say it wasn't so much what you done, but what you didn't do. You had no armor, you got no training, and yet you come out of that scrape in the skinny trees without much of a scratch to speak of. Now, I heard Hewspear say you handled yourself better than you had any right to in there, and stood when most would have pissed themselves and run like rabbits.

"But Mulldoos, all he sees is someone that survived that got no real right surviving when those who maybe should have lived just didn't. Nothing personal, though."

"Oh, no," I was finally able to speak without burning in my belly, "nothing personal. He just wishes it was me dead, instead of Tomner, or Gless—"

Vendurro's smile disappeared again as I stopped myself, but too late. I tried to think of something that might act as a balm, but only stumbled some more, "I'm sorry, Vendurro. I didn't, that is, I didn't mean. . . "

He ran a hand through his thick head of hair. "It's alright, bookmaster. But you hit on the thing square. Cap ain't the only one that takes losses hard. And I ain't meaning the battles, neither. We either won that or scrapped to a draw, depending on who's keeping tally. But the men. Losing the men. That rubs them both raw. I had a few men under me, back when we were a big company, full squad. Few of them, two younger, two older. But we weren't at war with nobody just then, so only got into a couple skirmishes, not much chance of anybody dying on my watch. So I can't pretend to know what it's like for them, not real like. But I've seen them, and Hew, too, all three, seen them lose men, and it's a hard, bitter thing, it is."

Vendurro let out a long slow breath. "So it's no kind of personal. Just rankles the lieutenant you lived when men he trained, knew for years, didn't make it back."

It was difficult to tell if he wanted to say more or wished he'd said nothing at all, so I left him to it, not wanting to interrupt if he truly wanted to go on, not wanting to press him if he didn't. But he wasn't done. Though you would have thought he was the one who'd just been punched in the gut by how halting it came. "I shouldn't tell you to keep your mouth shut with Mulldoos. I mean, it's sound advice and all, but I know you probably won't heed it none anyway, and I didn't much neither. Still don't know when to clamp shut half the time. I got myself in a ton of trouble over the years with my flapping yap. Thing of it is, Gless, he'd get me out of those scrapes when my mouth got to running faster than my brain. Always had my back, he did. Counted on that, which was half the reason I'd let my mouth go on like I did. Now. . . "

He trailed off, and there was an awkward pause that I broke by saying, "Mulldoos, was he. . . that is, when I came up on the landing, it looked like he was talking to you about Glesswik."

Vendurro nodded slowly. "Yup. That he was."

I waited quietly, figuring if he felt comfortable enough to offer more, he would. Vendurro stared off down the hall, past my shoulder, as if he expected Mulldoos to come back and spare him. Or maybe Glesswik. Finally, just when I was about to excuse myself and proceed to Captain Killcoin's room, Vendurro said, "The thing of it is, soldiers lose other soldiers. Part and parcel of the deal. No getting around it or prettying it up. And the Syldoon more than most, on account of us being full timers. Always on campaign, or on patrol, or invading, or repulsing, or some action or other. Not much time to watch the moss grow, if you see what I'm saying.

"So sooner or later—and mostly on the sooner—you see a Towermate or three go down. Just the Syldoon way. You lose your brothers. And there's nothing worse than that, because there's no tighter unit in the known world than a Syldoon Tower. So, it ain't never easy when it happens. But Gless and me. . . " his forehead wrinkled. "You got any brothers?"

I had no siblings that I knew of, though there were likely some out there. But I shook my head.

He smiled again, small and sad. "Shame, that. Man ought to have a brother or two. But us, the Syldoon, the boys in our Tower, we are brothers, no less than those of blood. Maybe more. And Gless and me were the closest. Just never figured on seeing him go down, is all. Never figured on that." He trailed off, staring down the hallways again.

I felt as if I should put my hand on his shoulder, or offer some condolence or other, but gestures and words both felt hollow, clumsy, even if delivered sincerely. So, hoping to at least lead him away from his grief rather than toward it, I said, "And did whatever Mulldoos say, did it help any?"

Vendurro rubbed the back of his neck, as if remembering Mulldoos's huge hand there, and his eyes got a touch wetter. "Told me to grieve my grief—weren't nothing wrong with it—but then put to it in the ground and armor back up, because my other brothers needed me alert. And we were running mighty thin on quality sergeants just now." He laughed a little, and then, unexpectedly, laughed some more. "Not one for ornate speeches, Mulldoos. But he has the right of it."

I nearly pointed out it had only been a day, and such a recent wound would need time to close and heal, but I was clearly no soldier, so maybe Mulldoos was correct. With lives in the balance, maybe performing your duties with a grief-stricken heart wasn't the best idea, or at least the safest. Who was I to suggest he should allow himself a heavy heart?

It made me glad I was no soldier. It seemed a rough, rough world.

I did put my hand on his shoulder then, impulsively, and said, "I can't pretend to know what it's like to have a brother, let alone lose one." And then, pulling my hand away, added lamely, "I'm sorry."

Vendurro smiled again. "Thanks, Arkamondos. Gless was a mean bastard, and always looking for a way out of a job if he could find it. Figures he'd leave me with double duty."

I nodded. "You can call me Arki. No one did, before the captain that is, but I'm getting used to it now. And it's far better than quillmonkey, scribbler, or—" we both said the next in unison, "horsecunt." And then we laughed together as well.

But like sun obscured by clouds, that merriment left almost as fast. And these clouds seemed thicker and slower to move past than the last bank. Again, I didn't want to intrude, so waited him out.

After staring at his feet for a minute, Vendurro said, "Told you he was a shit husband too, didn't I? Hardly there at all, especially the last few years with us campaigning all over Anjuria. Even before, when we were stationed in Sunwrack, he only seemed to head home long enough to father two brats of his own."

Vendurro ran his hands though his hair, shifted his weight from one leg to the next, then leaned against the wall, kicking it with his heel when he did. In that one motion, he seemed to lose ten years, but they came back just as suddenly, and brought friends. "Good lass. Leastwise, not bad. Mervulla. Native Thurvacian. Tower Commanders always telling us to settle down with the locals, make nice. Who can say what she saw in the bastard. Womenfolk are queer as cats."

He pressed his head back into the wood, closed his eyes. "The Syldoon, they'll provide something. For her, and her young, on account of the marriage at all. And she got some income. They owned some olive orchards, rented the land out to those that worked them. So, seeing as she's from the capital herself, can't see her selling. Still collect the rents, most like. So she won't need the bread line or to turn prostitute. But still."

"Bread line? Prostitute?"

"Yep. Plenty of widows got no livelihood to call their own, nor chance to make one after a certain age. Lose their men, lose their coin. Only options are charity or selling what wares the gods gave you. Syldoon widows luckier in that respect. We take care of our own.

"Still, whatever she felt for Gless, can't see her liking the news she's a fresh widow none. Can't see nobody liking that news, less they hated a fellow. And he might have been a bastard, but he wasn't totally wanting for good qualities. On the whole. So can't see her liking that news much at all."

"And you. . . you have to deliver it? You have to be the one to tell her?"

"Have to?" He banged his head and looked up at the ceiling. "Nope. Ain't no have to. But I knew him better than anybody. And she knew me some, too. So it's got to come from me. The news and the widowcoin. Got to."

Before I thought about what I was saying, the words came of their own volition. "Would you like me to go with you?"

Vendurro pulled himself slowly off the wall and looked at me. "You'd do that?"

Now that it was out there, I wished I'd thought it through first. I was sure that would be painfully awkward and. . . just painful. To witness anyway. But there was no recalling it. I nodded and he seemed to think it over before replying. "Can't ask you to do that. Not to her door. She never met you, she'd know right off something weren't right." He suddenly seemed young and small again as he added, "But if you want to head with me most of the way. And wait to down some drinks after. A lot of them. That would be something, that is, if you—"

"Of course. I'll accompany you as far you like, and I'll buy the first round or two. Well, provided the captain pays me ahead of time."

Between the offer and my halfhearted joke, he seemed in slightly better spirits. Before we dwelt on it much longer though, I asked, "Speaking of the captain, is he in his quarters?"

Vendurro replied, "Yup, that he is. Returned a while back. Told me to make sure he was left good and alone. Figure he's fighting off whatever it is he fights now that Lloi ain't here to spell him. Plus, he didn't seem like he was all too pleased about how that parley with the baron played out. Guessing you should give him some time, unless you like dodging pitchers or platters."

"Well," I replied, choosing my words carefully, "I can't say that I do. But there's something. . . that requires his attention. And I think he'll thank me for rousing him. Well, after he screams or throws something at my head."

Vendurro thought about it for a few moments, then fished the key out of his belt pouch. "Better you than me. Hoping you're right about it being all fire important, though. Getting real thin on company scribes in these parts, too." He took the last steps toward the door.

I have always been a study of the way people walk. Their posture, stride, the swing of the arms, the tilt of the head, if they are rigid or relaxed, pigeon-toed. Posture and gait can be very telling, saying a lot about what the person has endured, attitude, mood, mobility, quickness. You can usually tell a fresh limp from an old injury that the person has become so accustomed to they hardly notice.

When I met Vendurro, he strode as if each leg was trying to outdo the other in pushing him off the ground, a springy, rambunctious, youthful gait. But now, he walked as if he were twenty years older, hadn't slept in days, and was wearing lead boots. Which wasn't surprising, given his loss, but I wondered in time if he would ever fully recover that bounce, or if someone who met him in a year or two would never have the chance to see him that carefree.

Vendurro unlocked the door and I thanked him as we stepped inside. He sat down on a stool near the door after locking it again, and watched as I took a few steps toward the captain's chamber and then hesitated. Once I told Braylar what I knew, there would be no untelling it. It was tempting to walk to my room instead, or even back out to the Fair, under the pretense that I simply was following Vendurro's advice not to disturb him, but I knew if I did that I might lose the nerve to go through with it at all. So, with a quick look back at Vendurro, who shook his head and mimed ducking quickly, I knocked quietly on the captain's door.

I didn't hear anything. No raspy threats or pejoratives, no stirring at all, really. I rapped on the door again, louder this time, and waited, but still nothing. I looked back at the young sergeant, who only shrugged, and then I tried the door, expecting to find it locked. But it creaked open as I pushed. I poked my head in, ready to pull it back if anything came flying. The interior was dim, heavy curtains mostly blocking out the horn blinds and the last day's sunlight beyond them, and it took a moment for my eyes to adjust.

I called out the captain's name, and still hearing nothing, walked inside and pushed the door shut behind me. I saw his form on the bed, lying on his back, and slowly made my way closer. While the room was too dim to make out much, I saw his chest rising and falling slowly. Also that he was holding Bloodsounder with both hands on his stomach, the way a drunk might cradle the empty flask or leather bottle that had done him in.

I called out his name again, and still no response, physical or otherwise. It appeared he had sunk into his depths again, and this time without Lloi to rescue him. I sat down heavily on a bench against the wall, not worried that it scraped loudly when I did. Captain Killcoin didn't stir at all.

In the Green Sea, he said each time was a little different, that it was impossible to gauge his response to the stolen memories that must have been flooding into him now. Perhaps this condition was temporary. I was reluctant to head back to the common room to tell Vendurro—certainly he'd seen his captain laid low like this before, so it wouldn't come as a shock, but I doubted it would be welcome news either.

But from my experience in the steppe, it was unlikely I was going to do

any good sitting there. I had no skills to assist him, and my presence surely wasn't any kind of relief, even if he felt it at all. So I sat there, unsure
what to do. I waited for a while, my anxiety growing by the moment,
especially as I had little enough to distract myself with. Braylar's room
was small enough, and little had changed since we left it earlier in the
day. Someone, no doubt a terrified boy or girl, had swept up the mess and
removed the remnants of the ale, probably at Vendurro's behest. Besides
some chests and clothes on top of them, and the table and chairs near the
bed, the only other object in the room was the long container we'd lugged
and stowed away for so many days, the same that the captain appeared
determined to protect at all costs.

Looking at it, I still wondered at the whole business. Even given the
Anjurians' superstitious nature and how much stock they put in ceremony and pomp, it still seemed decidedly peculiar the absence of royal
vestments would be alarming enough to cause uproar or upheaval of any
kind. Obviously the Syldoon had several schemes in play in this region,
and the stolen vestments weren't central to their machinations. Their play
on Baron Brune and High Priest Henlester proved that, and for all I knew,
other games were being played as well.

But it still struck me as odd that they would go to such lengths to steal
and transport something that was peripheral (at best) to their major plans
here, especially since I doubted such maneuvering was going to prove all
that fruitful, and I'm sure the Syldoon soldiers in their charge must have
shared those doubts. The Boy King's reign was off to a rocky start, given that
his regent was hardly loved, and there was such contentious blood between
the young monarch and so many of his barons, something inherited from
the king so recently buried. Perhaps those inclined to be critical could
point to the missing trappings and robes as one more sign that the boy
wasn't fit to rule, or that his reign would only end in calamity. But while
I was hardly an expert on court politics, that still seemed somewhat shaky
to me. Even with all the importance attached to the rituals of ascension.

Perhaps you simply had to be Anjurian to appreciate the finer points.
Perhaps some missing robes were enough to undermine an already rickety
transition of power and title. Who could say?

I'd only read about such a transfer, as old King Xefron had reigned for
at least forty years, long enough to outlast the war with the Syldoon and

negotiate a truce, but not long enough to ensure his heir would inherit a stable kingdom or had the prowess and acuity to manage it. Were the robes and whatnot ancient? Surely they wouldn't want a new monarch to appear in public with tattered vestments, yellowed and threadbare. Hardly an inspiring image. But then again, maybe that was part of the ceremony, the cloth that so many ancestors had worn, ugly as it might have been, signifying that a legitimate succession was occurring. But just how old were they? Who had been the first to wear them? They must have been in a vastly different style and cut from the current royal fashion.

Before I'd thought it through, I found myself kneeling before the container, casting a quick look back at Braylar's unmoving form before pulling the canvas back.

A lock. Of course there was a lock. I nearly sat back down on the bench, but my curiosity was fully roused now. While a large part of me knew doing anything else was pure foolishness, I really wanted to see the vestments, just once. I would probably never have another opportunity like this. And I told myself I already knew what was inside, so there was no harm in taking a quick peek at the contents. So I walked over to the clothes, found Braylar's belts and pouches, and picked out the one that I was sure contained the long key.

I was breathing fast as I fit the key into the lock. The tumblers were well oiled, but still clicked loudly enough I worried Vendurro must have heard. But he was doubtless trying to put his grief in the ground, and surely I'd hear voices if anyone else returned.

With the lock undone, I lifted the lid, which was less well oiled, and creaked loudly. Even in the dim light, it took only a moment to realize that there weren't clothes inside at all. Not a one, not a stitch. Instead, there were countless scrolls of various sizes, some large and bound by tiny chains, others smaller and secured by leather cords, or a few with silk ribbons, and there were several cracked leather tubes that I assumed contained still more. Some scrolls had thick wooden rollers on each end, and even those had distinct differences, a few being plain and simple, others with elaborate designs carved into wood that seemed stained various colors. Some scrolls appeared to be papyrus, others thicker parchment that looked so old I feared to even breathe too close lest they crumble into dust. There were clay and waxed tablets in the container as well.

I'd been breathing fast before, but now I stopped altogether. These looked to have been gathered from a number of places, and spanned the ages. What *was* this?

"I hadn't realized the Fair was canceled today. Pity."

I dropped the lip and it slammed shut on my fingers. It was all I could do not to howl in pain.

With his voice unused for hours, it was even more coarse and raspy, but there was no mistaking the fact that Captain Killcoin was indeed awake, and not swept under the currents of stolen memories.

I pulled my fingers clear, stood up, and turned to face him. I felt like a child again, caught by my mother stealing a coin from her small purse. The blood rushed to my face, and I heard my heart pounding in my ears, both from hot embarrassment, fear, and also anger from having been deceived again. "There are no royal vestments."

Braylar was sitting up in bed and it was difficult to read his expression in that light. How he had moved so quietly, especially without rattling the chains of the flail, was a mystery. He set Bloodsounder on the bed and clapped three times, slowly. "Oh, deftly done, Arki. Truly. Caught literally red-handed—I hope it leaves a deep bruise, by the way—and you have the gall to lay an implied accusation at my feet. Very nice redirection. There might be hope for you yet."

Shame, fear, and anger coiled tighter. With my voice as controlled as I could make it to mask all three, I asked, "Do you ever tell the truth?"

He laughed then, followed immediately by a cough. "As seldom as I can manage, and only when other recourses are exhausted. Or as it suits my purpose. Which is rare enough, but noteworthy."

"But why? Why the story about stealing robes? Why did you tell me anything at all?"

Braylar rose slowly, and it was obvious now that his stupor was due to ale, as he teetered just slightly. He must have managed to keep some down without vomiting. "I have a question of my own, more pressing as it happens—where are the flagons? I don't recall sending them away. Is this your doing, because you will have more to answer for that heinous crime than the transgression of opening a locked box. Oh. Yes. I will take the key back now. Just after you snap the lock shut again."

I did as he bade and walked toward him slowly, feeling unsteady on my feet as well. Fear seemed the only strand left now.

"Come now, I'm not some brutish Grass Dog to cut off half your hand.

Frankly, I'm so utterly stunned at your initiative of late—or utterly drunk at last, I'm not entirely certain—that I find myself more amused than enraged. But I can't promise how long that shall last." He snapped his finger. "The key."

I handed it to him, happy he let me take my hand and fingers back whole and unbroken.

Braylar said, "As to your query, I wanted to see if word about stolen vestments started circulating, or if you carried the tale yourself to unwholesome ears."

"So it was a test? A trap?"

"Oh, yes. A testy trap."

"You had me followed then?"

"Well, it would not have been much of a test if I couldn't monitor the outcome, now would it?"

I stood there, stunned, wondering if my tail had seen the young Hornman, or my reaction to him, anyway. "And?" I asked, slowly, quietly.

"Well, if you had run to the good baron, you can be sure this conversation would have a much different tenor. I had hoped you would prove yourself leal, and you have. Well, until you broke into my things, that is."

I looked back at the chest, barely trusting my voice. "What are these documents then?"

He dropped the key into his pouch and closed it. "My permissive mood is passing. Leave me. Now. And send in more ale. Immediately."

While I had countless other burning questions, I knew I'd used up as much goodwill as the captain was likely to offer. And while I'd come into the room initially to tell him about the Hornman, that suddenly seemed the worst idea I'd ever come up with.

I turned to go, and Braylar rasped, "Oh, and the next time you filch something from me, young scribe, you can be sure I will batter you to the floor, kick your ribs in, and spit on your wailing face. If I am feeling permissive. And worse if I am not. Are we clear?"

Yes, now was not the time for admissions of any kind. It appeared Mulldoos had been right about this being my lucky day. Without turning around, I nodded and left the captain in his dim chamber as fast as my feet could carry me.

Vendurro watched as I shut the captain's door behind me. "No bloodstains. Guessing he didn't break nothing neither, or you hid your screaming real good." He was spinning his long dagger or short sword—I could never decide which—on the table in front of him.

I figured the best chance of saying nothing damning was to say as little as possible and shift the focus quickly. "What is that?" I asked, pointing at the blade. "I mean, it's a weapon, but is it technically a dagger or a short sword? It looks like it could be either."

Vendurro stopped spinning the blade. "Called a suroka. Never much thought about it. Just know how to stab people with it."

"Well, then. Suroka. I learned something new. Anyway, the captain was none too pleased about his missing ale. He asked for you to order some up. Immediately, was the word he used, I believe. Emphatically is the word I'd add." Vendurro got off his stool, though the very action seemed to deflate him again. He turned to leave, then stopped. "Was Cap looking OK? I mean, of course he weren't, not really. Seen him battle this thing before we found Lloi. Whole lot of ugly. But how is he faring, truly? Is it bad, yet?"

I shook my head, wondering how long Braylar could maintain himself with drunken stupors. And what it would mean if he couldn't. Would Hewspear take command? Mulldoos? I shuddered at the second thought. "He's thorny and issuing orders, so I'd say he's doing as well as can be expected, given the circumstance."

Vendurro accepted that, or at least appeared to. I wasn't so sure.

I returned to my room, marveling that things could change so radically, so swiftly. Yesterday, we were foiling the efforts of what I thought was an assassin-bent cleric and losing the one member of the company who could manage the captain's affliction or curse or whatever it was, and today, I discovered that not only was very little of what I believed true, but when the lies were lifted and replaced with truth, even that was suspect. Lies upon lies. And the baron was either ensnared or ensnaring us, and I'd seen a Hornman who could potentially end every scheme in play here, and quite possibly, our lives as well, and I missed my chance—or neglected to use it—to report what I'd witnessed. It was a lot to take in. With my head spinning, I got out my pen and ink and writing desk. After bringing the account current, I considered heading back down to the Fair while I still had opportunity. With dusk at its duskiest, and lantern light filling the spaces the weak and tentative sun no longer reached, Fairgoers were trying to eke out every last bit of joy or debauchery or forgetting or whatever it was they had hoped to find in Alespell before curfew was called. But I had no idea what that rattled and bruised Hornman might do—had he reported sighting me to his superiors? Probably not, in all reality, or he'd face the lash for not reporting it sooner. But if he was frightened enough? Was he in his barracks, or his own room, running through all the possibilities, just like me?

For a mad moment, I considered leaving the Grieving Dog, not to disappear in the currents of the shifting crowd of Fairgoers, but to head to the Hornmen barracks. I thought somehow if I could just speak to the young soldier, I might be able to. . . what? Remind him of the oath he made when he was so terrified he nearly pissed down his leg? Surely that wouldn't result in him turning me over to his superiors on the spot.

No, it would have been utter foolishness to leave the Dog just then, even if I wasn't so stupid as to try to find the solider. Any moment I could have been picked up for questioning by the Hornmen if the boy had already reported me. They had purview of the road and waterways, allegedly protecting Anjurian travelers (though as the captain and I found out, just as often preying on them) and collecting taxes, but their jurisdiction got muddy elsewhere. Beholden only to the king, the Hornmen were generally beyond the scope of barons and burghers on travel routes, but did they have the right to question me, execute me, particularly while I was in one of the largest cities in the kingdom? There were plenty of instances when Hornmen and the barons disagreed about who had authority over inns, especially those in cities, and jurisprudence was divided.

The dead Hornmen in the grass might give them the most legitimate claim to hang us, but even if the Hornmen chose to turn me over to Baron

Brune, that would likely end up with me strapped down on one of his tables in the depths of the castle, howling out despair as I was mutilated or torn, the horrible stench of vinegar stinging my eyes and nose as I cried out and told all I knew, hoping only for it all to end.

No, leaving the inn was a horrible choice now. Though staying might not prove much better.

And while I had sputtered out most of my scallops and ale and should have been starving, my stomach refused to sit still, so there was no reason to even head downstairs to the main floor of the Grieving Dog. While the idea of finding a corner to hide in had some appeal, watching the patrons come and go and argue and dice and maybe even sing—yes, a song would be nice, even croaky and slurred by the drunkest lout in the establishment—I suddenly had little motivation to do anything except lay back in my bed and stare at the rafters.

Which I did for far shorter than expected before falling into a thankfully dreamless sleep and waking up to a new day and the sound of voices in the common quarter outside my room. It sounded as if Hewspear had returned. I got up to join them, stopped at the door wondering if Mulldoos was there as well, and then swore at myself. It didn't matter if he was—if I was going to seclude myself in my room, it would be my choice, not because I was afraid of a bully with a big blade.

I stepped out. Captain Killcoin and Vendurro were sitting in chairs and Hewspear was leaning against a support beam, stiff and favoring the side with the wounded ribs. Vendurro stopped mid-sentence when he saw me, then continued, "Told me to tell you he was following up on some rumors, be back by nightfall. Told me you were the luckiest son of a whore he ever met. Begging your pardon, Cap, just relaying."

Braylar had washed a bit, changed tunics, and oiled his hair back to appear somewhat presentable, but he still had an obvious pallor and his eyes were shot through and rimmed in red. He took a slow swallow of his ale and said, "Well, even thin rumor is better than none at all. And you, Hew, what do you have to report?"

Hewspear glanced at me briefly and replied, "I found someone to transport Lloi back to the steppe. There is a group of pilgrims leaving on the morrow."

Braylar slammed his mug down and laughed, though it pained him to do so as he lifted his hand to his throat. "Pilgrims have a queer fixation with the steppe this time of year. I do hope they have a guard or two. Not that anyone would be interested in thieving a dead body." He lifted the mug and stopped before it reached his lips. "One of them wasn't a large woman in a large hat, by any chance."

I held my breath but Hewspear shook his head, coins jingling in his beard. That was good. One bad coincidence was already one too many.

Braylar took a long drink and the group was silent for a moment. I joined the two Syldoon at the table and pulled out a chair. Braylar took another swig, doing his best to drown his demons in drink, and gestured at the pitcher and a mug.

I accepted it and filled my mug as Vendurro said, "Remember, in Rivermost, we were talking about worst ways to go out? Well, I forgot one. We all did, as it happens. Just remembered it, in fact. Though can't for the life of me figure out what made me think of it."

"Oh?" Braylar asked, not sounding especially interested, but happy to entertain any distraction just now.

Vendurro replied, "Yup. Wheldon. Remember that poor bastard?"

Hewspear groaned. "Sadly, yes."

Vendurro looked at me, and while his heart didn't seem to be entirely in it, he spun the tale. "Well, Wheldon was always bellyaching about a bellyache. Wheldon the Whiner we all called him. Not a day didn't go by when he didn't tell one of us about his sore bloated belly, leaky shits, weird cramps and the like. Not one plaguing day. Might have been the first thing he ever says to me. 'Name's Wheldon. I near shit myself today.'

"This went on the whole time I knew him. And right up until his last. We got in a scrape on the western border, some hill tribes. What were they called? The Masukas? Marlukas? Something like that?"

No one seemed to remember, or inclined to correct him if he was wrong.

"Gless would have remembered. Always had a keen mind for that sort of stupid detail." He waved the thought off and continued. "Anyway, we drove those bastards back up into their caves, away from the good people they were murdering in that valley. Not many casualties, that I recall. But Wheldon took a mighty crack to the back of the head. Stone axe, I think. Felled him in one blow. Split that skull square down the middle."

I said, "That does sound a bit gruesome, but I have to say, that doesn't quite compare to some of the other stories you all told. Especially about Rokliss."

Vendurro smiled. "Oh, it wasn't the felling itself that was awful. It was what happened just after. You see, that whole time Wheldon was bellyaching when he was alive, he had something else alive in him causing him all kinds of trouble. Not long after he hit the dirt, long pale worms started crawling out his ears, his nose, one or two wriggling out his mouth. Seems they weren't too keen about having their meat house falling down, decided to look for some other place to hole up. Must have been twenty of the squidgy little bastards, near tying themselves in knots in their hurry to get out of poor dead Wheldon."

Hewspear laughed and took a drink. "You are a gross little man, Sergeant."

Vendurro shrugged. "Weren't me that had worms in his gut. Wheldon was the gross one."

The Syldoon all shared a chuckle, and I smiled. There was a brief pause and then Braylar looked carefully at the faces around him before asking, "Who among you has seen a good death?"

Vendurro took a drink from his own mug. "Guessing it depends on what your meaning is, Cap."

"Nothing altogether clever. I mean only this: we've covered the worst possible ways to die. At great, gross length now. We have all seen enough men die in a myriad of horrible ways, this was an easy enough diversion. What I am asking for is, who here has witnessed a man dying a good death? I suspect this is more difficult to answer, yes?"

It was hard to tell if he was asking a rhetorical question, or positing something simply for us to mull over, but Vendurro took it at face value. "Before the Syldoon got a hold of me, I was along at the back end of a raiding party. Zenvugo—that was the name of our tribe, that much I do remember—they was fixing on hitting another tribe's camp. I was barely old enough to hold the spear and shield at the ready, especially on a horse, but my da, he believed in getting us in the party as early as possible. Should have been an easy run—hit them fast, take off with some cows, maybe a horse or two, scoot back through the woods. Word was, most of the men in their camp was on the other side of the valley just then. Only seems they figured we was coming, cause they had a party of their own armed to the teeth, plenty bigger than ours. They surprised us good. We tussled best we could, but we just didn't have the numbers—plenty of my tribe were injured or hitting the dirt never to get up. Though none spilled worms just after that I recall.

"Anyway, the captain—that ain't what we called him, of course—*survote* was the word in my tongue, but that was what he was doing, sure enough, captaining, so I'm sticking with that on account of clarity—he saw right quick that we didn't stand a chance, sounded the retreat. They were making up the ground in the pursuit though, especially with us hauling our injured. We splashed across a ford, half the party dragging the other, and I looked back at the horse on our heels, coming out of the woods on the other side of the river. We weren't making it, not back to our camp, just too far, and they was just too fresh, and ten kinds of angry we were trying to steal some of their cows. I was near ready to piss myself, heart beating like a rabbit's, when one of the Zenvugo—can't remember his name for the life of me, though, plaguing memory—he got off his horse and waded out to the middle of that ford, slamming the pommel of his sword against his shield. Calling for one of their champions to fight him."

Hewspear nodded, as if he both expected that and approved, and Braylar was listening intently, red-rimmed eyes still bright.

Vendurro went on. "Bought us the time we needed to clear out. I stayed, hidden in the woods, eyes locked on what was happening in the river. The Nontir—that was the other tribe—they argued amongst themselves on their side of the river, shouting, while most of our party rode out fast as they could, until finally one of their warriors dismounted and strode out to meet the Zenvugo."

I asked, "Why would the Nontir risk losing the opportunity to take revenge on your tribe, especially when they had you? Obviously, they knew they were giving your party time to flee. Didn't they?"

Hewspear replied, "To most tribes and clans, honor is next to sacred. And turning down a challenge like that would have incurred a great deal of lost face."

Vendurro nodded. "That Nontir, he was brave, and full to the chin of that honor the lieutenant just mentioned, but that don't win fights. Fight hardly lasted more than three blows before he hit the water, bleeding out of a big old hole in his side. I was still watching from the woods, as our man started banging on that shield of his again, calling out their next champion.

"Well, the Nontir must have figured they'd honored their foe just about as far as they were willing to. A second later an arrow flew across the river and took that Zenvugo in the neck. He dropped his sword and shield, fell to his knees, and another arrow took him in the chest as he toppled over into the current."

Vendurro looked at Braylar and shook his head. "He saved our party, wading out on the ford to issue his challenge. Wish I could recall his name. But he knew he was picking a fight he couldn't win, did it anyway, to save the lot of us. On that count, he died a good death. But sprouting arrows, that was a shit death, shitty as they come. So I'm thinking that canceled out the noble sacrifice, left him just flat out dead. Ain't no good deaths, Cap. Not a one."

Braylar gave a sad smile, but Hewspear brought two of the coins in his beard together like tiny castanets. "I'm afraid I'm going to have to disagree with you, dear Sergeant." Vendurro started to interrupt but the lieutenant raised a hand. "Glesswik died yesterday not only fighting like a lion and following orders—I would argue that alone makes it meaningful, and therefore, 'good'—but he saved at least two Syldoon lives before he was struck down. And I would contend that beyond fighting for family, there is no greater honor in this world than fighting to keep your brothers in arms alive. Your nameless tribesman did that, years ago. And Glesswik did the same, just the other day. He stood his ground and fought for his brothers. He died a good death, Vendurro. Do not forget that."

Vendurro took a quick drink of his ale, eyes wet, and tried to discreetly rub them dry.

In my mind, I saw a horse biting flesh, and a woman sliding down a tree, screaming. Throat catching, I said, "I assume good deaths aren't solely the province of men. Or Syldoon. Because yesterday, Lloi died saving your life, Hewspear. Her death was awful. Heinous. But by your definition, no less good."

Hewspear smiled, reached down and took up a mug, and hoisted it as Vendurro and I followed his lead. "To good deaths, then."

The three of us took a drink, while the captain stared straight ahead, shoulders slumped, mug in hand but still on the table, as if it had suddenly grown immeasurably heavy. Without looking at me, or anyone, he rasped, "What of the captain of the priest guard, Arki? In the ruins? You were the only one to see him die. What of him? Would you say he died well?"

As was often the case, it was difficult to determine if he was truly interested in an answer, or if he had the answer already and was simply trying to figure out if anyone else in the room had been sharp enough to figure it out. I thought about what I'd seen before replying. "He was brave. Or indomitable. I'm not sure which. Maybe both. But he didn't have to die. He could have surrendered, and simply waited until you left. He chose to face you, knowing he would die, but it didn't serve any real purpose. It didn't save anyone's life. He was no longer fighting to defend his brothers, or his lord, or even an important patch of ground. So, I'm not sure. How flexible is this definition? Because I'm thinking, while he was brave, he was also foolish."

Braylar continued staring straight ahead, fixated on a distant point or image that no one else could see. He breathed in and out slowly, and with his noose tattoo laid bare, I could see it ripple on his throat as he swallowed, and then watched him flinch, pained. As we all waited to see what he was about to say, he closed his eyes, nostrils flaring as he let out a deep breath, and I instantly recognized the expression, the same that he'd had when his haunting threatened to overwhelm him in the steppe.

Eyes still closed, he said, "His name was Dargus. It is a strange thing, to know someone's name when you have never seen his face."

Vendurro looked from Hewspear to me and back to the captain again. "His name, Cap? He stopped to make an introduction before you two got to scrapping?"

Braylar's eyes remained closed, and the lids twitched, and the scars above his lip did the same. "I heard it. In his memories. I've seen and felt more of his than usual. Too many. So very many." The chains rattled as he lifted Bloodsounder up and laid the weapon on the table. "Long before the captain of the guard set foot in a temple, he was part of a mercenary company. Young. He joined young. He was the last of four brothers, tanners, the lot of them. But that wasn't the life he wanted. So he signed on with a company that came through. This was. . . ." The eyelids flickered again. "Thirty years ago? More? Hard to say. The Syldoon and Anjurians were at war when he joined. That does little to date a thing—until this recent truce, we have been warring for longer than any man alive.

"The Anjurians, having no standing army, and unable to maintain forces for extended periods, have often resorted to mercenaries. That is their way. But two years in, there was a truce. The sellswords hoped it would be temporary, as these things often are. But it was not so in this case. It was an outbreak."

Braylar tilted his head. "Was this the plague of your youth, Hew?" He asked this as if Hewspear weren't even in the room to answer, as if he were speaking to only a memory or shade of his comrade.

Hewspear sat down slowly, grunting, and then laid his large hands flat on the table and leaned back in his chair. "I cannot say, Captain. I cannot say." Though his eyes were intent on the younger man in front of him, he spoke quietly, as if he didn't expect Braylar to truly hear him either. Vendurro looked at me questioningly but I had no answers of any kind and only shrugged.

"It does not matter, yes? All that matters, it was an extended truce. And what happened is what almost always happens in such a case. A large group of armed men who have no other vocation, and no legitimate means of using their talents without an opportunity for sanctioned bloodletting, resort to banditry. They terrorized the countryside, just as unemployed sellswords have done since the dawn of mercenaries.

"Our captain who was no captain yet, only a young solider, he went along with the crew. I. . . feel that he had reservations. But along he went. They raided and pillaged, striking high and lowborn with equal fervor, no less a plague than the ones that have sprung up to ravage the world from time to time, practically a violent force of nature. Local militias couldn't hope to capture and punish all such crews. They were everywhere, more experienced at war, and remorseless. So the company continued thieving and eliminating any who opposed them. And Dargus robbed and raped with the rest of them, waiting for true war to break out again, to give them some real purpose."

Vendurro said, "Cap. . . are you, that is. . . " but stopped himself when Hewspear raised a hand.

Braylar continued, oblivious, running his fingers across the chains of the flail, lifting the links off the table, letting them fall back. "They could not assault any large strongholds—that is, they could have, but laying siege was nowhere in their plan. Hit a place hard, take what they could, and move on. Occasionally, they offered their services as protectors to defenseless villages as well, pledging to fight off any other roving bandits, but at a steep price.

"At one such village, the elders were resisting them. Had they been foolish enough to expect clemency, or rescue from some quarter? I can't say. But they told the company to leave. They needed no protection. The mercenary captain, he laughed, and ordered a sellsword to kill one of the captive villagers. Which he did. That was not a good death.

"The elder went ashen, but still did not relent. The captain grew impatient, and ordered Dargus to kill the captive he was holding. A girl. No older than a tenyear." The twitching lip and eyelids. "Dargus looked at the elder, praying he would see reason, agree to terms, but the man's lips might as well have been nailed together. The captain swore, told him to do it, and Dargus didn't want to. Wished he had never left the filthy stink of the tanners for adventure in the wide world. But he had been given an order in front of the rest of the crew, and he knew if he failed, his would be the next throat opened by a dagger."

I couldn't imagine what it was like to experience these memories. And was exceptionally grateful I would never find out.

"The girl, she started struggling, squealing and crying, but Dargus tightened his grip, still hoping the foolish elder would speak. When he did not, Dargus closed his eyes and tried to draw his dagger across the girl's exposed throat quickly, to just be done with it. But the girl had been growing wild in her efforts to escape, and was wriggling everywhere as she screamed, so the blade mostly sliced the bottom of her jaw, which only made her scream all the louder. The captain told Dargus to finish the job as he ordered another captive brought forward. Dargus did then, slashed twice to be sure it was done. The girl went limp in his arms, and fell to the floor of the hearth when released."

Braylar lifted one of the flail heads up a few inches off the table, turning the spiked and tormented Deserter God visage over to inspect its eyeless face. It was still bizarre to see a weapon designed to spill human blood shaped in likeness of the gods who had abandoned humanity to whatever ills might befall it. Was Bloodsounder some instrument of punishment the Deserters had left behind to torment us? To remind us of our proclivity for murdering each other? Or perhaps that was what had convinced them to leave us in the first place a millennium ago: men killing children, innocents, even other armed men. Murder and still more of it. Maybe that was why they had abandoned us and erected the Godveil in their wake to prevent us from following. We were simply that damaged and hopeless.

Braylar continued, "The elder, sensing too late that his resistance would only end in more executions, finally did acquiesce then, tears streaming down his face. But too late for the girl. And too late for Dargus. He followed the orders after that, but hated himself for doing so, and looked for the right time to slip away in the night. And with every dawn he failed to do so, he hated himself all the more. But he swore to himself, even if he was too much of a coward to leave, he would never be such a cretin to do such an awful deed again."

Braylar's face tightened, as if he were struggling to either understand the flood of memories, or resist them. "The pillaging and extortion continued for many months, until the company was robbing a temple. A temple of Truth. They had the underpriest at sword point, asking where they had hidden the wealth. Braziers, candlesticks, urns, whatever might have been worth something, but especially gold or jewels. The underpriest swore they had none, but the captain was convinced he was lying. And so he resorted to his familiar tactics once more. He ordered some men to bring initiates in, Dargus one of them.

"But Dargus was finally done obeying orders. He walked up to his captain. The captain looked at him queerly, irritated at the delay. He started to speak, but didn't get very far. Dargus cut him down." Braylar dropped the Deserter head onto the table with a thunk.

"He cleaved his skull in twain, wrenched the bloody blade free, and ran. Ran for his life. The underpriest and initiates were running too, and it was chaos in the temple. The bandits were shocked at seeing their captain cut down by one of their own, and no one took command. In the pandemonium, Dargus escaped. And the underpriest did as well. Dargus came across him shivering in the woods later, hiding in a log, and told him to climb on his horse. The underpriest came out without a word, and got on, and the pair rode off.

"That priest, he was even younger than the bandit who had miraculously saved his life and delivered him from harm. When they made it safely to another temple several miles away, the priest was wise enough not to miss the opportunity. He asked the bandit with the dead eyes to swear off evildoing, and promised him a life, a purpose, an exalted calling if he did."

Braylar lifted both flail heads in the palm of his hand, and though his eyes were still closed, he held them up in front of his face as if he were examining them. Vendurro almost interrupted again, but Hewspear stopped him, so the three of us waited in silence until Braylar spoke, a rasping whisper now. "So, two tenyear later, the priest and priest's man had risen through the ranks of their order, and found themselves in a weedy, toppling temple. And when the captain of priestguards saw I had slain the halberdier, he got up. He was bloodied and broken and had no hope of defeating me, but Captain Dargus, whose face I never saw, forced himself to his feet to challenge me once more. And do you know why?"

I wasn't sure if he was speaking to Bloodsounder, himself, or us, but then his lids snapped open, red-rimmed eyes narrow, but alert and looking at us. "He gritted his teeth as broken bones shifted, and blood flowed fresh down his limbs, pooling in his boots. He stumbled to his feet to charge me one final time, because in me, he saw the sellsword bandit captain. The one who ordered the death of innocents and children and the underpriest he had sworn his life to protect. The captain he'd murdered in a different temple so many miles and years distant that had somehow come back to haunt him. He would rather die fighting that captain than live knowing he had lacked the will again." He dropped the flail heads and I did jump this time.

Braylar fixed his stare at me, and it seemed somehow filled with equal parts rage, sadness, and a haunted desperation I couldn't name or understand. "So, the question of a good death or bad is not so easy to answer as it might appear."

With that, he rose unsteadily and made his way to his chamber.

There was little to say after that, but that didn't stop Vendurro. He looked at me. "You heard him go on like that before. I could tell you must have heard him recounting something similar like. You didn't seem a lick surprised. Had to have been in the grass. That right?"

I nodded. "One of the Hornmen he killed. Though the soldier didn't die right away. The wound the captain gave him, it took a while to kill him. Then the memories came on him all at once. This priestguard captain, he died right away, so Braylar has had more time to be. . . poisoned by the memories. That's how Lloi described it."

Vendurro shook his head, then looked at Hewspear. "And you, Lieutenant, you didn't seem surprised at all to hear the telling. You seen this before too, I reckon."

The older man's posture was rigid, as he moved only when he had to—his ribs were clearly still paining him. But it was hard to imagine a man sitting more upright with a more slumped demeanor about him. "I've seen this before. While no one in our company is unaware that he is afflicted with something, we do try to keep the worst details shrouded. It's gotten worse the last few years. Lloi helped him for a time, but now. . . " Hewspear let the thought trail off.

Vendurro bore the same expression he had when we were all standing before the Godveil at the ruined temple, torn between wonder and fear, contemplating something beyond our scope of understanding. He shook his head. "Ain't natural at all, what's happening to Cap. And it ain't natural that someone's got to fix him. Like you said, I always knew he was battling something queer, something unnatural, but seeing it, or hearing it rather. . . " He asked the next question to both of us. "We came by Lloi by luck alone. What happens if Mulldoos can't find another Lloi? I know we can't get no Memoridon, but seems like the choices are growing mighty thin."

Hewspear slowly rose to his feet. He took a shallow breath and said, "Perhaps this won't be a bad spell. Some are worse than others. He seems to be managing well enough for now. Perhaps that will continue."

It was difficult to tell if he believed that or was merely reciting it for our benefit—I doubted he was as skilled a liar as Braylar, but then I didn't think Braylar was as skilled at deception as he actually was.

Hewspear walked out of the common quarters, maybe before Vendurro had a chance to ask any more questions, though he seemed to have exhausted them, as he simply stared down at the table, took a small drink of ale, shook his head, and continued staring at the moisture ring there.

Part of me was tempted to stay, to talk to him about it, perhaps to listen as he worked through what he'd heard from his captain. But I also sensed that he was uncomfortable, and so I stood up as well, considered saying something else, and then realized I didn't know what to say, and that even if I had, I wasn't particularly in the mood to say it.

I headed to my room, staying there the remainder of the day. With evening coming on, and my stomach grumbling, having only eaten some wrinkled fruit and stale cheese in my room, I decided it was time to stretch my legs. Maybe leaving the Grieving Dog wasn't the smartest idea, but that didn't mean I had to stay holed up like a trembling bird. I could at least head to the ground floor and take a proper meal. Hopefully there would be somewhere I could sit without having to force conversation with anyone else, but either way, it would be good to be among people who didn't have a surplus of secrets, grief, or shadowy curses.

The Grieving Dog filled up quickly enough, and even with all the vaulted nooks and small shadowy alcoves, there was still a real shortage of secluded places available, so I took my plate of fried meatballs and grape leaves stuffed with rice and boiled egg, and made my way out back to the garden.

The tall oaks provided such a dense canopy above, and the wall around the perimeter of the garden was so high, it was easy to forget we were in one of the busiest cities in Anjuria. Even the noise of Fairgoers passing by the street seemed like something distant. While most of the benches were occupied, I found a small table against a tree and leaned back into the trunk. Even with the buzz of dozens of drunken conversations all around, punctuated by the odd boisterous shout, it was still probably the most peaceful spot in Alespell, and should have been easy enough to block out everything that had happened in the last few days. But even after several glasses of heady wine, and the lantern light blurring and shimmering slightly, it was still a challenge to forget the present circumstances. The departed, the schemes, the suspicious and brutal baron, the haunting with slim chance of reprieve, the Hornman I rescued who might just doom us all.

I got up to find a beer maid, laughing drunkenly to myself when I thought they were never referred to as wine maids. I was reluctant to lose my spot, but finding more wine was an absolute necessity, so I started winding my way around benches and pockets of people toward the doorway to the interior.

As I got closer, stumbling over my inebriated feet, I saw Mulldoos walking through the crowd toward the stairwell. He hadn't seen me yet, so I considered turning right back around and disappearing. But the figure immediately behind him stopped me short.

He was leading a small girl through the inn, and her hands were tied together. She had hair so fair it was nearly white, but in complete disarray, and her face and arms were covered with bruises and more ominous welts. She had a cracked lip, and was wearing a tunic that had several bloodspots on the chest. Her shoes—or what passed for shoes, at least—were torn and tattered, and one seemed tied together with twine.

In short, she was a complete mess. But that didn't stand out so much as her demeanor. Where most beaten children would have kept their heads fixed on their feet, or worked hard not to make eye contact with the dozens of strangers in the room, this bruised, bloodied, and bound girl held her chin up, and gave anyone glancing her way a challenging look back, as if daring them to say something or lay a hand on her.

My chance to disappear was gone—Mulldoos saw me. The crowd parted around the strange pair, largely due to his usual liberal use of elbows and angry glares, but also as people stepped aside to get a better look at the strange prisoner.

Mulldoos jerked a thumb toward the stairs as he got close to me, and I followed them up. The lieutenant called out and knocked on the door, and a moment later Vendurro unlocked it and opened it. Mulldoos pushed his tiny charge through first, and while I couldn't see Vendurro's expression, I heard him exclaim, "Plague me! Where'd you get this drowned cat?"

Again, instead of being cowed, the girl looked in his direction and hissed.

"And feral on top of it," he added.

Mulldoos looked at Vendurro as he entered and showed his arms, which were covered in scratches and what looked to be teeth marks. "Vicious little hellcat, more like."

The girl started turning to face him but he grabbed her firmly by the back of the neck. "Face forward, hellcat."

"Lay off!" she yelled, struggling as best as a small girl with her hands tied could against a massively muscled soldier who wasn't pretending to be gentle.

He turned to Vendurro. "Best fetch Cap."

Vendurro knocked on the captain's door. When Braylar didn't respond right away, he knocked again and called out, "Mulldoos come back, Cap. Got hisself a prisoner. Maybe half a prisoner, truly. Guessing you'll want to see her though." He turned around and looked at the group, then whistled, long and low. "Guessing you'll hold for Cap, but this story ought to be ten kinds of entertaining."

Mulldoos smiled, which was almost disturbing. "Oh, you'll hear it soon enough." He looked at Braylar's room and then back to Vendurro. "He doing alright?"

Vendurro didn't answer right away, glanced at me, then at the tiny battered prisoner as if gauging how much he could say. "Been better, I'm thinking. But to hear Lieutenant Hew tell it, or Arki here, been worse, too. So holding steady. For what that's worth."

"You seen Hew? Where's he at?"

"Cap said he might have gotten good word about the whereabouts of. . . " Vendurro looked at the small girl and added, "That fella we been after. So off to check on that. Be back short like."

Braylar stepped out of his room, eyes still bloodshot, but otherwise looking no worse than before. Still, as Vendurro said, that wasn't anything to feel tremendously good about. It was difficult to tell which ailed him more—the ale or the demons he was trying to drown.

He looked ready to issue a biting remark of some kind when he stopped himself, noticing the small and scruffy newcomer in the room. Then he looked at Mulldoos. "Well. This is the rogue witch, is she?"

Before Mulldoos could answer, the girl said, "No witch at all. Told them that, told this bastard that, and now I'm—"

Mulldoos cuffed her behind the ear. "Being right disrespectful. This is a captain you're speaking to."

She shook her head and said, "Could be the king hisself and I'd tell him the same plaguing thing. Whatever they said I done, they lied. Bunch of lying shits, the lot of them, and I hope when the plague comes through again it hits Ash Walk first."

Braylar grinned. "And here I thought Lloi was the most irreverent dream thief we'd ever run across." He looked her bruises over and said, "It's good to see that you were careful, selective, and discrete."

Mulldoos shrugged his shoulders. "Most of that was on her already. And as I recollect, seemed our situation called more for results than tip-toeing around. It's nothing but dumb chance I managed to turn this hellcat up at all. Villagers were fixing to kill her dead when I rode up. You want me to send her hissing back into the wild, though, you just say the word. And you want her drowned in the river, that works as well too."

She stomped back, trying to strike his shin or foot, but mostly hit floor. He grabbed her by the neck. "Settle down there, you little bitch." Which only made her thrash more until he gave her a firm shake.

Braylar said, "Oh, she'll stay a bit longer. At least until I've determined her use. Or lack thereof, more likely."

Which set the girl to kicking and squirming again. "You put your cock anywhere near me, I'll bite it off and spit in in your face, I will. Just see if I don't."

Mulldoos cuffed her behind her other ear and Braylar replied, "Oh, I have no doubt about that. But do settle down. I prefer my concubines quite a bit older, recently bathed, and decidedly less hostile."

She glared at him but stopped struggling. For the moment.

Braylar walked to the table and took a seat. At least he hadn't stumbled or wobbled overmuch. He folded his hands on the table, still staring at the angry young thing in front of him. "I know you're simply bursting to tell me the details, Lieutenant. So please. Share how you came to find this vicious, little, scruffy creature that you somehow believe might be allowed anywhere near me if I was prone and helpless. This story, I would love to hear."

Mulldoos smiled again, the kind a cat might have with the mouse's tail poking out of the corner of his mouth. "Me and the boys, we hit every inn and tavern in the city, hoping to hear word of a witch out there, expecting not to. Thirsty work, that is. But Alespell is big, with more villages and communities around than most. Heard tell of two sightings, one in Tenvale, the other in Ash Walk. Most rogues get found out, they get done for pretty plaguing fast, so we rode out in a hurry. Would have split up, but Tenvale wasn't far off the path to Ash Walk, so we just hit there first."

"But clearly that did not pan out."

"No, they stoned their witch. Been dead a couple of days already, nailed to a tree. So we kept riding a half day for Ash Walk, figuring to find a similar outcome. But Ash Walkers, they must not get much in the way of excitement, decided to have themselves a trial. Would have ended the same way, for sure, but it delayed killing the girl long enough for us to ride into the square."

Braylar leaned forward. "Please tell me you paid for your prisoner and didn't kill everyone in Ash Walk."

"Nope. That is, yep, no killing, just passed some coin across. Seemed the village elders weren't too keen on losing their chance for a little fun. Stoning, drowning, burning, whatever else they had in store for the lady here." The girl turned and scowled at him, but held her tongue, and Mulldoos continued, "Asked a pretty coin for the release, so not charging by the pound. I thought about cleaving one of those bastards, to help the bargaining speed up a bit. But I paid up. No blood."

Braylar looked closely at the girl. "And you think she possesses the requisite. . . skills?"

Mulldoos shook his head. "No plaguing idea. But the villagers seemed right certain she was thieving dreams."

"Liars!" she spat.

Mulldoos looked ready to smack her again but didn't. "True or false, they claimed she had a way of creeping into people's skulls, especially when they were sleeping. Knew things she ought not to. So she's got as good a chance as any of having some rogue blood in her. Which is to say, probably none. Villagers are superstitious whoresons who don't know their asses from their faces. Still, she was the only one in the area. Me, I say we send for a proper Memoridon, and fuck the consequences. Bound to be one close. Guessing the Empire's got one hounding us."

Braylar didn't respond with the venom I expected, especially given how he had dressed Mulldoos down only a few days ago. "No, Lieutenant. This is what we have to work with. Such as it is." He stared at her. "So, girl, you deny being a dream thief, do you?"

She pushed some greasy hair out of her face. "Answered you already."

Braylar rapped on the table. "You aren't dim, lass. That much is certain. Which is good. I have absolutely no use for dimness. But impertinence will get you nowhere good here either. My man there might not be the most delicate solider alive, but he did rescue you from a decidedly bad fate. You would do well to cooperate now, lest you find yourself in equally dire straits tonight. What's your name, girl?"

She tucked another strand behind her ear, and I thought she was close to feeling the back of the lieutenant's hand again, when she said, quietly. "Junjee. Junjee Millstone."

"Very good, Junjee. So. Your fellow Ashians, friends and family all, were ready to string you up, accusing you of sifting through dreams, and taking what you wanted. Yet you maintain you were completely innocent, yes? But let me put it to you one more time: can you do these things? I ask, not wanting to kill you for it, or punish you at all, but to preserve you, to save you, so that you can assist me. So answer, lass, and speak true."

Junjee tilted that proud little chin up, looked him directly in the eye with the poise of a woman two or three times her age, and said, "I got no other answer for you but the one I gave already. Gave it and gave it and gave it. Got nothing left to say. So do what you do. Only know if you violate me, I'll—"

"Bite my cock off. Yes. I do believe we've covered that." Braylar glanced down, and the direction told me he was looking at Bloodsounder somewhere under the table. "You see, it so happens that I have dire need of someone with the skills you deny having. While it is true most of the known world would string you up for admitting to them, I am a Syldoon. I don't know if you know much about Syldoon—"

"My ma always said you were murdering dogs."

"Well, your mother wasn't entirely wrong. But she also didn't protect you behind her skirts when they came to string you up, did she?" He waited for her to answer, but she only maintained the haughty tilt of her chin. "Knowing a little of the Syldoon, then, you might also be aware that we make use of women who demonstrate this forbidden aptitude. So, now without family or friends, a penniless stranger in a huge city that will devour you at the slightest chance, I give you final opportunity to reconsider. I could offer you not only life, but a livelihood. You would be rewarded, highly regarded. So if it is fear that stops your tongue, girl, then—"

"My kin almost killed me yesterday. I got plenty to be afraid of. Terrified. Of everything. Got nothing now, just like you done said. So if I had what you asked for, or could fake it enough to fool you, I would. I'd give it. But they were going to string me up based on rumor and untruth. I can't see dreams. And red as blood, I can't steal none. Never stole nothing in my whole life."

Braylar watched her face intently as she spoke, weighed her words for the truth or falsehood. Then he exhaled long and slow out his nose and nodded before getting to his feet and stepping back from the table. I had the terrible feeling he was going to have Mulldoos take her out and kill her in the alley or drop her in the canal. Only Mulldoos wouldn't object like Dargus did.

Instead, Captain Killcoin said, "Very well, Junjee. Cut her free, Lieutenant. Give her some small coin and set her loose."

Surprise flitted across Junjee's face, and then whatever anger had been sustaining her drained away, and the chin fell a little. Mulldoos drew the long-bladed suroka, worked it between the ropes, cut through them. She continued looking at the captain the entire time. "Got nowhere. . . just letting me free?"

Braylar gave her a cold look. "Would you rather he cut your wrists instead of the rope?"

"No. Course not. It's just—" She sniffled, then started to reach up to wipe her nose before Mulldoos snatched her hands and pulled them back down so he could finish the rope. "I thought. . . I figured I was your prisoner. Where do I go?"

Braylar replied, "That is entirely up to you. I would not recommend Ash Walk. You will have enough money to buy some clothes, and a few hot meals. After that. . . "

"You're an army, ain't you? Heard armies need pot scrubbers, needle pushers, and the like. I'm handy, I could—"

"We are not an army just now, and not on campaign even if we were. We have no use for you. You were only brought here on the chance that you could do what you were accused of. Nothing more." He started to turn away to head back to his chamber.

The look on her face—the fear, desperation, anger, all washing into each other and not quite blending—was heartbreaking. I said, "Captain? What of the Grieving Dog? Couldn't they use an extra hand sweeping, mucking stalls, fetching water? Something? If you put in a good word. . . "

Braylar stopped, still not turning around. I looked over and saw hope flash across the girl's face, snatched away as Braylar said, mostly over his shoulder. "It amuses me you think we are clerics caring for the neglected and forgotten, archivist." The rope was free and she rubbed her wrists slowly, looking defeated and lost and truly young for the first time.

The captain sighed and said, "Still, it doesn't pain us to inquire, now does it? Vendurro, check with Gremete. Ask on my behalf, and see if they have need of a grateful and. . . spirited youth. Junjee, accompany him. If the Grieving Dog will have you, you will know immediately. If not, again, you are in a huge city. Opportunity around every corner." He failed to mention the thieves, murderers, and rapists around every corner as well. Still. She was alive, and that was something. I hoped she would find a home here, or at least a start.

Junjee wiped her face on her sleeve, wincing as it crossed her bloodied nose and split lip. Then she straightened and said, "Awful thing when strangers are kinder than kin."

"Sadly, you are not the first to say so," Braylar replied. Then he started toward his room. "Mulldoos, it appears you still have hunting to do, and I still have copious amounts of alcohol to consume. Let us not dawdle." And then he disappeared in the gloom and shut the door.

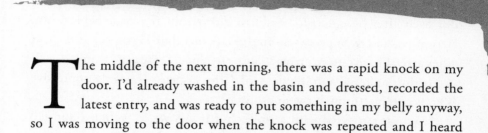

The middle of the next morning, there was a rapid knock on my door. I'd already washed in the basin and dressed, recorded the latest entry, and was ready to put something in my belly anyway, so I was moving to the door when the knock was repeated and I heard Vendurro say, "Quick and quicker, if you please, Master Quills."

Stepping out, I saw Braylar and Mulldoos seated at the table in the common room, plates of pepper sausage, honey cakes, and a bowl of sliced squash and peas in front of them. Braylar seemed no worse than he had the previous few days, but certainly no better. Mulldoos looked at me briefly, his pale eyebrows bridged by a deep wrinkle, but he said nothing.

I was about to ask Venduroo about the urgency, but Braylar was three words quicker. "Very well, Sergeant, now that our truant scribbler has joined us and we are all accounted for, you mentioned having important news."

I had a moment to wonder if Vendurro suggested I should join the group or if the captain had sent him to fetch me. Either way, the fact that he allowed me to be included was surprising, given that he caught me pilfering, but Vendurro stopped those thoughts entirely when he said, "Yup, got something that surely passes for news, though I won't be the one to truly deliver it. Hewspear be here short enough, and I'll let him tell you hisself, but he sent a runner ahead. Won't be the only one joining us to break fast."

Something in his tone and expression said this someone was not going to be especially welcome.

Mulldoos stopped mid-chew, cheeks bulging with food, two-tined fork halfway to his mouth with another bite, and Braylar straightened in his chair, left hand instinctively dropping down to Bloodsounder. "Out with it, Sergeant—who is this unexpected guest?"

Vendurro scratched at the tuft of hair on his chin and blew out a lot of air, clearly not liking being the bearer of this news at all, but he was spared just then, as there was a knock on the door to the hall. He looked relieved when he walked over, and getting confirmation of the man on the other side, undid the lock.

Hewspear stepped through the entrance, saluting as he saw his captain. But even after he entered, Vendurro didn't shut the door behind him. He waited, and even peered around the corner, but Hewspear said, "Our other arrival hasn't quite arrived. Shut the door, Sergeant."

Vendurro obeyed and Braylar said, "The suspense is utterly oppressive. Who is coming through the door next?"

Hewspear struggled with a smile, but it was weak, wobbled and fell. "Soffjian is in Alespell, Captain. She will be here shortly."

If Braylar was shocked, he hid it well enough. His irritation, however, less so. He immediately glared at Mulldoos, who raised both hands in the air. "Don't look at me, Cap. Had nothing to do with it." As he slowly lowered his hands he added, "Might not be the worst turn, though. The hellcat didn't work out. But even if she had, wouldn't have been any kind of full on solution. And whatever I didn't like about that half-hand whore of yours—and there was plenty, she was like a burr in my prick—she managed to fix you up as good as you got fixed. Enough to function, leastwise. But might be she mucked things up real good inside, too, so maybe Soff showing her skinny ass is—"

"A harbinger of pain, suffering, or outright disaster. And those are the best outcomes." Braylar turned back to Hewspear. "That would explain all the uneasiness in delivering the news. Well then. That does complicate things. How much time?"

Hewspear walked over to the table and accepted a cup Mulldoos offered. "She found me in the streets two hours ago. Not all that shocking, of course. But still, unexpected. And she wasn't keen to divulge anything. Also not shocking. I'm not sure why she didn't strike for the Dog immediately. So, not knowing her business, I can only hazard a guess. But unless she plans on taking in the pleasantries of the Fair, I would expect her soon. As much as you can expect something of one who makes the unexpected her business." Again, the wobbly smile, as he drained some wine and sat stiffly.

Braylar swirled the ale around in his own mug. "Very good. Well, less than good, truly. But we work with what we have, yes? And just now, I suspect we suddenly have less. Time, luck, resources, something, but less, to be sure."

I hadn't recalled hearing that name before. But the exchange, the tone, the way the Syldoon suddenly seemed on edge and eager for drink, in the context of other conversations, other edginess, all clicked together for me. Before thinking it through, I blurted, "She's your sister, isn't she? This Soffjian."

Mulldoos clapped twice, slowly. "You might be a weasel and a cowardly horsecunt, boy, but you're half-clever, I'll grant you that."

I wondered if that was designed to prompt me to try to defend myself—would that raise me in his estimation if I did, or simply give him an excuse to knock me to the floorboards and kick in my teeth? But at least he confirmed I was right. I pressed on, ignoring Mulldoos. "And she's a Memoridon, your sister. But why is she so unwelcome? I thought the Syldoon controlled them. What reason do you have to—" I nearly said "fear" but knew that would end badly for me—"dislike her presence here so?"

Mulldoos shook his head. "Half-stupid, too."

Braylar looked beyond irritated now, though whether that was due more to my questioning or the arrival of his sister, I couldn't say. But before he could chastise me, Hewspear replied, "The Memoridons are controlled by the Tower Commanders. Just as the soldiers in the field are controlled by the Tower Commanders. We both answer to the same Commander. So, when the Memoridons and Syldoon operate in the same theater, they are. . . parallel. They have their agenda, and we have ours."

"Problem being," Mulldoos said, "those agendas don't always cozy up to one another."

"That would be perpendicular," Hewspear offered.

"Well, the Memoridons are plaguing perpendicular then, you old goat. Only thing I know is seeing one show up's not like to be a good thing. Cap's got the right of it, there. They bring nothing good most days. Unless of course your superior officer got himself a peculiar cursed flail that steals memories. That thing Memoridons tend to know more about than most. Might be the only time one showing up unannounced ain't the worst thing that could—"

"Enough!" Braylar slapped the table. "She is here. We will survive her presence as best we can until she is gone. That is all. But if anyone so much as whispers another word about Soffjian being a boon, I'll nail his tongue to a door. With or without the head. Depending on mood. Are we clear?" Everyone nodded, though Mulldoos a second slower than the rest.

I'd read that Memoridons were used to gather intelligence, interrogate, even assassinate—the books noted little else was known about them, besides the fact that they were shadowy and dealt in memory magic, all of which justifiably earned them dangerous repute. But those accounts were written by Anjurians, or Gurtagese, or the odd Ulldesian.

But given that they were controlled by the Syldoon, not the other way around, I always assumed the trepidation was felt only beyond the borders of the Empire. Even if Memoridons had some autonomy, they still answered to the same commander the soldiers did. I didn't understand how these seasoned and generally callous and crude veterans could be so disturbed simply by one being in the same city. Even before the arrival of the captain's sister, the mere mention of the name seemed to rankle the Syldoon unlike anything else. But clearly Braylar was in no mood for more on the topic, so I held my tongue. Which was always a wise move, especially on the heels of the nailed-to-a-door threat.

Braylar turned back to Hewspear. "Now then, Vendurro tells me you have less. . . troublesome news as well. What of it?"

Hewspear set his cup down. "Well, I imagine the other news changes the complexion, but I have word of Henlester."

Braylar leaned forward. "Indeed. We have his whereabouts, then? I thought our ears in his house had been. . . stuffed?"

"If Dothelus or Mikkner yet live, I've heard nothing of it. I suspect, as you do, that the high priest has culled his household significantly. Still, we haven't turned up their bodies, yet, so they might survive. But if so, they've given no word of any kind."

Braylar's forehead wrinkled and then he asked, "So, then, we have word from the castle?"

Hewspear nodded. "We do. Obviously not verified for a certainty. But it seems Henlester has fled the barony, and is holed up in a hunting lodge. The reports suggest it's one of three spots. The southern portion of the Hedgeleaf Forest, or possibly further west, one of two lodges in the Forest of Deadmoss. It's quite large."

"Not his own lodge here in the barony then. The man is a cheat, a liar, a murderer of whores, but at least he isn't stupid. These other lodges, they are owned by. . . ?"

Mulldoos jumped in. "Brother priests, am I right? These righteous bastards always stand shoulder to shoulder when it comes to defying the lord of the land."

Hewspear chuckled. "You do have such a way with words, Mulldoos. True eloquence, It's rather inspiring, really, a poetic gust. But you do have the right of it. Both lodges belong to High Priests in their order, though in another barony."

Mulldoos tilted his chair, balanced on the back legs. I had the dreadful urge to nudge him under the table until he fell on his ass. "See there. Brune's a brutal bastard with an ass tighter than a peanut, but he's the legal lord of the land, and hunting a fugitive. Those priestly pricks—"

"Live in another barony, as I noted," Hewspear corrected. "So, if they owe allegiance to any baron, it isn't Brune. Segwiss, was it, in the south?"

Vendurro chimed in, "Segrick, Lieutenant. Thinking it's Segrick."

"That's right! Segrick. So—"

Mulldoos broke in, "Doesn't much matter who the baron is, when brutal Brune figures out where Henfucker is holed up, I expect he won't be too happy with the dumb sons of whores who harbored him. Point of fact, I expect Brune won't be in the mood to care too much about borders and boundaries, neither."

"Borders are boundaries."

"Point being, you wrinkled old cock—"

"All cocks are wrinkled. Until they aren't."

"Well, you're always wrinkled, so there's that. But the point being, priests are making an awful error harboring one of their own, priestly disposition to slime together as they do. If Brune doesn't take them out himself, he'll be complaining loud and long to this Segwick, and—"

"Segrick," Vendurro corrected.

"Bite my hairy jewels," Mulldoos replied. "Segrick is a baron, and they have a peculiar way of sticking together, too, least when it comes to sticking it to the priests."

Braylar had heard enough bickering. "We aren't concerned with baronial or priestly relations or protocol just now. When is Brune moving? When he verifies the location for a certainty?"

Hewspear nodded. "If the information is accurate, I imagine so."

"If?"

Hewspear leaned back, cringing as he moved and his ribs, sore or broken, shifted as well. "Brune might be vicious, in his pampered way, but he is also crafty. And after the incident in the theater, he knows there are eyes and ears in his house. He might believe they are Henlester's. But if he believes they are ours—and clearly the man isn't overly inclined to trust us just now—well, a cunning man. . . "

"Yes, well taken." Braylar's hand drifted down to one of the flail heads, intentionally or by reflex, I couldn't say. "If he were hunting for ears and eyes, he might skip the ruse of three sites and fix on one, but as you say, he is not a fool, so anything is in play here. Send six men, one pair toward each hunting lodge. Have them hold for any sign of Brune's scouts returning. If the news is accurate and not simply setting a trap, he would have dispatched men already to ascertain the truth of Henlester's whereabouts. So, let's determine for ourselves, yes?"

Hewspear drained his glass. "Very good, Captain."

He started to rise when Mulldoos asked, "And if the crafty, cocksucking baron is baiting us? We leaving then?"

Braylar dropped the Deserter flail head he'd been holding and it clinked against its twin. "We don't rise to the bait. As I told you the other day, we have sacrificed much to put things in motion here, and I won't simply abandon it because the man has a suspicious mind. If he truly had damning information, we'd be strapped to tables in his cellar, not debating tactics here. So, if it is a trap and doesn't spring, that will go some length to perhaps dimming his suspicion, or redirecting it. He is willing to believe his priests are plotting against him, which is exactly why we can't allow Henlester to fall into his hands. He must be ours or eliminated. I hope I've made myself abundantly—"

There was a rapping on the door, but when no one called out from the other side, hands dropped to weapons around the room as everyone jumped up from the table, and I was equally relieved and distraught that I was unarmed. Vendurro whisked his sword out of the scabbard, Mulldoos drew his falchion, Hewspear pulled his mace off his belt and Braylar had Bloodsounder in hand.

Braylar looked at Vendurro and gestured toward the door, and then seeing me standing there, hissed to get my attention and motioned toward his chamber. I didn't immediately understand the intent. I raised my shoulders, and his dark look somehow darkened, and he pointed to his chamber once more. It took me a moment to remember the crossbow in there, and I rushed in and after a panicked search found it and the quiver.

I fitted the devil's claws to the thick string and worked the mechanism as quickly as I could, dropped a bolt in place, then rushed back into the common room, reminding myself to be careful not to trip and accidentally loose the thing. Even with all the training and drilling, it was a wonder soldiers didn't accidentally kill or injure more men on their own side than they did.

But either I had taken longer preparing the crossbow than I thought or Vendurro had verified the person knocking more quickly than expected, because when I entered the common room again, he was already opening the door, though he still had his sword in hand.

Two women stepped through the doorway, as different as day and, well, dusk at least. The first was tall for a woman, taller than me and Mulldoos, and nearly on even height with Braylar. Two other things immediately stood out about her. First, her dress and armament were exceptional. She was wearing armor—a cuirass of silver scales, not unlike what Braylar had worn in the Green Sea, though slightly less tarnished, with a scale fauld around her hips, and scale bands encircling her upper arms as well. She had a short red cape, fringed along the bottom, and trousers ending mid-calf, her lean calves bare to the dusty sandals on her feet. While the woman was thin, there was no mistaking the muscle everywhere, even without her moving overmuch. She wore her armor well.

On her left hip, she had a suroka, seemingly standard issue of the Empire, and I assumed she must have been Syldoon, but her neck was bare, unmarked by a noose or anything else. Still, it was impossible to ignore the polearm she carried, a ranseur longer than she was tall, with a red tassel beneath the head that matched the color of her short cloak. She might not have been a Syldoon soldier, but she clearly knew how to take care of herself.

But while the arms and armament were striking, her face and expression were more so. Her auburn hair hung mostly loose, though with some seemingly random braids pulling enough away from her face to reveal it in full. A narrow nose, full lips, cheeks unmarred by scars or divots or obvious blemish. By most estimations, she would have been accounted very attractive, and in some circles, a true beauty. But those same plump lips seemed disinclined for humor or anything erotic, pursed in something between distaste and an arrogant sneer. And the eyes under the thin, dark brows weren't pools to be stared into. In fact, I got the impression that looking at her too long or attracting her attention in return would be a very bad thing. The eyes were cold, harsh, measuring. And while she didn't share many features with her bother, and seemed far more martial than I imagined any Memoridon being, it was clear she had to be Soffjian. The eyes gave it away.

The woman who followed her into the room, however, was radically different. Short, and if not especially pudgy, pillowy with full hips, she also wore trousers that stopped short to reveal her calves, which were thick and rounded with muscle. But besides the long-bladed suroka, she had no weapons, no armor, only the modest ash-colored tunic and coat, a burnt orange sash around her waist, and a pewter badge on her breast, a running jackal.

Her skin was darker than Soffjian's, though not nearly as much as Hewspear's, which was like the inside of a lantern. No, hers was the color of sandnuts. Her hair, not quite black, wasn't long enough to be braided or pulled back into a bun or a tail, but still required a wild assortment of silver pins and clasps to keep it in some semblance of order. She reminded me of the river wrens I'd seen as a child, wild feathers sticking out in nearly every direction at once. She had silver rings on each eyebrow, and several along the rims of her ears, and at least one stud flashing on her nose. And while Soffjian's eyes were dark and dangerous, this woman's were so pale it was hard to tell they were blue at all, but still worlds warmer. There was something impish about her expression, as if the sight of several armed men was amusing for some reason. Dimples, bubbly cheeks, a small nose that had a fetching almost squared off tip, a hint of mischief in those peculiar eyes—if Soffjian was far more martial and imposing physically than I expected from a Memoridon, this other woman was far too puckish. Assuming she was a Memoridon.

Soffjian looked around the room, taking everything in in that all-too familiar way. When she lit on Braylar, she said, "Brother." She laid her ranseur on her shoulder, almost lazily. "I might be offended being welcomed by so many sharp and pointy objects, but Hewspear here tells me you've all suffered some scratches and bruises in a recent scuffle with the locals, so you're a bit on edge. Understandable, of course. And to be expected. But still. The lack of an embrace is a little hurtful."

Braylar smiled, utterly humorless, and while he slowly slid Bloodsounder back on his belt, he made no move at all to approach her. "Soffjian, sweet Soffjian, I hope all of my missives these last years have found you well."

She smiled in return, equally devoid of any warmth, and Braylar looked at Vendurro. "Sergeant, you haven't neglected to send them, I hope?"

Vendurro looked as confused as he appeared uncomfortable. "Missives, Cap?"

Soffjian replied, "I do believe your captain is having some fun at your expense. Always baiting and berating the underlings, eh brother? Ever the bully. But I am well, thank you ever so much for the concern, feigned or not. You, however, are looking a bit peaked. Jagged cheekbones, overcast complexion, some alarming bruising around the neck there, and yes, so many new scars. I would say, if you'll forgive me, that you look particularly unwell."

The other woman stepped closer. "Oh, Soff, always so critical. Would you rather he looked like a swineherd? He is a Syldoon captain, after all. I know they discourage us from fraternizing with you boys, but I must say, all the steel and scars are quite fetching. Exciting, really." When she smiled, it was clear her mockery was good-natured. "Hewspear, Mulldoos, Vendurro, so good to see you all again." She stopped when she saw me at the back of the room and waved. "And you, too, stranger with the crossbow. Though I do hope you lower it a bit. We are all friends here. Or at least not open enemies. Well, unless I'm getting that wrong. I do do that on occasion. And it seems we received our mandate so long ago, I hardly remember why we rode all this way."

I lowered the crossbow, embarrassed I hadn't already. Then Braylar looked at his sister and said, slippery with sarcasm, "While I am clearly overjoyed to see you again, I am anxious to be enlightened. Why did the two of you make such a trek? Surely it must be taxing already. I would have prepared a more suitable celebration of your arrival had our Tower Commander sent notice." He made no effort to disguise the bite in the last line. It was difficult to tell whether the arrival of Memoridons, the fact that his sister was one of them, or the surprising nature of the visit irked him more. It very well might have been a tie.

She smiled, thin and tight. "Very well. Cutting right through the pleasantries. My arrival is notice, of a sort. It seems you and your retinue have caused all the mayhem you're going to in the region. You have been recalled."

Braylar raised one eyebrow. "Truly? That does strike me as. . . odd. We are here by command of the Tower Commander himself. You do realize we have spent years in this region, orchestrating and preparing, and finally putting things in motion. Our orders were clear. Are clear."

She matched him eyebrow for eyebrow. "Mayhaps you should have followed them more quickly then."

"If Commander Darzaak has cause to be concerned or displeased, I assume we would have heard of it already. From him. Directly."

"Had the recall come by way of Commander Darzaak, I assume you would be right. But this recall comes from Emperor Cynead himself."

"Directly," the shorter woman added. When the siblings both glared at her, she said, "Well, just aiming for clarity. These kinds of messages often get muddied carried from place to place. Details get left out, conflated, what have you. Just want to be sure no one is confused about any of the particulars. I'm often confused. It's an unpleasant way to go through life."

"Shut it, Skeelana," Soffjian ordered. Again, sounding eerily similar to her kin in the room.

Braylar looked at Soffjian. "And the good Emperor is aware that these plans are part of a greater Imperial mandate, and endorsed by his admin-istration? Surely these facts have not slipped his mind, even as pressed as he is by mundane Imperial matters? Details get lost in the capital from time to time as well."

Skeelana nodded. "Excellent point."

Soffjian tapped the butt spike of her ranseur on the floorboards. "Not his mandate, brother. The predecessor he ousted. And while he did noth-ing to stop them, I would hardly call that a ringing endorsement. But in any event, he is recalling your company, as well as most others in Anjuria, if rumors are to be believed. But I don't trade in rumors. Only in fact, cold and cruel and often transcribed for posterity. Even Memoridons don't always trust in memory." She retrieved a scroll from her belt pouch and handed it to Braylar.

Braylar did not examine the seal for authenticity, but broke it quickly, bits of blood-colored wax falling onto the floor. Mulldoos and Hewspear exchanged a look as Braylar read the contents, eyes darting quickly across the lines. I wondered if it was coded or written simply in Syldoonian.

Vendurro asked, "They really pulling out the other companies here? A lot of Syldoon in the region."

Soffjian replied, "Rumor, Sergeant. Rumor's the slut you bend over a chair and never see again. Truth's the lady you wed."

Mulldoos slid the falchion back in his scabbard. "Truth usually turns out to be a bitch. And twice the trouble. Give me a bed full of rumors any day."

Skeelana laughed. Soffjian did not. She said, "Ahh, yes. Your lot does have a penchant for whores and barmaids."

Mulldoos burped, loud and long, as if he'd been saving it for rebuttal. Or the preamble, anyway. "Better company than most. Only consort with ladies and other powerful bitches when we got little enough choice."

Soffjian didn't take her eyes off Mulldoos that I noticed, and there was heat behind them. But she kept her voice level, so much so that it was difficult to tell that the jovial tone was counterfeit. "Bitches, witches, so difficult to tell if one is truly more flattering than the other. But 'powerful,' Mulldoos? You are far too kind."

Before their exchange had an opportunity to escalate, Braylar rolled the scroll back up and said, "Well, Mulldoos, you and anyone else in the company tired of Anjurian politics can breathe easy. It seems there is no wiggle room to speak of here. We will be returning to Sunwrack. Anon, as it happens." His tone ran at cross purposes to his words—he didn't seem particularly pleased or at ease.

Soffjian slowly spun her ranseur in circles, watching the tassels flutter above her hand. "I am hurt, brother, that my word alone wouldn't persuade you on this point, but hardly stunned. Which is why I was relieved to have the documentation. You have been abroad for so many years, I expect that this must come as a welcome surprise."

Twin scars at the corner of Braylar's lips twitched. "It is indeed surprising. But no less so than the fact that an esteemed Memoridon should be sent to deliver the news. Were my Jackal brothers so very occupied that none could be tasked with serving as courier? Certainly you haven't misbehaved and earned Commander's Darzaak's displeasure. Again."

The ranseur stopped spinning and now it was Soffjian's turn to force a hastily counterfeited smile. "Oh, no. I volunteered. Not wanting to miss the opportunity to reconnect after so many years, Bray."

There were undercurrents I didn't understand in the exchange but didn't have a chance to parse them out when Braylar gave a feral grin. "Much longer, and you might not have been able to track us at all."

Soffjian's eyes flashed with something closer to hate than love, but her false smile didn't waiver. "Oh, dear brother, I will always be able to track you. Always."

"A keen comfort. Truly."

Skeelana added, "Between the two of us, I'm sure we could find your company just about anywhere." She said this casually, impishly, but there was something else veiled there as well. A warning?

Braylar sat down in his chair. "Well, with this unexpected turn of events, we have plans and preparations to make. We cannot simply pull out of the region without undoing so much of the good work we've done here."

Soffjian lifted the ranseur, briefly inspecting the divot in the floor-boards the butt spike made. "I have not read your orders, of course, so can't speak to the specifics, but I was under the impression that Commander Darzaak was himself following imperial directive when he issued them. So I imagine there will be some urgency in obeying."

Braylar's smile seemed a touch more genuine now, though no more pleasant. "Ahh, yes. I imagine you need to return to Sunwrack very soon. So far afield, sister. It must be quite. . . uncomfortable for you. Don't feel the need to wait on our account. If you must go, by all means, go with speed. We won't be far behind."

Skeelana answered before Soffjian could. "Oh, I just don't think we could do that. No, no. You see, we have orders to accompany you every step of the way. Commander Darzaak was most insistent on that point. So there will be quite a bit of time for the two of you to catch up. Which is wonderful, if you ask me. Just wonderful."

"Truly moving," Hewspear offered.

Braylar ignored both of them, eyes still locked with his sister's. "All those skills, all that power, and still as much a pawn as the rest of us, yes? Never fear, we will move shortly. Just after I have followed the rest of the orders that prefaced the recall. The particulars of which, I will still leave to your vaunted and vaulted imagination. Now then, we have a great deal to do in a very short amount of time. So, if you will be so kind as to leave us to it. . . ?"

Soffjian seemed to like being dismissed as much as Braylar liked being recalled, but she nodded and replied, "Of course. Far be it from me to interfere with the work of soldiers and saboteurs. That is, I imagine, what you are doing in this region, is it not? Being but a pawn, I so rarely have fulsome information to operate with."

I wondered which parent the siblings had inherited their biting rejoinders from.

Braylar's smile didn't fade, though it seemed held there more by rigid force of will than any emotion. "I have so missed our engaging repartee, sister. Truly. But we will continue another time, yes?"

Soffjian held onto the ranseur, and performed an exaggerated bow and curtsy. "As you will, brother. Only remember, the recall originated with Cynead, not Darzaak. So you would be wise not to dawdle overmuch. I suggest you make your final maneuverings soon. This Emperor has never been much of a forgiving sort. Though which of them has?"

She turned and headed to the door, but before exiting, stopped in front of Vendurro and laid a hand on his shoulder. "I am truly sorry for Glesswik's death."

If anyone thought it strange she would know such a thing, having only arrived, no one gave any indication. Vendurro nodded and said only, "Appreciated."

Soffjian let Skeelana leave first and then pulled the door shut behind her. We all listened as their footfalls receded down the hall toward the stairs, then Mulldoos broke the silence. "What are you fixing to do, Cap? Want me to round up the regulars and get them pointed home?"

There was an edge to the question, as if the answer he expected and the answer he wanted weren't likely to be the same.

Braylar didn't disappoint. Exactly. "I have no wish to give my sister the satisfaction of vacating so quickly. But she is right on that count—the Emperor is not the most patient of men. So, we ride out tomorrow. Tell the rest of the men to prepare the wagons and supplies. We will meet them after."

Mulldoos looked at Hewspear, then back to his captain. "After?"

Braylar stood and started toward his room, only seeming to realize halfway there that Mulldoos had asked him a question. I wasn't sure if this was due more to him calculating several moves ahead, or if the stolen memories were taking their toll. He looked at Mulldoos. "We are going for the High Priest tomorrow. Have twenty men ready to ride out with us. Twenty-five, if that leaves enough to handle the wagons. No, no, twenty will have to do. I have no wish to leave our cargo poorly attended."

It was obvious this didn't sit well with Mulldoos, but he paused long and hard to chew over his objections before finally saying, "The High Priest, Cap? What for? Brune was ready to plunk us in his toy room already. Sure as spit he'll figure we were in league with Henlester or worse once we pull out. What's the point going after the priest? Won't matter if we silence or even capture that holy horsecock. Nothing will win Brune's good graces now. Can't see we got much to gain there, Cap. What am I missing? Am I looking sideways again?"

I expected Braylar's temper to flame up anew, being questioned by his lieutenant so soon after their recent dustup, but he appeared calm enough as he slowly made his way back to the table. "You are correct. The good baron will no doubt presume the worst. Thanks to a rash and foolish Emperor, a great deal of effort will have gone to waste here, and I suspect in the other baronies as well. Lives spent and lost over nothing now. You are absolutely right—we have no more to play out with him. Not just now. But Henlester is another piece on the board. And still a valuable one. If we can procure him without additional loss, we will do it."

Mulldoos seemed ready to argue the point, but perhaps remembered the recent dressing down he incurred out in public and thought better of it. Instead, he looked to Hewspear in mute appeal.

While Hewspear didn't share the pale boar's hot blood, he still seemed to be of a similar mind, at least as far as this single topic went. Everything else was a point of contention. "Captain, as we discussed, there is still the possibility—perhaps a strong one at that—that Brune is baiting us with the leak of the High Priest's whereabouts. He could be waiting for us to march right into that trap."

Mulldoos couldn't help adding, "Like the ruined temple, Cap? You said you thought we would spring one there, but I didn't listen. Turned out you couldn't have been more right. I couldn't have been more wrong, you couldn't have been more right. There. Said it loud and clear. So why risk another trap?" Braylar twitch-smiled. "We wasted life enough in this region, Cap. Said so yourself. And that was before Cynead's little summons. Now that waste is bigger, and worse. Nothing at all to show for it. Nothing, and—"

"That is precisely why we make a move to obtain the High Priest. Or at least close enough to see if there is a trap waiting for us, to see if he is even there. If there is a chance to take him, we can at least leave Anjuria with something to mitigate the losses. If only a little, yes? But if we don't at least ride to see, we surely will abandon Anjuria with only Syldoonian dead on the ledger. And that is unacceptable. We cannot ignore an Imperial mandate, much as I would like to, but neither can we leave with nothing. I will not allow it."

Mulldoos looked ready to press on, as he was wont to do, but Hewspear seemed to sense that and wisely interrupted. "Very well, Captain. But it does raise the question, would it be not wiser to keep our forces together? If Brune is attempting to ensnare us, we are doing half the work for him by splitting our men. And we do have something else for the ledger—those scrolls and maps, those ancient volumes. We risk losing those if we leave them behind to chase down a rumor."

Braylar smiled, "As the good lieutenant says, he prefers those. But we don't know precisely what we have compiled. It might prove to be nothing of value, antiquated scratch marks on piss-poor parchment of no interest to anyone. But there is a very real chance that Henlester might be ours for the taking. And if there is something useful in those dusty scrolls, he could also be instrumental in ciphering the meaning and piecing things together.

"The rest of the men will be behind us only by half a day, a day at the most. We have a chance to seize the High Priest and double the value of our prize. We go on the morrow. Prepare the men. That is all."

Hewspear rose, sensing the futility of arguing the point, but unable to completely help himself. "Soffjian did mention the Emperor was expecting us to withdraw at haste."

Braylar replied, "And so we shall. As it is, she's likely not expecting us to depart for a few days. I'm sure she imagines I will do my best to frustrate her, as I know she would me. So, given that Deadmoss isn't too far out of the way, we might even make a better pace for home leaving tomorrow. Anything else, or are you two layabouts willing to follow orders now?"

Mulldoos shook his head, his thick neck rippling, and appeared ready to dig in, but Hewspear gave him a look, and he kept his reply to, "And if you sniff another trap? What then, Cap?"

Braylar's smile disappeared. "If I sense a trap, you will be the first to know, and the first to remind me of what happened the last time we didn't retreat when we had the chance. I will not lead us to our destruction.

If our scouts, flesh and blood, or steel—" he tapped the haft of Blood-sounder, "give the slightest hint that things are amiss, we regroup with our wagons and our dead, and head home, ledger be damned, yes? Now ready the men."

His lieutenants saluted and left. Perhaps more grudgingly than they had in Rivermost, and no doubt grumbling and grousing. That did seem to be the life of a soldier.

Braylar was eyeing me, "Yes? You have something to offer as well? Out with it. Why should my trusted lieutenants be the only ones to question my every move or motive? With Lloi gone, you must pick up the slack, Arki. I see you wish to add something, so add it."

I did, though I intended to bring it up another time. Still, no time was likelier to result in an answer I wanted, so I said, "You mentioned the scrolls you scavenged."

He stared at me. "I do not recall using the word scavenged. Despite the sigil of our Tower, we are not jackals or crows. But what of them?"

"And they are old, ancient even?"

His gaze shifted into a glare so I hurried on. "I have a good working knowledge of a handful of languages, contemporary, as well as older iter-ations. And if you scav. . . discovered them mostly in Anjuria, I can make out Middle or even Old Anjurian well enough. I could decipher them for you. Or try at least."

He gave me an impenetrable look. Those worried me the most. "An interesting proposal. And do you make this offer out of your commitment to our cause now, or because you cannot resist a scholarly mystery?"

Sensing an opening, and without thinking, I replied, "I still don't know what your cause is, or whether the thing you do and purport to do are even the same. But I do like a good mystery. You wouldn't need to involve someone else. And I already know the penalty for any treachery. You've made that abundantly clear."

Braylar didn't answer immediately, a half-smile on his lips, no doubt weighing the benefits of involving me deeper against any mistrust he still harbored. I waited anxiously until he finally replied, "The Syldoon are the ultimate pragmatists and utilitarians, Arki. We recognize talent, use talent, and reward talent. That is one secret to our success and superiority to kingdoms where bloodlines are all, no matter how thin, diluted, or poisoned. So you see, I am encouraged you arrived at the proposal on your own. It saves me the trouble."

When he saw my expression, my slow recognition, he laughed, and for once it sounded not only genuine but free of mockery or bile or any other nasty thing. I said, "That was why you hired me, and the previous scribes as well, wasn't it? After testing me, after I passed, you were going to open that chest and ask me to start sifting through the contents. Right?"

He switched to Syldoonian. "Oh, I still have my misgivings. Have no doubt on that score. But yes, you shall have your crack at the mystery, bookmaster. Let us see what you see. But not tonight. Tonight you pack, and we leave early on the morrow."

Braylar waited to see if I comprehended or not. I'd never admitted that I studied and could understand Syldoonian well enough, though butchered it when I attempted to speak it. So I opted for sticking with Anjurian in responding. "Thank you, Captain Killcoin. I will prepare for the journey and look forward to unraveling the treasures you've gathered."

He laughed again, almost a bark, and shook his head. "I should have known. More fool me." Then he turned and headed to his quarters. I stood there, stunned that I'd scored a victory, of sorts, and thrilled that I would have something to occupy my time and exercise my skills besides simply recording the murky doings of my patron and his retinue.

After preparing my things to head out in the morning, I stared up into the rafters as I listened to the revelers in the beer garden below, my mind alert and jumpy, as I imagined what secrets or knowledge might be contained in the material the Syldoon had gathered. They wouldn't go to such lengths to collect them if they were just lay subsidy rolls, or a catalogue of a larder, or anything trivial or mundane. They'd traveled far, and in secret, to gather them, so there had to be something fabulous on some of those pages. Surely some of them. Or at least the strong possibility. But what? What would I discover? Provided I hadn't overpromised in my linguistic abilities. What secrets would I unravel?

The possibilities were delicious enough to keep me up for hours. Soldiers might have been that excited on the eve of a battle, or courtiers before trying to conquer the chastity of a lady, or maybe sailors before departing on a voyage. I knew my ambitions were modest, even silly to most men. Especially those lacking in education. The idea of spending any time at all sifting through dusty tomes and arcane quill marks would seem the dullest enterprise known to man. But to me, that was what I missed about university the most—the opportunity to explore knowledge, recent or crumbling with age, that those who had come before saw fit to pen to the page in an effort to preserve and protect. There was a certain thrill about coming across even an old subsidy, working out the translation, exercising the mind. And nothing so keen or sharp an excitement as coming across something that had, for whatever reasons, gained a certain value or currency over the years, something lost or critically important or of such significance that men would pay handsomely, or even kill, to obtain it.

I would never be a man of martial prowess, or wealth or power, or even an important one in most circles. But if I could uncover some treasure in the midst of all those pages, then, for the moment at least, I would be worthy, practically invaluable. Yes, Braylar could find another scholar, but he'd already gone through some, and I'd managed to secure a spot in the company, even as I broke into the crate. Maybe because of it. Maybe the captain had even been waiting for me to take initiative. But either way, whether I'd passed a test or he'd forgiven me my failure, he was giving me a grand opportunity. And no matter how few men would understand, or appreciate, it was one that kept my mind abuzz. It felt like I was finally realizing my purpose.

Perhaps tethering myself to the Syldoon hadn't been the most foolish decision I'd ever made after all.

It seemed like I had only just drifted to sleep to that thought when I felt a hand roughly shaking my shoulder.

I opened my eyes, blinded by lantern light. "What. . . is it. . . what's happening?"

Vendurro stood back, though I recognized the voice before the blurry silhouette came into focus. "Got to move, Arki. Cap says we got to move."

I looked out the window, and didn't see the faintest hint of dawn, which didn't stop me from asking, "It's not dawn—is it? I thought. . . the captain said we were leaving sometime tomorrow. Later today, I mean. During daylight, that is. What's changed?"

Vendurro started for the door, looked over his shoulder, the lantern casting wild shadows on the wall as it swung in his hand. "Bloodsounder." Said alone like that, it sounded like the ominous clap of a great leaden bell. "Cap says there's a fight of some kind coming to us. Right quick, from the sounds of it. Cap ain't like to rouse us and set us in motion unless he had real good cause. You know that as good as any. I can't explain it, not a lick, guessing you can't, nor nobody else for that matter, but we all seen that when he feels a thing, it's got as much chance as coming true as not. Better, if he feels it strong enough. And if you saw his face just now, you'd know there weren't nothing subtle or slight about it. So we're heading out to meet it. All of us. Get dressed, grab your things."

He left the lantern on a hook, still swinging crazily, and pulled the door shut behind him. I heard voices on the other side, as no doubt the rest of the Syldoon were up and ready to move. To head out. To meet some unknown foe in the dark.

All thoughts of scrolls and happy translations disappeared faster than spilled water in the sand. Precious, and gone in an instant, as if it never existed at all.

I jumped out of bed, tripping on the blankets, nearly landing on my face. I hoped the captain was wrong. He'd been wrong at the Three Casks. Well, half wrong. Violence had come, it just hadn't involved the Syldoon. And when they were ambushed in the temple ruins by Henlester's soldiers, he hadn't been able to discern or decipher whatever flickers he might have sensed. Braylar had misgivings, those borne of a naturally distrustful and calculating nature, and he'd certainly expected something. But Bloodsounder hadn't given any warning at all, or not enough to persuade him.

However, the captain had been right out on the steppe. Eerily so. That was impossible to dismiss as coincidence. And he'd been far more certain before that violence occurred. So if he was equally convinced now. . .

Dressing as quickly as I could, I still clung to the thin hope that maybe he was mistaken, but dreading the reality that he likely wasn't. Fortunately, I'd already stowed my writing supplies and clothes in advance of our planned trip, so it didn't take very long. When I had it all together, I took one last look around, and was about to head to the door when I saw I'd nearly left Lloi's curved sword behind. It was in its scabbard, leaning against the wall at the foot of the bed.

I knew I was likely to do more damage to myself than any opponent, but it would feel good to have some means of defending myself. Plus, I couldn't simply leave it behind. Well, I could have—no one else would have known or cared. But it was hers, which made it mine by default now. So along it came. I set my writing case down long enough to buckle the scabbard belt around my waist, gathered everything again, and suddenly felt a sharp reluctance to leave.

There shouldn't have been any pull at all—it wasn't that great a room, and I'd only been there for a few days. Part of it was the fear of whatever unknown threat was not far beyond the door, the bloodshed I'd see or be a part of. But it was more than that. Maybe it was the fact that I was only slightly less nomadic than the Grass Dogs, never inhabiting a place for long. It was foolish—I knew the Grieving Dog was a temporary abode, and we wouldn't be in Alespell forever. But even accustomed to being on the move, I wasn't prepared to quit the room yet.

Vendurro's voice startled me. "You about ready? Doesn't matter, either way, time to go." He poked his head in the door and saw that I had all my belongings and nodded. "Alright then. Let's have at it." And then he disappeared again.

The common room was a flurry of activity. Syldoon I'd only seen once or twice were carrying supplies, and doing it in a hurry, shouldering past each other, armor jingling, boots scuffling, cursing in harsh whispers when there was an impasse at the main door leading to the hall. It was amazing the whole inn wasn't awake. Maybe it was—I heard a door open down the hall and someone start to tell the Syldoon to keep it down before being shouted at and shutting it quickly. Clearly, Braylar wasn't intending to slip off in the night like wraiths or overly worried about appearances now. He must have been certain indeed to put all his soldiers into action before dawn. That didn't bode well at all.

I held my writing case to my chest, a satchel slung over my shoulder, conscious that I was the only unarmored man in the room. And the only one standing still.

Braylar marched out of his quarters, and I noticed immediately that he was more heavily armored than at any point I'd seen him. Where he'd worn his scale cuirass underneath a tunic both in the grass and during the battles around the ruined temple, he now had on a mail byrnie with a lamellar cuirass on top, and vambraces of an unusual splinted design on his forearms, and splinted greaves on his lower legs. Clearly, he was expecting a full-on fight, and in no hurry to disguise his intention to meet it head on. Captain Killcoin said something quickly to Hewspear, who nodded and headed out into the hall as well. The captain saw me and strode over, eyed me up and down, stopping only briefly on Lloi's sword. I almost expected him to tell me to unbuckle it right then and there, but instead he said, "Ahh, so good to see a seasoned veteran in the command room. Always inspires the troops. Given that you are ready for the road, I take it Vendurro briefed you."

I looked around quickly, bearing in mind Hewspear's point about revealing only what was necessary about Bloodsounder. "Vendurro told me violence was coming. And seemed certain. Or certain you were certain. Which amounts to the same thing, I suppose. Is it like. . . the Green Sea, then? You are certain?"

He took a step closer—his breath wasn't as fouled by ale as it had been of late, but wasn't free from the vapors either. He managed a whisper and growl together, "Very little in this world is certain, but my temper is one of them if you don't keep your voice down. As to what is coming, it is enough that I am unwilling to gamble on being wrong."

Two soldiers bumped into us, carrying the case of scrolls—my treasure!—and mumbled and apologized to the captain before colliding with the table.

"I've seen newborn calves with better balance. Careful, you whoresons."

One said, "Sorry, Cap!" and they hustled out, letting another Syldoon in the room before tromping into the hall.

I was about to ask Braylar what we were doing, but Mulldoos appeared next to us and I shut my mouth. "Boys are near to ready, Cap. Main battalion are heading out with you, the remainder are holding back with the wagons, like you ordered. Got ourselves a problem, though."

"I imagine we have several. Anytime you rouse the troops in the middle of the night to tell them plans have moved up, many things can go awry. What, specifically, are you referring to?"

Mulldoos glanced over his shoulder, and seeing no other soldiers coming or going, replied, "Got to figure we're up against Brune's bunch, right? I mean, you didn't say as much, but then you didn't have to. Now, the gates are supposed to be open just after dawn, Fair hours. But if it's that prick Gurdinn or any other Bruneboys come calling, even if we leave their corpses in the street without a casualty and break for a gate, real good chance we might find it shuttered tight. But even if we win free, the wagons and stragglers will be, well, straggling. Maybe we should have them trail close behind. If it's a lock in, our best chance is to break free in force."

Braylar nodded. "Perhaps so. But while the good baron has no doubt attempted to gather some intelligence about how many Syldoon he has in his city, we've done an even better chance of disguising our number and keeping ourselves scattered. He will be expecting us to try to flee in a group. Those wagons are going to go slower. Even if we abandon some supplies, the bulk even, we're not leaving the recent cargo. Too big for horse, so wagon it is. If most of our force litters the street with their bloodied soldiers and makes for a gate, locked or otherwise, they will not be looking for the rest to come in a smaller party."

"Fair point, but—"

"I wasn't finished, Lieutenant. Mobility is our greatest ally. Always was and will be. So we ambush the ambushers and take flight, but the wagons would only slow us down. Our one chance to really see them out as well is to take the risk of them leaving separately once the gates are clear, and reconnecting well outside Alespell. Once we've assured ourselves we have lost or beaten any pursuit."

Mulldoos nodded vigorously. "So they go separate. Fine. But we should at least provide some other kind of diversion. Beyond just us killing Bruneboys in the streets, I mean. If we do win free—"

"When."

"When we win free, then, even if they ain't looking real hard for more Syldoon, they won't be half-asleep at the gates neither. Might be checking wagons real close. I would. And you'd check them twice as close."

Braylar nearly smiled. "Very well. What did you have in mind?"

When Mulldoos didn't reply right away, it was obvious he had been operating in extemporaneous mode. Once again, my words came out before I'd examined them carefully beforehand. "The ripper."

Both men looked at me in surprise, clearly having forgotten I was standing right there. I pushed on, "The other day, I saw a ripper caged near the main plaza. On display. About as terrible a creature as Lloi described, maybe more so. Tore a boy's hand clean off like it was. . . a page from a book. If someone freed it. . . "

I left the thought unfinished, because I hadn't really considered the consequences of the suggestion, and when I did, it was impossible to say them out loud.

Braylar seized on it immediately. "A ripper running free would cause chaos. The very kind to draw the attention of every city guard in the quarter."

Mulldoos nodded. "Like to kill a few folks, for certain. Anybody who wasn't would be heading for the gates right quick. Brune couldn't double his damage by impeding them neither." He smiled, showing several shockingly white and uneven teeth. "That's vicious, scribbler. Right vicious. Didn't think you had it in you." He turned back to Braylar. "Wish I'd thought of it myself, but it's plaguing perfect."

Braylar agreed. "Near to it. See it done."

Mulldoos's looked at me again, but something akin to grudging appreciation instead of the ready disgust that so often sat there. He saluted his captain and headed to the door.

When I blurted out the suggestion, I had an image in mind of the beast running loose, roaring, scaring everyone in the city, but foolishly, I hadn't imagined that it would be killing as it went. But of course it would. It attacked a boy through the bars—if it had run of the city, even for a short time before the watch or soldiers cornered it and took it down, surely more bodies or pieces would be left in its wake.

I felt my stomach twist and said, "Captain, about the ripper, I—"

"Very clever, Arki. Exceedingly, truth be told. Mulldoos is right—a surprisingly cold and calculating design. You have been in our company too long already, I fear. You are becoming more Syldoonian than the Syldoon."

He clapped me on the shoulder and turned to head back to his quarters when he heard a voice that stopped him short. Soffjian's. "Brother, I must say, I hadn't expected such compliance. In fact, I was prepared for the likelihood that I was going to need to repeatedly remind you of the Emperor's very limited leniency. And yet here I discover you and your men scrambling around as if in preparation for an invasion. Curious."

The captain turned around, making no special pains to remove the sneer from his face. "Nearly as curious as you appearing here before the dawn."

"You weren't trying to leave without me, I hope. The Emperor and Commander Darzaak were quite clear. Skeelana and I escort you to the capital. The entire way. And as to my sudden, and early, arrival, surely you haven't forgotten—"

"You have your ways. Of course. And of course I could not possibly have forgotten. So let us both dispense with the theatrics, sister. You know we are preparing for an unexpected fight. There is very good reason to believe our enemies are moving against us this morning. Very soon, in fact."

Soffjian drove the butt of her ranseur into the floorboards. "Oh, dear. And what enemies are those?"

Without missing a beat, Braylar replied, "The kind that carry swords and grudges, my dear. And they will be upon us presently if we are not on the move. So, as I can see you are already armed and fed, you are welcome to join us. In an Imperial escort capacity, of course. I would never expect

Memoridons to get involved in a conflict not of their making. Or you can remain behind and take the Fair in for a few days. Catch up after, as I know you are infinitely capable of. But either way, my men will be leaving without me in a moment, which would hardly be very captain-like of me. So if you'll excuse me, I have some martial matters that require my attention."

Soffjian didn't look particularly satisfied with that response, but wasn't prepared to push the issue either. I had the feeling she was trying to determine if her brother was playing her in some fashion. Which, if true, was a healthy skepticism to have. I would have been better served with a healthier dose of it myself along the way.

She nodded and bowed ever so slightly. I wasn't sure if that was appropriate or mocking and Braylar gave no indication. "If it's all the same to you, I will accompany as you leave to meet your foes. And do my best not to get in the way. If you've seen one grand Fair, you've seen the rest, true?"

Soffjian didn't wait for his response and left the room, deftly sidestepping a Syldoonian soldier coming through the door. Braylar looked at me and my possessions. Much less than most men, but too much for one horse. He said, "Store your extra clothes and writing supplies in a wagon in the stable, and be quick."

"It sounded as if it might be a few days before we meet up with them again. Should I bring my writing desk with me? I'd like to, if that's fine?"

Braylar replied, "As you wish. If I give you a crossbow, do you think you can avoid shooting your horse, yourself, or one of my men if you ride with us into combat?"

At hearing "combat" I resisted the urge to swallow hard or shift my weight from one foot to the other. "The last time I had one, Captain, I managed to distract one of Henlester's men long enough for you to kill him. And hit a horse. Though that was even luckier than nearly hitting you and the guard. So, does that count as acquitting myself well enough to handle one again?"

The words were out too fast, and I almost started to apologize and recall them as he stared at me before saying, "Stow your gear then, Crossbowman Arkamondos. And I will arm you once more."

It seemed the more I was around the measured and calculating captain, the more rash and impulsive I was becoming. Not a very good combination.

I started toward the door and he said, "Stay close to Vendurro. I gave him no explicit instructions to keep you safe, but I suspect he actually likes you, so he might protect you a bit. I would advise you to stay near me, but I will be in the thick of it, and will have no patience for you if you get in the way."

With that lukewarm assurance, I headed out of the common room, forcing myself not to look around to take it in a final time. It wasn't so very special, and it seemed to invite ill luck. It would be my final time here regardless, but there was also utter finality, and I didn't want to dwell on that possibility. I walked quickly though the door and made my way down the stairs, nearly colliding with another Syldoon, moving around him only half as smoothly as Soffjian had managed. I'd never felt particularly dexterous, but this crew made me feel clumsier and less sure of my footing than at any other point in my life.

Unlike the Three Casks in Rivermost, the Grieving Dog didn't let commoners pay half-rent to sleep on the common room floor, but Gremete was up. As the owner of the inn, she probably rose before dawn most days, anyway. She was standing in the middle of the room, arms crossed over her meager chest, and didn't look particularly happy about the very early traffic of soldiers going up and down the stairs, but it didn't appear to be the irritation of someone roused from sleep.

Braylar leaned over the railing above, his mail and lamellar and weapons jingling, if such deadly accoutrement could be said to jingle. "My apologies for the disturbance, Lady Proprietor. The lodging has been exemplary, on the whole."

Had she been in a smaller city, or a road inn, seeing armed men moving early might have given her pause or concern, but Gremete seemed entirely nonplussed. "And you've been a good patron. Exemplary might be a bit strong, but you never stiffed me, were tidier than most, and minded your manners. On the whole. For soldiers." She had mastered the half-amused, half-exasperated tone that could have only come from being a mother.

This wasn't lost on Braylar, who smiled, more genuinely and longer than normal. He walked down the stairs, gloved hand still grazing the bannister ever so slightly, making a slithering noise as he went. When he reached the bottom, he tossed a small pouch jingling with coins. Gremete caught it, and though never having been stiffed, seemed in no hurry to begin now. She opened it and thumbed through the coin, squinting in the scant light. Then she looked up at Braylar. "I'm better with sums than most, but it looks like you overpaid a bit. More than a bit, truth be told. Looks to be about double what you owe. Something I should be worried about?"

Braylar's smile never left his face, held there so long it was worrisome. "A Syldoon never overpays, Lady Innkeep. Under on occasion, and accurate to a penny the rest of the time, but never over. Food and lodging, as discussed. The extra is to cover the damage."

Gremete looked up at the second floor and back to the captain. "About to recant on the good patron part. What all did you do to my rooms, Syldoon?"

"The rooms are in fine shape, Gremete. Never better. Some repairable damage to overall business I imagine. I expect it will be readily apparent soon enough." He regarded me, smile gone. "I had hoped all the armor and weapons and what not had alerted you to a pending melee. Were those hints overly subtle? Move, Arki."

He headed out the door, as Gremete started asking another question and just as quickly stopped when it was obvious he was in no mood for more discussion. She looked at me and I shrugged my shoulders. "The man does know something about damage, but I have no idea what he's talking about either."

She tucked the purse into her apron, threw a towel over her shoulder, and disappeared into a dark hall, shaking her head as she went.

Hurrying after Braylar, the writing case, satchel, crossbow, and quiver all bounced in various directions.

I walked into the stalls, the hint of the sun flaking the roofs and eaves to the east, but generally still blocked off from all but the castle in Alespell right now. The half-moon and its half-ring was still half-visible above one roof, delicate and white, like some fragile bit of crystal that had already been cracked in two, the missing half crushed to dust or fallen behind the horizon. A lantern hung on a hook just inside the stable door, otherwise we'd be in near darkness still, even with dawn upon us, but it was shuttered most of the way, and so the interior was gloom. Most of the Syldoon were mounted already, and Soffjian and Skeelana were as well.

It was a larger party than I expected, certainly more than had been staying at the Grieving Dog. I did a quick count and came up with eighteen:

fifteen soldiers, two Memoridons, plus myself. With the chill in the air, everyone's breath was ghosting in front of their faces at irregular intervals, and the effect was nearly mesmerizing. All these soldiers, armed and armored and saddled up for some skirmish or battle that only a handful of them had any understanding of, simply trusting that their captain had roused them in the middle of the night with good cause. Which was likely true. So when I shivered, it had less to do with a chill outside the skin as in.

I secured my gear on my horse as best I could, and it looked only marginally less clumsy on the animal than it had on me. But at least it wouldn't have to bear the added weight of armor. Though if Captain Killcoin was right, I'd probably find myself wishing I had some. When we headed to the temple, I expected I might witness some combat, but never imagined I might be in the thick of it. And there was little question I would be this morning.

The captain turned his helm over, spread the aventail drape out, then tipped his head down as he lifted the helm over, the riveted rings spreading about his shoulders and obscuring every part of his face save for his eyes. It gave him an even more fearsome look than usual.

Mulldoos approached Braylar and reported, "All the men are ready. And the wagons will move out later today, as ordered."

Braylar nodded and pulled one glove tighter on his hand, flexing the fingers. "Very good. And the rest?"

Mulldoos nodded. "Timing's like to be tricky, Cap, but the ripper'll show on cue, or the man that cocks it up will answer to me."

Braylar nodded. "Who do you have assigned?"

Mulldoos called out, "Lugger, Brunzlo, over here, now."

Two soldiers came jogging over, lamellar plates clacking.

Mulldoos said, "Cap's got some questions for you." Then he moved off to inspect one thing or another, possibly for the third or fourth time, was my guess.

Braylar turned to them. "You boys up to this?"

The taller soldier who had a pronounced dent in his nasal helm said, "Aye, Cap. Got it squared away, no worries."

"And the keepers?"

The shorter Syldoon chuckled and ran a finger across his neck in a sign that hadn't required interpretation since the dawn of time. I thought about how angry I'd been at that family for profiting off a caged beast and the foolishness of yokels, but that didn't mean they deserved to get murdered. My stomach flipped and wrestled with itself.

Braylar nodded. "Timing is critical. Open the cage too soon, and you're like to spoil the surprise and probably get killed in the bargain. Too late, and you will still end up dead. By sword or claw. Or Mulldoos. Either way, succeed and you're heroes, fail, and. . . " he drew a gloved finger across the mail drape, right around throat level.

Both soldiers saluted and walked their horses out of the stable and into the alley leading to the main street. I got my horse moving and sidled alongside the captain. I glanced at the rear entrance to the inn and seeing no one, asked as quietly as I could, "Is this really wise, captain? I've seen this creature—it isn't a trained—"

"It was your suggestion. And safer than the alternative."

"Which was?"

"Fire."

"Fire?"

"An element. The hot one."

I thought about the stables, the hay, the wattle, daub, and old wood in nearly every building. Yes, even a small fire would be more dangerous than a ripper running free.

"But, what if it kills patrons here? Shopkeepers? Fairgoers?"

"It is a ripper. I would be disappointed if it simply nuzzled them and showed its belly for a good rub." Braylar was trying to make light, but between knowing that the man and his sons were lying in a pool of dried blood somewhere, and the likelihood that others would be soon enough, I felt sick again.

"Is that why you paid Gremete extra, because—"

Braylar lowered his voice, whisper-rasping, "Gremete has been compensated. Grossly, unless I misjudge. I imagine she will be safe indoors in any event. While your affection for battered soldiers, plump pilgrims, scarecrow girls, and flinty old innkeeps is commendable and duly noted, you seem to forget, I do what must be done to protect my men and our mission. And if that required all of Alespell to be turned to ash, I would gladly do it. But with any luck, our enemies will serve as the main course, and the beast will be hunted and killed before it can cause any serious mischief."

Braylar looked up at the dawnlight, more prominent on the shingles on the upper portions of the roof now, creeping down like a silent thief. "We have to move. Now. But rest assured, my tender scribe, this will likely save lives. Ours, at least. And in the final tally, that is all that truly matters." He called out to the other soldiers in the barn. "Lead your horses. We go."

We all rode out onto the main concourse, Broadbeef Lane, and headed east away from the Grieving Dog. It was largely deserted at this early hour, but even if curfew hadn't been lifted and the first Fairgoers hadn't crossed the bridges and gates, some Alespell denizens were already up and moving through the streets, though most darted into the shadows or down a side street at the approach of a large party of men on horse, so I never got close enough to make out their purpose. Likely some were bakers or craftsmen, and some thieves or drunkards, though if the latter, sobering up remarkably well, and moving to safer avenues.

Many of the buildings in this district, a mix of commercial residences with the merchants living above the storefronts, were full of variety, the corbelled houses and shop fronts with a wild mix of facades. . . chipped paint and whitewash, ornamented by irregular paneling, faded murals, enamel mosaics, and decorative tiles both cracked and new. In the still dim light, the colors were muted and largely gray or grayer, but the diversity of construction and decoration still caught the eye, as did the range of signs hanging for the illiterate to make out the purpose of the shops—some wooden silhouettes, like the scissors hanging from the tailor, the saddle from the saddler, and others with the object painted on simple signs, like the boot for the shoemaker, the candle for chandler, and on and on. Some were simple and without frills, but a few merchants had employed talented artists to render hats and purses and wagon wheels and locks and gloves and every other thing someone might sell or buy.

Vendurro rode up alongside me, helm and lamellar reflecting very little with the sun still only peering over the highest rooftops. He started to say hello, yawned loudly enough to draw a dirty look from Mulldoos over his shoulder ahead of us, and took a big bite out of a hardboiled egg. Bits of crumbly yolk caught in the tuft of beard on his chin, then fell down his armor and onto the saddle. He brushed them off and grunted, seemingly more bothered by the spilled food than the likelihood of spilled blood that awaited us. . . ahead somewhere.

I leaned in close and said, "Has the captain said where we're going?"

Vendurro offered me an egg, thankfully not the one he'd bitten. I was about to decline and then realized I hadn't eaten anything yet to break fast. Even so early, and with the possibility of death and destruction closer with each step my horse took, I was still hungry. I took the egg and Vendurro replied, quietly so as not to draw anyone's ire, especially Mulldoos's, "Don't have to ride with Cap too long before figuring out he's not one to let loose the wheres and whatnots until he's good and ready, and I'm guessing he's neither just now, as I ain't heard a thing. You could ask one of the lieutenants just there, but I figure you're in no hurry to get cuffed in the ear, which is an altogether real strong likelihood, which is probably why you asked me, ain't it?"

I nodded and took a bite of the egg—it had a grain or two of salt still pressed into the white on the outside, but was otherwise as plain and generally tasteless as a boiled egg could be. Still, it would quiet my stomach for a bit. "Did he say anything about what he. . ." I looked around at the other Syldoon riding around me—I certainly didn't want to get punched in the stomach, ear, or anywhere else Mulldoos might decide on. I was about to attempt to rephrase the question when a soldier on my other side who I didn't recognize said, "I'd snap your lips shut, scribe. Unless of course you wanted them so swollen they don't open real good on their own." I thought he was issuing the threat from his corner, but he tilted his head to the front, where Braylar, Hewspear, Mulldoos and the two Memoridons rode in a tight group. I'd been so busy thinking how to pose the question I hadn't seen Soffjian or Skeelana ride up.

Yes, silence did seem to be a good choice, especially when I realized I was the only one even whispering.

Soffjian had mentioned abstaining from any fight, but she still had on her scale cuirass, where Skeelana wore nothing more protective than a half cloak over her sashed jacket. I noticed that both of them were behaving a little strangely. While everyone else looked straight ahead, or occasionally toward a noise coming from one of the darkened buildings or side streets, the Memoridons' heads were in constant motion, though very deliberate, as they very slowly turned in nearly every conceivable direction. Not as if they suspected a threat, or in response to any particular sound, but as if they were trying to make sure they saw everything everywhere and took it all in. It was unnatural, and I noticed Vendurro watching them as well, and when he glanced at me, he shrugged his shoulders. "Plaguing queerest company you'll ever hope to ride with, scribbler."

I couldn't argue that point.

However, my question about our destination was soon answered. Braylar led us down a cross street, Bulwark, and it was narrower than Broadbeef. Several houses down, a figure stepped out from an alleyway, and I immediately tensed up and almost reached for my crossbow, but no one else seemed remotely alarmed. Once we got closer, it was obvious it was another Syldoon, and two more emerged behind him.

Braylar dismounted and handed the soldier his reins, and Mulldoos and Hewspear climbed down as well, pulling their crossbows and quivers from their horses. I followed their lead right after Vendurro did, and the three soldiers took turns leading the horses into the alley. I hadn't even noticed the entrance at first, as a wagon blocked it from view from the north, and a large number of crates accomplished the same feat on just the other side of Bulwark in front of the opposite alley, preventing anyone from immediately seeing that either in the gloom.

All the Syldoon spanned their crossbows, and half of them walked into the alley as well, disappearing into the shadows, while most of the remainder moved off into the opposite alley. Clearly, we were intending an ambush of some kind. Assuming he was correct and there was someone to ambush.

Braylar summoned Vendurro over, and having nowhere else to go and following the advice to stick close to the sergeant, I jogged after, careful to keep the crossbow pointed toward the ground, but not directly at my feet. I'd nearly discharged the weapon accidentally more times than I could count, so if it ever happened, hitting my own foot was preferable to shooting a Syldoon or Memoridon, which would result in a great deal more pain for me.

The captain was having a low conversation with his two lieutenants and remaining sergeant, the mail drape still obscuring most of his face, which was no less disconcerting out here in the open as it had been in the confines of the stable. I overheard Hewspear ask, "Do you expect them to come down Broadbeef Lane, Captain?"

Braylar nodded, his mail tinkling ever so slightly. "I do, though I can't be entirely certain they won't approach down Furl Street. In the very crooked and maddening layout of Alespell, it also leads to the Grieving Dog, though at an angle to Broadbeef, intersecting just east of the inn. But all. . . indications are they come down Broadbeef." He turned toward Vendurro and pointed toward the alley where the horses had been led. "You made sure that actually leads somewhere, yes?" Vendurro nodded. "Good. I hope not to have use of them, but should we need to retreat, it proves awfully difficult in a dead end."

He led us to the other alley, opposite the mounts. While I had no wish to fight at all, as I was clearly only marginally better than inept, and would only be more of a danger to our company if I attempted to do so from horseback, I had misgivings about leaving my horse, even in another alley. It tolerated me, and it was far faster than I would be running if it came time to flee.

Braylar stopped just inside the entrance to the alley. Mulldoos was a little further in, and when a rat darted out from behind a barrel, he stepped on its back, breaking it with a crunch, ending its life with nary a squeak. If it had brethren, they were smart enough to stay put. I moved next to Braylar, but not so close that I crowded him. "I don't presume to know much about combat—"

"Truly? You carry yourself like a puissant champion of a thousand battles."

"But why have you chosen to dismount and fight on foot? If we have to fight, that is."

His hand drifted to his left side, fingers idly tapping the haft of Bloodsounder. Even with his face and scowl hidden by the aventail, there was no disguising the irritation in his voice. "We will have to fight. Make no mistake. It is more. . . absolute now. And as to the how of it, perhaps you failed to notice, but the chief virtue of a horse is speed and mobility. Neither of which you can put to any use in these narrow and crowded avenues, especially once the denizens start milling about. We would only get in each other's way here, unless we headed to the thoroughfare, by the central plaza. But then, hiding twenty horses is awfully challenging, yes? Which makes setting an ambush decidedly difficult. Now be silent. Idle chatter also proves an impediment to surprise. Beyond which, it is incredibly annoying."

We waited, and much like waiting for Henlester's underpriest to show himself at the temple, it was about the least calm anticipation I could imagine. I tried to distract myself from the fact that our lives were very likely hanging in the balance or could be snuffed out in mere moments by focusing on the small details around me, but given my state of mind, all I dwelt on were things unpleasant, uncomfortable, and nearly unbearable. The heavy stench of urine in the alley from animals, drunks, or thieves, that was like a damp blanket wrapped around my head. The dead rat's siblings, nibbling away at decay and rot in the deep shadows and the droppings and most rotten leavings even unfit for them. The pocked and crumbling wall at my back that had surely been pissed on, as it felt like barely congealed powder and paste. The fact that the last time I sat waiting like this, I at least had Lloi there to keep me company, but now there were only the deadly Syldoon and even more mysterious or perplexing Memoridons.

It was almost better to think of the impending battle and bloodshed.

Braylar turned to me. "Ready your weapon, Arki. When we move out, stay near Vendurro until that proves impossible, then remain in the rear. But do not loose the bolter unless you absolutely have to and you are in mortal peril. And maybe not even then. I'm still not sure I trust you not to shoot someone I like in the face."

Or maybe urine and decay were preferable.

Suddenly Braylar raised a hand. I wondered if he sensed the approach through Bloodsounder, but then I realized why—the very faint but detectable sound of many feet on the cobblestones of Broadbeef Lane. They weren't marching or tromping, and any other time of day, the sound would have been lost amid the clamor of other noises. As it was even with all senses alert, it was still very difficult to hear the approach of the men. I looked between some crates, saw them heading west on Broadbeef toward the Grieving Dog, passing the intersection with Bulwark. They were armed men, to be certain, and many in mail hauberks as far as I could tell. Just as the captain had predicted. Foreseen. All of them were moving as quietly as men could while in armor in a city before it truly wakes up.

I was counting them as they passed and disappeared from view when I noticed something else that threw me off. They were all wearing baldrics. As most of them were right-handed and had their swords and daggers on their left, I did catch one of them turning to look down Bulwark and glimpsed the horn handing on the end of the baldric on his other hip.

So it was Hornmen and not Brunesmen approaching stealthily with intent to capture or kill us—there were at least thirty soldiers. Possibly more. It seemed the Hornmen thought their jurisdiction included Alespell inns after all, or at least they were willing to risk Brune's wrath in taking the Syldoon.

I was certain Braylar must have noted the baldrics as well, but just in case he hadn't, I heard Vendurro whisper from right behind my shoulder, "Not Brune's boys at all, Cap. You sure do know how to piss off them Hornmen, though. Real glad we ain't still in bed."

Braylar turned toward me as he responded. "It would indeed be a bad day to still be abed." While the dawn light was working its way down the buildings, it didn't penetrate the alley at all, and even if it had, with his face obscured by mail and his eyes lost in shadow, I couldn't make out the slightest expression, but I could feel the malevolence in the stare. The fact that I only heard it somehow made it even worse.

I had advocated sparing the young Hornman in the grass, and I had been spotted by him in the bazaar. I had trouble swallowing, realizing that whatever blood was spilled this day would be in large part due to me.

"Where are their horses?" I asked in a croak.

Vendurro replied, "Probably got them stowed a couple blocks away. Figure easier to sneak up on foot, guessing."

A Syldoon stepped out from a doorway near the intersection that I hadn't even known was there. He'd been ten feet from all the soldiers who'd passed. He gave some hand signal that meant nothing to me, which clearly put me in the minority, as it immediately set us in motion. Braylar stepped out into Bulwark, crossbow still relaxed but ready to dispatch death from a distance. We followed him out, and without another word, he turned away from Broadbeef and started walking pretty quickly in the opposite direction. This didn't seem an oddity to anyone else except me either, as the Syldoon fell in behind him and we were all on the move, even if it seemed to be going the wrong way. I tried holding my crossbow like the soldiers around me, so if it somehow discharged, it would angle up and away from anyone in the company. Though the same couldn't be said for anyone who happened to pop their head out a second story window to empty a chamber pot or see what the commotion was about. Still, it was smarter than aiming it at my feet.

When we got to the end of the block though, the decision to head in this direction made more sense. We turned onto Furl Street, heading northwest, and kept up a brisk pace as it slowly angled toward the Grieving Dog as well.

Closing in on the intersection, Braylar slowed down and crept closer to the facades and locked doorways which were still resisting the dawn with all the stark shadowiness they could muster. As the street slowly curved toward Broadbeef, I had to fight off the sudden and mad urge to laugh. Skulking through the shadows was like being a boy, playing Stalk the Stalkers, only the men were armed with real weapons, not sticks, and blood was about to be spilled. Quite a bit of it.

As we approached the intersection, I was sure we would be heard, just as we had heard the Hornmen. While our party wasn't as large, and we were attempting to move with stealth, armor can't be quieted completely, and there were still quite a few of us. But as we crept to the end of the building on Furl street, I realized two things: we had been expecting them and listening intently, while they were expecting to raid an inn without men sneaking up on them; and the Grieving Dog seemed to be occupying the Hornmen's complete attention.

They all had their backs turned to us, as they stopped in front of the main entrance, with the leader gesturing toward the stables we had recently left.

We stepped out onto Broadbeef and approached. The moment was at hand. As commanded, I stayed near the rear of the group, not far from the Memoridons, careful to keep my hand away from the long steel trigger, even if the crossbow was pointed up.

The Hornmen seemed ready to begin their raid to capture or kill the handful of Syldoon they assumed were inside. They clearly didn't expect those same men to attack them from the rear just then.

Syldoon spread out into a single line, and Braylar brought his crossbow up and sighted down the length, and the other Syldoon did as well. That left the Memoridons and myself as a much smaller second line. Skeelana looked at me, and seeing that I still wasn't aiming my crossbow at a Hornman, raised both pierced eyebrows in surprise before returning her attention to the silhouettes in front of us as the first volley was loosed. She seemed remarkably calm for someone unarmored in an armed conflict.

We were less than a hundred paces away, but the Syldoon were excellent shots on horse, and twice as able lining up their aim on foot—I don't think many missed their targets, even without much light to aim by. While the Hornmen Braylar drove off in the Green Sea had been poorly armored in gambesons, many in this group had hauberks. So while more than a dozen of them were struck by bolts and cried out or grunted, only a handful dropped to the ground, most in the gambesons as far as I could tell, though some in mail appeared to have been hit in the backs of the legs. It took the Hornmen a moment to recover from the shock of being ambushed, but they figured out the threat was from the rear quickly enough, all of them spinning around, shields up.

Meanwhile, the Syldoon worked the devil's claws on their weapons with frightening dexterity. I'd seen Braylar and two other Syldoon manage the speed spanning on horseback, but without that added difficulty it was amazing how fast the crossbows were loaded again, the bolts dropped into the slots and the ropes drawn back with alarming alacrity, and the claws folded back out of the way as the crossbows came up to bear again.

I expected to see the Hornmen run, or at least scatter for cover, sidling up against the buildings or hiding behind posts and barrels. But the leader of the Hornmen ordered those with shields to form a wall and the rest with only spears to fall in behind, and the wall was already moving forward when the second volley hit home.

At this range, there was no possibility of arcing any bolts over the shields in hopes of hitting the men behind. Several bolts thunked into the shields low and high, but a fair number made it past, some skipping off the tops of the helms, but one taking out a spearman in the second line, striking him square in the face, and he was done. Others were hit in the lower legs, below the hauberks, and one man fell to his knees and broke the shield wall completely, and another was hobbled badly enough to disrupt it. The Hornmen slowed briefly, closed the gap, pressing forward again with renewed urgency and leaving the wounded behind.

The Syldoon still managed to span and loose a third volley, and while it wasn't synchronized, most flew at approximately the same time, they were so practiced and fluid. It was like they weren't facing a larger group of armed and angry men at all, just performing some training exercise, they were that smooth.

Two more Hornmen fell, one with a bolt in his neck, the other with one in his knee. The Syldoon dropped down to set their crossbows aside, gently almost, and drew their shields and swords, falchions, slashing spears, and one particularly vicious flail, and got ready for the charge, forming a longer line in front, with a smaller group several paces behind.

I was the only one still holding a crossbow, but in no hurry to attempt to shoot between or around the Syldoon to strike the Hornmen. Soffjian readied her ranseur though made no move to step forward, and Skeelana stayed close to me, as she was the only one less prepared for a fight than I was. And yet she still looked more focused than frightened or even nervous, and didn't seem to be fighting off panic like I was. She continued looking in several different directions, and not solely at the large group of men charging toward us. I looked where she did and saw only signposts, darkened doorways, and the Grieving Dog. Nothing that should have attracted more attention than the armed men who so clearly wanted to cut us into pieces.

Once the Hornmen realized the threat of more bolts was gone, they closed faster, shields no longer locked together, shouting curses and unintelligible roars, angry they were taken unawares instead of the other way around, furious their numbers had been cut down before they even had a chance to engage the enemy, and now filled with a bloodlust, sensing their superior numbers and ferocity would simply overwhelm their foes, and it didn't look like they were mistaken. The Hornmen came on in a mad, undisciplined rush.

The Syldoon held their ground, though, maintaining the first line stretching across Broadbeef, too few to form a proper shield wall to repel the foe, but not allowing any room for the Hornmen to rush around them and flank them either, with a handful of soldiers behind them, waiting. The Syldoon in front blocked or avoided the first blows and let the Hornmen's momentum carry them through the first rank, striking them as they passed but trusting their comrades to take care of them. Mulldoos's falchion chopped into the back of a Hornman's neck, biting deep, unleashing a spatter of red, and that soldier was down and twitching; Mulldoos turned his attention to a Hornmen who had been struck in the arm by another Syldoon as he passed through, injured but not incapacitated, who was spinning around to face him when Mulldoos moved in, the falchion coming down fast. The Hornman got his shield up just in time to turn the blow, but left himself open to the other Syldoon, who slashed across the back of a hamstring, just below the mail. With a howl, the Hornman fell over. Mulldoos kicked the shield and knocked him on his side, and the other Syldoon moved in, sword arcing down twice before the pair of them moved quickly to aid their brothers.

This action or something similar happened up and down the line, as the overly impulsive Hornmen allowed through were cut down in short order. In the line ten paces in front of me, the Syldoon let a Hornman rush past, tripping him as he did, but neither scored a decisive blow. The Syldoon couldn't engage and had to help a comrade alongside who was fighting off three Hornmen harrying the front line, exchanging a series of blows and blocks, shrugging off the first and second that struck mail.

The Hornman who made it through wasn't set upon immediately, as the other Syldoon behind the front line were all occupied, so he considered me for a moment, and seeing a non-soldier pointing a crossbow mostly in the sky, chose to attack the exposed Syldoon who let him through. He would have had his choice of open targets, but as he stepped forward to deliver a blow, a ranseur shot out, the long tip striking him in the side of the knee, and the curved blade catching the back of his leg. He nearly crumpled, regained his balance, and turned to face Soffjian. She thrust twice more, high, then low, and he blocked one and managed to sidestep the other, though it was clear he couldn't move quickly on a badly injured leg. Even though her polearm wasn't quite as long as Hewspear's slashing spear, it still afforded her better range than the Hornman.

He stepped forward to close the gap, but his leg briefly buckled, and Soffjian picked that moment to lay in. She raised the ranseur as if she were going to slash down at his head, and the Hornman saw the potential blow and lifted his shield to protect himself. Which was exactly what she'd been counting on. She dropped the tip and it lashed out like a viper, the long spike hitting the soldier in the thigh of his good leg, penetrating the gambeson. As the Hornman's legs gave out, he braced his fall with the knuckles of his sword hand. But that sword wasn't doing him any good down there, and Soffjian had already closed, the curved cross blade flashing in dawnlight as it slashed across his face.

The Hornman rolled in the dirt screaming, hands trying to hold his face together, blood soaking the front of his gambeson down to his sternum. Soffjian turned to give me a baleful look. I wanted to protest that I'd been ordered to stay out of it unless there was no other recourse, that I should have been holding a quill, maybe surveying the battle from the relative safety of a second story window, but obviously she wouldn't have cared. She stabbed the wounded Hornman twice and finished him off.

Even with their disorganized charge and the casualties they'd sustained in the first exchange, the Hornmen still had the advantage, and while the Syldoon were more competent, supporting each other and drawing their opponents into slips or exposure, numbers still mattered, and the Hornmen seemed to be forming up better now and attempting to flank the Syldoon soldiers. I saw two of Braylar's men dead or dying as well.

I looked over to the far side of the street and saw Hewspear facing two Hornmen, one with a sword and shield, the other with a longsword in two hands. I thought with no shield to hide behind, damaged ribs, and having only his long slashing spear for offense and defense, he would be taken out quickly, even with the advantage of slightly greater range. And he would have been dispatched had the Hornmen worked together better as a team, forcing him to divide his attention, or striking together as one, the longsword-wielder using the man with the shield as buffer until he closed. But they did neither. Instead, they advanced haltingly, side by side, but uncertain, not taking advantage of the situation, unwilling to make a move. Even if they had simply charged in, one of them might have been struck down, but they still probably would have overwhelmed Hewspear. But it was clear they counted him a skilled opponent, and neither soldier wanted to be the one dead in the dirty street. So they came together, with little space between them, but too slowly.

Hewspear feinted at the man with the sword and shield, caused him to stop and stay out of range, guard up, but the longswordsman took another step forward. Hewspear's slashing spear shot out, the tip slipping past the soldier's guard, brought to bear too late, and striking him in the folds of mail around the base of the throat. While it was hard to tell if it penetrated the mail at all, it struck him hard, and he doubled over, letting go of his hilt with one hand and clutching at his neck.

The soldier with the sword and shield thought this was his opportunity and came in fast, shield in front, eyes peering over the edge. Hewspear seemed to anticipate this, but instead of trying to maneuver back or to the side to maintain his range, or attacking immediately to possibly force him to halt, he let him come two steps. And as the soldier started his attack, Hewspear unexpectedly stepped forward to meet him, changing his grip as he did, spear nearly horizontal, the tail and butt spike rising, then turning to intercept the blow, catching it low on the blade. At the same time he used the haft to check the shield, pressing into it hard before the soldier could have a chance to use it as a weapon to pummel or bash, and then Hewspear was taking another step to his left, forcing the sword and the arm out of his way as he moved passed the edge of the shield. The soldier tried to turn with him, but his momentum carried him forward, and it was obvious he hadn't expected such an aggressive move from the taller man.

Hewspear kept the sword pinned out of action just long enough, spun one step ahead of his opponent, worked the haft around the edge of the shield as he did, and used it as a fulcrum as he set up his next shot, sliding forward, turning the spear, and striking with the butt spike all in one fluid motion. The spike was much shorter than the slashing spear head, but it caught the soldier square in the face, just left of the nose and south of the eye. While it didn't kill the soldier, it effectively ended the fight, as his first instinct was to reach up and protect himself, which proved impossible with a sword in one hand and a shield in the other. Hewspear used the lapse to step in, delivering a wicked blow straight down to the Hornman's collarbone. The soldier dropped his sword and flailed with his shield in desperation, but it barely connected with Hewspear as he kept moving, and his final blow was a horizontal one across the Hornman's lower jaw that did considerably more damage than the butt spike had. The Hornman was down, still moving, but spastic, and not for much longer by the looks of it.

Hewspear looked like he was considering whether or not to finish him off, but then recalled the Hornman with the longsword, and was turning to find him. He saw him at the same time I did, with Vendurro standing over his prone body, his own shorter sword red with the man's blood. Or someone else's. But in either case, the man with the longsword was still as stone in a pool of dark red-black.

He nodded at the younger man, and looked around for his next foe. There were plenty of choices, too many, but before joining another part of the melee, Hewspear saw a Syldoon fighting a spearman off ten paces away, with another Hornman about to attack him from the rear. Hewspear moved the slashing spear into one hand, pulled his flanged mace off the belt with the other, and flung it at the second Hornman. It spun end over end, and I'm not sure if it was weighted to be thrown or if Hewspear only got lucky, but the flanged end struck the soldier directly in the back of the helm. It seemed to stun the Hornman for a moment, and when he wheeled around to face his foe, Vendurro was already closing the distance to engage. Hewspear leaned over on his spear, the tail in the dirt, holding his injured ribs that he had managed to hurt more with the throw than the toe-to-toe fighting with the Hornmen.

This seemed to be the one thing the Syldoon had in their favor—I'm not sure if they drilled for this kind of chaotic street battle, but they obviously worked together exceptionally well as a unit—even when splintered, they protected each other, and seemed to keep their eyes open so they could aid one of their brothers-in-arms in trouble as they battled a foe with superior numbers.

Still, Hewspear might have been killed, standing briefly like that, bent over, head hung, holding his ribs as they broke or shifted or maybe even tore something deep inside, as a pair of Hornmen were advancing on him, one in mail, one in a filthy gambeson, both with spears up and level and ready to ride him through. But just as he'd helped rescue a fellow Syldoon, he was rescued in turn, though not in any way I could have ever expected to see.

Soffjian stepped forward to intercept them, but even having seen her in action, I didn't know if she could take on two herself. The Hornmen saw her, and changed direction to meet her. And when she brought her ranseur back with one arm, cocked almost behind her in what appeared to be the least helpful guard imaginable, with her other arm straight ahead, fingers splayed as if she was trying to somehow ward off the attack, I was sure she was dead.

But then something happened so unlike anything I'd ever witnessed, I wondered if I actually perceived it accurately or not. The Hornmen closed the gap, almost in range to strike, and she hadn't moved an inch. And then both Hornmen suddenly stopped where they stood, and an instant later, they dropped their spears as if the hafts were on fire, the one in the gambeson reaching up, clawing at his face and eyes, the one in mail stepping back as he yanked at his hauberk, trying to tear it free, swatting at his limbs and sides as if he were being stung by a swarm of insects all over his body, though there were none to be seen. He tripped over his heels and fell backwards, and switched from fighting off an invisible pestilence to covering both ears with the mail mittens of his hauberk, and then crawled away from Soffjian as best he could, digging his feet into the dirt and trying to propel himself backwards.

I listened closely, and heard nothing save the sounds of combat—men grunting and yelling and screaming, metal striking metal, metal striking wood. No new noise, and while the existing noises were awful, they weren't anything to injure the ears. But still, he crawled away and covered his ears as if he heard demons shouting his name.

Soffjian remained fixed in that pose, though she pivoted slightly, fixed on the Hornman who was still in front of her. He was still digging at his face, so furiously that he'd torn his flesh, rivulets of blood running between his fingers. And he let out a shrill scream, horrendous, and I would have thought his comrade was attempting to block out that noise, except I was certain he had covered his ears and begun his mad scramble before it broke the air.

The Hornman in the gambeson dropped to his knees, still emitting the single, piercing note, rising even higher, the sound of someone anguished and terrified and confronting something not of this world, and he continued to scream as he clawed, blood pouring down his face below his hands, and he gouged an eye out, which brought the scream to another more horrified level briefly, before he suddenly, and mercifully, stopped and fell over, hands clenched in claws in front of his ruined face. But he wasn't moving. And it was clear whatever awful thing tortured or possessed him had finished him. He was surely dead, his life and scream snuffed out as if they never existed at all.

Hewspear was upright again, mostly, staring at Soffjian, face pale, though from his own pain or from seeing the same thing I saw, I couldn't say. But he regained his composure quickly enough, and then he drew down on the other Hornman, who was sitting now, and looking around, bewildered. That soldier never had the opportunity to shake off whatever Soffjian had done to him, as Hewspear moved directly behind him and drew the edge of the slashing spear across his throat.

Soffjian slowly relaxed her pose and stepped away from the action, shaking her head slightly as if to clear it. I have no idea what she did, but it was both awesome and terrible to behold. I knew Memoridons were rumored to possess unholy powers, but seeing it right in front of me, crippling two men and apparently driving them mad, one to the point of death, was something else entirely, and made the fact that I had just watched Hewspear slit someone's throat seem pleasant by comparison.

Skeelana was still near me, content to leave the fighting to the soldiers or give herself an escape route if things turned as ugly as they appeared, as the fight still seemed to fall in the Hornmen's favor, even with the Syldoonian discipline and the Memoridon's aid. Despite Braylar admonishing me to hold off, he had armed me, and recognized that I'd played a part in saving his life. Clearly now was the time to get involved if there was one.

Raising my crossbow, I was careful to keep my fingers off the long trigger until I knew what I intended to do with it. The melee had broken down into small unit affairs, clumps of men here and there, with formations having no place in a street brawl now. I looked at the closest group—four Hornman forcing two Syldoon back. While the Hornman appeared to get in each other's way more than anything, the Syldoon couldn't overcommit or expose themselves, so mostly deflected, blocked, and gave up ground as they fought shoulder to shoulder.

I waited for them to move, to present the best Hornman target with the least chance of accidentally killing a Syldoon. They didn't cooperate, so I moved to my left, closer to the building, trying to maneuver to a spot for the best shot. I heard a noise right alongside me, spun and nearly unleashed the bolt, when I saw a wrinkled man standing in his door, his curse stuck in his throat as he saw my crossbow, and more importantly, the dozens of men killing each other in the street. He slammed the door without uttering a word and I spun back to the group, hoping I wasn't too late.

If I held for the perfect shot, it would never happen, so I sighted down the crossbow, turning with them as best I could, lifted three fingers to the long trigger, and squeezed.

The bolt flew across the small space faster than I could see. I hit a Hornman in the upper back, and while I couldn't tell how deeply the quarrel went, it bit enough to cause him to spin around, reaching for it with one hand, spear in the other. He stopped though, realizing it was lodged in far enough that he'd only cause more damage trying to yank it free, but he also realized whoever loosed the bolt was there reloading another as well.

Or would have been if I hadn't been staring at him, dumbly expecting him to simply fall over. When he saw me, he grabbed the spear in both hands and came for me at a run. Whatever damage the bolt had done wasn't enough to slow him down.

I reached for another quarrel then, fumbling with it as I had trouble not looking at the man charging at me and ready to run me through. I nearly dropped it, slid it home on the stock, and started to work the lever of the devil's claw, knowing he was going to reach me before I had a chance to span the crossbow and loose again—he was going to ram the spear through my belly and out the other side, and I'd fall to the dirt, dying slow, dying fast, but dying for certain. But it was too late to run, so I worked the lever and the claw pulled the hempen rope back, dropping it behind the nut, all I had to do was work the claw free, just as Braylar had shown me, get it out of the way, lift and loose. I heard the Hornman's feet, nearly on me, but I kept going, it was the only thing left to do, expecting any moment to feel an explosion of pain in my belly.

And then suddenly the running stopped. I looked up, wondering why I wasn't skewered. The Hornman was there, standing five feet away, but instead of driving the spear home, he was raising one hand in front of his face, shaking his head quickly, as if trying to dislodge a bad dream.

Then I realized why. Skeelana was just off my shoulder and a little behind, her own hand raised, fingers splayed as Soffjian's had been, mouth knit tight in concentration, eyes closed. Only this time, the soldier wasn't clawing his own eyes out or screaming, just shaking his head, looking confused, slowly waving one hand in the air.

Skeelana whispered, "Finish loading, Quills. Quickly, if you please."

When the Hornman heard her voice, it was as if the spell had been broken, or diffused somewhat, as his eyes cleared, and it was obvious he saw the pair of us. He drew the spear back with both arms, took a step forward, and I wasn't sure which of us would die first, but Skeelana raised her other hand, fingers out as well, and the Hornman paused, lips drawn back like an angry hound's, eyes darting, confused again. He did thrust then, and it went through the air in the space between the two of us.

I finished working the lever just as he drew the spear back again. It was clear he couldn't see at all, or saw something that wasn't there, but even a blind or mad man can still kill with a spear if he jabs it enough times.

The Hornman did thrust again, this time missing Skeelana by inches. Reflex forced her to jump to the right, away from the thrust, and then the soldier's eyes cleared again and he cocked the spear back.

But before he impaled her, he jerked back, a bolt protruding from the side of his neck, above the mail, below the nasal helm, in all the way to the fletching. He dropped his spear, took two steps back, hands scrambling for purchase on the bolt, eyes wild with fear. His fingers touched the fletching, jerked open as if feeling the bolt really embedded in his flesh made the doom more real. Then he dropped to his knees, looking at me the entire time, now in accusation more than panic, as he tried once to pull the bolt free before opening his mouth, gurgling blood all over his armor, and falling onto the ground, the bolt I'd hit him with earlier protruding from his back. A link might have broken, but it hadn't punctured the mail that much, and probably hadn't gotten too far past the gambeson underneath. No wonder he hadn't been slowed down any. I'd only scratched him. Well, before shooting him in the neck, that is.

I turned to the side, stomach roiling, glad he'd landed on his face, so the accusation was at least in the dirt now, but still unable to stop ale and some undigested egg from spewing out my mouth. I was careful to keep the crossbow clear. Braylar would not have been happy about a crossbow caked in vomit. Such a good day for crossbows. I heaved again, though it was mostly spit and bile, and put my free hand on my leg to keep from falling over, not surprised to find that both leg and arm were shaking violently. After all, it's not every day you shoot and kill someone for the first time.

Blinded by tears, I heaved again. And when I felt a hand on my shoulder, I spun and raised the crossbow, unable to see any better than the spell-stricken Hornman. Before I shot him in the neck.

Skeelana had taken a step back to avoid getting hit with the crossbow as it came up, and said, "I'm not an expert, but it tends to work better when it's loaded."

I started lowering it, and wiped at my eyes, feeling weak, ashamed, and still quite sick.

She said, "That wasn't really an invitation to put it away, Quills." She gestured at the men still fighting further down the street. "You might have cause to loose it a time or two more."

Her hands were empty. Not even a weapon. And yet she'd managed to keep a very angry armed man from gutting us, only through the use of some Memoridon sorcery. I was beginning to understand why the Syldoon respected and distrusted them. I was glad to be alive, but what she'd done simply wasn't natural.

I asked, "Why. . . why didn't you simply kill him, as Soffjian had?"

Skeelana looked irritated. "Why didn't you draw that sword on your hip instead of fumbling with the crossbow? And more importantly, why haven't you loaded it again, lord protector? Plan on throwing it at them?"

I worked the lever again and spanned the device much more deftly, now that I wasn't in immediate danger of being run through. I shuddered, burped, and tasted the refuse of my own stomach's rebellion. With my crossbow again loaded I waited on her, expecting her to take the lead.

She shook her head, "Don't look at me, Quills. I know even less about war than you." She glanced at the crossbow. "It just seemed more useful having the thing loaded. If you're looking for a recommendation, I say the two people who know the least about combat stay right here, as far from it as possible."

I couldn't very well argue that point. I had nearly gotten us killed by getting involved moments ago. But as I looked at the clumps of men still fighting, trying to make sense of it, it seemed the better-trained Syldoon had fought off the Hornmen as best they could and whittled their foe down considerably, but attrition was taking its toll and they looked like they were about to be overwhelmed.

It seemed futile, but I raised the crossbow again, tried to pick another Hornman to shoot—I would probably die with the rest, but better to try than hang back and watch it happen—when I heard it. Something between a roar and a shriek, so ferocious and alien it stilled the blood. Everyone seemed to stop, even the Hornman and Syldoon grappling against a barrel who had dropped their main weapons and were trying to draw daggers.

The ripper bellowed again from behind the Hornmen. I looked down Broadbeef, past the Grieving Dog, and saw it. Lugger and Brunzlo had almost waited too long, but during the melee they had managed to wheel the stolen wagon into the middle of the street and pulled the large canvas covering off, revealing the bars. And the open gate. And the giant nightmarish bird beast hunched at the rear, looking out the opening, sniffing the air, and eyeing all the combatants in the street ahead of it.

Did it see steel and danger? Or just meat? I thought it might turn and attack the pair of Syldoon, or race to freedom down the deserted street, but they stabbed it twice with spears from behind, and then with another bellow, the ripper made up its mind. It ran out of the wagon, again moving far faster than I would have imagined, hulking legs propelling it forward. In four strides it was among the wounded Hornmen who had been left behind. One saw it coming and tried to crawl away, but the ripper knocked him into a post. The massive beak closed on the man's helmeted head. He screamed, and when the ripper realized it couldn't bite through the iron, it used its short talons to rip the helm off, then crushed the man's skull in its beak, cutting the scream in half.

The Hornman commander glanced at the Syldoon and then decided which threat was greater. "Form up and advance," he ordered, with only the tiniest quiver.

The men looked at each other, realizing they were facing a creature that had stepped out of an awful bestiary, but tentatively turned to face it, forgetting all about the Syldoon they had been fighting. We all watched one of the wounded Hornman with nowhere to hide try to ward the creature off with his spear; the ripper hissed, batted it aside with the long scythe-like talon, leapt on top and pinned the soldier's shoulders to the ground with one thick leg and slashed the man's throat out with one long curved talon.

The Hornmen wavered as their commander screamed at them, and a few started forward, then stopped as they realized they were advancing alone. Even with so many men between, I was terrified, so I don't know how they didn't simply flee, but the commander called them cowards and worse and ordered them to line up, and whatever training they had overcame their fear—as the ripper started coming closer, blood dripping from its maw, the ends of its beak clattering as it hissed again, the Hornmen stepped out to meet it, having forgotten entirely about their human foes, perhaps thinking the Syldoon would join them in driving off the beast before continuing the battle where they left off.

They were mistaken.

The Syldoon let them take a few hesitant paces to face the ripper before laying into them from the rear. If the previous melee had been confusing, this was utter chaos. Men yelled, the ripper shrieked and pounced, the Syldoon slashed and stabbed and cut the Hornmen down.

And then, after several prolonged moments of screaming, shouting, bodies filling the street, it was over. The Hornmen commander was lying on his side, trying to hold in the guts that were sliding through his fingers, and without him, the remaining Hornmen morale broke. They started to flee in all directions. Some away from the ripper, some around it, others scrambling for doorways, some simply trying to get away from the Syldoon.

The ripper chased a pair of Hornmen down a side street, and the rest kept running too, but that didn't stop the Syldoon from mowing them down. Several Hornmen died with wounds to their backs. Vendurro cut one deep in the calf as he tried to run past, and Mulldoos stepped in to strike the Hornman several times across the shoulders, the back, the arms, driving him to his knees. None of the blows sheared mail—it looked like doing so with a one-handed weapon was nearly impossible, if the mighty Mulldoos couldn't manage it—but he and Vendurro pummeled the soldier into submission. Or what would have and should have been submission. Only Mulldoos wasn't much interested in taking prisoners just then. He stepped over the moaning figure that was slowly trying to push himself up, and chopped down across the back of the neck. The figure slumped back down, not even twitching, and even from that distance I could see the exposed and mangled spine.

Mulldoos spit on the dead Hornman's back and looked around for others to cut down, but most had escaped, running free. I saw that Braylar wasn't any more forgiving of a fleeing foe. His opponent was trying to back away, fending off blows from Bloodsounder, looking over his shoulder to make sure he didn't trip. But when he saw Hewspear closing in on them, he had no choice. It was obvious he was waiting to deflect a final blow before turning to run, but Braylar must have sensed that. Instead of striking again, he held Bloodsounder at the ready, just on the inside of his own shield, and stepped forward.

It would only take a moment before Hewspear closed the distance, so the Hornman changed tactics. He slashed out with his sword toward Braylar's helm, hoping to either drive him back or force the shield up long enough to block his vision and provide an instant to go. But Braylar anticipated and stepped into the blow, deflecting the sword up into the air and swinging Bloodsounder in time. After starting to swing the flail, he jerked the handle up to the left, and then when the Hornman's shield moved to intercept, it proved a feint, and Braylar brought the flail heads down low, a blur. The spiked heads struck the Hornman in the side, hard enough they either broke bones beneath the padding or completely knocked the wind out of the soldier. Either way, he bent over, shield down, and Braylar raised Bloodsounder to finish him off.

Hewspear shouted something I couldn't make out, but it stopped Braylar before he could deliver the blow. The captain looked at his lieutenant as he ran up, moving awkwardly.

The Hornman threw his sword on the ground, and was struggling to get his arm out of the shield straps, favoring his busted ribs, clearly surrendering, when Hewspear lashed out with the slashing spear, striking the Hornman in the side, shearing the baldric strap. The mail hadn't given way, but something underneath had, as the Hornman doubled over as his horn fell into the dirt. He was starting to raise his head, likely to plead, but he never had the opportunity. Hewspear had stepped in, and almost casually ran the long edge of the spear across the Hornman's throat. The soldier collapsed, and at least didn't suffer longer, as his blood dyed the beaten earth darker.

I walked over to them, angry, watching as the remaining Hornmen escaped. At least the Syldoon didn't pursue them and cut them all down. I was ten paces away, and while I intended to hold off and share my protest quietly to the captain alone, I found myself instead shouting, "Why did you kill them like that? They were defeated! Unarmed!"

Braylar was still staring at the last of the Hornmen as they disappeared around a corner and then looked at the body of the soldier Hewspear had just killed. He slipped Bloodsounder onto his belt, bent over, and pulled his helm and aventail off his head, the mail slithering. His hair was slick with sweat instead of the usual oil, and red across his forehead where the helmet padding had pressed tight. Finally he turned to me and replied, each word hotter than the last, "I seem to recall another defeated, unarmed opponent who was granted reprieve. Do you? Do you recall him? Because," he gestured around Broadbeef and the dead and dying, "that was a triumph of stupidity. And you can be sure I do not intend to allow it to happen again. Now shut your mouth, lest I think you the dumbest shrunken cock ever born."

All anger drained away immediately, and my cheeks flushed, reminded again that this ambush, the casualties, the mortalities, were all tied to my moment of mercy in the Green Sea.

Braylar put his helm in the crook of his arm and said, "Anything to add? No? I thought not." The he called out to his men, voice more hoarse than ever. "To the horses. We have overstayed our welcome in Alespell. And Mulldoos, make sure Lugger and Brunzlo get something extra on their next pay. Also, be sure they have to wait at least a tenday longer than usual to get it."

Braylar led the way, with Mulldoos limping on one side, and Hew-spear using his spear as a staff and support on the other, having aggravated his rib injury and possibly compounded it. Two Syl-doon ran ahead to be sure the path to the horses was clear, and two more hung back to be certain the Hornmen hadn't regrouped, or the city watch or Brunesmen hadn't been alerted to the bloodshed in the streets and come exploring. I kept looking everywhere, expecting to see more soldiers storming down on us, or the ripper plunging out of an alley and tearing someone to pieces.

I hadn't even noticed Vendurro alongside me until I heard him say, "Saw you back there, when you took out that Hornman. Only thing I caught, but saw you do that. Acquitted yourself real good, Arki. Real good. You keep it up, might end up a better shot than most Syldoon. Not me, of course. But most." He winked and I nodded, not trusting myself to say anything else. I was trying very hard not to think about what happened. I glanced up at the shuttered windows to see who was spying on the group of bloodied, armed men tromping through the mud below.

But when Soffjian walked past me quickly and fell in alongside the captain, I moved forward as well, wanting to be just close enough to hear but not so close to draw a rebuke.

I heard her say, "Your intelligence was quite something today, brother. Exceptional even. You seemed to know which route those soldiers would take, even before they did. Very impressive. Even Memoridons can't man-age communication with such skill and precision. As ever, I am in awe, Bray. Though I do wonder how it was you pulled that off."

Instead of replying to her, Braylar turned slightly in Mulldoos's direc-tion. "Who am I?"

Mulldoos didn't pause in the slightest before replying, "Meanest plagu-ing bastard to stalk the world."

"Fair point. But professionally speaking."

Mulldoos looked over. "Captain of a Syldoon company."

"Ahh, yes. Thank you. I sometimes forget that. Since I seem to constantly field questions about every little tactical or strategic decision I make, and the conduct we engage in to carry them out. Peculiar, yes?"

Soffjian tapped her butt spike on the ground as she walked, approximating Hewspear's gait somewhat, though without needing to support her weight or suffering pain with every step. "I was merely appreciating, brother. One professional to another." With that she fell silent, though I got the distinct impression she was merely biding her time for more questions, or trying to taunt her brother into a misstep or thoughtless revelation.

I turned to say something to Vendurro but he had moved off again, and was talking quietly to one of the men. Maybe complimenting him on exceptional bloodletting skills. The knot in my stomach pulled tighter.

Even with Hewspear trying to spare the captain, Bloodsounder got bloodied once again. Was Braylar feeling the effects already, absorbing a memory or two? More? I couldn't ask, not with his sister nearby, and he likely would have only scolded me for acting the nursemaid anyway.

We made our way to the horses without incident, mounted up, and headed to a wider street that intersected Broadbeef, so we spread out a bit and weren't riding nose to tail. When I realized someone was riding alongside me, I assumed it was Vendurro again, and turned to say something to him, surprised when I saw Skeelana's pierced heart-shape face instead. She was looking straight ahead, expression blank. But she didn't move off when she felt me watching her, saying only, "Must be a welcome change, not having to stare at an unshaven ape for once. But still, you are staring. Just so you know."

I was tempted to turn away, but I knew if I stayed alone with my thoughts I would only dwell on throats being slit and men being dispatched in the mud. One of them by me. So I said, "Skeelana, is it?"

Half her mouth rose in a grin, the other couldn't be bothered. "Always been, always will be."

I tried to think of the best way to frame the question, but gave up, saying simply, "I'm curious. . . back there by the Grieving Dog, when you did. . . whatever it was you did to the soldier."

"Most curious people ask questions. Was that intended to be question? It felt like it was going that direction, but then. . . just sort of didn't."

"Yes. Sorry. Why didn't you simply do what Soffjian did? Why distract him, or whatever you did, rather than simply. . . take him out."

"Well, that's a question at least. Impolitic, to be sure, but a question. They call you Arki, right? On account of you being an archivist?"

It was my turn to smile. "On account of my given name being Arkamondos."

She looked over then, surprised. "Arkamondos the Archivist? Well, that's fortuitous, isn't it? Or did your parents just think that passed for clever to push you into the role?"

My smile disappeared. "I never knew what my father thought, and my mother thought only of herself. Maybe I chose the path because I thought it passed for clever."

Skeelana let that go. "Oh, exceedingly. But you are an archivist, correct? A chronicler of sights and sounds, a cataloguer of all you survey?"

"That might be overselling things a bit, but I witness and record, yes."

"So now you're trying to make sense of what you saw, in order to better record it later. Sound about right?"

I nodded. "About."

She tilted her head at the Syldoon riding ahead of us. "Well, you might not have noticed, but the Syldoon aren't particularly fond of our kind. Memoridons, that is. In fact, they're about as unfond as you can get. And if you're seen consorting with me too much, getting chummy as it were in order to puzzle out what it was you witnessed back there, well, you might find yourself losing some station, archivist."

"And you must have failed to notice, but I'm not exactly held in high regard. Hard to fall in station when you occupy the bottom already. Or near enough to a Memoridon to make little difference."

Skeelana laughed, and then seemed surprised she had, camouflaging it with a cough and her hand.

When the nearest Syldoon turned back around, I said, "So answer the question, please. Very difficult to record what you don't understand."

"I could, and probably should, really, tell you to ask the Syldoon. They could explain it well enough, and maybe it would help your relationship."

It was my turn to nearly laugh. "By pressing them about their least favorite subject? Somehow I doubt that."

She didn't answer immediately, and seemed to be considering it. Finally, she replied, "I'm not sure how Soffjian would feel about this. We might both end up in poor estimation."

"We'll keep each other company then." I tried to finish with a smile, but the thought of an angry Soffjian turning her attention my way made me very uncomfortable.

"Fair enough." After a pause to mull it over, she said, "I didn't do what she did for the same reason the infantry, cavalry, generals, cooks, grooms, and prostitutes all do something different in the army. Each player has a purpose, and skills. Memoridons are no different."

I thought about that. "So, does that make you the cook?"

An uneven grin tilted on her face again. "More like the sutler. I try to stay as far from any front lines as possible. Not even a fan of the back lines. But orders carry us where they will."

She might have been brighter than Lloi, but it seemed she would prove just as difficult to redirect in conversation. "So, your skills are different than Soffjian's then. What did you do to the Hornman who seemed so very eager to pin me to a post?"

Skeelana said, "You noticed me looking around quite a bit, before the battle? Of course you did—you gave me at least two queer looks."

"I noticed."

"Well, I was memorizing."

"Memorizing?" I tried to recall what there was in that narrow deserted street worth recalling. "What? And probably more important, why?"

Skeelana made sure he voice was just low enough for me to hear, though as she pointed out, most Syldoon already had a grasp of what the Memoridons did, even if they'd rather not. So it wasn't exactly like she was spilling something secretive. Was it? "As you might have gathered from the name, all Memoridons have keen memories, more precise and deep than any untrained. And some of us are remarkable, even for Memoridons." She broke into a broad grin that was alarmingly charming. "So, when I say memorizing, I mean nearly everything. I could tell you which shop signs had been most recently painted, where the rust spots were on the hinges, the single wooden awning that was most warped and in need of repair, the exact location of each puddle, and on and on. And I did that looking in as many directions as I could, but especially behind us, away from the Hornmen."

If anyone else had been making the boast, I would have been skeptical, but given what I'd seen Skeelana and Soffjian do, I was more than willing to suspend disbelief. "Behind? Why is that?"

"I needed to remember what every portion of that deserted street looked like when it was actually deserted. Even with none of us in view. Completely deserted."

I waited for elaboration; unlike Lloi, Skeelana obviously knew I was waiting, and seemed to delight in raising my curiosity, but also appeared just as perfectly content to let the conversation die whenever I did, so I pressed on. "Why was that important?"

"Do you remember the expression on the Hornman's face, just as he was about to spear you, and I intervened? Confused? Dazed, disbelieving, and afraid?"

I nodded. "Hard to forget a face like that. Even for us non-Memoridons."

"Well, I planted a false memory in his head, just as he cocked that spear back. One second, he saw a thin archivist who was very close to pissing his breeches—no insult intended—and then next, he saw the shop, the doorway, the horn shutters, and everything else behind you. As if you weren't standing there any longer. As if he were staring at a deserted section of street."

"A false memory? Truly?"

"No, a false memory, falsely." The grin jumped back into place. "The problem was, it was hastily cobbled together. And not made to hold or stand up to prolonged scrutiny for very long."

I tried recalling his face, bleaching out all the terror I was experiencing in the moment, and attempted to simply recall the exact expression he wore. It did seem as if he saw a ghost. Or sorcery at work, at least. And was equally frightened, but incensed as well. "Why. . . why wouldn't it hold?"

"Far too many reasons. As I said, done in haste. I hadn't studied the scene behind us from every possible distance or perspective. I caught most details, but hadn't had time to get every single one. And then there's the matter that all of our memories are branded with our own storylines and histories. You look at a squalling child in the middle of a crowd, maybe it reminds you of your own babe, so it makes you smile a little, and you recall it fondly later. I look at the same red-faced infant, maybe it reminds me of the babes I've lost in birth, so it's a melancholy memory. You see?"

Though I didn't entirely, I nodded and she continued. "If I know a subject, can study him, tour his own memories and the storylines they're lodged in, I have a decent chance, well, some kind of chance anyway, of possibly creating a falsehood that is convincing. Feels real. Contours, texture, validity. Dovetails with his own experience. You get it?"

I didn't, but before I could say as much, she added, "And the height issue, of course."

"Height issue?"

"He was tall, if you recall. Not like your friend Matinios. Sorry, Hewspear. So, not freakishly tall, like him, but this boy was tall enough, and I'm freakishly short, so it doesn't take much for the difference to register. I'd looked at the building and street from my perspective. I would have needed a stool to see it from his vantage. Always irked I wasn't born taller, but never so much as when I try to plant a false memory and it fails on account of short parents."

I thought about it, again remembering the Hornman's various reactions. "So what he saw. . . or didn't see . . he knew it wasn't real?"

Skeelana replied, "Exactly. It stopped him cold for a moment, but the illusion was spoiled fast. He couldn't see either of us, but he knew it was just a trick. We hadn't disappeared, not really—his mind knew that—and what he saw, the deserted street, flickered around the edges and wouldn't hold true. That's why he kept attacking. Now some, dealing with memory magic, will turn and run, illusion or not. But he seemed more angry than afraid. Until you shot him in the neck, that is."

That did stop the conversation for a moment. We turned onto the broader street, Olive Way, and began heading west. There were more people about now, here and there, opening awnings, throwing open shutters, pouring out night soil in the tight alleyways, but it was still relatively quiet and calm. Braylar was leading us toward a broad, low fountain. I tried not dwelling on the bolt in the soldier's neck, or the fact that I was the one responsible for putting it there. "You mentioned different skills. Among Memoridons. I take it that means Soffjian wasn't creating or planting memories like you did."

Skeelana suddenly looked more serious than she had before. And I couldn't be sure, but she might have even shivered. Which could have been attributed to the damp chill, but she hadn't done it before that I noticed. She opened her mouth to respond, when we both realized we'd gotten to the fountain.

Braylar said, or rasped rather, "Nothing draws unwanted questions at a gate like fresh splashes of someone's else blood on your hands and armor. Rid yourself of any. And be quick about it. A bunch of soldiers bathing in a fountain also tends to make the natives quite nervous."

This earned a few chuckles and most of the Syldoon dismounted to at least rinse their hands and forearms, as that seemed to have been the likeliest target for blood splatter. I looked around the small plaza—while it wouldn't get near the traffic of any of the more significant ones, there were several merchants already setting up their stalls around the perimeter. The gloom and early hour would hide the fact that the Syldoon were turning the shallow pool all kinds of pink, but Braylar was right—the less attention we attracted the better.

Skeelana and I looked at each other at the same time, as if to check for any stray sprinkles of blood, but we were clean. That was one of the benefits of a crossbow, after all.

Since neither of us dismounted to wash up, I said, "I've only ever read about sorcery, and never expected to meet anyone actually practicing it, but I always imagined if I did, it would involve glowing runes in the air, or fireballs lighting up the sky, or. . . "

"Something flashy?" She laughed.

"Right. And as far as I could tell, you and Soffjian adopted the same sort of stance, did the same kind of thing with your hands, but the results were. . . different, to say the least. So, my question still stands: what did Soffjian do? How did she strike that Hornman down without so much as touching him?"

Skeelana's eyes were fixed ahead. I looked where she was, and saw Soffjian crouching down around the edge of the fountain, dipping her fingers in, tips only, and rubbing them delicately along some scales on her armor. Her cloak disguised any blood that might have landed there. Without taking her eyes off the other woman, Skeelana said, "Oh, she can do a bit of memory planting as well if she has to, though frankly not as cleanly or clearly as I can. That isn't her strength. Her skills are far more. . . aggressive in nature."

"She does seem pretty comfortable in combat."

"What makes you say that? The shiny armor or the long pointy weapon she totes around?"

I saw the gently mocking grin and mischief in her pale eyes. "So, Soffjian is some kind of. . . martial Memoridon then?"

Skeelana's smile tilted across her lips. "Never heard that before. I like it. Catchy. Yes, something like that. Like the Syldoon, we are trained according to what talents we seem to possess in abundance. Soffjian showed early on that her mind was. . . very sharp."

It was my turn to smile, as I looked at Braylar on the opposite side of the fountain. "Runs in the family, doesn't it?"

"That it does. So in addition to being trained in a different branch of memory magic, she also underwent quite a bit of combat training as well. She might not be fully-fledged Syldoon trooper, but—"

"She can hold her own well enough."

"That she can." There seemed to be a mixture of both pride and trepidation there. "And as for what she did to those poor Hornmen who made the mistake of thinking her easy prey, well, I'm not even sure if I should say."

It was hard to tell if this was earnest or if she was enjoying baiting me. "As you said, the Syldoon know a fair amount about how this works. Or its effects anyway, right? It's not as if I'm asking you to reveal secret details about your arcane instruction. Though you can if you like."

We watched the others climb back into their saddles, and then we were moving again, across the plaza and over to Canal Street, which led to the western gate. Or so I thought. I still hadn't mastered reading the trails of ceramic tile markers above all the avenues that were supposed to designate what district you were in and where you were headed.

I hadn't noticed it from the far side, but there was a pillory in one quarter of the plaza, very close to the entrance to Beacon Street. I was hoping it was unoccupied, but as we closed in on it, I saw a man there, head and hands sticking through one end, body the other, kneeling on the stones. His head was hanging, and I wondered if he was dead—while the temperatures at night hadn't plummeted and the heat during the day wasn't completely oppressive, that was with the options of taking shelter. Who knows how long he'd been out there in the elements, or how frequently they fed him or tended to his ailments. He looked gaunt—not quite skeletal, but surely not subsisting on much. His head jerked up at our approach, face stubbly, eyes in dark hollows but still hopeful. He licked his chapped lips and said, "A bit of water? Gods defend you, just a few drops?"

There was a wooden placard hanging around his neck that had one work on it: "Thief." There were worse words to wear around your neck. But better, too.

When he realized we were soldiers, the hope seemed to ebb, and when he saw the Syldoonian noose tattoos on the necks, it disappeared completely. But some perverse courage remained, just the same. "My lords, you ain't no friends to the Anjurians, and—"

Braylar said, "You are Anjurian, thief."

"True as rain, but I was meaning the barons, the king. Fancy lords sitting on high seats. You got no more love for them than I do. Spare a few drops, I beg you."

Mulldoos said, "Be grateful I don't piss on you face, you stupid prick. Next time, don't get caught."

The prisoner's head fell in despair, a curtain of dark greasy hair covering his face.

We started forward again. Humans really were ingenious when it came to devising ways to cause pain, discomfort, and death. I was actually wrestling with whether or not to turn back and offer the man water. He was likely guilty, but there was always the chance he wasn't. And even if he was, lopping off a hand probably would have been less cruel. But then Skeelana leaned toward me a little, though not so much that it looked like conspirational whispering, and said, "I will tell you a little, archivist. Though this has less to do with any of your rhetoric, and more to do with my large mouth and inability to keep it shut long. If you wish."

I got the feeling she somehow guessed what I was about to do and spoke up enough to distract me until the pillory fell behind us.

"I would like," I replied, forcing myself to forget the poor wretch.

"Very well. It would be too difficult to explain in full, and I'm sure I'd need to violate several precepts in order to give you enough information to make complete sense of it. And since you aren't even a Syldoon, you're less than a bumbling neophyte."

"Thank you kindly."

"You're most welcome. But it goes something like this. Everything we sense—with eyes, ears, tongue, nose, and skin, it seems like this is the entirety of the world. Our thoughts, memories, experiences, they are all defined by our senses, filtered through them, right?"

I nodded. "Following you so far."

"Right. But that's just it. It's filtered."

"No longer following you."

Skeelana anticipated that. "Or course not. But that's one of the first things you're trained to recognize as a Memoridon. To know that we all have a veil."

"A veil?"

"Several, in fact. And they filter out more of those sensations than you possibly know, letting only a small number of them actually through."

This certainly wasn't anything taught at university. Though again, given the source, I was willing to lend it credence. "And why would we have a veil? Veils?"

"Because the gods aren't always cruel?" She laughed. It was a pleasant sound. Contagious. "See, if we didn't have them, we'd become overwhelmed. Completely, utterly overwhelmed. Immediately. At least without the kind of instruction Memoridons receive. We learn how to slowly pull back layers of the veil, allowing more and more through, without being damaged by the deluge of sensations. It takes years to accomplish this, but it's the source of most everything else we do—understanding how the veils work, and how to manipulate them."

This was a heady idea, literally and figuratively, and I wasn't sure I had a complete handle on it, but I knew I couldn't press her about it indefinitely. And I'm sure there was only so much she could or was willing to divulge. "So Soffjian did, what, exactly? To the Hornmen?"

We left the plaza, turning down a street and heading toward the city wall and some gate or other. Skeelana leaned in my direction a bit and smiled. "Uninitiated or not, I figured a bright boy like you would have pieced that together. There's an art to it—Soffjian could have pulled aside just a layer or two, knocked him unconscious or disoriented him, as he was overwhelmed, unused to the increased sensations. She could have been really precise had she chosen to. But the martial Memoridons, as you aptly put it, they're a lot more like the Syldoon proper than the rest of us. So, not needing a prisoner or leaving him for someone else to finish off, she didn't hold back.

"She ripped the veils off the Hornmen altogether. Especially the first, the one she focused on. She tore his to tiny pieces and it blew away like it never existed at all, and there was no repairing it, even if someone had been there with the power and inclination to do it. Poor bastard was bombarded by thousands, maybe tens of thousands of sensations he just wasn't equipped to handle. Would have driven him mad if she left him a layer or two, but with nothing there to protect him, it simply killed him."

She fell silent, and I looked at Braylar at the head of our company, and Soffjian riding a discrete distance behind. "They might not look that much alike, but the resemblance is still uncanny."

Skeelana grinned, briefly, but it was grim, and accompanied by another shiver. The next question was out before I knew it was coming. "You've never been in combat, have you?"

Her eyes darted to me and back to the rider in front of us. "No. No, I haven't." This admission seemed grudging, as if she felt lessened by it. It was strange to think that I actually had more experience in these things than one other member of our small company. Even Lloi had been in a number of battles, and likely seen a fair number of men die, before and after leaving the Green Sea.

Skeelana pricked a hole in any satisfaction I was feeling. "I'm also guessing you've never shot and killed a man before, have you, Arki?"

I briefly considered lying, and then for no reason I could explain, opted for the truth. "I've shot *at* men before. A few times now. Out of necessity. But no, I've never killed a man. Until this morning."

Saying it out loud, I felt a strange mix of relief and desperate horror swirling together. I'd never be able to say I'd never killed a man again. No matter where I was headed, there was never any going back.

Skeelana nodded, once, quickly, but somehow firmly. "Then we are both a bit out of place in this hardened company. I suggest we stay in the rear."

I felt the nausea die down. A little. "Agreed. Or maybe one row in. You never can tell when we might get attacked from behind."

Even as she laughed, I fought the urge to look over my shoulder. But unless the ripper was just about to leap up and tear me from the saddle, the most pressing danger was ahead. Immediately ahead. We were almost to the gates.

We slowed down as we crossed the bridge. Unlike the Hero's Bridge we'd originally entered Alespell from, this wouldn't take nearly as long. The traffic was still very thin at this early hour, as we seemed to be the only ones leaving and only those in the closest outlying villages and farms could have made it to the city this early. Since the Fair still ran for a bit, there was no cause for anyone to camp outside the walls waiting for entrance. So, there wouldn't be any delays due to passage of people or carts or livestock or wagons, or any random checks.

In theory, we'd be gone soon enough. Assuming we weren't detained. And as our horses carried us forward, I thought of a dozen reasons why that might happen. A telltale bloodstain someone missed washing off. The likelihood that an alarm had been raised, and someone had reported Syldoon killing scores of men in the streets, or the Hornmen who escaped had sought help or regrouped. The fact that a large band of armed Syldoon was in the city at all. Leaving was better than entering, but our presence would make any guards uneasy, no matter which direction we were going.

We reached the first gate, the portcullis up, the guards walking out of the gatehouse to see why a large group was departing so early in the day. There were two of them in soiled gambesons and boiled leather, neither looking especially anxious or on edge, both holding their spears as if they would rather lean on them than use them. Until they realized who they had in front of them.

When the younger guard saw Syldoon soldiers, armed, armored, with nooses on full display, he stopped, stood up straighter, tightened the grip on his spear, and immediately looked at the older guard for the lead. That man also seemed to have tensed up, but then some recognition flashed across his face, and it took me a second to place him. He was one of the guards who had allowed us to leave the city before curfew when the group had headed for the temple ruins with Captain Gurdinn and the Brunesmen.

He had large tufts of hair sticking out of his ears and below the rim of his iron helm, and gray stubble on his face, which marked him as a seasoned soldier, but probably more accustomed to breaking up the odd scuffle or running down a thief like the one in the stocks than any kind of real combat. Or facing a potential threat like the Syldoon or deciding what to do with them.

I didn't envy him.

He recovered quickly enough though, eyes narrowing. "Saw you leaving the city the other day. Less of you, leastwise. And I recollect you were dressed a mite differently then."

Braylar moved his helm from the crook of his right arm to the other, casually, the mail draping over his vambraces, but I had the sense that he was just freeing up his good hand to pull Bloodsounder off his belt, or the crossbow off the saddle if need be. Still, he blew on his right hand and answered nonchalantly, as if the Syldoon always trafficked in and out of an Anjurian city just after dawn. "That's a fine memory you have. You must be quite good with faces."

"Aye." The older guard gave the younger a stern look, his wiry eyebrows drawn down, eyes nearly slits. The younger guard nodded as if spoken to and hurried back into the squat guard tower. It occurred to me that they surely weren't the only two housed there, just the only two assigned to the damp and chill of inspection.

The older guard nodded. "Also recollect you were riding with the baron's men." Several wooden shutters above us opened simultaneously with a loud creak and I just about jumped out of the saddle. They were propped open and a fair number of archers looked down on us. Arrows were knocked, but no strings pulled back that I could tell. Still, as one of only two *not* wearing armor, I immediately began to sweat, chill be damned. Skeelana didn't look any more at ease alongside me.

Continuing as if he hadn't heard those shutters at all, the older guard said, "The baron got use for your kind here, he must have his reasons. Can't fathom what they'd be, but that ain't my place. So, guessing he wouldn't be too pleased about a gate guard waking him up to ask about your kind skulking about. So there'll be none of that."

Braylar responded as if he, too, were oblivious to the arrows above. "Sounds as if you have a fine appreciation for your liege lord's temperament. Restraint and good at placing faces. It's no wonder you were given this prestigious post."

The guard took a step forward and patted Braylar's horse on the muzzle, as if the men were just having the friendliest exchange in the world. "No need to involve the baron none. But I'll tell you this, Black Noose, with peace on for a while, some men in Anjuria might not have lost any to your kind, but I ain't one of them. You and yours took my brother, just north of Brassfield. Border raid. By you cunts."

Braylar replied, "Hmmm, I don't recall having been to Brassfield." He called over to Hewspear, "Did we ever raid a Brassfield, Lieutenant?"

"No, Captain. I can't say that we ever did."

"I thought not." He turned back to the guard. "So I can't take any credit or blame for that particular engagement. Did your brother fight heroically? Some men do, some men don't. In fact, some simply shit themselves, trip over their spears, and get trampled in the mud by their own side. I do hope he died more nobly than that. Those who die gloriously are often remembered in song, but they tend not to compose too many tunes for the ones who shit themselves."

The gate guard grabbed the reins tight, knuckles white, and looked up at Braylar. I heard bows straining as arrows were drawn back and it took all my willpower not to look up or kick my heels into my mount and run for cover. "Weren't but two and twenty at the time, he was. Married a year. Just had a daughter. So I'm working real hard here to come up with a reason not to let my boys fill you full of arrows, Brune be damned. Figure out cause later."

With the distinct possibility of an arrow plunging into my chest depending on the next words out of Braylar's mouth, I was more than terrified. The captain leaned down and said, "You carry out your duty as you see fit. I can never fault a military man for acting decisively. Even if it turns out such a decision is rash in the extreme. You see, I expect the baron would not react so kindly to news of us being cut down at his gates, particularly since he summoned us to Alespell in the first place. I had the pleasure of attending the baron just the other day, in fact, as he interrogated one of his men who'd made the unfortunate mistake of acting rashly and disobeying orders. Have you been to Baron Brune's dungeons or met his interrogator? Lovely man, though not especially chatty, with a delightful purple birthmark on his face?"

The guard didn't respond but slowly loosened his grip on the reins. If he didn't know the man personally, he obviously knew him by reputation. Braylar continued. "No, I expect not. Only traitors and malcontents are brought before him. With the only occasional audience being evil bastards like myself, summoned here to root out and deliver those working against your good baron. So, by all means, if you'd like to experience those cells and the delightful methods of passing the time therein, give the sign to you men, loose your bows. Cut us down to a man. Be decisive.

"Or be prudent and don't condemn your men to torture and death. Entirely your call, gatekeeper."

Braylar slowly straightened back up, and the older guard stood where he was, rigid. Unlike a crossbow that did the work for you, you couldn't draw a bow for long—they would need to shoot or release the tension. I held my breath, waiting for the twang of the bowstrings and the horrible pain to follow.

But the guard released the reins, took two reluctant steps back toward the guard tower, and then slammed the end of his spear on the cobblestones, the crack reverberating, echoing off the walls of the gate and making me nearly piss myself. But when I glanced up a few seconds later, the archers had withdrawn, and the shutters were closing again. Without another word, the guard turned and headed back in the tower, no doubt choking on rage at the inability to unleash some personal vengeance on the men he held responsible for his young brother's death. I hadn't envied him before, but I definitely didn't envy the next man or woman who did the slightest thing to irk him later that day. They would pay a hefty penalty.

Skeelana looked at me, face pale but forcing a smile. "Well. What an exciting morning. And still so early."

"If nearly soiling yourself is exciting, then yes. All kinds of excitement."

I wondered if either Memoridon had been readying to do something to help us escape the potential disaster Braylar seemed inclined to invite. But I imagined there was very little they could have done to stop the first volley of arrows.

We started moving again, passing underneath the gate and over the drawbridge and I breathed easier. A man, a woman, and a donkey moved as far aside as they could as we approached, the people wide-eyed as they saw the inked nooses, the donkey oblivious to it all.

Sometimes, just sometimes, I wished I was a donkey.

As we headed west down Rover's Road, away from Alespell, presumably for good, the couple and the donkey weren't the only ones to shy away or give us the road entirely as they made out the noose tattoos. The Syldoon didn't seem overly concerned with hiding now, as none of the soldiers wore anything over their armor, and their necks were entirely too visible. I supposed there wasn't much point anymore. We were out of Alespell and heading to Sunwrack, capital of the Syldoon Empire. Nevertheless, we were still in Anjuria—and as the guard at the gate had proved, Syldoon were not loved in Anjuria, truce or no—so I wondered why the captain didn't order the men to hide the nooses for a bit longer. But it seemed a foolish thing to risk wrath over, so I kept the question to myself.

Everyone was quiet for the first mile or so, until we'd put Alespell truly behind us. Braylar instructed two men to fall back and screen the road to the rear, and he sent two Syldoon ahead of us as well. We pressed on and I had to resist the urge to look over my shoulder, to see if the Syldoon were racing to catch up and alert us of pursuit. More Hornmen, maybe Brunesmen, possibly even someone else Braylar had inadvertently or intentionally offended, stolen from, lied to, or encountered slain relatives of. It wouldn't have surprised me if a mad mob of pilgrims was kicking up a cloud of dust on our heels.

As we put more distance between us and the city, bloody fountains, and beaked horrors, with the farmlands and homesteads slowly coming and going, soldiers began chatting together, here and there, though briefly, and without much enthusiasm.

One soldier ahead of me with a big pulpy nose that had seen more than its share of breaks said, "Did you see the look on those Horntoads when the ripper ripped into them? Plaguing hells, but they shit themselves good!"

The solider alongside him, who had sleepy eyes and a bit of a drawl, replied, "Only reason you didn't brown your breeches was you knew it was coming. Don't tell me that thing didn't shrivel your balls. You're a liar if you do."

The first sounded offended. "Weren't nothing but an animal. Weren't nothing more."

"A giant animal that liked tearing people in two like wet paper."

"Yeah. So. Still nothing but an animal. Just bigger and meaner is all. Weren't like it was a monster or nothing."

"If that wasn't a monster, than I hope to never see one."

Pulp-nose paused and then said, "Should have brought it with us. Some kind of secret weapon, eh?"

"That secret weapon tore Bulsinn's arm off, you plaguing bastard."

Pulp-nose looked at Bulsinn up the line, slumped over, but still riding. "Yeah. Well. His hand mostly, weren't it? But that's my point. Thing deals some serious damage. Maybe we should get an egg. Hatch it, raise, it, train it. Turn it loose when—"

"Plaguing idiot."

"What?"

The second soldier shook his head. "You're a plaguing idiot with pig shit for brains."

"Well. Make a hell of a weapon is all. That's all I'm saying."

That was that. Most conversations seemed to last that long or less before lapsing into silence. I didn't overhear anyone whispering about the Memoridons or their part in the battle. Or paying them any attention as they rode in the company now. The pair of them might as well have been wraiths. Soffjian had fallen back from the head of the column, and Skeelana had ridden forward to keep pace with her.

I watched Bulsinn wobble a bit several riders ahead before another Syldoon moved over and steadied him, asking him something as he offered a flask of wine or water. Bulsinn shook his head, but then took the proffered flask, reaching across his body awkwardly to take it with his off hand. Well, what used to be his off hand. His only hand now. I wondered if he would live. I'd seen plenty of scarred and broken veteran soldiers in Rivermost, on the dole from the burghers who ran that city—missing digits and limbs, talking about old battles with rheumy eyes and sandy voices. They'd lived. But I wondered if they'd had to ride right away after losing a hand. I suppose so. It wasn't like battles or wars would stop for a single soldier. Or ten thousand of them.

It was strange—when I witnessed Braylar's alarming behavior in the

Green Sea, nearly got stabbed to death in the wagon, and watched the captain beating down his foes and crushing them, not with rage or even anger, but simple cold viciousness, and later saw Lloi tend to him, I'd been shocked and unnerved beyond anything I'd ever experienced. But today, I'd seen things that were beyond any reckoning at all. A giant predator tearing armored men to pieces, setting bladders free with its piercing screech. Most animals, suddenly free from captivity, would run, or fight their way to freedom. But the ripper had been far more interested in taking vengeance out on the humans in front of it, killing as many as it could. There was malice there. Maybe even hatred.

The second solider had been right. It was a monster.

And then there were the Memoridons, using some kind of invisible sorcery to melt men's minds like wax, driving them mad or striking them down without so much as a touch. . . that was something I could do without seeing ever again. Or not seeing. And that actually made it worse—if fire had leapt off Soffjian's fingers and set the man's skin ablaze, or if lights had danced in front of the Hornmen attacking Skeelana, blinding him not with illusions in his mind but something real, something I could have seen. . . it would have still been unnatural, awful, but at least it would have made some semblance of sense. What the Memoridons did was beyond unnatural. No wonder the Syldoon wanted as little to do with them as possible.

And even beyond those things, I saw a man die in front of me, by my hand. Maybe it would have been worse if I'd driven a blade between his ribs or cut his throat. Of course it would have. But his life ended by my hand. Did he have a family? Children? He had parents, at least, unless they were in the ground waiting for him. Friends, no doubt. Whoever he left behind would never have the opportunity to say goodbye to him, to tell him a kind word. Had he been kissed on the lips by a lover before riding through the predawn streets of Alespell to his death?

I was very glad I didn't possess Bloodsounder. It was difficult enough to think about the man I killed without knowing the first thing about him. If I'd known who he really did leave behind to grieve for him, what his passions had been, fears, dreams, compulsions. . .

It was too much.

My silence clearly wasn't companionable—downright inhospitable, truly—so I took the opportunity to move alongside Vendurro, who was riding alone. I'm sure he would have been arguing with Glesswik about one thing or another. Had Glesswik been around. I forced myself to smile as I called out Vendurro's name.

Vendurro nodded when he saw me, freckled face briefly breaking into a grin. It wasn't the broad and engaging smile I'd first seen, but that was several battles and one lost friend ago, so it was better than the grim greeting I expected. I shifted in the saddle, my legs and back already uncomfortable, and then realized that there were some benefits to not wearing armor. Although these soldiers were no doubt accustomed to the extra weight pulling on the shoulders, extra load was extra load.

I wondered how much blood Vendurro had to clean off. How many men had he killed? In Alespell, just that morning. Ever. It seemed a question better left unasked, so instead I opted for, "How long since you've been to Sunwrack?"

That did cause him to brighten a little. "Been a fair bit. Longer than any of us would like, I'm guessing." He stopped, calculating. "A few years now. Seems longer. Always seems longer when you're away from home."

"Home? I would've thought that. . . "

I stopped myself, but Vendurro wasn't as cooperative. "What's that?"

"Well. . . some of the other soldiers, they've spent decades in Sunwrack. Or, at least returned there when they weren't on campaign I'm guessing. So, more of their lives there than where they grew up. It makes sense they would consider the place home. But you can't be much older than me, if any. What was it Hewspear said—you were chosen when you were still children?" He nodded. "So, you've spent half your life or thereabouts as a Syldoon. But that means half your life was with your family." His bright look disappeared. "Your blood family, I mean. Where you came from."

I could see I'd either overstepped or pinched a bruise, as he looked straight ahead, smile gone altogether. I did seem to have a knack for that. I was considering whether or not to try a completely different topic or wait for him to ride ahead or fall behind, or excuse myself if he didn't, when he replied, "You're on the mark about the timing of it. Half in one means half in the other, not much sense arguing the sums. But you can have yourself a loaf of bread, half still good, half given over to mold and rot, so two halves ain't always equal. What do you do with the half that's gone green? You cut it free and drop it in the dirt and eat what you got left. Unless you like eating mold. Can't think of too many who do, though. You a big fan of mold, are you, Arki?"

"It's not my favorite. So. . . is it really that easy to cut that part of your life free? The life you had before? Where you grew up, the people who raised you?"

Vendurro didn't pause in responding this time. "A few things might help clear it up some. Firstly. I didn't truly cut that part out altogether. I was using the moldy bread for effect."

"Figurative then?"

His smile returned. "No, I literally used it for effect." Since he talked like a tough half the time, it was easy to forget that he'd been educated, like all Syldoon. I'd have to remind myself of that. Especially in Sunwrack. Very bad to underestimate these men. "Fact of it is, I still send some gold to my old clan from time to time."

"Really? Just the gold? Or do you send message or communication as well?"

"I'd send a letter, too, but what's the point? They'd just use it to start a fire. And the message is the gold itself. Means I'm alive. And so long as I am, I'll continue to send some. I don't even ask who's there to receive it. Don't want to know who's still alive on that end. That's part of cutting things free. Figurative like. But I'll never be free of them completely. Those folk gave me life, taught me how to fight, and milk a goat, and herd sheep. And most any other skill I had when the Syldoon took me. But here's where we come to the second point."

"What's that?"

"You can't help what family brought you into the world, and they're in your blood, to be sure. They are your blood. But once you fall in with the Syldoon, there's no falling out. It's for life. You know that the minute your manumission is done. You signed on with all the blood you got and more. And that's something different, to be sure. You chose the bond, and dedicated your life to it, promised to protect your brothers and your Tower-mates so long as you got breath to do it. You see and do things as slaves that brings you closer than you ever get with any family, and once you get set free, accept the commission, take on the noose, there ain't no taking it off."

Vendurro realized he'd been speaking more passionately than I'd ever heard him, and seemed a little embarrassed, but then shrugged his shoulders and added, "Sunwrack is the only home I got, Arki. No matter how long I been away. It's a hard place full of harder people, but it will always be where I took the noose, so heading back there is about the sweetest ride I can imagine."

He looked over at me as I thought about that and then asked, "What about you, Arki? Mulldoos nailed it true—you weren't from Rivermost in the original. You miss home any, the one you grew up in? How's it feel to be heading in the opposite direction?"

If Mulldoos or almost any other Syldoon had posed the question, it probably would have been with intent to wound or rile up, but one look at Vendurro's expression told me he hadn't meant it that way. And yet it had stung, if only for a moment. "No, I'm in a situation far different from your own. I don't miss the home I grew up in, as it hardly counted as one. So it wasn't all that difficult to cut free. But I've never found anything like what you experienced. The university came closest to a home, but I always knew it was temporary, so I never allowed myself to form any lasting attachments. And everything after that has been a journey. With stops. So, no chance to create a home. Worthy of the name, anyway."

I never imagined saying this, but there wasn't any reason not to. At least to Vendurro. "I suppose I envy you that. Well, I know I do. You have something I'll never experience. Maybe someday I'll find a place that becomes home. I'd thought Rivermost might have been it, but I sort of knew the entire time that was temporary, too. I doubt I'd have ridden off with Captain Killcoin otherwise. But what you Syldoon have. . . The intense bonds. The allegiance. The blood oaths to your comrades. That's truly unlike anything else I've seen or heard of, even among other soldiers."

"No lie, that. None at all."

I sighed, and got angry at myself for doing so. "No matter where I set down roots and make a home out of, I'll never know the world as you do. It's quite. . . something." The conversation had turned much too earnest, probably for either of our tastes, so I added, "If I could have that without having to be a slave for a tenyear, and then kill men routinely after, well, that would be lovely."

Vendurro laughed, loud enough that the soldier in front of him looked over his shoulder before seeing me and wondering if his comrade was laughing at me, then assuming he must have been, faced front again.

"Plague me," Vendurro said. "When you put it like that, I kind of do miss my family." Then we laughed together, earning a scowl over the shoulder from the same soldier in front.

It felt good to laugh after witnessing the battle in Alespell. Not just witnessing, I reminded myself. I had participated in the worst way possible. Even if it had been defending myself and Skeelana, I had taken a life. And what's more, suggested freeing the ripper, which had surely ended several more. I almost felt guilty laughing, but still, it felt good.

We were quiet for a minute after the laughter died away, and while I was reluctant to ask or say anything that might spoil the moment, I never knew when I would have another opportunity, so I gave it a go. "You said you've been in Anjuria for three years?"

Vendurro nodded. "Something like that. Wasn't counting the days. Ought to ask Hewspear. That man knows something about practically everything. The lieutenant could probably tell you down to the minute."

"And Lloi had been in the company for two? Or close to?"

Vendurro thought about it, then replied, "Near enough."

I glanced over my shoulder to be sure no one was immediately behind us. "And how long has Captain Killcoin had Bloodsounder then?"

Vendurro said, "About four years, give or take. About a year before we come to Anjuria. Thereabouts."

"And how did he come to have it? Lloi told me he unearthed Bloodsounder. But she wasn't with him, obviously. What did she mean by that?"

Vendurro looked at me, lower lip moving back and forth, dragging that patch of sandy hair on his chin with it, as he seemed to be wrestling with how to, or whether to, respond. Then he looked ahead to make sure no one was close enough to hear. As the company had the road to ourselves, we had spread out a fair amount—someone would need to drop back or ride forward quite a bit to make out our conversation. "I was there, as it happened. Kind of wishing I hadn't been. But Cap, guessing he's wishing the same right about now."

"Where was 'there'?"

"We was riding screen for the army. In—"

"Riding screen?"

Vendurro stopped himself. "Easy to forget the only things you know about soldiering you read in some book or other. You seen the captain sending scouts ahead, behind, all around?" I nodded and he continued. "Well, an army, they do the same thing, only bigger like. Usually send a small unit. Scour the countryside for stores of food, signs of the enemy. Sometimes sent out to destroy crops, or poison wells, or work up some other kind of mischief. That's what the crossbow cavalry was best at— scouting, gathering intelligence, taking what needed to be taken, breaking what needed breaking."

"Crossbow cavalry? I take it you mean this unit?"

Vendurro tapped the side of his long nose. "Yup. Nailed it true, Arki. But this is only a portion of it. Anyway, the army was on the move. This was in the hills of Gurtagoi. We weren't at war with the Anjurians just then, so this wasn't the army entire or nothing. Just a few battalions, set to check out reports of some movement from uppity Gurtagese bandits. Worst kind of screening there is—just getting a lay of the countryside, not expecting any scrapes, not stirring up trouble of any note. Just riding. Sleeping. Riding. Sleeping. So when we come upon a burial mound, and Cap said he wanted to take a closer look, we were half bored out of our minds and all curious as cats."

I'd read about burial mounds, but never seen one. "You said Gurtagoi? There weren't any tribes or clans in the vicinity, were there? If memory serves, this province had been settled for some time, right?"

"Yup. A lot of open country, still, but no active tribes that I know of. Any that lived there were wiped out or moved on a long time ago. Why?"

"Well, my studies indicated that burial mounds in active tribe lands might have something worthwhile in them. But since this was in a settled region, open or not, I'm guessing it would have been looted a long time ago, wouldn't it? So what caused the captain to want to investigate?"

Vendurro scratched at his stubbly neck with two fingers. "Can't rightly say. You weren't the only one who had that thought. A few of the men said the same thing. Mulldoos the loudest. But you seen the Cap—when he gets a thought lodged proper in his head. . . "

"A blacksmith with tongs couldn't pull it out."

Vendurro chuckled. "Right. And you got to remember—well, maybe you don't, since you probably didn't know this in the first of all, but Cap, before he was with the Syldoon, him and his sister—" he looked up the line at Soffjian. "They were something of experts when it came to robbing burial mounds. To hear him tell it. So maybe he gleaned something in the flowers and dirt, or the slope of the land, or devils know what he saw—but he seemed real certain this mound was worth exploring for a bit. And since we weren't in a bull-busting hurry just then, most of the men were more than happy to let the horses graze and lay in the thistles while the Cap and a few of us investigated.

"We followed his lead as we walked the perimeter. Looked like a big mound of grass most of the way, until we came to the entrance. A big old stone slab in place, bunch of squiggly carving worked into the face. Cap told us to find some logs to bust in there. Mulldoos, he looked at Cap, you know, like he does, and said, 'Cap, what makes you think somebody else ain't busted in here in before now? Why are we playing in the dirt? Let's get back to camp.'

"But Cap, being Cap, said, 'Have you no spirit of adventure, Lieutenant?' Well, Mulldoos weren't one to have the size of his manhood questioned, so he helped fetch some logs and pry that stone slab off the entrance. Heavier than it looked. Took some sweat from all of us, but we finally worked it free."

"Did you have torches?"

"Well, I wouldn't have thought to bring none, it being midday and all, and the mound didn't look all that big, figured enough sun would come down there with us to see what was what. But Cap insisted we get some ready, which earned him another of those Mulldoos looks. But we went about it, worked something up, started inside."

I asked, "Did it. . . smell?"

Vendurro laughed. "Now that you mention it, it did. But not like death or rot. Just a stale, trapped sort of smell. Like the earth had belched but never had a hole to let it out. So we hoisted those makeshift torches, started in. The dirt floor was packed tight, covered in dust of the ages, and there weren't footprints that I could make out. Didn't look to me like no one had broken in there before us. As we started down the incline, Hewspear must have been thinking on that and said, 'Captain,'—you know, never have heard him shorten it, just wouldn't sit right with him, I suppose—'Captain,' he says, 'I do have a spirit of adventure. But don't you find it peculiar that a crypt like this would have been undisturbed for so long?'"

Vendurro managed a good impression of nearly everyone, capturing the rhythm and cadence. "Well, Cap looks at him and says, 'Perhaps, but it's most definitely disturbed now. Do you really wish to turn back before seeing what's inside?'

"There wasn't one of us that said much to that. So in we went, following a tunnel down. And Cap was right, after we turned away from the entrance, the sunlight would've known better than to follow us, so the torches proved mighty useful."

"Thought they might," I said, smiling.

"Real right head on them shoulders, you got. Anyway, we kept walking until we got to the burial chamber. It was big, bigger than I would have expected. Ceiling about fifteen feet high, so Hewspear could straighten up again. Bracketed with wooden beams. The ceiling, that is, not Hewspear of course."

"Why was it so big?"

"Well, I might've asked the same question, never been graverobbing myself neither, coming from a clan that didn't do burial mounds."

"No?"

"Nope. Burned the dead to ash, high and low. Can't say why, for a certainty. Always just been done that way. But Cap said this mound likely belonged to a warrior of note. And if it was anything like where he was from, that warrior didn't head into the afterlife traveling light.

"And he was righter than right about that. All along the outer edge of the chamber, all manner of things. Jars that once had oil, or mead, or who knows what else. Some flutes that got Hew's attention—always did like his windy instruments. A small table with some sort of game board on it, the pieces caked in dust so much it was hard to tell what they were, besides lumps. Blew the dust free, choking on it, found onyx, started stuffing them in a pouch. Trays for food. Wicker baskets, drinking horns, combs and brushes, fox-fur blankets. On and on. I saw Mulldoos grab some old brass torcs, getting into the spirit of things. We were circling around, examining this and that, pocketing anything that wasn't too warped or cracked. But Cap had already made it across the chamber to an open door on the other side. He called out, 'Baubles. Come on, men,' and disappeared into the next room without waiting on us."

Vendurro stopped talking for a second, looking down at the pommel on his saddle, the reins loose in his hands. He glanced at me, and he might have shivered, though I might have only imagined the last. Or not.

"What is it?" I asked.

"You know me. Well, not really. But you know I ain't a coward. And not one to get real superstitious like. But as I walked toward that open door, I felt like we ought not to have been there at all just then. It wasn't just that we were about to meet the dead man who owned that hole in the ground. It was something. . . else.

"I stopped just outside the doorway, watching Cap's torch play across the wall inside, heard him shifting through the dust, and it just felt. . . wrong. Real wrong. Tough to put to words. But just then, Hewspear seemed to have the right of it. Maybe there was a good reason we were the first ones to pull that slab aside in a good long while."

"Bloodsounder. And it's. . . " I hesitated to use the word, but nothing else sufficed. "Curse."

"Didn't know it at the time, but yup. And it was too late—Cap was in, we were out, and even though I knew it was foolishness, I put my hand on my sword stepping through the door, just the same.

"There were three stone tables set in the middle of the room, bigger than the one we just left. On one side, the skeleton of a horse. Had what once must have been one hell of a pretty saddle, bells all up and down the harness. On the opposite table, there were two skeletons in rags. Again, probably real pretty gowns at one point. Cap must have sensed our questions. As he was circling the tables, he said, 'They send the warrior to the afterlife with his best horse and two finest slaves. Well, that would be my guess. We had a similar practice in my homeland. It's supposed to be an honor, but I don't imagine the horse or slaves shared that view.'"

Vendurro scratched at his stubble again, and continued. "And in that center table, that was the big chief hisself. Bones and some embroidered death gown mostly in tatters. Must have been something to see at some point. The gown, I was meaning. And on the side, his wargear. Big scaled cuirass of bronze, iron helm with a faceplate in the shape of a screaming bearded man, a shield—the leather face rotten away—sword in a scabbard, a spear, iron head black and haft as curvy as a scared snake. And . . . well, you know that already. Cap saw that wicked flail, drawn right to it, traced his finger along it in the flickering light, gently shook the dust free from the chains, and slowly hoisted it. It rattled down there, links clinking, sounding louder than it had any right to. Cap cleaned Bloodsounder off—though of course didn't know the name just then—examined the heads, and the whole thing was free of the patina or warping that had waylaid so much else in the crypt. It didn't look new, but you could tell that weapon would have no problem working just fine, with a quick cleaning. Wasn't rusted like it ought to have been."

I tried to imagine the scene. "Did Captain Killcoin seem to sense anything wrong?"

Vendurro shook his head. "Not that I could tell. But he's about as hard to read as a blank book most days. If he did, didn't stop him from giving us leave to gather whatever loot was salvageable to distribute among the men. We set to it, moving awful quiet, even though wasn't nobody left to disturb. And Cap just sat there, leaning against the edge of the stone table, turning those Deserter heads over and over. So can't say that he sensed something was amiss, but his actions did seem mighty peculiar. Seemed right fixated on the thing, and while he was a man of moods, can't rightly say that I've ever seen him locked in on something like that. Never knew him to have any sort of affinity or interest in the Deserters, so to see him turning those awful heads over in his hands, the torch light seeming to slide right off that dark metal, was queer, to be certain. But still, never thought to think something real awful was about to befall the man. I never would have guessed."

Well, it was difficult to imagine the mood of the men or women who had interred the body, as the pain of the Deserter Gods abdicating this realm and leaving us alone behind the Godveil must have been sharper and fresher for them. But even now, so many centuries later, I know if I uncovered a wicked looking weapon shaped in their awful image, that would be an absolute deterrent and send me fleeing in the other direction immediately.

Vendurro said, "And even if we got some kind of warning or other, can't say that would have held up Cap. Might just have intrigued him fiercer."

He had a point. When Braylar set his mind to something, it just wasn't like him to allow anyone else to push him in a different direction. With sparing the Hornman being the lone exception, efforts to persuade or dissuade the man seemed to steel his resolve in whatever direction he was already going in. "Lloi mentioned that at some point, he was beset by those memories Bloodsounder stole. And that you all tried to bury it back in the ground. That wasn't the same tomb though, was it?"

Vendurro shook his head. "Nope. Fair distance from it, if I recollect right. He'd killed men in battle with the thing, after stealing it from the grave. Can't say the count, but more than two or three over the next year or so. But Bloodsounder seemed to take its time working its evil magic on him. Real gradual like. We all noticed something was strange. Leastwise, me and Gless and the lieutenants, knowing him better than most, and spending more time in the man's company. So we saw a change. The upchucking after combat—that was new. Always a hard bastard, Cap, not one to get wobbly-kneed over any killing that needed doing. Leastwise, before using the flail.

"And he must have been bloated with the memories of the dead for some time before he finally fessed up to having them. Curses are a tough thing to believe in overmuch. Unless it's you bearing the brunt of it. Coming from anyone else, we would have thought him mad. But it was Cap, we could see him suffering. Spells come over him. Drifting like a tiny branch in a big eddy. Only it were one no one else could see or do anything about."

"What about the other men in his command?"

"What about them?"

"Didn't they notice that their captain was. . . unwell?"

Vendurro nodded. "Ayyup. Sure they did. And once whispers start, real hard to unwhisper them. Luckily, Mulldoos wasn't one to brook any nonsense like that. First time he caught someone talking about it, shoved that man's face into a tree until he choked on bark and practically gouged out his eyes, told him to shut his hole or Mulldoos would do the shutting himself. You know. Like he does."

"Like he does."

"So that's when we tried burying the flail, middle of the night, off on campaign. Only that seemed to make the Cap worse off than holding the thing in his hands, tortured him, made him scream and thrash like he was on fire. So we dug it up and brought it back. And just like that, things seemed to improve all on their lonesome. For a while, leastwise. We started to think maybe severing the tether like that, even in the temporary, broke whatever hold it had on him, stopped the affliction cold. Of course, it didn't work out like that. Took some more time for it to start deviling him again, but less than before, and he was worse off. I heard one of the men openly wondering if it were the plague, or something worse, only I didn't bash him into a tree, just told him to bite that tongue before I carved it out. That was when we happened upon Lloi."

I considered the timing of everything. "It sounds like you were on campaign in or around Anjuria the whole time this happened."

"That's right."

"So. . . " I looked up the column, to where the women were riding in a pocket by themselves. "His sister, the other Memoridons, they have no idea then? About Bloodsounder. What it does to him. The stolen memories. The warnings it gives him. None of it."

Vendurro leaned over toward me and lowered his voice, though the pair weren't anywhere near close enough to hear anything except the tromp of their horses' hooves. "No. And I expect Cap is real eager to keep it that way. Real. Eager. So don't go mentioning the first thing about it around no female ears. Memoridon nor otherwise, when it comes to it. In fact, best not to talk about it much at all to anyone, excepting me, the lieutenants, or Cap. And Mulldoos might make you eat bark or drop you hard if you do. And Cap, well, harass him too much on that front and could be your memories deviling him next. Though he does seem to like you more than the last couple archivists we had. Still, best not to test that overmuch."

With a wink, Vendurro rode ahead, leaving me to my thoughts. Which was always a dangerous proposition.

Braylar called for a brief halt to water and feed the horses. We moved off the road, and I followed the Syldoon lead of hobbling my horse and allowing it to graze on the grass, which wasn't billowing in the breeze like any found on the Green Sea, but still seemed plentiful enough to feed the horses of a very small company on the move. I left my horse where it was and joined Braylar. He was absently patting Scorn's neck while his other mount moved off a short distance, chewing some grass.

I had specific questions in mind, but hesitated to bring them up. Of course, I shouldn't have approached until I was really ready, as my silent looming seemed to annoy him as much as someone shouting in his ear. "I have the uncomfortable feeling you intend to speak at some point, and yet there you mutely stand, like a nervous actor waiting for the curtain to rise, shifting feet, wringing hands, trying not to draw attention to yourself, and managing to do exactly that. Well, consider the curtain up. Out with it."

Did the man always have to be so irascible? "I was just wondering, Captain, when we were going to reconnect with the wagons?"

His hand dropped from Scorn's neck and he finally turned and faced me. "Were you? And why were you wondering that, exactly?"

"One thing in particular. Well, two really."

"Are you sure it wasn't three?"

I took a deep breath. "I'd been thinking about the crate you have, that you showed me. With the scrolls."

He took two quick steps until our noses nearly touched. Braylar lowered his voice. "Now that I have shared the contents with you, all but two here know what lies inside. Can you hazard a guess as to the two ignorant parties?" He didn't wait for a verbal answer, but continued when he must have seen it in my eyes. "I would like to keep it that way. Indefinitely. And before you insist on asking why, as I know you are wont to do, let me address that briefly: Do. Not. Ask. Now, the second particular thing? Provided it wasn't connected with the first."

I lowered my voice. "Well, without discussing the specifics of any contents, I was wondering when it was my services could prove useful."

"When we reunite with the wagons, you shall have your opportunity to prove you are a better translator than sleuth. Though there is more than one crate to go through. Anything else? My horse is wandering."

I looked off into the grass, and he had sensed the beast shuffling away from the road, or heard its munching growing fainter. This time I looked around to be sure no one was listening. "You struck someone down. In Alespell."

Braylar's eyes narrowed. "You do know what it means to actually ask a question, yes? Let me provide an example: are all learned boys so obtuse?"

I tried again, speaking quickly, "Are you. . . are you well? Hewspear tried to save you from using. . . " I looked down at Bloodsounder. "Back there. But you did strike someone down with it, didn't you? I ask because, well, it seems without Lloi, drink is the only thing that helps. And not especially well. And you can't exactly captain the company drunk, can you? So, with that girl Junjee failing to work out, and no chance to find another, might you consider—" I looked around before spotting Soffjian pasturing her horse some distance away from the others. "—asking for assistance?"

Braylar gave me a stare a ripper would have been proud of. "Several questions, at last, and yet each more ill-advised than the previous. Amazing. You truly should have stopped with the first unasked question I had to puzzle out myself. You're the man who wins two coins at a gambling table, and then loses four more, never knowing when to walk away." He shook his head in disgust and showed me how that was done, moving off quickly.

That wasn't an answer, or even a semblance of one, but pointing that out couldn't have led to anything good. So I headed back to reclaim my own grazing horse. I still didn't fully comprehend the dynamic that was at work between the Memoridons and Syldoon—and with the way information was parsed out, it could be some time before I did—but clearly now wasn't the time to ask about it, and the captain surely was not the person to ask.

I undid my writing case, sat in the grass, and proceeded to record everything as accurately as I could. Sometimes time passes slowly when writing, other times quickly, and this was certainly the latter. It felt as if I'd only settled down to record when Braylar gave the order to mount up again.

There were a couple of occasions I made eye contact with Skeelana, wondering what her slant would be, or if she would be more forthcoming. In university, there was no shortage of texts concerning the Syldoon. Mostly written from the Anjurian perspective, or other similar peoples who had been pillaged, conquered, decimated, or absorbed by the Syldoon Empire, so hardly flattering. And suspect, as far as veracity went. But the documentation about the Memoridons was far less voluminous, and what existed much more sketchy.

Who better to ask than a Memoridon herself, especially one that wasn't openly hostile or capable of melting my mind into steam or mush or whatever it was Soffjian had done to the poor Hornman. Soffjian was probably a worse choice than her brother, but perhaps Skeelana, when I got the chance?

Then again, maybe I was just trying to find an excuse to speak to her at all. She was easy to chat with, warm and playful, even as she teased me. The prospect of doing so again was somehow both exciting and daunting. But she was also a Memoridon. I had to remind myself of that. And she was probably only humoring me, besides.

Braylar called out, "You are tarrying, scribe. You do not get paid to tarry. Mount up."

After packing my quills in haste, I snapped the case shut, slid it back into the leather harness on the side of the saddle, and climbed back up, the insides of my thighs chafed and sore already.

I wondered if steady riding would result in calluses on my legs. I hoped not.

The column rode in silence. I was the only one shifting and sitting the saddle so poorly—even Skeelana seemed a more competent and comfortable rider. I tried not to look behind, trusting that the two riders Braylar had screening would ride up and announce any sign of trouble or pursuit. Still, we had fled Alespell with countless dead Hornmen littering the street, a ripper running loose, and a baron who didn't take kindly to being disobeyed. Surely, someone must have been hounding us by now.

I fell back behind Vendurro, Mulldoos, Hewspear, and Braylar, not so close that I would intrude or crowd them (or draw more than the dark stare from Mulldoos), but near enough I'd be the first of the remaining men to know what was happening. Should anything noteworthy happen. Which of course it did, given who I was riding with.

We approached Martyr's Fork as one road veered almost due north, and the other branch continued into the west. While I fully expected us to head north, as that was the direction Sunwrack lay, we stayed west. Away from Thurvacia. Clearly I was missing something. Again.

Soffjian rode past me, not tarrying in the least. I wasn't sure if it was a cantor or a gallop, but it wasn't slow. Skeelana followed, though not riding quite so hard, with the spare mounts behind her. I gave her a questioning look as she passed and she only raised her pierced eyebrows. I picked up the pace a bit as well, closing the distance between myself and the Syldoon officers, though as discretely as I could manage.

Braylar's sister passed him, wheeled her horse around with a whinnying protest and then stopped directly in his path. While he could have chosen to go around her—this was an open road, not an alley—he halted and waited her out.

She seemed adept at masking her emotions when it suited her, perhaps no less so than Braylar, adopting expressions and demeanor for effect, but looked genuinely angry now. "I couldn't help noticing you are no longer headed home, brother. It's been some time—I do hope you haven't forgotten the way?"

Braylar met her stare. "Your heartfelt concern for my faculties is appreciated, as always, but—and I realize this might surprise you—I do in fact know where I am headed. Thank you for checking, just the same. Truly touching."

For the briefest moment, I thought I saw the anger flare up into a smoldering rage, but her usual mask slid into place so quickly, it might almost have been a trick of the shadow of a fast-moving cloud playing on her features. Almost. "While the Emperor and Commander Darzaak didn't see fit to share the actual script, it was made very clear to me that you were to quit Alespell as soon as you were able and return to Sunwrack immediately. Was the message more muddled on the actual page? Some ambiguity there? Please, explain what I missed."

I nudged my horse forward a bit to better see his face. Yes, he was smiling. That didn't bode well. "Oh, no, you are quite right. The mandate to return was spelled out explicitly. No uncertain terms. No room to misinterpret."

Soffjian laughed, which was as humorless a sound as I'd ever heard. "Truly? So, you're simply disregarding an Imperial order?"

"Our return to the capital will involve as much haste as we can muster. Exactly as instructed."

Soffjian glared, the unfriendly smile still on her lips. "Oh? I remain mystified."

"The order allowed for us to complete whatever final action we deemed necessary here before quitting the territory and returning. That particular segment is open to interpretation."

Mulldoos broke in, smiling as well, though he seemed to actually be enjoying the confrontation. "Cynead ought to have buttoned that one down better. Cap has room to wiggle, you can be sure he'll be using it."

Soffjian's eyes never left her brother. "That's Emperor Cynead, Syldoon. And I suspect the *Emperor* will not be amused at your delays."

Mulldoos didn't back down either, which wasn't shocking, but still spoke volumes about his bravery, stupidity, or indignation. "Guessing in all his imperialness, he forgot it was an imperial order sent us and every other squad into Anjuria in the first place. Emperors don't like getting dirt or blood under their fingernails—that's what grunts are for. None of us are here by our own volition, Memoridon."

Soffjian moved her horse forward, and part of me feared she would extend her splayed fingers and drop Mulldoos in the dirt. Another small part of me hoped to see it, at least if she only put him in his place instead of churning his brain like butter. But instead, she reined both her horse and herself in, voice level and cold. "Your political commentary isn't particularly relevant or interesting to me. But perhaps the Emperor will be more intrigued—you will have ample opportunity to share your views back in Sunwrack."

If Soffjian was a potential lightning strike, Mulldoos was happy to hoist his sword in the air and march around in his armor. "Cynead's a plaguing fool. Giving us marching orders home, when we were finally making some headway." He spit in the dirt. "Emperor or no, man's still a horsecunt and a half. That ain't a view, it's fact."

Given how much he'd argued with Braylar before on this very point, insisting the Syldoon needed to pull out, I was surprised to see Mulldoos taking essentially the opposite position now. But maybe Vendurro was right—the losses mounted up in ways you couldn't calculate. Or maybe he just despised his emperor that much. Or enjoyed bating a Memoridon who could destroy him without a touch.

Soffjian gave the pale man a flat, opaque look. "Your successes, failures, or losses are not my concern. My sole purpose here is to ensure you comply with Emperor Cynead's mandate and Commander Darzaak's directive and return in a timely fashion. Which it seems your captain intends to disobey, if not in the entirety, at least in spirit."

Mulldoos started to reply, but Braylar broke in. "The good lieutenant is in the right. We have lost men in this region at imperial behest, sweet sister, and we can never reclaim the fallen or our lost years. That is a soldier's lot. We receive commands, we obey commands to the fullest of our abilities, and on rare occasions, we receive some commensurate reward. We accept this. And Cynead—" Soffjian started to interrupt but Braylar raised a hand and pressed on. "My apologies— *Emperor* Cynead has been absent from the front lines for so many years he might have forgotten what the common soldier risks and endures in a dangerous territory far from home. A forgivable lapse, perhaps. But given the cunning intrigues he plays at on a daily basis in his own courtyard, it is surprising he would insist his agents abandon their maneuvering on his behalf."

"Bray, you overstep—"

"So, while he might have eaten some spoiled fruit, suffered a severe bellyache, and decided to suddenly reverse policy, threatening to under-mine everything we have worked so hard to engineer here on his behalf, that is his fickle prerogative, yes? But I will be thrice damned if I will quit this region before doing something to guarantee all of the blood spilled here was not in vain. And I expect when he sees how conscientious we are in our withdrawal, he will appreciate the lengths we have gone to. All for the glory of Empire. And Emperor. Of course."

Soffjian moved her horse alongside the captain's, and I thought Scorn was going to bite its face off. Or hers, if it got the chance. "You are involved in a very dangerous game, only you are merely pieces on a board. The only true player who matters is the one who ordered you to return. Promptly. And you can be sure he doesn't appreciate his pieces suddenly declaring their autonomy or refusing his moves. You would do well to remember your position and role. Brother."

Braylar laughed, coughed, and rubbed his bruised throat. "Oh, I can tell you without flattering myself in the slightest that my memory is nearly as sharp as a Memoridon's, Soffjian. You can be sure I have difficulty forgetting anything of import. So never fear. Our detour will not be long, and we'll return to the road north soon enough. I have no intention of ignoring our mandate or running afoul of our overlord."

Skeelana watched, mostly with curiosity it seemed to me, as her fellow Memoridon spun her horse around again, laid her heels into its sides and rode off, heading west. And she had a small mischievous smile teetering on her face as she nodded in Braylar's direction and said only, "Siblings," before following Soffjian.

Braylar and his lieutenants watched the pair ride ahead before Mull-doos offered, "Be nice if she was riding all the way back to Sunwrack. Only she's going the wrong way. Same as us, only faster. I wasn't about to take her side—"

"Greatly appreciated, Mulldoos."

"And it pains me to admit it even without her here—"

"Your angst is palpable."

"Seems to me she might be wrong on some score, but she got one thing right. Even if she's an evil bitch in her delivery. Why are we going the wrong way here, Cap?"

Braylar was still watching the dust settle after his sister's departure. "We aren't going the wrong way in the slightest, Lieutenant. While I might be suffering other ailments, my sense of direction is remarkably intact."

Hewspear said, "As much as it would pain me to side with my temperamental young cohort—"

"You wrinkled cock," Mulldoos interrupted, "only reason there's two of us is so we can side together once in a while and talk sense into the man."

Hewspear ignored him. "But I can't help wondering about the wisdom of this particular venture, Captain. We do risk the emperor's wrath, even if we arrive only a few days later than expected. And as much as Mulldoos would like your sister to disappear over the horizon, she will be with us the entire journey home. And gods know you have no reason to suspect she will go out of her way to paint a favorable portrait of any of your decisions or actions, whether questioned by commander or emperor."

Braylar looked at his officers, clearly accustomed to their skepticism, though no less annoyed by it. "Insolence begets insolence. We still have an opportunity to seize High Priest Henlester, and we will explore it before quitting Anjuria."

Mulldoos and Hewspear gave each other a look, the pale boar clearly perplexed, and the older, darker man pensive. Mulldoos replied first, though more carefully than I would have expected. "I figured with the way we left Alespell, we were done with that business."

For the first time Braylar seemed to notice I was still present and his eyes were as hostile and piercing as spear points. "With the Hornmen driving us from our nest, we wouldn't have had much longer to do anything in Anjuria as it was. Even if the Memoridons hadn't arrived."

I tried very hard not to let my cheeks color, which probably made them flush darker, as he continued, "So, we go after Henlester, because there is no telling if or when we will return to this region. This is our best, and last, opportunity. This is not a discussion. I am sorry for your confusion if you mistook it for one."

Mulldoos looked at me, obviously not comfortable with me privy to this non-dialogic dialogue, but holding his tongue about it.

Perhaps riding with the Syldoon predisposed me to always look for a hidden secondary or tertiary reason behind every little thing they did, but suddenly I was almost certain that capturing Henlester was more complicated. I said, "This isn't about Baron Brune, or causing unrest in Anjuria, is it? Not now, not since you've been recalled from Alespell. This has something to do with the scrolls you—" I nearly said "stole" and caught myself, "procured. Doesn't it?"

Hewspear smiled, his bare upper lip curling. "Congratulations, Arki—you are our first scribe to actually live long enough to divine our other purpose here." He turned to Mulldoos. "See, I knew he was a good wager. I have a nose for these things."

"You have a nose for sticking in the dusty cracks of old crones. Plaguing goat." Mulldoos looked at Braylar. "I'm guessing if the scribbler had broken into your chest, you would have brained him by now. Meaning, you must have told him what we were hauling around. Meaning, there's one more thing I don't fathom."

Braylar replied, "Arki would have discovered—needed to discover—the nature of our cargo eventually. We do need them translated, better sooner than later. Especially since we have been recalled."

His left hand drifted toward Bloodsounder's chains, the tips of his fingers tracing their contours as he looked at me. "Yes, Arki, our pursuit of the nefarious high priest serves more than one end. Our operations in Anjuria might be over, for now anyway. But a hostage, particularly one so caught up in all kinds of blackmail, betrayal, and alleged assassination, well, he could prove quite useful, even sitting in a comfortable cell in Sunwrack."

That seemed plausible. But piecemeal. There was too much unsaid, as always. I was about to ask more when Vendurro rode up to our group. I expected him to ask why we hadn't moved forward at all, or something else of import. But instead he said, "Anybody here ever taste copper?"

Everyone looked at him, Braylar flatly, Hewspear with mild amusement, Mulldoos with the hints of exasperation already brewing. Vendurro continued, "Asking, on account of Yargos. See he got elbowed in the face back there in Alespell by one of the Horntoads. Lost a tooth. Bleeding like a stuck pig, he is. Still moaning about it like it's going to make his plaguing mouth or our ears hurt less. Anyway, Yargos was going on about how blood tastes like metal. People always saying it tastes like metal. Copper usually. Heard that a lot. Everybody says it like it's some kind of truth. But anybody here ever taste copper?"

Mulldoos shook his head. "Horsecunt."

Vendurro looked confused. "Blood tastes like horsecunt? Or copper does? Or. . . ?"

"You."

"Thinking I don't taste much like any of those things. Hope not, leastwise. Got some kind of problem if I do."

Mulldoos looked at Hewspear. "We really got to talk to the recruiters about who we let in this outfit. Seems standards are slipping more every year."

Vendurro smiled. Mulldoos shook his head and spat in the grass. Then he dismounted and walked his horse off.

Vendurro laughed and called after him, "You sure are the plaguing prickliest bastard I ever met. No question about that." He looked at the rest of us, stopping at Braylar. "So. . . . looks like we're stopping here, then?"

I laughed, and when everyone looked at me blankly, not knowing why I found this funny, I chose not to explain.

Braylar looked up the road where his sister had disappeared. "We could put a few more miles behind us today. But just now, I'm not feeling any urgency. We stop here."

And so we did.

If the Syldoon were surprised we were stopping a little earlier than usual, they hid it well enough. Perhaps they were simply accustomed to their captain's mercurial moods, or maybe they were glad not to be pushing too hard after a battle earlier that day. Or maybe they were wondering if Braylar was succumbing to the effects of Bloodsounder. They might not have all known the particulars, but there was no disguising the fact that he was afflicted by something unnatural. Which surely was disconcerting. Did they doubt the soundness of his judgment at all? While I understood why Hewspear and Mulldoos tried to prohibit the spread of information, not knowing all the details might have actually made it worse, leading his men to quietly conjecture more or question his fitness for command.

Then again, the Syldoon seemed more loyal to their superior officers and their Towermates, as Vendurro called them, than any men I'd ever met. Everyone else in the world, chief among them the Anjurians, considered the Syldoon as untrustworthy a people as ever walked the world, capable of any deception, scheme, or enterprise that was designed to ruin or cripple anyone outside the Empire's borders. None of which was wanting for accuracy. And yet, to hear Braylar's retinue tell it, the various Towers seemed just as intent on outmaneuvering each other, with only a modicum more restraint used in doing so. But to their own—their single faction, their Tower—these men were the staunchest, most stalwart allies imaginable.

They squabbled and bickered with passion, mocked and ridiculed each other with rare enthusiasm, and still, there was no denying they would defend their own against anything and anyone, without remorse or complaint. Which was amazing—I wanted to complain loudly and often. My thighs were chafed and raw, the muscles in my back sore, and it hadn't even been a full day in the saddle. I cringed at the thought of how many more it would be.

The men unsaddled their horses and let them graze in the long grass on the right side of the road before leading them all off into a copse of trees that would provide some cover for the night. Most soldiers took the opportunity to check and perform minor repairs on their armor where they could, sharpen their blades, stuff some dried meat or fruit in their mouths.

I unloaded my writing case and set to recording, wanting to stay as current as possible.

Progress was slow and halting, as I nibbled on cheese and nuts and seemed unable to focus on capturing the recent conversations and revelations, my mind pulled back to Alespell and what I'd seen there. And done. Though I tried very hard not to travel far down that road.

Eventually finished, I closed my case and then closed my eyes, head against my saddle, a blanket pulled tight. I thought sleep would be a long time coming, given the events of the day and the vulnerable state we were in, hidden among some trees alongside a road that could be filled with Hornmen or Brunesmen at any moment.

Before I knew it, Vendurro was rousing me at dawn and it was time to mount up again. I felt anything but well rested.

We began putting more miles behind us, the sun rising higher, the chill of morning long gone, as the day would prove to be a hot one. I looked up at the endless sky. It seemed artificial, something painted on the interior of the largest dome in creation, the blue of the backdrop almost too brilliant, too pure, the numerous clouds almost perfect in their rendering, with ashy shading counterbalancing the stark whiteness, and of every size and shape imaginable, as if the artist had been charged with cataloguing clouds in all their infinite variety. They didn't seem to drift in the slightest either, fixed there as if they'd remain until the paint chipped and cracked and fell down on every cloud-gazing fool. The air was hot and still, without even the slightest breeze, let alone anything to get those clouds moving again, and I wanted nothing more than to close my eyes.

But as usual, my curiosity wasn't sated. I kept running over the conversation we had on the road the previous day, and still had more questions than answer.

When we stopped to rest the horses, I spotted the captain and his lieutenants off to one side, as usual, separated from the rest of the troops, but not distant.

Mulldoos was leaning against a tree, his eyes closed, Hewspear was working away at his flute, and Braylar was fiddling with his helmet strap.

Braylar looked up as I stopped in front of the trio. "You have that pensive look about you that always prefaces disquieting questions. Out with it."

Well, directness did save me the trouble of trying to wheedle my way into a conversation before asking anything. I glanced around to be sure no one else was in earshot. "The scrolls you want me to translate? How is High Priest Henlester connected with those? You said they were from ancient collections and libraries."

Mulldoos opened his eyes and sat up. Hewspear stopped working on the flute. I expected one or all three of the men to silence me, either with sharp rebukes, brutal mockery, clever evasion, or oppressive silence. But, after a moment when the lieutenants looked at their captain and he looked at each in turn, some strange unspoken thing must have happened. Captain Killcoin glanced up the road, as if to make sure Soffjian was not storming back down it, and then he turned to me. "You know the Syldoon Empire is comprised of factions, yes? Constantly maneuvering and politicking against the others, soldiers loyal to the Empire in theory, but only deeply loyal to the Tower they belong to. Well, the Memoridons are the same way—beholden to Towers. The Tower Commanders, in truth."

"I know very little about what they can or can't do. Only what I've read in university. Which is sparse and—"

"Total horseshit," Mulldoos offered.

I couldn't argue that point very well, so ignored it. "But I saw Soffjian, and Skeelana too, for that matter, in Alespell. They did things that were. . . amazing. How is it the Towers control them, keep them in check?"

Hewspear replied, "As the captain noted, they are fragmented, as we are. Memoridons from one Tower are secretive and competitive and reclusive—they don't congress much with their sisters from other Towers. And there are other factors that keep them in check, as you say."

Mulldoos said, "What the wrinkled cock here is getting at is, every Tower is different—some bigger or smaller, depending—but there's only one Memoridon for every fifty Syldoon, at best. No Tower gets more, not even that prick Cynead's. The ratio is the ratio. And they might be bitches and witches, but they ain't all powerful."

I considered that. "That makes sense. A cap on numbers certainly is a natural limiting factor. But what's to prevent them from capturing your Tower Commanders or assassinating them? Or fleeing Sunwrack? They obviously don't have the numbers to overwhelm you by sheer force, but that doesn't seem to be their strength anyway. Well, with exceptions like the captain's sister. So there must be something more, then?"

Mulldoos's very pale brows closed ranks. "Figured that out all on your lonesome, did you? Must have missed the part when Hewspear said 'factors,' huh? Meaning plural. Sure with your fancy education you know about plurality?"

I tried not to grit my teeth as I said, "That was my way of asking what the other factors were."

"Maybe next time, how about you just say, 'What are those other factors the old goat was going on about?' See how that works? Real direct like. No confusion. Doesn't invite nobody to question your intelligence at all. Stick with that. Lot safer for you, scribbler."

I fought off the urge to engage him and turned instead to Hewspear. "I believe you mentioned something about other factors?"

"See, there you go!" Mulldoos said. "Though you forgot the goat part."

Hewspear replied, "The Memoridons are bonded to the Tower Commander. It's not a process most Syldoon are knowledgeable about, only those in the commander's immediate circle. So I can't reveal much. Only that the Tower Commanders do not practice memory magic themselves, so the bond is an unusual one. There is a construct involved. And the mechanism, the ritual, the binding, it not only protects the commander from any sorcery the Memoridons wield, but prohibits the witches from being away from the frame—" I started to ask a question but he anticipated it, "That is, the construct—for very long. Part of the reason they aren't assigned to accompany units like ours for extended periods of time. This binding, and the relative scarcity of Memoridons, together ensure their compliance. Though our understanding of the process is limited. And I suspect even those intimately involved know less than they believe."

Mulldoos chortled. "Wait, before that, did you just admit there was a topic known to all the tribes of the world that you weren't some sort of expert on? Did you just say that? You said that, didn't you? With witnesses and everything? Plague me, that's a first."

"Alright," I said, excited to be getting some straight answers, but still floundering a bit in making sense of it all. "So what does this have to do with dusty tomes from other kingdoms? And Henlester?"

Mulldoos nodded in an exaggerated fashion. "See, real direct, boy. You're learning. Slow, but you're learning." I wasn't sure if he was mocking me. Well, of course he was, but it seemed slightly less biting than usual. That seemed like progress.

Hewspear answered, "The Syldoon are reviled for a number of reasons, as you well know, and employing the Memoridons while all other kingdoms hunt them to extinction certainly does us no favors. But the Empire is relatively young compared to most kingdoms. And the memory witches have been around for far longer, burnt and drowned and hated and feared. No one knows for sure where those powers come from. But some believe the Deserter Gods instilled it in men."

Mulldoos said, "Before deciding they wanted nothing more to do with all these broken toys they were playing with and left us high and dry to fend for ourselves, that is."

Hewspear gave Mulldoos a look that was equal parts paternal and pitying. "Such a shame to have such a narrow scope of imagination or appreciation."

"Such a shame to be a prattling old windmill. But don't let me interrupt your history lesson. Bleat on."

Hewspear ignored him. "There are many regions who catalogued their experiences with hedge witches, for centuries. Mostly this consisted of anecdotes about what they were accused of, and how many were strung up or otherwise murdered and when, but some scholars in some parts of the world chose to actually investigate the witches. Compile accounts of their behavior, origins, descriptions of their unnatural abilities."

It was my turn to interrupt. "Let me guess—you've discovered a higher concentration of them in Anjuria."

Mulldoos whooped. Actually whooped. "There it is! All kinds of clever!"

I started to reply but thankfully Hewspear interceded. "That's correct, Arki. The most useful of them are written in Old Anjurian, though some in Middle as well."

"And you have reason to believe the Temple of Truth has such records, or something like that?"

"There you go, boy!" Mulldoos said. "Direct as a bolt to the face. Cleverer and cleverer."

I forced myself to ignore him. "But why all this effort to obtain and translate these scrolls and reports in the first place? What could you hope to learn that you don't already know? The Empire has used Memoridons for centuries now—certainly you have intimate and voluminous knowledge. You know far more than any peoples in the world about what the Memoridons are capable of." Then I undermined the strength of the statement by asking, "Don't you?"

Braylar nodded. "What they are capable of? Absolutely. But we are discussing origins. Original experiences and impressions of memory witches. And while most tried to destroy them, as Hew said, there were some very few who studied them. And the Syldoon are not the only ones to attempt to control them. Only the most systematic and successful. So, it is possible we might unearth some information that we don't know, something ancient and buried and useful, some of those earliest efforts that might give us advantage now."

"But. . . you already control them. Advantage how? Over whom? I don't. . . I don't understand."

Mulldoos replied, and I expected him to belittle me, but he chose Hewspear as the target instead. "Not hard to see why. All that blathering puts me to sleep every time, too."

Hewspear mostly ignored the jibe, saying only, "Limited," before responding to me. "Each Tower controls its own Memoridons."

I still must have looked painfully confused, as Braylar said, "What my circumspect lieutenant means is, we are trying to see if there is any way to gain control of those belonging to the other Towers. Not only controlling our own, but all of them. And the priests of Truth might prove useful in doing so. Or not. We speculate, based on limited information. But with any luck, your translations will push our examination of things in the right direction."

I was about to say something else when I heard hoofbeats. We all looked up to see a rider coming down the road from the east. From the direction of Alespell. Not galloping, so if it was a Syldoon scout, it didn't look like we were in danger. Not immediate, anyway.

B raylar and his officers stood and so I did as well as we waited for the rider to rein up. I wondered if the other soldiers begrudged me my position in the company. Until remembering that I was only a scribe, and likely barely registered in their field of view. Vendurro must have seen the rider as well, as he approached our group, burped, and announced, "What do you suppose, good word or bad?"

No one answered as we continued to wait.

The rider was one of the pair that had remained behind us. He halted his horse and saluted.

Braylar took a few steps forward. "Report, Syldoon."

The scout pulled off his helm, face red and sweaty. "Our wagons made good time, Cap. Coming up behind us. Few miles back yet, but be here soon enough." He looked around. "Didn't expect to catch up to you so quick."

Braylar twitch-smiled and replied, "One of the perks of being captain, soldier, is that you can occasionally goad a Memoridon without suffering severe repercussions. This is doubly true when the Memoridon in question is your sibling. Though sometimes half as true. But in either case, she provided me an excuse to slow down, appreciate the scenery a bit." He extended a sweeping arm, taking in the generally unremarkable pines and uneven dirt road.

The scout didn't quite seem to know what to do with that information. "Uh, just wanted to bring word to expect company soon, Cap."

"Very good, soldier. Rest for as long as you need. Then return to the road and keep a vigil eye."

"Aye, Cap." He saluted again and rode off into the grass toward the other soldiers.

After he was out of hearing distance, Mulldoos did what he seemed to do better than anything besides killing people—questioning orders. "Cap, you know me. I got little love for any Memoridons."

Braylar pivoted, clearly sensing what was to come. "Nor for crippled whores with Memoridon-like tendencies. Or reedy scribes. Or rusty mail. Or much of anything that does not involve ale, loose women, vulgarity, or the opportunity to carve up Anjurians. Go on."

Mulldoos took that in stride. "But seeing as how she's already likely to report you dawdling a fair bit, and parsing out an Imperial directive how you choose to, is it really smart to keep jabbing her with a sharp stick like you are? Maybe we ought to send a rider to let her know we're waiting on the wagons, or—"

"Does my sister command this unit, Mulldoos?"

The lieutenant waved off a big bloated fly. "Course not, Cap. But—"

"Very good. So until I am forcibly relieved of duty, I will command as I see fit. And when our Memoridon escort storms off like a spoiled child, I am less inclined to do anything to appease, placate, or otherwise mollify her. We wait for the wagons. Here."

Mulldoos looked at Hewspear, who sighed and grudgingly took the cue. "And like that, the escort returns." We saw him looking down the road in the opposite direction, at two figures barely visible on a hilltop, leading some spare horses. "But might I suggest, Captain, that while feigned deference might be too difficult, cordiality might serve us well. In this instance. Given previous history and relations. Respectfully, Captain."

"Your 'respectfully' is clearly feigned. You see, that is the difficulty with false pretense—it is so easy for a skilled and suspicious liar to see through. I will forge nothing false with my sister—that would serve only to heighten any hostilities and suspicions further. But your concern and suggestions are duly noted, the pair of you."

Mulldoos laughed, nearly a snort. "Like to see this notebook with all the counsel he's logged and ignored over the years. Thicker than my forearm, I'm guessing."

Braylar looked at Hewspear. "You see—nothing counterfeit there. Insubordinate and unruly grousing, laid bare and naked for all the world to see."

"Just you, Cap. And the old goat." He jerked a thumb at me and Vendurro. "Couple other witnesses, maybe. But never more public than that."

Braylar turned to face his brawny lieutenant, and it was hard to tell if he was planning on applauding him or lashing out when Vendurro jumped in. "Begging your pardon, Cap, but—"

"Lodging apology on the front end only serves to put me on edge. What is it?"

"Sorry for that too, then, Cap, and sorry for being sorry upfront, but—and this ain't meant as no kind of insubordination, or any kind of ordination, for that matter—but what do we have to gain by baiting your sister? Is pissing on her boots a ploy of some kind? Just trying to see the upside, is all."

The captain smiled, devoid of humor, not even a hint, and said to me, "Betwixt the tall man's slippery smarm and the pale man's brusque belligerence, we find Vendurro, either the cleverest in the group, or the only one unable to commit to one stance or the other. Be grateful we do not need ditches or latrines dug, as you would have the first three shovels."

Braylar walked off in one direction, then Mulldoos slapped the trunk of a tree and went off in the other.

I knew the other two were likely one step behind so took the opportunity to ask, "Why is there such obvious discord between the captain and his sister? Is this how Syldoons and Memoridons normally engage? Because I get the distinct impression it's more than that."

Vendurro looked at Hewspear and the older man kept his gaze on the distant horizon, and I knew there must have been a significant story there, but I also sensed that it was very unlikely I was about to hear it.

After a pause, Hewspear looked at Braylar, still walking away from our makeshift camp. "You have the right of it. There is indeed a great deal more than that. But this is something best heard from the captain himself, provided he felt like sharing the details. Which I suspect he will not. So," he looked directly at me, his eyes registering the severity of the warning, even if he chose his words more carefully, "I suggest not pursuing this line of questioning with any of his men, and I'd wager you avoid any wroth unpleasantness by thinking twice about putting the question to him either."

Hewspear stalked off, and even as I started to look at Vendurro, he raised both hands in the air and starting backing away as if I held a loaded crossbow trained on his chest. "Nope. Nuh uh. Don't even think about. You heard the lieutenant—when you're standing over a really nasty snake hole, real bad idea poking your pecker in to see what happens. Best just to walk off and leave well enough alone." And with that, he left me alone as well.

Well, my curiosity was only inflamed more with that kind of response. Despite waiting to ask until Mulldoos left, in retrospect, he might have been my best hope of hearing some unvarnished or unguarded response. Though it just as likely might have resulted in my landing on my back in the dirt with his boot on my chest.

Still, even as I'd learned quite a bit more about the Syldoon in the last few days, there was something oddly comforting about being completely excluded from some information. If they suddenly divulged everything I asked, I would have suspected they were lies in the entirety or my life was about to end.

Soffjian and Skeelana arrived before the wagons, and the former was as happy as a cat dunked in a barrel of water. Though, in her case, it was a jungle cat from Thulmora, and even that animal might have been less of a threat to the dunkers.

Braylar had returned from his brief trek into the woods, and was sitting near Hewspear and Mulldoos, and the three of them were talking— arguing, more like, as that seemed their preferred form of communication—and while Skeelana veered off and headed to an unoccupied spot alongside the road with the spare mounts, Soffjian rode directly toward her brother. Even from a distance, and with her being generally guarded in her expressions, it was obvious she wasn't going to hand him lilies.

I started walking in their direction as well. I had no obvious reason for attending, other than satisfying my curiosity, but that was enough for me, and I suspected the heated exchange would distract anyone from my appearance anyway.

Swinging one leg over her horse's neck, Soffjian dropped to the ground. "You might have told me you intended to stop unexpectedly, Bray."

Braylar stood up as he replied, "And you might have asked before storming off like an intemperate child. Our wagons are nearly here—my scouts informed me they made much better time escaping the warrens of Alespell than expected. So it was pointless to continue."

"And you couldn't be bothered to send a rider after us?"

"I didn't imagine you'd ride halfway to Drivenfort. I assumed, being preternaturally alert, you would notice we weren't directly behind you and eventually return. And see—here you are."

Soffjian took a step forward. Like Hewspear, she always seemed to have her pole arm with her, and unlike a traditional sidearm that was sheathed, scabbarded, or on a belt and posing no immediate threat, a pole arm always seemed one quick motion from spilling blood. Or perhaps it was the size. Either way, with her ranseur held in one hand, and the look on her face, I half expected the other hand to come up and the fingers to spread as she assaulted him in that unseen and terrifying way she was capable of. Or to simply stab him with the thing.

Instead, she said, "Needle me as you like, Syldoon. Thwart me as you choose on this road. And the next that leads us home. Your prerogative. But do not think you will do so unscathed."

Braylar stepped in to meet her, stopping only when they were close enough to smell each other's breath. "Home, is it? Even now, so many years later, I never imagined you would espouse such affinity and affection. Rigid obedience, yes, but I always suspected you would withhold your heart. It seems I was wrong." She started to reply, but he tilted his head toward the road and cut her off, "And our wagons are in sight, so we can be homeward bound soon enough. You are welcome to sit in one. Give your horses a rest."

She didn't look where he indicated and hadn't cooled in the slightest. "The only thing I'd welcome is a chance to see you laid low. And every moment journeying together convinces me I won't have to wait long."

Soffjian plopped the ranseur on one shoulder, nearly poked Hewspear's eye out as she spun on her heel, grabbed her horse's reins, and headed over to Skeelana.

Braylar turned to his retinue. "There," he said. "You see what being cordial gets me. Ready the men. Once the wagons are back in the fold, we head out. Arki, you will ride with me in the lead wagon."

As the captain moved away from us and unstoppered a bottle of wine, I wondered if staying in the saddle might actually be more comfortable after all. The captain seemed to be weathering the unseen things he endured, but I suspected he was going to need quite a bit more wine or ale to maintain that, and while he could be prickly sober, he was even less predictable and pleasant drunk.

The wagons joined our small caravan, and after the drivers reported their departure from Alespell had gone without incident— apparently the ripper running around eviscerating townspeople was exactly the distraction the Syldoon had been hoping for—we got set to keep moving. Besides Yargus and his bloody mouth, and Bulsinn losing a hand to the beast, the casualties in the pre-dawn battle had not been as high as I expected. Certainly, plenty of Syldoon were nursing injuries, but none as serious as Bulsinn's that I could tell, and the small company had lost four in the fighting. Which, considering the odds, wasn't nearly as bad as it could have been. But now with the soldiers in the two wagons, the total was a fighting force of twenty-five men, the two Memoridons, and myself. I wondered how many of the Syldoon had been involved in infiltrating the various temples and baronial households, and how many had been assigned to uncover the scrolls and parchments.

I joined the captain in the lead wagon. It was much like the one we'd used to travel across the Green Sea—a bench in front, a long, simple wooden bed that was unremarkable except for the faintest traces of blue paint the rain and wind had beaten into submission, a patched and stained canvas cover, large wheels, and the usual assortment of barrels, chests, sacks, and miscellaneous instruments hanging from hooks inside that made moving around more than a challenge and just short of impossible. While the Anjurians tended to favor the smaller all-wooden wagons, either open or enclosed with walls and flat roofs, frequently carved and embossed and stained or ornately painted, the canvas tops weren't unusual enough to elicit notice or comment. Which seemed to be exactly what the captain was going for—something large enough to haul the Syldoon supplies and completely innocuous.

The captain made it abundantly clear he wished to be left alone with his wine, and sentenced me to the interior of the wagon. I might have been glad of it if the wagon had been hauling the scrolls he wanted translated, as I could have at least gotten started, but the supplies were all entirely mundane, and the chests were all in the wagon behind us. So I moved to the rear and watched the mostly uninteresting countryside roll by, hills and woodlands occasionally broken up by small villages and communities tucked away in them, with farmsteads here and there surrounded by narrow pines, broad lindens, and stern oaks.

The further we got from Alespell, the less traffic there was heading in that direction, particularly since we were more than a half day's ride away. No one was going to risk traveling the road at night, even given the alleged protection of the Hornmen who rode and patrolled. The few travelers we did encounter hastily gave way to the large armed party.

We continued heading southwest, away from Alespell, away from the road north to Sunwrack we'd chosen to pass up, and toward. . . something. Henlester holed up in some hunting lodge somewhere, and likely Brunesmen trying to dig him out, and almost certainly more combat and casualties. I couldn't believe it, but Sunwrack actually seemed like the safer, preferable choice at this point. Even with the alleged poisonous politicking and vicious infighting among the factions there, it was unlikely combat would spill into the streets. Often, at any rate.

But it didn't really make much sense to be bemoaning my fate. I had made my choice to ride with the Syldoon and their captain, so I would go where he led, for good or ill. Though ill seemed more likely.

I massaged a sack of grain in an unsuccessful attempt to make it resemble a pillow or anything remotely comfortable, laid back, and decided to try to sleep the miles away if I could. I twisted and shifted, and it felt like my eyes had just shut when our wagon slowed, which seemed odd, since I didn't think we had traveled far enough to require a reprieve—Braylar mentioned we would arrive at our stopping point around dusk, and it was still in the center of the afternoon. And that's when I noticed the two Syldoon sitting in the wagon with me. They had tunics over their armor and hoods covered their inked nooses. They were both cradling crossbows.

They were familiar, but only vaguely, as most of Braylar's men were strangers to me—waking up to unexpected armed friends would have been disconcerting enough. Clearly, I'd slept harder than I imagined, but was fully awake now, and suddenly very nervous.

One with large ears protruding almost straight out of his head said, "Sleep well, princess?"

The both laughed and I made my way through the supplies to the front as quickly as I could, pulled the canvas aside, and leaned over the bench.

A hundred or so yards ahead, there was a tower constructed of wood and stone, with a few smaller one-story wooden buildings around the base. The tower looked old and was leaning ever so slightly. I shaded my eyes and couldn't make out much more. "What is it, Captain?"

Braylar pointed at the banner hanging limply on top of the tower. "Unless one of my scouts has grossly deceived me, we are approaching a Hornmen outpost."

He said this calmly and without care, as if he were commenting on the quality of the gravel beneath the horses' hooves.

The captain had covered up his armor with his tunic and scarf as well, and as I climbed over the bench and sat next to him, looking around, I noticed our company had thinned considerably. It was the captain, myself, the two in the wagon, and whoever was in the wagon to our rear. That was all.

Braylar didn't have a blanket on his lap, so at least I didn't have to worry about him shooting anyone. Just yet.

I looked ahead at the small cluster of buildings, watching a thin line of smoke listing out of a crooked chimney, and imagined the Hornmen inside. I suddenly craved wine. A lot of it. "Captain?"

He didn't look at me, eyes still trained on the Hornmen outpost, assessing, measuring, calculating. "Archivist?"

"Is it. . . that is. . . is it wise? To approach a Hornmen tower like this? What if they know what happened in Alespell?"

"One of the buildings is likely a stable. I strongly suspect that houses Hornmen horse. Do you recall a Hornman on horse racing past, its mouth foaming, the rider slathered in sweat, wide-eyed as he passed a company of the very men he was about to report to the border patrol? No, of course not, you've been sleeping. But I can assure you, someone in my company would have noticed just such a rider. We are tremendously observant like that. Quite a bit of intense training, just to ensure we don't miss these little details. I also see no rookery there, so the odds of a winged messenger somehow beating us here are also nominal."

"So you don't think they'll be suspicious?"

"Of what? Two wagons and a few men? They encounter such things every day."

"Where are the rest of the Syldoon?" I looked around both sides of the road, clear of trees in both directions, with a large bank of woods on the opposite side of the Hornmen outpost, several hundred yards away.

He saw me and replied, "Your deductive reasoning is exemplary."

"Why not simply take the wagons through the woods, though? Avoid the outpost altogether?"

Braylar rapped his knuckles on the bench. "You see—that is what a lack of expertise and training gets you. The woods are too dense for wagons. At least to move quickly. And there are probably patrols besides. So it didn't warrant spending an extra day just to navigate around a lone watch tower. And as to why those men aren't with us, a smaller, poorly guarded caravan does not seem quite as threatening as twenty-five armed men on horse."

"Has Bloodsounder. . . have you felt any—"

"Cease your nervous prattling. They've seen us in any event—we would rouse a great deal more suspicion if we suddenly turned about and sped off in the opposite direction, wagons and horses in a mad flight of terror. Now, whatever you do," he turned at me and twitch-smiled, "don't act as if you killed one of their brave soldiers in Alespell. If you think you cannot calm your nerves enough to manage that, I suggest hiding in the back under a large sack of figs."

He laughed then, and slapped me on the back. All I kept thinking about was where they would execute prisoners out here. They didn't have any gallows—did they hang them from the gnarled apple trees, or cut off their heads in back? Perhaps they were target practice for bolts of arrows. That would be fitting.

"Even the chronicler who betrayed me wasn't so dour. You're a mystery to me, little scholar. A mystery."

We rolled closer and I saw two soldiers above the crenellations at the top of the tower, watching us as we approached. A small breeze stirred the banner just long enough for the white horns on the green field to show. The tower appeared to have been built for observation across the fields and the solitary road rather than for defense, as the gate and walls surrounding the compound were wood, and not high or thick. But the outpost looked like it could still house a fair number of men, and my nerves were jangling as three Hornmen stepped out of the barracks and walked over to the road, hailing us.

Braylar waved back, smiling, and then turned to me and said, very quietly, "I don't suppose I need to remind you to keep your mouth shut? I know it shouldn't be necessary, but I somehow feel as if I still should."

I shook my head.

"Very good." He kept waving and smiling.

A Hornman with yellow teeth, a yellowed surcote, and an old yellow horn hanging from his chapped baldric addressed us, looking around at the wagons and horses tethered to the side, "Any difficulties on the road?"

He sounded much more bored than threatening, but the first Hornman in the Green Sea hadn't appeared overly hostile initially either, and every one of them since had tried to kill us. So there was that.

Braylar shook his head. "No, my lord. Thank you very much for your concern though."

The Hornman nodded, clearly unconcerned. "You the leader of this outfit?"

Braylar nodded. "I am, my lord. Though 'outfit' is probably too generous a term."

The Hornman seemed completely disinterested. "Coming from the Great Fair, I expect?"

"Yes. Our fourth time."

The Hornman glanced at me, and I tried to smile, though my lips suddenly felt like wriggling worms that moved of their own accord, so I stopped trying immediately.

He asked what we were hauling. Unlike the Hornmen in the grass, who were no better than bandits themselves, this man seemed perfunctory and eager to be done with questions.

Braylar regaled him with an abridged version of the quill merchant speech he'd used on the Hornman in the Green Sea, which seemed a very poor choice considering how badly that had ended, but aside from making one slightly sympathetic noise during the tale, the Hornman didn't seem to even be listening.

The captain concluded with, "So, my lord, is this a tax station then?"

"That would at least give us counting coins to while away the hours. No, it's a watch station."

Braylar asked, innocently, "To what end?"

The Hornmen responded slowly, as if he were speaking to the dullest of dullards. "To keep watch." When Braylar looked at him as if he still didn't entirely understand, he added, "Brigands. Grass Dogs that lost their way. Whatever other evil element there be."

"Ahh, I see. And so you patrol this territory then?"

The Hornman was clearly done with of the conversation. "Patrols patrol. Watchers watch. And merchants should move on instead of flapping their lips if they hope to secure any trade down the road."

Braylar waved. "Good day to you, my lord. I'll alert you or one of the patrols should I encounter anything nefarious on the road."

"You do that." The Hornman was turning away and heading back to the barracks, the other two soldiers behind him.

I started to breathe easier, cursing myself for being so skittish, when another Hornman came out of the tower, rubbing his hands together and blowing on them, and headed in our direction. While age didn't always equal a higher command, in addition to greyer locks and a more grizzled face, he had the bearing of the more senior officer as he addressed the soldier who had been questioning us. I overheard him say, "That's it? Not even a cursory inspection?"

The other man shrugged, then looked over his shoulder at us as he responded. "Judgment call. And I judged I wanted to be back in front of a fire sipping sour wine, not out here wasting our time inspecting a wagon we got no reason to be inspecting."

"The reason," the older man replied, voice filling with disdain, "is it is your job. Your duty. Your sworn vow. And if you shirk it, you can be sure I—"

The other threw his hands in the air. "Fine. Waste of plaguing time. But fine. No need to go reporting nothing now." He turned to the two Hornmen next to him. "Be quick about it."

As the younger soldiers approached the wagon again, clearly irritated and put out, the two senior Hornmen stayed back.

Braylar whispered, lips barely moving at all, "You will walk to the back. When I give the order, pull the flap and get out of the way." Then he turned to me and said loudly enough for the Hornmen to hear. "Be a good lad—jump down and show them in through the back gate, would you? Let these fine soldiers be about their business so we can continue."

He was smiling, but it didn't come anywhere near his eyes, and barely even touched his lips.

Looking at him, I dreaded what I was about to do, but knew there was nothing I could do to stop it either. You ride with the Syldoon, you ride with the Syldoon.

I gave the smallest of nods and climbed down. It felt like my short boots were lined with lead as I hit the ground, my heart lodged in my throat, my blood pounding in my ears as I slowly walked toward the rear of the wagon. And yet, even though I was moving, it seemed like time had almost ceased unspooling altogether.

I looked over my shoulder as I got to the end of the wagon. Captain Killcoin had jumped down and was standing nonchalantly alongside the bench, looking at the older Hornman watching the proceedings, the false smile still on his face. How could they fail to see through it, to suspect nothing at all? But they watched their cursory inspection happening, no sign that anything was remotely amiss. Even the soldiers at the top of the tower had disappeared to get out of the wind that had picked up, blowing suddenly cold and fickle.

The two Hornmen looked at me as I stood there dumbly, waiting for something, a sign, an order, anything. One with piercing green eyes glared at me. "Well? Let's get on with it. Open her up already." The moved around me so they were standing directly in front of the gate.

I nodded and reached for the canvas flap, when I suddenly heard pounding hooves—four Syldoon were galloping out of the treeline, riding hard for the tower, clumps of dirt and grass erupting behind them.

Braylar yelled, "Now!"

Even being ready for it, I wasn't quite ready for it, and nearly let the flap slip free before jerking it open. Two bolts flew out and I nearly pissed myself. One of the Hornmen fell on his rear, staring dumbly at the fletching sticking out of his chest. The other stumbled back several steps, trying to grab the bolt in his belly with one hand, fumbling for his sword with the other. He looked over at me as the blood started to spread across his gambeson, a dull almost drunken expression on his face, when another bolt shot out and struck him in the chest. He toppled over and curled into a fetal position in the dirt.

I glanced in the direction of the watch tower—the senior Hornman was also down, a bolt sticking up from just above his sternum, and he didn't look to be struggling at all. The other Hornman with the yellow surcote was crouched down and frozen, apparently torn between running for the cover of the tower and charging Braylar, who was working the devil's claw with expert efficiency, spanning and reloading it with devilish speed.

That indecision proved his undoing. The Hornman started toward Braylar with his sword finally drawn, saw that he couldn't make it in time, and turned and ran for the door. But he didn't get far before Braylar's bolt caught him in the small of the back. He fell forward, nearly collapsed but somehow maintained his balance as he took another few halting steps. Braylar cursed.

But the Hornman didn't make it to the door. There were two Syldoon in the rear wagon, and they had been ready to attack as well, both taking aim at the wounded man. Each crossbow loosed with a hard twang, and one bolt caught the fleeing Hornman in the leg, the other in the shoulder. He dropped to his knees, coughed, and kept crawling.

Something whizzed by me and I ducked down, looking around wildly, thinking a Syldoon had accidentally shot at me. Then I saw the arrow in the ground between the Hornmen, still vibrating, and remembered the tower. There was a Hornman shooting out of an arrow loop midway, and several on top, taking aim from behind the crenellations at the Syldoon below and those riding for the compound. Arrows were flying everywhere, as the archers were able to shoot more quickly than the Syldoon could reload.

The Syldoon next to me who'd jumped out of the back broke for the tower, running hard. Two more arrows flew down, one missing and hitting the earth near a wagon wheel, another striking a Syldoon in the side, but then continuing on at a different angle, having been deflected by the lamellar plates under the tunic.

I dove behind the wagon and looked around the corner. Braylar had already closed the distance to the tower, apparently unmolested, and he was standing over the Hornman still on all fours just outside the door. The Hornman looked up, three bolts sticking out of him, clearly doomed but not yet believing it, and he shook his head, and put his hand on the door, reaching for the handle.

Braylar's long suroka was out then. He grabbed the Hornman by the hair and drew the blade across his throat in one quick motion. Luckily I didn't see the wound, but the blood spattering on the door told me Braylar wouldn't need to strike twice. The Hornman fell onto his stomach, fingers sliding down the door before his hand came to rest on the bottom.

The two Syldoon from my wagon joined him there, dropping their crossbows, drawing their swords and bucklers. Braylar wiped his suroka clean on the dead man's sleeve, sheathed it, and pulled Bloodsounder off his belt along with his own buckler.

Overhead, three Hornmen turned their attention on the group of riders galloping toward them and loosed arrows. One was leaning over the crenellations to try to get a shot at the Syldoon at the door, and the other two were keeping the Syldoon at the rear wagon pinned down, with several arrows thunking into the side or tearing through the canvas. The Hornman in the arrow loop was shooting wildly, and missing widely.

The Syldoon in the rear wagon were sending bolts back, and the Syldoon racing toward us were shooting as they galloped as well. Several struck the stones of the battlements, sending dust and small stones raining down, one flew just above, and another found the Hornman who had exposed himself trying to shoot at Braylar and the soldiers at the base of the tower. He fell back behind the battlements and didn't pop up again.

Two Hornmen came running awkwardly at a crouch out of the stables, swords in hand, but they clearly hadn't been expecting combat, as they had no shields, and carried a long bench for protection. But between the Syldoon on horse and those shooting from the wagon at the rear, neither Hornman got to the tower before bolts made it past the wood and into flesh. One stumbled and fell. The other slowed, tried to cover him with the bench, and took a bolt in the neck for his trouble.

One of the Syldoon tested the door and shook his head at Braylar. The horsemen reined up and threw their legs over their horse's heads, dismounting and hitting the ground in a fluid motion, with Mulldoos and Vendurro among them, dropping the crossbows and running forward, falchion and sword in hand. The other two stayed back and ducked behind the barn as they loaded their crossbows again—it truly was amazing how quickly they managed that—and along with the pair of Syldoon shooting from the wagon behind me, they kept the archers nervous enough that they couldn't loose arrows with impunity.

Braylar yelled something and three of the Syldoon ran out to grab the long bench the two Hornmen had been using to shield themselves.

One of them got shot in the shoulder, but they managed to make it back and the crossbows provided some cover. Two Syldoon started striking the locked door with the bench. Had the tower been designed to resist a serious siege, that front door would have been too thick to withstand a makeshift ram like that, but clearly the Hornmen never imagined they would be attacked. The wooden door didn't splinter, but the Syldoon were able to knock it most of the way loose from the hinges before the bench fell to pieces in their hands.

One Syldoon pushed the door in as far as it would go, and two arrows flew out of the gap, one striking him in the arm, the other sailing off and past the group.

The Syldoon dodged to either side of the door as several more arrows zipped out. Braylar whistled behind him, and the two Syldoon in front of the tower ran over, spanning their crossbows as they came. The archers at the top of the tower used the brief respite to shoot more frequently and would have pinned the running Syldoon to the ground but the two Syldoon behind me loosed their crossbows again. One of the archers fell behind the battlements screaming and the arrows stopped long enough for the Syldoon to run to the base.

Mulldoos moved his buckler in front of the open door as three more arrows came out, one clanging off the steel, and then the Syldoon with crossbows stepped in front of the door and shot into the interior of the tower. Braylar led the charge as he forced the door out of the way, buckler up, Bloodsounder at the ready, the others following him at a crouch, with the two in the rear dropping their crossbows and pulling out their sword and axe.

I looked up at the tower and didn't see any archers, so I assumed they ran downstairs to meet the threat that had invaded, but one archer behind the arrow loop must have seen me peering around the corner of the wagon and shot at me. The arrow thudded into the side of the wagon a foot from my face, splinters striking my cheek, and I ducked behind again, cursing my stupidity and wondering at his. Clearly I was the least threatening threat around—I wondered why he hadn't run down the spiral stairs with the others, or at least kept shooting at the pair of Syldoon behind me who were shooting back.

Half-hidden, I heard shouts from inside, a scream, a grunt, and the noises receded. The door was still open, half hanging, but I didn't want to look too long as there was no telling if the Hornman was still hidden behind his arrow loop, just waiting for me to expose myself.

The air felt colder than it had all day, but that still didn't stop the sweat from coming as I waited. Then I saw someone up top again. The Hornman circled the rooftop of the squat tower like a trapped animal, as if he might happen upon an escape that hadn't immediately presented itself as he raced upstairs. Seeing no new exits at all, he drew an arrow from the quiver at his waist and nocked it, retreating from the trap door on the roof until his back was against the crenellations on my side of the tower, having completely forgotten about the Syldoon with crossbows below.

The Hornman yelled something, maybe a warning to the Syldoon first through the trap door, and drew his bowstring back. But then he must have realized his situation was untenable, and any arrow he loosed would be his last—there was nowhere to go, and apparently he was the last Hornman standing. The Syldoon behind me shot at him, both missing high, but then the Hornman had enough—he threw his bow and arrow down and raised his arms above his head, clearly surrendering.

Three Syldoon joined him on the roof, Mulldoos among them, his falchion already edged in blood. The Hornman said something as Mulldoos took two strides toward him, and started shaking his head when he saw the pale Syldoon raise his weapon.

And then—maybe seeing the total lack of mercy in the eyes of the man in front of him, maybe overcome by pure panic—he threw himself over the edge rather than be struck down, hanging from a crenellation before Mulldoos appeared above him, and then releasing the stones and falling through space.

He landed on his legs, and I heard a loud crack as he crumpled under his weight and lay there groaning, his leg broken, and from the horrible angle underneath him, badly.

Mulldoos shook his head and then the Syldoon disappeared back into the tower. A few moments later they all filed out. One was wrapping a makeshift bandage around his arm, and another was limping a little, but they seemed to have survived the assault with no other serious injuries.

I stood up and walked slowly toward them, giving a wide berth to the Hornman on the ground with the bolt in his chest, still wheezing and alive, but eyes closed, his entire tunic soaked in blood.

The Syldoon were chatting amongst themselves, one joking about how the Hornmen needed to train a little harder to resist an actual attack. I overheard Vendurro say, to no one in particular. "Holy hells. That went to shit in a huge hurry."

Mulldoos wiped his blade clean and replied, "Always turns to shit sooner or later. Mostly sooner. Could have been shittier though."

Braylar was surveying the scene and stopped when he saw the Hornman with the broken leg. Mulldoos looked in the same direction and sighed in disgust. "Just wiped her down, too." Then he turned to Vendurro again. "Best thing about being an officer is the delegating bit. See to it, Sergeant."

Vendurro looked at the man groaning in the dirt, saw the bone jutting out of his leg. "Plague me. He *jumped*?"

Mulldoos laughed. "Like a baby bird that didn't know it couldn't fly."

Vendurro shook his head. "Plague me."

A Syldoon was walking by and Vendurro grabbed him by the shoulder and turned him in the direction of the badly wounded man. "Best thing about being an officer is delegating the shit jobs. That right there is a shit job. See to it."

Mulldoos barked a laugh as the Syldoon sighed and started marching toward the broken Hornman, drawing his long-bladed suroka.

Braylar saw me as I approached, and no doubt recognized the sentiment in my eyes, because he cut it off brutally. "Before you even consider pleading for another life, Arki, recall, if you would, that a great deal of blood was spilled in Alespell two days ago all because of the life I foolishly spared at your pleading. There will not be another. No prisoners. No witnesses. That is the Syldoon way."

I heard him, but couldn't pull my stare away from the Hornman at the base of the tower, his horribly shattered leg preventing him from even crawling as he saw the man coming to finish him off. The Hornman pulled himself up to a sitting position against the tower wall, screaming once as he shifted. As the Syldoon got closer, he raised his hands up, palms out, supplicant, and started pleading for his life as he shook his head.

I heard Mulldoos mutter, "Pathetic little baby bird."

The Syldoon stopped a foot in front of him, said something I couldn't make out, and the Hornman was still shaking his head, more violently now. When the Syldoon repeated it, the Hornman very slowly lowered his hands to his sides. The Syldoon said something else to him, and the Hornman closed his eyes, lips barely parting. I wondered if he was praying or saying goodbye to someone.

After dropping down to one knee alongside the wounded man, the Syldoon was bringing his blade forward to kill him when the Hornman was suddenly overcome with panic again, and tried to grab the blade. The Syldoon sliced him across the palm and the Hornman yelled and flailed even more, trying to grab the Syldoon's arm and protect his neck and face at the same time.

I heard one of the soldiers around me laugh as the Syldoon tried to free his arm and was pulled off balance by the victim's surprising surge of strength.

Mulldoos shook his head. "Gods." Then he marched forward as the other soldiers watched the pair struggling, blood from the Hornman's wounded hands and leg smearing both men as the Syldoon tried to wrestle him into submission, unprepared for the sudden and furious resistance.

The pale lieutenant pushed the Syldoon out of the way and kicked the Hornman in the temple. The man immediately went limp, his head dropping to his chest after bouncing off the stone behind him. Then Mulldoos chopped his neck nearly in half with the falchion and stepped back quickly to avoid the blood.

The Syldoon wasn't so lucky, caught in some of the spray as he scrambled to his feet, sheathed his long suroka, and went to rigid attention, clearly expecting a serious dressing down. Mulldoos didn't disappoint, yelling, "Clean yourself up, you stupid horsetwat. Seen battlefield surgeons less bloody than you. And while we're on the topic, we're not in the mercy business. You weren't sent over to ease that dumb cunt's suffering or passage to the great beyond. You were told to finish him off. Quick. Clean." He looked him up and down, shook his head at the blood spatters. "So remedy that right quick, son. And when you're done," he grabbed the soldier's wrist and pulled his arm up. The soldier's eyes widened, but Mulldoos slapped the hilt of the falchion into the palm and yelled, "Clean and hone this thing until it shines like you just picked it fresh from the armory."

The soldier gave one quick nod and Mulldoos turned on his heel and started back toward the captain, glowering at the rest who stopped to watch the scene. "And you lazy lepers better find something to do besides gawking or squawking, or I swear to every whore that made the mistake of birthing you miserable wretches, you'll wish you had."

Most said "Aye, Lieutenant," and started back to their respective horses before Braylar halted them. "It so happens, I have just the thing. Pluck the bolts out of these bodies and take the Hornmen to the stables. Set the horses loose and burn the thing to the ground."

One of the Syldoon—the one with the face that looked like it had been hit by a shovel, eyes set too far apart, nose flat and pulpy, said, "Fire, Cap?"

"Aye. Fire. The thing that burns other things."

Pulp-nose said, "Begging your pardon, Cap, but what I meant was, the tower's stone. Not like to light up real well."

Braylar slowly pivoted to face him and hissed. "The stable and barn, you ass. Large wooden buildings, just alongside the tower there, full of four-legged beasts. That you will set loose first. Set fire to that. And be quick about it. I want to be away from this place immediately."

The Syldoon saluted and set to work.

Vendurro scratched the back of his neck, still staring at the Hornman at the base of the tower covered in blood with a pale bone jutting out of his torn hose. "Shit job, that. Shit job."

Mulldoos turned on him, about to shout something at him as well, but then reconsidered, cursed, and stalked back to his horse. Maybe he was going to harass him for passing the job off before he remembered he'd done the very same.

I turned and watched as a Syldoon approached the Hornman that was behind the wagons. He grabbed him under the arms and started to drag him toward the barn, heard him groan, and dropped the body. Then, not wanting to repeat the bloody performance from a few moments ago, the Syldoon spanned his crossbow and nonchalantly planted another bolt in the middle of the man's chest. The Hornman jerked once and went still for good.

The Syldoon swung his crossbow around out of the way on its strap, and went back to work moving the body to the barn.

I felt my stomach twist. The captain was right, as awful as it was—those deaths in Alespell were my fault. In saving one life, I'd managed to end several more. Though Braylar had clearly chosen to try his luck with the outpost. I couldn't be held accountable for the aftermath of that.

The captain was eyeing me, measuring my expression. "I can see it on your face, Arki. Writ as clear as if put there in ink by a stylus."

I readied myself for mockery or a cruel jibe. "Oh?"

"Yes. It's the quills, is it not?"

Worried I was only being baited, I asked carefully, "I'm sorry—the quills?"

"The lack of them, to be precise. In the Green Sea, I could tell you thought it a poor choice for a cover story. And now you're absolutely certain of it, yes?"

I didn't reply, sill fearing that he was ready to verbally ambush me.

"Well, it pains me to no end to admit it, but you might be on to something. I still feel the story itself is credible, and my delivery impeccable, but it has failed two performances in a row. So. You must help me think of something else the next time we have Hornmen, Brunesmen, or any other nosy men poking around the wagon. I leave it to you." He watched his men hoisting the dead. "Put that creative mind of yours to use, and leave off whatever it is that weighs heavy on you here."

Did he suddenly regret being so hard on me? And if so, was it only because he thought me too weak to be able to take it? Or was it because he believed he was overly harsh? As always, I had difficulty determining what it was that motivated him from moment to moment, but he was offering me a reprieve. Or trying to, at the least.

I felt my throat clench and nodded. "It could be that, no matter how flawlessly you sold the tale, the fault might have been only poor timing or odd circumstance."

"Perhaps." Braylar climbed up onto the bench.

I did the same. "Or it could be you just don't look like someone who sells quills for a living."

Braylar looked at me, and I thought I might have spoiled things, and was about to hastily add something else, when he laughed and slapped me on the back. "Entirely possible. I was going for innocuous."

"That, Captain, might have strained credibility. Just a bit."

He nodded, a small smile still there. "So then. What would you suggest, oh learned scribe?"

I thought about it as he got the team of horses moving, forgetting for a moment that the Syldoon were hiding a fair number of bodies and getting ready to burn everything to ash. "Well. You need a ruse that arouses no suspicion and seems entirely plausible. How about gravedigger?"

He gave me the sharp look that usually prefaced a sharper rebuke, stopped as he realized I was joking, and slapped my back again. "Very good, Arki. Very good."

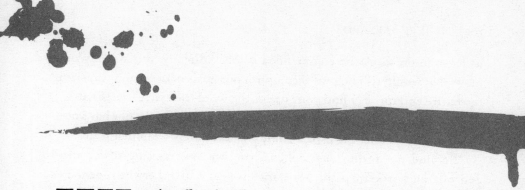

We rode off as hastily as the uneven and stony road would allow. I looked behind us, saw the dark smoke rising above the trees, the burning stable hidden as we rounded a small bend. I wondered what would have happened if any other travelers had come by just after the attack. But I knew, really, and just gave silent thanks it was only Hornmen corpses burning in the barn. At least the captain had spared the horses. He did seem to have a soft spot for animals.

It was silent for the next hour or so, and some of the smoke must have wafted onto the canvas, or my clothes, even though I hadn't been all that close to the flames, as the smell stuck with us the entire time. Muldoos and Vendurro flanked our wagon, and the other Syldoon rode alongside the one behind us. We rounded another bend and saw a large group of horsemen waiting for us. I nearly choked on the wine I was drinking until recognizing Soffjian and her red cloak among them. We closed the distance and the riders fell in among us, rounding out our small caravan. Not surprisingly, Soffjian looked particularly perturbed as she sidled up next to our wagon.

Looking straight ahead, she said, "You do seem to court a great deal of conflict wherever you go."

"I am a great courtier, it is true," Braylar replied, eyes also fixed straight ahead.

"Are you sure your quarry is worth all this excessive maneuvering and effort, brother? We could be halfway to Sunwrack by now, but instead, we are riding through the woods in the wrong direction, with the likelihood of you incurring imperial wrath growing every mile. Nothing would delight me more, of course, so I ask only out of idle curiosity."

"There is nothing idle about you, sister. And never has been. But as to your question, we could have come up with a multitude of plans that would not have involved us going out of our way, had the Emperor given us leave to do so. As he commanded us back directly, this was my only move that would still help us accomplish our goals here without capsizing the entire enterprise. I find your use of the word 'excessive' excessive."

She smiled, and though the physical resemblance might not have been strong on the whole, the joyless smile was absolutely a familial trait.

"Remind me again," she replied, "why we are traipsing so far afield and off the northern path? My curiosity—idle or otherwise—demands parley."

"Does it now? Very well. I will tell you this. Most of our machinations in Anjuria involved setting one caste against another, aggravating what were already volatile conditions between them, and seeking to destabilize things, in advance of the emperor's invasion."

"That has not materialized."

"That has not materialized," Braylar agreed. "But still very well could. Likely will, in fact. The ravages of the plague are still felt, but I suspect Cynead believes we have recovered enough that we no longer need to work in the background setting the stage for assault. But if so, what he is neglecting to realize is that Anjuria has recovered as well. And while they are still fractured, and ruled by a very young monarch, it is foolish to abandon everything we've achieved here without doing one final thing while we have opportunity. A rare opportunity."

Soffjian considered this, or made a show of considering anyway, before saying, "And if your brilliant hunch is off, and he has no such plans? What if he doesn't intend to invade now? What if never?"

Braylar laughed. "The Syldoon are either invading, planning on invading, or paving streets in conquered lands. Even the most atypically peaceful emperor doesn't sit the throne long without giving us some martial objective or other. We tend to resort to killing each other in the streets if we grow bored, Soff. Or deposing emperors."

"Be that as it may, given that you are operating solely on supposition— unsupported supposition, in fact—it seems odd you would be so eager to risk his wrath for capturing one piece on the board, when he could have moved onto a different game entirely."

She was looking in our direction now as she waited for a reply. No. Not "our," I suddenly realized with a lurch in my chest—she was looking at me. Only me. With those dark, very dangerous eyes. While she surely knew how gifted her brother was at subverting the truth and probably wasn't looking for tells from him, she seemed to suspect—rightly so—that I was far closer to transparent than opaque.

If I glanced away quickly I would arouse suspicion, and if I locked eyes too long, it was like challenging some wild beast. Her gaze appeared casual enough, but I felt like she was slowly peeling layers of my face away the longer I looked at her.

I turned to Braylar, as if I were waiting for his response as well, and not at all like I was trying desperately to do something casual and blameless.

He ignored both of us, or at least what we were doing, and I feared he might not reply at all, which would leave me trying to manufacture some other innocent gesture, or excuse myself and head back into the wagon as nonchalantly as I could. But then he said, "It's true, I'm far from Cynead's inner circle. In fact, I'm somewhere in one of his outermost circles. I cannot know his mind. Just as you can't. So everything we do here is fraught with risk. Everything. That is simply the way of it."

She sniffed and said, "As you say." Then she rejoined Skeelana further ahead.

Keeping my voice low but avoiding the urge to lean in and whisper, I asked, "Do you think she suspects? That there is more to you going after Henlester?"

"You mean because you fidgeted like a small child about to piss himself the second she so much as looked at you?"

I started to fumble a reply when he continued, "But even if you hadn't behaved like a complete ass, I always suspect her of being suspicious. It's in our natures, you see. And her more than most."

Hewspear and Vendurro had warned me to bite my tongue, but I nearly ignored such sage advice and queried the captain about whatever poisonous past they shared. The timing seemed ideal, in that I'd just seen the siblings engage in some more verbal sparring, but the timing was equally terrible, in that I'd obviously irritated Braylar again, and his sister doubly so.

Would there ever be an opportunity to deftly weave it into conversation when he didn't look ready to chew stones and spit the pieces at me?

Unlikely. Most unlikely.

⊕

As dusk approached, I wondered where we intended to make camp for the night. When we were in the Green Sea, we simply camped where we stopped, and little different on the road to Alespell. But having killed a large host of Hornmen in Alespell, and a small tower full of them not long after, we couldn't possibly be sleeping just on the side of the road. Too dangerous. We had to turn off somewhere. The only question was where, and if the captain had selected the spot ahead of time. I supposed it was too much to hope we would find a small village that had an inn of some kind.

We headed off the main road, onto a much smaller rutted trail only wide enough to accommodate one wagon. I wondered what we would do if we encountered any traffic coming the opposite direction, but there was none. The track was overgrown and nearly as grassy as the wild areas around it. And there wasn't any noise at all, besides the chirping of birds or the ever-present buzz and hum of insects, drawn to fresh flesh before being repulsed (somewhat) by the herbs strewn all over the wagon and hanging from the tack and harness.

A fox darted out of the brush, looked in our direction for a while, and then scampered across our path before disappearing on the other side.

When we finally made it around a small bend and saw a horseman standing in the middle of the track, I tensed, fearing it was a bandit, or a Hornman, but no one else even seemed surprised.

The Syldoon rode up to us and reported the site was clear. I wasn't quite sure just how clear until we rounded the bend a bit further and came across the village. The most deserted village I had ever seen.

Judging by the fences that had fallen and the encroachment of weeds and grasping roots and other aggressive vegetation, it had been for quite some time. But what made it especially odd wasn't the state of desertion, or the way the wilderness had sensed its opportunity and begun reclaiming the area as its own, but the fact that most of the structures looked solid and still in good repair. As we entered the outskirts of the village, I noticed several doorways open, windows as well. Peering inside as we passed, I saw a fair number of the usual items you would expect to encounter in any home—hints of chests, dressers, tables and chairs, rugs still on the wooden or dirt floor.

On the road to Highgrove University, heading there the first time, nothing but a frightened boy, I remember we came across a settlement that was equally abandoned, but it had clearly suffered the ill-use of whatever bandits or marauders had driven the inhabitants off. Buildings burned to the ground, everything that might have contained anything of value cracked open or shattered, other objects that were completely utilitarian broken or smashed out of spite or some vindictive lust. The entire village was ransacked. We'd hurried on, as it felt like the damage might have been done recently, and the thieves might still be prowling around.

But this was something altogether different. This place didn't seem like it had been attacked. In some ways, it reminded me of the temple by the River Debt. But while those ruins had been foreboding, the area devoid of most sentient life, filled with a heavy spirit of desolation, it had the shimmering, endless, and horrible Godveil to explain why it had been forsaken, destroying the minds of any who ventured too close.

There was no obvious reason this village was utterly empty, or why it had not been looted. It was different from the temple, but no less eerie. It felt like all the inhabitants were spirited away right in the middle of whatever they'd been doing.

My mouth went dry and I fumbled for some wine before asking Braylar, "What happened here?"

We kept rolling along and he didn't reply, only looked around the deserted village, trying to find something. Finally, he pointed at a plot of land behind one house that contained graves. Several, and of varying sizes. "The plague."

"The. . .?" I looked everywhere at once, and the truth of it was suddenly so obvious it hurt. The place was so abandoned because people had tired of burying their own, and the survivors had moved on as quickly as they could, afraid to contract the same, or so overcome by the quiet destruction that had claimed so many they simply couldn't remain. Maybe they even suspected their possessions were tainted, as so many had been left behind and left undisturbed.

That was why the place felt so haunted. It probably was.

"But. . . is it smart to stay here? Some physicians claim the plague runs its course in short order, but others mention the possibility that whatever causes it might be lying dormant, simply waiting for the fools to stumble in and startle it awake again. Is this. . . foolish? It feels foolish."

Braylar gave one of those hard looks that made men exceptionally uncomfortable, me more than most. "We will be absolutely undisturbed for the night here, because fools believe as you do. I am far more worried about armed men hunting us than some dormant plague rising like a vengeful spirit. Is there anything else you wish to add? No? Very good."

The community was a tiny hamlet and it didn't take us long to reach the center of it, which is about where we stopped. Braylar guided the team of horses into a barn that had either been left open by the plague survivors or by his own men who had ridden here ahead of us. While most people likely avoided the village, he wasn't taking any chances either. The rest of his men followed his lead and moved their horses and the other wagon inside, though it couldn't house all of them, so several took their horses elsewhere.

Braylar lit a lantern, hung it from a hook, untethered Scorn and started tending to her, and I did the same with my own ignoble steed. My horse hadn't been ridden during the day, so I was tempted to rush through it, but the captain's steed hadn't been worked any harder and he still treated her as if she had nearly been blown galloping the entire day, so I mirrored him as best I could. Even my horse looked at me as if I was being over-zealous, but I wasn't going to stop brushing until he did. Which seemed to take far longer than it should have.

When we were done and led the horses to some stalls, we unhar-nessed the team that had been pulling the wagon and gave them their due attention. Never having owned a horse and needing to care for one before accompanying Captain Killcoin, I was still somewhat surprised by just how much handling they required. I suppose I always imagined you simply rode until you were done riding and then got off.

Braylar was right—I could be something of a fool. I just hoped he was equally right about the plague no longer being in the empty village. I found myself breathing as shallowly as possible, with my heart beating like a startled hare, before realizing that if there was a danger it was likely too late. We were here. And would be for the night. If the plague would claim any of us, it had probably already chosen its victims and begun working our demise.

When we were finally done with the horses, I followed Braylar out of the barn and across the thoroughfare, over a small stone bridge over a dry streambed choked with branches and dried leaves from seasons past.

I thought he intended to stay at what appeared to be the manor house, home to whatever mayor had died or otherwise departed, but he kept walking.

Then Braylar stopped, swayed, reached out for the nearest wall and nearly missed it. I put my hand out, reluctant to grab him outright, but not wanting to fail to offer aid of some kind either. He rubbed furiously at his temples as he steadied himself against the wall, then gritted his teeth, nearly gnashing them, before his head lolled to the side. I was sure he was going to fall and did grab his arm, but he caught himself, shook me off, and slapped himself in the side of the face.

"Captain, are you—?"

"Fine," he said, eyes still closed. "I am fine."

"Is it—?"

"Of course it is. Whatever else could it possibly be? The dreaded plague?" Without waiting for an answer, he pushed off the wall, took a hesitant step, shook his head once, and then kept walking.

A short time later we stopped in front of a nondescript timber building, the only one besides the manor house that was two stories. Unlike in a large city, every inhabitant in this small village had surely known what each and every building was, and any visitors from the main road would have had little chance of getting lost, so there was almost no signage. This building was the lone exception—it had a faded, warped sign hanging from one iron loop that had an image impossible to misinterpret: a flagon of ale.

Even though there were no wenches, pretty or ugly, no ale, fine or muddy, and no other attraction, overt or covert, the Syldoon seemed to have difficulty resisting the allure of a tavern or inn. But as I stopped at the door, it struck me that it might not just have been familiarity or affinity—the beds here had been home to countless people. The beds in the homes up in the village had only belonged to the dead or the heartbroken who'd left them behind. It was probably easier to bunk down in a place like this.

Of course, when you stopped to consider how many people had stayed a night here on the way to Alespell and carried the plague with them, it didn't seem like such a safe place. But it was where we were staying, so again, there was little to be gained from mediating on it too long. For good or ill, we were in the village and in the inn, so there it was.

The place looked as it must have before the plague ravaged the village, generally undisturbed, trapped in time. While the innkeeper, if he survived, must have taken valuables and whatever he could carry to start over, the tables and chairs were still here, covered in a patina of dust, and several tables still had plates or cups strewn across them. There was a rag here, a spoon carved from horn there, a black iron poker hanging in front of the empty fireplace. Messy, yes, evacuated in some haste, but not looted or vandalized. Simply abandoned, like every other building in the hamlet.

I stood there watching the Syldoon make themselves at home, admiring the way they seemed mostly oblivious to the fact that they had killed so many Hornmen, and were now pushing benches and tables aside to bed down in a dead community. They seemed to focus on the immediate and the known and little else, trusting their captain and his lieutenants to make the decisions regarding anything beyond that. I wondered how they did it.

I saw Vendurro chatting with another soldier I only vaguely recognized, and Skeelana off to the side and watching it all, much like I was, and Mulldoos barking an order at a younger soldier, and tried to decide which direction I would head in or if I would find my own secluded spot. I had to admit, the largest part of me was drawn to approach Skeelana, but I wasn't sure if that was because she was the most appealing or the least threatening. She was half as physically beautiful as Soffjian and twice as attractive. I felt myself warming to her whenever we spoke, even as she gently chided me.

Hewspear was sitting at a table by himself, away from the other others, back rigid, breathing shallowly, his brow deeply lines as he carved away at a flute with a very small blade.

For some reason, I decided to approach, hoping I wasn't interrupting. Hewspear looked up at me, and then pointed to a spot on the bench. "Sit, Arki. If you are so inclined."

Hewspear didn't seem the kind of man to make his own space awkward by placating others, so I sat and looked closer at the flute. It was a little shorter than his forearm, and he'd made remarkable progress since I'd seen him start whittling several days back. Before, it was rough in shape and form and devoid of anything resembling a flourish, but now it was covered in intricate strands of vines, sharp-edged leaves, and delicate flowers scattered among them. It was quite fine, really, and the level of detail he'd achieved was far greater than I would have expected. I had no carving skills to speak of, so perhaps I was easier to impress than most, but I'd known a student at university who was exceptionally skilled, and Hewspear's work was easily a match, possibly surpassing it.

He noticed me staring and smiled. "Not expecting a veteran killer to have a light touch, eh, Arki?"

"No," I replied quickly. "That is, I mean, I don't consider you a veteran killer."

He went back to his fine work, still smiling. "You are as ingenuous as they come, young scribe. And if you aren't yourself convinced of the lies you spin, you can be sure your audience will be equally skeptical."

I started to respond, caught myself, and then started again, "Obviously you are a soldier. And clearly a seasoned one. No offense," I hastily added.

"None taken," he replied, smiling.

"And I know soldiering technically involves killing, but 'veteran killer' seems to imply. . . someone who commits the acts wantonly. Or with malice. Or enjoys them too much. I don't see you like that." I paused, and then asked, "Is that naïve?"

The tiny knife nicked away a thin curl of wood and he blew it off the blade, watched it float, undisturbed by any breeze, turning of its own accord, spinning gently to the floor. "Are not all the Syldoon bloodthirsty killers?"

I looked over at Mulldoos on the other side of the room. He had his arms folded behind his head, leaning his chair back against a post, calm, possibly asleep. And still somehow seeming like coiled danger. "No, I don't think all. That is, for your cause, I don't think you'd hesitate to use whatever means were necessary. But it seems more. . . "

I struggled to find the right word or phrase.

"Yes?" Hewspear blew another tiny shaving away, following its twirling path to the floor.

"Pragmatic, maybe?"

He looked up. "I wouldn't argue that point. And while I wouldn't presume to tell you what context means to you, or argue the semantics of the thing, all I'll say is, I have killed men. Less than some, but more than many. On account of my advanced years and crafty nature." He winked at me, but the good humor seemed to drain away as quickly as it appeared. "But a man who kills is a killer, no matter the cause or circumstance, regardless of whether it is a pitched battle among troops who are aware of the risks, or after too many ales in a tavern. So, a veteran killer is a veteran killer, no matter how you dress it up or embroider it."

Hewspear held the flute up, blew down its length and dusted it off with his dark hand, before examining it closely by the light of a nearby lantern. While it wasn't perfectly sanded or polished as yet, and he hadn't finished his carving, the craftsmanship was exemplary. "Let me assure you, they were not all righteous kills that allow me to sleep like a babe."

I was struck by the juxtaposition of his words with the wooden art he had worked so nicely in his hands. They seemed completely incongruous, and yet, somehow fitting. So very. . . Syldoonian.

"That is a beautiful flute."

"Many thanks. It will probably sound like a strangled bird—I'm a far better woodworker than musician—but it is quite nice to look at, I will grant you that."

"Who is it for?"

Hewspear's face clouded over, but only for a moment. "For my grandson. Luhosiba."

I waited, but that seemed the sum total of the answer. "I'm sure he'll love it. It is a fine gift."

Hewspear turned the flute over in his hands, still inspecting. "It will be, once it is finished and stained and lacquered. Assuming it plays. But I'm not sure I'll have the chance to give it to him."

Again, there was nothing to follow, though the silence was full of portent. Was Luhosiba sick? Was Hewspear worse off than he indicated—could he feel his lungs leaking blood into the cavities of his body? Was there something else, something worse?

I obviously didn't know, and couldn't guess.. A little hesitantly, I asked, "Is Luhosiba. . . is he ill?"

Hewspear looked at me. "No. No, nothing like that. At least, not that I know of. I haven't seen the boy in several years now, but he was healthy enough when I left."

Still half-fearing the answer, I pressed on. "Then, why are you worried you might not have opportunity to give it to him?"

Hewspear set the flute down on the table and slipped the small knife into an intricately worked leather case. "My son's wife and I are what might charitably be called . . . estranged."

"Do you mind if I ask why? If you do, I—"

"No," he replied. "It is sad, but no secret. You see, for a Syldoon soldier everything is in the now, and the limited future. But especially the immediate. What we achieve in this lifetime is all that we achieve. It is a distinct difference between us and nearly every other kingdom. While we might accumulate wealth soldiering, establish a farm or a fishpond or a mill in our dotage, and can pass on money and some measure of security to our families, we do not pass on title or rank."

"So, the offspring of a Syldoon doesn't automatically become one?"

He held up a long finger. "Correction, Arki. Can *never* become one. It is one of our oldest traditions. What's more, it is law."

"But why? Wouldn't that be easier to have someone join already familiar with the culture and its expectations, than having to recruit from far-flung villages on the edge of the Empire?"

"Easier, yes. More effective, no. You see, we recruit from the hinterlands because those people are hardy—they grow up in constant strife and warfare. Simply by virtue of surviving, they've proved they are as tough as they come. What's more, their relative ignorance of how the Syldoon operate is one of the boons of the system. Can you imagine a pampered Syldoon child, having grown up in the privilege and culture of Sunwrack, being willing to submit to the intense and sometimes deadly rigors of the decade of enslavement? Or Syldoon parents allowing it?"

He answered his own question without waiting for mine, "No. The Syldoon are strong only so long as they have a steady influx of robust and resilient stock, hungry to prove themselves, to compete, to endure, to survive. That is what makes the Empire the most powerful in the world, and promises it shall remain so."

It was a peculiar system, to be certain. "And so how did this lead to estrangement?"

Hewspear sighed, and leaned back. "My son, Vedmurrien, wanted to be Syldoon, burned for it in fact. He didn't understand why he was forbidden when he was younger. It made him furious when he saw new Syldoon boys and a few girls come into Sunwrack his age, and I had to explain that they would be able to become Syldoon while he could not. I tried telling him he would be safer, and healthier, and likely live longer. Explained he could do anything else in the world he wanted. Become an artist, apprentice in a trade, manage a date farm," he touched the flute. "Even a musician. But being denied this one thing, he became fixated."

I wasn't sure how long ago this was, and didn't want to interrupt now that he was talking without pause. "Still, as years passed, Vedmurrien stopped asking about it. He'd see a new caravan of caged wagons full of recruits, or a manumission ceremony, and he'd silently fume, but he didn't talk to me about it anymore. The law was the law. And frankly, I was glad of it. The soldiering life is a hard one. And while he was a good lad, he just wasn't built for it. Sickly, not the strongest of limb. Poor eyes as well.

"And I made the mistake of thinking he had accepted it and moved on, that as he approached adulthood he would settle into some craft or other pursuit. He had other interests, girls among them, and I was hopeful he would find his own path. Be happy. And when he got married to Adjunna, I celebrated with him. But the very next day he announced he was joining the auxiliaries."

"The auxiliaries? But I thought he couldn't join the army?"

Hewspear sighed. "While the Syldoon are the core component, the largest and most prestigious, the Empire maintains a standing army, and even in times of relative peace, the Syldoon soldiers are not enough to man all fronts, provinces, and cities. The offspring of Syldoon can never be Syldoon proper; however they can sign up as clerks in the army, engineers, or auxiliary soldiers."

"I take it from your tone you didn't approve."

He laid his head back and stared across the room, to the empty tables and benches that once were occupied by countless patrons. "No. I did not. As I said, he wasn't cut out for it. And what's more, his young wife Adjunna approved less. She hated the idea of her betrothed serving the Empire in any capacity, especially if he risked his life doing so."

"Why? I mean, I can understand her fearing for his safety, but it sounds like there was more to it than that."

Hewspear looked at me and then smiled. "Ahh, apologies. I forget—you might be educated, but that is a far cry from actually growing up in the Empire. It is an odd arrangement. Thurvacian citizens, even those born and raised in Sunwrack—perhaps especially those—have a mixture of reactions to the Syldoon ruling over them, of course. Fear, hatred, bitterness, apathy, and in the best and rarest of cases, mayhaps appreciation or respect. The Syldoon proper—those who survive their ten years of slavery and join a Tower—are outsiders, barbarians from far-flung lands. Rough, ill-mannered, illiterate when they arrive. And yet, after their own intense and somewhat brutal education, in time they all assume power in every corner of the Empire, and control the interests of all other members of the society."

"So. . . Thurvacians are merely subjects?"

"They might occupy civil posts, and they keep the Empire running, but they will never rule themselves. So you can see why the indigenous citizens might not have a tremendous fondness for their overlords, especially those who rule with a cruel hand."

I nodded. "So, Adjunna was Thurvacian, and she didn't especially like you as a potential father-in-law anyway, but when she learned your son wanted to enlist in the army—"

"Livid doesn't begin to do it justice. And, in what must have required a great deal of pride swallowing, she approached me privately and begged me to talk Vedmurrien out of joining."

"But you probably had, hadn't you? Tried to dissuade him, I mean."

"Of course. Loudly. Often. Until veins nearly burst in my throat. But while the law prevented him from becoming a Syldoon proper, nothing would stop him from becoming a soldier, no matter how poorly he was suited for it. And now that he was married, the law also considered him a man, capable of charting his own course."

Hewspear suddenly looked and sounded his years, face drawn, wrinkles deeper, the gray in his beard and hair grayer. "So Vedmurrien enlisted. I did what I could to fix it so he'd end up with the lightest duty possible. And that worked for a while. He and Adjunna had a son, and though she was always cool toward me—never forgiven me for 'allowing' him to enlist—I visited the three of them when I could while I was in Sunwrack. For a time, things were good. For a time."

Even knowing the story was going nowhere pleasant, I asked, "Until?"

"There always seems to be an 'until.' That is one of life's harsh lessons. We—that is, our company, the crossbow cavalry—we were making plans and preparations for coming here, to Anjuria. Not two weeks before, I received a letter. Vedmurrien's unit had been sent to investigate a peasant uprising in Urglovia. It hadn't sounded particularly dangerous—the sort of thing even auxiliary forces could reasonably be expected to put down easily enough—and my only worry before scanning that parchment was that he might not return in time for me to say my goodbyes.

"As it turned out, he did not return at all. He was cut down in a small skirmish. Only a few casualties. They routed the rebels. On a ledger, just another rousing success for the Syldoon Empire." He closed his eyes. "Only a few casualties, after all."

Hewspear didn't continue, and for once I was in no mood to push the issue, as I had no idea what I could say to a man who'd lost his son. Had the body come home to Sunwrack? Had he had a chance to say goodbye?

We sat there in silence for a time, me utterly regretting my line of questioning, him probably regretting answering. Hewspear lifted the flute very deliberately, examined it a final time. "So," he said, still looking at it, "Adjunna refused to speak to me before we left on this campaign, blaming me, no doubt, for our shared loss. And she would not allow me to see my grandson. Denied every letter I've sent since." He rolled the flute across the table, testing for warp. "I hope the boy is still fond of music. And I hope I get the chance to deliver this when we return. We shall see. I have my doubts. Three years might have lessened the pain, or hardened the heart. I have no wish to strip a mother of her child. Truly. But the boy is my blood as well, the last link to my son. And a man can be denied only so long. A Syldoon less so. There is a reason we are veteran killers, after all."

He forced a pained smile and continued inspecting his flute, and there was little more I could add. I found the best reason I could to excuse myself without simply walking away. "I, uh, left my writing case behind in the wagon."

As I left the inn and crossed the bridge, the sun was gone for good now, with the sky still holding onto some last vestige of the light, and I headed to the barn. I hadn't thought to bring a lantern, so felt my way through the dark inside, listening to a horse snort in a stall nearby, my hand out in front of me in case I stumbled over something and started to fall. After reaching the wagon, I felt my way around it and climbed inside, eager to get my case and return to the inn as quickly as possible.

Careful to avoid all the objects hanging from the hooks, I hunchwalked as I cautiously made my way to the front, cursing myself for not walking around and entering from that side in the first place. I wondered if Braylar had ordered the cases with scrolls hauled inside, and hoped I would get a chance to start poring through the documents soon—even if I didn't find what the captain was looking for, it would be a welcome diversion, and a chance to exercise skills I hadn't used in some time. I found the cold brass lid and was picking my case up when the axle creaked.

I wasn't alone.

I nearly jumped and fought the urge to spin around. The only occupants in the village were us, so it had to be an ally of some sort, and still I felt my insides turn to liquid.

Slowly turning around, I tried to make out the shadowy silhouette that was slightly more black than rest of the gloom in the barn beyond, hoping I would recognize Vendurro.

Instead I heard Soffjian say, "I have been waiting for the right opportunity to chat. I do hope this is a good time?"

She climbed all the way into the wagon and sat down near the rear. Soffjian didn't have her ranseur for once, but its absence didn't make me feel any more secure. She could strike men down with no weapon at all.

I was usually nervous enough around women as it was, especially attractive women. I routinely made an ass of myself, fumbled my words, inevitably said the wrong thing, and regretted opening my mouth in the first place. Now, alone in a dark barn with one, who also happened to be Braylar's sister, who also had the capability of turning my mind to silt in an instant, or driving me absolutely mad (and not with love or lust), I was feeling as unsettled as you could possibly feel. Mulldoos would have been more welcome, and the phantom of a plague victim would not have been worse.

Still on my haunches, I leaned back against a barrel, wondering how far her unseen reach extended, and if I suddenly bolted out the front of the wagon, would I have any chance of making it out of the barn before she felled me.

Soffjian took my silence for concession. "Very good. Now then, I was hoping you might be able to clear up a few things for me."

She said this with the sly implication that she already knew much more than I could ever know, but was only looking for confirmation.

I took a deep breath, sought the right words. "I'm happy to help in whatever way I can. Only, the captain will be wondering where I've gone to shortly, so I don't know that we will have a lot of time. To sit in the dark and have a discussion, that is. And what's more—"

"Oh, never fear—I won't keep you overlong. I promise. And I would hate to do anything to jeopardize your relationship with the captain."

I had difficulty believing that. Perhaps she was less manipulative than her brother. But I doubted it.

Soffjian continued, "I'm curious, though. What exactly is your relationship with Bray? Sorry, familial casualness. Your captain. Clearly you aren't from the Empire. How is it you come to find yourself in his service?"

I weighed a number of answers, most designed to obscure as much as possible. But I suspected a Memoridon could learn the truth easily enough, even if she hadn't already. I opted for selected truth. "I am Vulmyrian originally. Though I was trained at Highgrove University. I was a scribe and archivist for a number of patrons over the years, which brought me to Rivermost. It was living there when I heard your brother was looking for someone with my talents. Honestly, if I'd been satisfied with my lot in life, I wouldn't have given a second thought to interviewing with the man. But I wanted more than what I had. A lot more. So I did."

The silhouette seemed perfectly relaxed. "How wonderfully direct and forthright. I have to say, I'm pleasantly surprised. This conversation is going to go very well, I can tell already."

I doubted that as well. "I'm not sure my new patron would approve me disclosing too much, however. He's rather particular about who knows what about his goings on. And you. . . the two of you don't seem to have an especially good relationship, if you pardon my saying."

Soffjian laughed. "No. That we don't. So pardoned. And I appreciate your loyalty. I do. Above all things, I appreciate loyalty." She folded her legs underneath her. "So, he clearly misplaced the original scribe that was assigned to his unit."

This clearly wasn't a question, so I didn't hurry to reply at all. In fact, I opted not to respond in the slightest.

That didn't slow her down any. "So, do you know what happened to the archivist who was originally in his company? Before you joined? Thurvacian, I believe, was he not?"

I weighed my words carefully, cognizant that, despite her casual demeanor, she was obviously measuring my every word, the tone of my voice, and the time it took me to fashion any reply at all. "I can't say that I do. Given that I wasn't a part of his company when that person was assigned. I imagine he didn't perform his duties adequately?"

Immediately after the words were out of my mouth, I wondered what else this woman could do. Was she secretly plumbing the depths of my memories as we spoke, to find the ones that proved the words a lie? Could she do such a thing?

Why had I left my writing case behind? Why?

Soffjian said, "Fair enough. Thank you for your candor, Arkamondos. Or do you prefer Arki? I've heard you referred to as both. And of course, much worse by Mulldoos. Foul beast."

Was she trying to bait me into joining her in decrying a member of Braylar's retinue? She seemed not to like the man any more than I did, but it was likely she was engaging in some verbal gambit or other. Was she attempting to position herself, align the two of us together in order to encourage me to speak more freely? If so, it failed. Despite my dislike for Mulldoos. "Well, I don't know the man all that well, only having been among the company a short time. According to some of the other Syldoon, no one rubs him the right way, so I try not to take it personally. As to the name, whatever you prefer is fine. I will answer to either."

"Amenable, loyal, forthright. My brother is incredibly lucky to have you, Arki."

Had any other attractive woman paid me so many compliments, I would have been equally suspicious. But I was doubly on guard, given who I was speaking to. "Well, many thanks. That said, I probably should return before the captain wonders if he needs to recruit yet another archivist."

Soffjian chuckled. "Only a few moments more, if you would. I don't know how many other opportunities we'll have to discuss things so openly and honestly."

"Very well. I stay at your pleasure." Even as the words were out, I silently groaned at myself.

"So," she said, "I know you've only been among my brother and his men a short time, but I was hoping you might be able to shed some light on something else for me. You see, despite occasionally wearing armor or serving our armies close to the front lines, I do not count myself an expert on anything military. But I couldn't help but notice my brother's new weapon. It is quite striking, if you'll pardon the pun."

My breath hitched in my chest, thrown off rhythm completely. I considered forcing a laugh, but knew that it would be the falsest move possible, so did and said nothing.

Soffjian continued, "He was always partial to more traditional side-arms, if I recall. It seems curious that he would suddenly opt to switch to a flail. Syldoon soldiers train at proficiency in all weapons of course, but like the rest of us, they are not immune to favoritism. And Bray—apologies, Captain Killcoin—was always partial to small axes. I do wonder why he chose to adopt a flail now. Do you have any idea?"

I did, and tried to clear my mind of that fact. "Again, this predated me some years, so I can't speak to it with any authority. And being armed only with quills—"

"And the occasional crossbow."

"And the occasional crossbow," I amended. "I'm less martial than you are, by a fair margin. So the proclivities of soldiers are a mystery to me."

She let that hang there for a moment before saying, "Be that as it may. It is equally curious—maybe more so—that the flail heads are in the likeness of Deserter Gods. Impossible to miss that."

"Impossible. For certain."

"And yet I never took Bray for an especially pious man. Even if he opt-ed to pick up a new weapon, challenge himself perhaps, certainly he could have chosen a flail less holy. Or unholy, depending on your vantage."

Again, I was left wondering how much more she might have known than she was letting on, but I got the distinct impression she wasn't merely toying with me, or trying to get me to incriminate myself in some fashion. I was nothing to her. She was seriously hunting for new information, or at least information that confirmed already formed suspicions.

I said, "While I suspect you and your brother have had a falling out of sorts and haven't seen each other for some time besides, I'm sure you know enough about the captain to know he is not really. . . communicative. Especially to one such as me. I'm no confidant. So I'm afraid I can't really tell you very much. All I know is that the flail is terrifying, and even if he chose to pick it up relatively late, he uses it to great effect. Beyond that, your best bet would be to question someone like Hewspear or Mulldoos."

She didn't reply right away, and in the dark, I had no expressions to try to read. I said, "This has been a lovely chat, but—"

Soffjian spoke up, suddenly sounding much less gracious and tolerant. "I'm sure you're right. I really am asking the wrong questions, or posing them to the wrong person. Let me try another then, before you return to your master. It's come to my attention that Braylar was interviewing a little waif just before I arrived. One accused of being a witch, rumor has it. I believe she found herself into the Grieving Dog kitchens or some such thing, at his request. So, still something else odd—why was he interviewing a hedge witch? And why did he extend himself to help her? Certainly the captain of a Syldoon company has not forgotten that recruiting Memoridons is the sole province of, wouldn't you guess, Memoridons."

My mind was suddenly buzzing with answers, each somehow a worse choice than the last. I swallowed hard. "A waif? Hmmm. I can't say. I don't—"

"Before you go down dissembler's road too far and spoil our little conversation here, I do want to tell you one thing. Being a Memoridon, I have certain. . . skills. For instance, I could step into your mind and sift your memories any time I choose. While Syldoon sometimes pick up tricks to frustrate us, I am sure you would pose no problems at all. Skeelana is much more deft at such things, and could do so gingerly if instructed, but I confess, I am something of a brute when it comes to sifting. So if I enter you looking for answers, I will rend you apart. Shred you. Destroy you, most likely, to discover what I search for. Not with malice, mind—I just don't happen to be especially gifted in this way.

"Now, you are my brother's ward, under his protections and purview, so unless I harbor serious suspicions, I won't do this thing. We are merely talking right now. Exchanging information. I do hope we can continue merely talking. Don't you?"

I gripped my writing case so tight I thought I might dent it and my mouth was drier than dirt ten feet underground.

Falsehoods would get me nowhere. But revealing even an inkling of what I knew would damn me forever in the captain's eyes, and most likely result in me pleading for my life in a ditch as Mulldoos laughed and put an end to it.

I was trapped. Utterly.

So, breathing fast, I did the only mad thing I could think of. I went on the offensive. "Do you prefer Soffjian or Soff? I've heard you called both. And of course much worse by Mulldoos. Horrible barbarian that he is."

She maintained a level tone and replied, "No doubt. Soffjian is preferable."

"Now, we are having a nice conversation, Soffjian. As nice as you can have in a dark empty barn in a plague-ravaged village, anyway. I do like a good conversation. I prefer it with mulled wine in front of a nice fire. But still. I'm glad you sought me out. Up until now, I'd been wondering why the Syldoon were so wary of you and your kind. But I think I'm beginning to understand. Captain Killcoin—my apologies, Bray—he obviously mislikes you for reasons that are his own. But the entire company tensed up the moment you joined them and probably won't unclench until you leave. And it makes sense now. I do understand."

"Do you?" she asked, and two words never sounded chiller. "And what—"

I pushed on fast before she decided to simply excavate my skull. "You asked a question, so in a good conversation, it is your turn to listen. You make soldiers nervous, but you terrify me. Silly to pretend otherwise. It is what you wanted, and you achieved that. But I will tell you something else. I am the captain's ward, as you said. And his man. And that loyalty you lauded, earlier? It is to him. Not you. Not anyone else. Him and his retinue and his company. That's it. I have nothing to hide, and frankly, I'm not sure how much he does. The captain is secretive, to be sure, but I am the last person to know anything in this company. So you are really having a conversation with the worst person possible if you are hoping to unearth anything. There is nothing I can tell you."

When I stopped, my head was pounding, I was shaking, and I was sure any moment my eyes would be filled with bright lights as she ripped my skull open and poked inside. I waited for her to do something, say something, but she sat there, frozen, silent, and it was all I could do not to jump over the bench and run for it.

So when I heard a voice calling from somewhere just outside the barn, my bladder almost voided. I looked at Soffjian, or her silhouette, and was at a total loss for what to say.

Vendurro yelled out my name again. I pulled the front flap aside, and croaked, "Here."

"That you, Arki?"

I nodded, then realized he couldn't see me, and said, "Yes. Me."

"What are you doing out here in a dark barn by yourself? Roping the unicorn?" He laughed at his own joke, getting closer. "No need to head to the barn, Arki. You're among military men, not plaguing librarians. Hells, even librarians and priests got to be forgiving of a man tending to his pent-up business, right?"

I didn't respond, glad my face was in the shadows so he couldn't see me shine up bright and red. Getting caught with my manhood in my hand would have been preferable to him stumbling on me speaking privately to the captain's sister. I didn't know what to say, and half expected Soffjian to speak up, incriminating me completely, though I wasn't technically doing anything wrong, as she had sought me out, not the other way around.

Looking behind me, I feared the worst, but she was gone.

Vendurro didn't wait for a response anyway. "Well, no time to finish, more's the pity for you. Pull your hosen up and get to the inn. Cap's got something he wants to talk to all of us about."

I grabbed my writing case and started fumbling over the seat. "What is it?"

"Didn't say. On account of wanting to talk to all of us. Inside."

I jumped down, the springs on the wagon squeaking as it rocked gently back and forth.

Vendurro looked at the case and then back up at me. "Like to write about it after you're done, do you?" Even in the dark I could see he was still smiling.

"What? No. That's why I came out here. I forgot my case."

He nodded in exaggerated fashion. "Sure it is. Why, sure." He grabbed my arm and pulled me along. "Come on then. You know the Cap don't like waiting none."

I hazarded a quick glance over my shoulder before the barn disappeared from view as we walked around the corner of another building. Soffjian was nowhere to be seen.

"Shouldn't we lock the barn doors, or shut them or something?"

Vendurro looked around the deserted village and said, "Think we're good." Then he punched me in the arm and broke into a jog, calling over his shoulder. "Come on!"

We ran down the empty street toward the inn, and crossed over the short stone bridge.

When we got inside, I knew it wouldn't be raucous, as it was a defunct inn with only half the company bedding down there, but I still expected to encounter boisterous jokes, someone spinning a tale of some kind, or dicing and cursing. And probably whatever stock of ale and wine they still had left on the table.

But it was strangely quiet. At first, I thought it might just be the spell of staying the night in a plague village, but then I saw the faces of the men, some talking to each other, but most staring into their cups or at the rafters.

Clearly something was wrong.

I saw Vendurro stiffen. "Alright, you bastards, what is it?"

The three closest soldiers looked at each other and Vendurro raised his voice. "Out with it, straight away." While he was younger, and smaller framed, he had obviously been paying close attention to Hewspear and Mulldoos and did a fair approximation.

The soldier in the middle stood up and, looking very uncomfortable, said, "Cap's. . . taken ill. Like he does sometimes. You know. . . ill." He pointed up the stairs. "Lieutenants took him up there. Is it bad, Ven? Looked bad and—"

"That's Sergeant, Craslo," he snapped. "Sergeant. And seeing as how I just got here and had to inquire with you as the whats and wheres, I'm thinking you're asking a plaguing stupid question. Ask another one, and I'll set you to digging latrines."

Craslo looked at the open door then back to his sergeant. "It's night."

"Say one more plaguing dumb thing, you lippy limp cock, one more, and you'll be digging them in the dark with your hands. Doesn't need to be a question, just the next dumb thing out of your plaguing dumb mouth. Go on then."

Wisely, Craslo held his tongue. It might not have been Mulldoos barking at him, but it was an officer, and an incensed one at that.

Vendurro looked at me, said, "Come on!" and started taking the stairs two at a time. Balancing my writing case, I didn't trust my balance or dexterity, so I hurried as fast as I could to keep up. I reached the landing, and saw another Syldoon standing guard in front of a room at the end of the hall. He looked at Vendurro, eyes wide.

"Head downstairs," Vendurro ordered. "No need to be crowding the whole lot of us up here. Go get a drink."

The soldier nodded, clearly relieved to be relieved. Without another word, he grabbed the railing and hustled down the stairs. You would have thought he was fleeing a fire.

Vendurro scratched at the tuft on his chin, glanced at me, suddenly seeming less confident than he had before the other men, looking young and just as nervous as I felt. That should have been comforting, but only served to make me feel worse.

He straightened his shoulders, pushed the door open, and said, "Vendurro and Arki, coming in."

The room must have belonged to the innkeep or been reserved for whatever prominent fieflord happened to stop for the night, as it was larger than expected, though mostly empty. A few cabinets thrown open, an empty chest with the lid up, a wardrobe, doors also open, and in the center, a large canopy bed, the posts carved with intricate scenes of deer being chased round and round by hounds and hunters. And in the center of that, the captain.

Hewspear and Mulldoos were standing there, looking down at him. Braylar was sprawled on his back, limbs outstretched, breath shallow and labored. Just as he had been in the Green Sea.

"He collapsed, didn't he?" I asked. "Downstairs?"

Mulldoos kept his eyes locked on Braylar. "What gave that away? The fact he's lying there senseless, all collapsed like?"

I tried not to sigh or roll my eyes, despite the fact that he wasn't looking at me. "What I meant was, the men, your men, they saw him collapse, correct? Which means they aren't—"

"Yeah," Mulldoos shouted, "the men, our men," he mimicked, "plaguing saw him go down, you dumb—"

Hewspear interrupted, "What Arki is trying to suggest, I think, is—"

"You taking his side, that it? This stupid little shit?"

Hewspear shook his head. "There are no sides to take. And you would scarcely find anyone except a Syldoon more overeducated than our scribe here. But the men have seen the captain go down several times now. And might be less than comfortable with that." He turned to me. "Is that in fact what you were driving at, Arkamondos?"

I nodded. "They looked. . . " Having already angered Mulldoos, I searched for the right word.

"Spit it out, you horsecunt!"

"Spooked," Vendurro offered. "They looked spooked. And with good plaguing reason. With Lloi gone, and that rogue witch not being one at all, well. . ."

Mulldoos looked ready to verbally assault him, or me, or even Hewspear, jaw clamped tight, muscles bulging in his thick neck, eyes big and wild, seeming even wilder under those misplaced pale eyebrows. But instead he took out his rage on one of the carved posts, kicking up dust, and moving the bed several inches. If anyone else had been sleeping there, he would have bolted upright. Even a drunk would have at least rolled over and slurred a complaint. But the captain didn't even stir.

"Never thought I'd miss that whore, Lloi. Plague me. Plague him." Mulldoos dropped down on a stool, not caring that it nearly broke with his bulk. For the first time since I'd known him, he didn't sound surly, angry, or argumentative. He sounded defeated.

Eyes still on the captain, Mulldoos asked me, "How long was he out like this? In the grass? Before Lloi finally showed her sorry ass and muddled through helping him?"

It seemed a bad time to state the obvious—that her muddling was the only thing that kept him upright and stopped the troops from questioning his status the last few years. "Not long. A few days? He started showing signs of the sickness earlier though."

Mulldoos looked at Hewspear. "We got no time, and less. Only reason I found the little hellcat was keeping my ears open in every tavern in Alespell. And turned out she still couldn't do shit. Out here. . . " He shook his head. "Grim odds of finding another one out in the wild. Mighty grim."

Hewspear leaned against a faded panel on the wall, the paint chipped and flaking off. He peeled off a strip with long, dark fingers, thinking, and let it fall spiraling to the dusty floor.

Vendurro didn't appear to have any idea how to behave. He stared at the lantern, as if trying to find the answer in its dim honey light.

Already on the wrong side of Mulldoos (was there a right side?), I was reluctant to speak up again, but with no one else shouting out ideas, I felt I had to try. I cleared my throat. No one looked, so I just spoke. "We could tell Soffjian." I thought about what she told me in the wagon. "Or better yet, Skeelana. They might be able to help."

Hewspear seemed to consider it, but then shook his head. "The captain forbade it. Expressly. We'll just have to send men to outlying villages."

Vendurro's shoulders fell a notch. "This is the outlying village. No big settlements out this way. A few other small villages here and there, but the chances of wandering into one just before a hedge witch gets hung? Mulldoos called it—grim and grimmer going."

Mulldoos gave me a long look, his blue eyes too pale to be flinty, but no less hard or unfriendly. The next words out of his mouth shocked me. "Never thought there'd be worse than admitting Hewspear might have the right of something, but this tops it. Scribbler's got the right of it. I told Cap he should've done this back in Alespell. And you did, too, you wrinkled goatcock. Only thing that makes any kind of sense. Especially now that we got no options left."

Hewspear pulled another long strip of paint off the wall and looked at it, balanced on his fingertips. "You know their history. And even discounting that, there are a number of reasons the captain wants to keep the Memoridon beyond arm's length. If we reveal his condition, we risk revealing more. And that we cannot do. Not yet."

I said, "She already suspects he is hiding something."

Hewspear blew the long strip off his hand. "Oh?"

Mulldoos turned on the stool, wincing as pain must have shot up his injured leg. "You talking to Soffjian, you skinny shit? That's ripe, it is. Real plaguing ripe." His hand fell to the falchion on his hip. He looked ready to rise and use it just then. "You trying to work your way up that witch's skirts?"

I shook my head quickly. "No! She doesn't even wear skirts! But no!"

"Real bad idea, trading information to try to bed that witch." Mulldoos drummed his fingers on the hilt. "Like to be a messy end for you, either way."

I forced myself not to take a step back, despite every instinct screaming that was the best idea. "No, it wasn't like that."

"No? The not giving up vital information, or the not trying to wet your dick in the driest hole on earth?"

"What? Neither. I wasn't doing either one." I quickly added, "She cornered me in the barn a little while ago, started asking me questions, about the girl, and Bloodsounder, and—"

Mulldoos rose. "And what'd you tell her, scribbler?" I imagined several other people looked into those same cold eyes just before being sliced open.

"Nothing! I dodged every question and delayed." I looked at Vendurro, "Luckily he came out, and she left before she could get very far. But she already suspects. That's the point I'm getting at."

Mulldoos looked at Vendurro. "That right?"

Vendurro nodded, looking very serious. "Yup. Came in there, just like he said, caught him with his pants down."

I shouted, "What? That isn't true!" I tried to keep the keening edge from my voice as I turned back to Mulldoos. "That isn't true!"

Vendurro laughed. "Nahhh, I'm just pissing on you, Arki. It's true, Lieutenant. Didn't even see her in there. Must have taken off when I come near. Soffjian scares the hardness out of him. Same as me, when it comes down to it. Any sane man. No way was he seeking her out, and he wouldn't have the guts to even think of bedding her, even if she weren't Cap's sister. Which of course she is. Just saying."

Not the most complimentary defense, but I tried to look grateful that he took my side as he went on. "He's telling it straight—went out to fetch that case of his, and got stuck in the wagon with her. Nothing more."

Mulldoos took a step toward me and I realized I was clutching my case tight to my chest. I tried to relax my arms, in case I needed to throw it at him and try to run. For all the good that would do. "So, not trying to get your gems rubbed, but still doling out information. Not sure, but that might be worse."

"I told you, I didn't volunteer anything. She caught me unexpectedly, and I tried to get out of there without looking like I was hiding something."

Mulldoos didn't advance closer, but his hand didn't drop away from his weapon either. "Course you are. Even though we ain't told you much at all, that's ten times more than we want that cold bitch to know. Shouldn't have told her a thing, you skinny prick."

I knew if he attacked I'd likely be dead before I hit the floor, but I was tired of being bullied and humiliated. "I didn't. She doesn't know anything. I said *suspects*. And just a second ago, you were saying we should approach her! Now you're saying we shouldn't trust her?"

"That was before I knew you were meeting in the dark with her."

Vendurro said, "She sought him out, Mulldoos. Not the other way round. And to hear him tell it, he didn't tell her nothing she didn't already know or think she knew."

Mulldoos didn't look especially mollified as he turned on the sergeant. "He been in the company a couple of tendays and you fall in love, Ven? Thought we taught you better than that. Only ones you can trust are your brothers. The rest of the world? Marks, victims, or enemies. Sometimes tools. Which one you think he is?" He jerked a thick thumb in my direction.

Hewspear clicked his tongue on the roof of his mouth. "Arki didn't need to mention meeting Soffjian at all. But he did. And his suggestion, much as I mislike going counter to the captain's orders, is the only one that stands a chance of success. As you yourself proposed before blustering about." He pushed off the wall slowly, nearly peeling himself. "Are we agreed on this then? We invite the Memoridons in, tell them all they need to know, and ask them to help the captain?"

Mulldoos nodded once, fast, grudgingly, still looking as if he'd prefer to cut someone open. Hewspear looked Vendurro's way, and the younger man swallowed hard. "Can't see no other choice. No good one, leastwise. If you're asking me, I say let's do it."

Hewspear nodded. "Very well. Vendurro—find Soffjian or Skeelana." He stared at the prone captain. "And quickly, lad. Quickly."

Vendurro looked as if he'd been asked to stick his hand into a viper's hole and wiggle his fingers, but he gave a quick nod and hurried from the room.

Mulldoos returned to his stool and kept vigil. For all the good it did.

I wished I could have said something to him to change things in my favor—remind him that I helped save the captain's life in the temple, or Hewspear's in the copse, or could have run when we were in Alespell and chose not to, especially after seeing the Hornman I spared. But of course I couldn't. And of course it wouldn't have done any good, even if I had.

If Mulldoos was right—if I was only a tool to the Syldoon, with never a chance to be more than that, then I was a fool to stand up to Soffjian to try to protect them. As it turned out, I was a fool regardless. She could have struck me down without blinking, even if I had good cause. And in the end, it didn't matter. With no other recourse, we were doing the one thing the captain had absolutely forbidden.

Now the only questions were: could she or Skeelana help him, would they, and what would it mean once they had access to the interior of the man?

The group sat in silence like that, watching nothing, waiting for what felt like ages, when there was a soft rap on the door. We all turned as it opened and Vendurro came in first, followed by Soffjian and Skeelana. Despite having no immediate use for it, Soffjian carried her ranseur. I suppose if being among the Syldoon (and now a combat Memoridon) taught me anything, it was that unexpected bloodshed could come at any time and from any quarter. Skeelana, as usual, had the bare minimum armament of a suroka, though on her it seemed a ceremonial weapon, at best. I'm sure I would have looked equally uncomfortable with it on my hip.

Soffjian looked around the room, taking everything and everyone in slowly, and again I was reminded of the way Braylar surveyed a scene or situation, calculating and either pragmatic or cold, depending on how you viewed such detachment. She stopped when she got to me and smiled, though it was hardly warm. "Well, Arkamondos. It seems all your efforts to maintain secrecy were undone anyway. Or will be soon enough. Though I do commend you for the great lengths you went to try to maintain the little charade." Soffjian looked directly at Mulldoos, and whether Vendurro had tipped her off or she was that masterful at gauging temperament, she said, "You should know, clumsy and artless as he was, your young scribe here did his best to reveal nothing of your captain's very unusual condition."

She might as well have been talking to the furniture for all the reaction she got.

Soffjian stuck the butt spike of her ranseur on the floor and gave it a slow spin, setting the tassels flowing like a dancer's skirts, and then she looked at Hewspear. "Vendurro tells me you have need of our services." She glanced at Braylar again, like a battlefield surgeon, determining whether a wound would prove fatal, result in amputation, or perhaps could be treatable. "While I appreciate your rigid brotherhood, tell me what I need to know. Spare no details. Not if you truly want us to save my brother. That is why you summoned us, is it not?"

Hewspear explained it all then, the necessary information at least. If it had been Vendurro briefing her, it would have been the opposite of brief and taken three days, but Hewspear was succinct, including only those critical facets—a pithy account of unearthing Bloodsounder, its peculiar debilitating effects, their thwarted efforts of breaking the bond between weapon and man, enlisting Lloi, her efforts to drain the poisonous memories out, subsequent death, and the failure to find someone else to take her place and help the captain.

Soffjian listened for the most part, asking for a small bit of clarification here, a little elaboration there, and though it all seemed designed to help her better assess his condition and her ability to aid him, having experienced her scrying firsthand, I felt as if her line of questioning served some other purpose as well. Though I couldn't fathom what that might be.

She seemed intrigued by all she heard, but not especially shocked, and only vaguely surprised by some of it.

I looked over at Skeelana once or twice as she sat apart from everyone else, hoping she might somehow reveal something, anything. But she only made eye contact once, and broke it just as quickly. I wondered if I was reading too much into things. Or perhaps not reading enough.

Finally, Soffjian seemed satisfied, and Hewspear had unspooled as much as he intended.

Mulldoos spoke for the first time. "We brought you in to take care of him. No secret I got no love for your kind, but—"

"Really?" Soffjian feigned shock. "I confess I'm as wounded as I am surprised."

"But I figured if some crippled barbarian whore could keep him from going mad, you and yours ought to be able to fix him good. Maybe cure him. Free him. But let me tell you something, witch—"

"Oh, do. Please."

"I watched Lloi tromp around inside him, finding those stolen memories, stealing them back out, so I know how long it took. And she had no real skill. So if I get the feeling you're strolling around seeing the sights, looking at more than exactly what you need, I swear to Truth, I'll cut you into pieces so small they wouldn't choke a rat. You understand?"

He had such a violent presence, and spoke with such horrible conviction, there was no doubting he meant every word, but it did not have the intended effect. Soffjian seemed unfazed. "Your loyalty and desire to protect your captain are both duly noted. But I do believe I take some exception to your tone, Lieutenant. At best, it could result in me simply refusing to aid him at all. At worst, it might invite the wrath of a war Memoridon who can blast you to madness without more than a blink. I'd advise you—and I'll only do so once—to adopt a slightly more congenial manner."

Mulldoos should have been terrified, but to his credit, if he was he completely masked it. "Advise whatever you plaguing want. Warning still stands. Cap didn't trust you to look him over, I sure as hells don't either. But we got no choice. Only do what needs doing. Nothing more."

She could have walked out or struck him down and neither would have surprised me, but after pausing for a few moments, as expressive as a reptile, she said. "Oh, I hear you, Syldoon. Make no mistake. But the memory of a Memoridon does not end. Do remember that."

Soffjian looked Skeelana's way, and the younger woman sprang off her stool and came over. Soffjian put her hand on Skeelana's shoulder. "As I told our anxious scrivener over there, this will require some delicacy. I am not good at delicate."

"Useful at last." While everyone else in the room was wound tight, Skeelana looked like she was ready to jump in a swimming hole on a hot summer day. "What would you have me do?"

"It's just like sifting through memories, searching for the truth. Only, as the good soldiers here have made abundantly clear, we're not looking for his memories. Only foreign matter that does not belong."

Skeelana nodded. "Finding it should be easy enough. But I've never—" She took a deep breath, and it was hard to tell if she was nervous or excited. "I've never extracted anything like that before."

Soffjian smiled, and for once there was some warmth to it. If only a hint. "Well then. You will be making some history. Memoridon history at least. An untrained was already trudging around there, muddying the waters. If she can do it, I'm confident you can manage."

I said, "You'll feel quite nauseous after." Everyone in the room looked at me as if they had completely forgotten I was even a bystander, and I immediately felt the flush in my cheeks. "That is, if previous experience holds true. The stolen memories, they're like poison, and drawing them out, you'll experience a little of what the captain has. But it passes. After you vomit anyway."

Skeelana said, "Why thank you, Arki. So good of you to look out for me. I can't wait to vomit."

Mulldoos snorted. "Got a real way with the lady folk, you do. Real charmer."

Soffjian gave me a look that sent shivers chasing each other across my skin. "Do you have anything *useful* to provide?"

I looked at Hewspear, and then said, "Lloi asked for fluids. Wine, water. But I think that was because she was chanting. Though perhaps just because it was arduous, and she was thirsty. I don't know. But she did want fluid."

"Nothing useful then." She reclaimed Skeelana's attention. "You are a Memoridon of the highest order. While you are attempting something beyond your normal scope, I have no doubt you can perform the task at hand. And without ridiculous chanting. Though if you do grow thirsty, you have only to ask, and Arki will run and fetch you something. Though I wouldn't suggest wine. Nasty coming back up."

Mulldoos laughed, and Soffjian ignored him. "Ready then?"

Skeelana nodded, and while it appeared she tried to stifle a smile, she couldn't mask it completely. She was excited. Almost giddy. "History it is."

There was no chanting, thankfully. And I didn't have to run off to fetch anything. Skeelana didn't even strip the captain's tunic off, or resort to any other primitive parts of the ritual that Lloi had employed. And she didn't take half the night to do what was asked of her either.

She sat on a stool by the captain's side, one hand raised just above his head, eyes closed, face calm for the most part, only occasionally shifting or jerking, as if she felt an unseen needle prick her or swallowed or smelled something foul. But otherwise, it was unremarkable.

No one seemed particularly at ease, but Vendurro least of all, and he excused himself, claiming the need to check on the men. Mulldoos paced a few times until Soffjian hissed at him and told him to be still. He seemed ready to lay into her when Hewspear caught his eye and shook his head, looking at Skeelana and Braylar. Mulldoos scowled but leaned backed against the wall.

It took no more than two hours, though they passed with excruciating slowness. When Skeelana opened her eyes, blinked them quickly, face pale, and announced it was done, Mulldoos leaned forward and asked, "That it? You sure you got it all?"

Soffjian tsked and said, "First, you worry about her dawdling and intruding into whatever horrible secrets my brother is hiding, and now you chide her for working too efficiently? You can't have it both ways, Syldoon."

Just the same, he echoed the question as Skeelana rose unsteadily to her feet. "Yes," she replied. "I did. Though I'm fairly sure this Lloi of yours didn't draw it all out before. Some vestiges were. . . old. Very old." Then she looked at me, growing paler by the moment. "If you'll excuse me now, I do believe I have to expunge something myself." She hurried from the room on wobbly legs, pulling the door shut behind her with a bang.

I heard her taking the stairs two at a time as Braylar roused. While he looked groggy, like a man deprived of sleep who finally was allowed some respite before being woken again, it took him only a moment to register where he was, and more importantly who was in the room with him.

He sat up straight in bed, eyes locked on his sister. She leaned against the wall and smiled. "Welcome back, brother."

Hewspear stood next to the bed and asked, "How do you feel, Captain?"

Whatever fog he had burnt off quickly. Without looking away from his sister, he replied, "I feel as if my loyal lieutenants have once again found it impossible to obey a direct command. I hadn't thought there was much ambiguity with this one. I would love to hear the justification for this latest bit of egregious insubordination. Truly I would. Right after my sister bids farewell."

Before Hewspear or Mulldoos could speak, Soffjian said, "Your men saved your life, Bray. They had misgivings about inviting me into your parlor, you can be sure, but they knew they had exhausted every other possible remedy. You were down and lost in a multitude of memories, none your own. They summoned me. Skeelana healed you. You truly are an awful patient."

"Unless quite a bit transpired while I was lost, Skeelana is still your kind, sister. And therefore, very, very unwelcome in my skull."

"Welcome or no, we saved you. Well, I had very little to do with it, in fact. But Skeelana saved you, and cleaned up quite a bit of debris your little grass fairy missed, despite you cordially inviting her in. I would think some thanks are in order."

Her smugness seemed designed to rile him up. Instead, he asked, quietly. "Why?"

"Why what? Thank us? That seems self-evident."

He shook his head slowly, leaned back against the rickety headboard. "No. Why help me? I know my men disregarded me entirely and entreated you. But why agree? Why help me?" This didn't seem like a gambit or repartee. Braylar looked genuinely puzzled. And distraught.

I expected Soffjian to offer a quip, or something soaked in sarcasm. Instead, she leaned against the wall, composed her response, and said, "Do you recall when the Syldoon came to our island, Bray? When the Sanctuary was. . . disrupted?"

After a long pause he replied, "Of course. What of it?"

"Well, then of course you remember what we saw, what happened there, right in front of us."

Braylar pushed off the headboard, back rigid, eyes bloodshot slits. But he kept his voice level. "There aren't enough years to be had to forget such things. I do hope you are arriving at something resembling a point."

Soffjian stared at him, or through him. "Oh, I believe, even muddled as you are, you know what point I am getting at. Unless you have somehow forgotten the vow you made after."

Mulldoos and Hewspear gave each other a curious look as their captain replied, "A vow was made. By a foolish, grief-damaged boy. Driven to greater heights of foolishness by his sister. What of it?"

She gave a cold smile. "Revenge was yours by right. I would have stood a better chance of pulling it off, truly. But not having a cock, that proved problematic. So I aided you, counseled you, helped you plan it—"

"Helped me botch it. One stupid child counseling another."

"Children or not, you swore over the body of our father, swore before our ancestors and gods—"

"That is why they call it a vow."

"Swore it would be done. You would kill the killer and then bring down their whole empire. Something melodramatic and impractical like that if memory serves."

Mulldoos slapped his good leg and laughed. "You really say that, Cap?"

Braylar snapped, "I did indeed. As idiot children are wont to do."

"You were a child," Soffjian said, "but a vow made is a vow made, isn't it? Only, you never fulfilled it. And a tenyear later, you swore a different vow, didn't you? To those selfsame fuckers who murdered our father."

Braylar said, "To the Tower. There is a distinction here. What—?"

"Oh, but you're all murderers at heart, aren't you? So, two vows, one to your kin alive and dead, the other to the bastards that abducted you. I was there for both, if you recall."

"Impossible to forget," Braylar replied. There seemed to be more meaning freighted to this, but I didn't know the import.

"And several years later, forced to choose between the two, you opted to keep the one made to the conquerors and plunderers. The murderers with nooses. Isn't that right?"

Mulldoos looked confused. "Cap, is she talking—"

"I did my duty, Soffjian," Braylar said, ignoring Mulldoos.

"To your new brothers. Your adopted kin. Yes. But to me, our father, our homeland, that vow, that promise, it no longer had meaning to you. Did you mean it, even back then? Right after our father had a blade buried in his stomach, did you mean it then?"

Braylar's teeth barely parted as he spoke, a throaty rasp. "You healed me, sister, or played a role. For that, I have an unfortunate debt. But that won't stop me from striking you down the second it is repaid."

She continued as if she hadn't heard him. "Who would hold a man to a vow he made as an enraged child, ancestors as witnesses or no? But it isn't solely father. You had a chance to save our people, Bray, and you failed. You chose your new murderous brethren over true kin."

"And you overstate and overheat things, as you've always done. I followed my Tower Commander's orders. Honored my vows. Nothing more. There was no opportunity to save anyone. Our people, who, I remind you, I hadn't seen in fifteen years, and were strangers to me—they doomed themselves."

"Your Tower Commander sought your counsel. And you sought mine before giving it. Exactly as you did when preparing your plan of vengeance so very many, many years ago. Only this time, you chose to ignore it."

"I told my Commander what he needed to know, Soff. All for the

Empire. You remember so much with perfect clarity. Save that. We are Empire now. You, me. Everyone in this room. There is no going back."

Soffjian leaned forward, looking every bit as predatory as her brother normally did. "You rejected your homeland, your ancestors, your people. Tell yourself whatever serves as a salve but do not pretend you did what you could for them. You could have persuaded the Tower Commander to a different course of action."

"I did what I could. This is ancient history, and has nothing to do with the now."

Soffjian gripped the haft of her ranseur in both hands, knuckles growing white. "You asked me why I helped you."

"Which you failed to clarify. Utterly."

"I swore an oath to my captors as well. To the same Commander. And part of that vow was to keep you alive at all costs."

He gave a half-smile, or the twitchy resemblance to one. "Commendable. See how rewarding maintaining your vows can be?"

Soffjian moved away from the bed. "But know this, brother. I, too, have another vow. Grounded in the fervor for Tower and Empire you conveniently espouse. And if a time comes when my pledge to keep you alive is superseded, and I am no longer restrained, you can be sure I will marshal my hate for you into action. I will not hesitate in the slightest to do so. I will ruin you. And *that* will be truly rewarding,"

The muscles in Braylar's arms were corded from keeping him upright, and he trembled ever so slightly with the strain. "I stand warned. Well, recline warned, really. But many thanks, just the same."

Soffjian marched out of the room, leaving a daunting silence in her wake. I had a hundred questions, none of which I could ask. Hewspear and Mulldoos seemed to be steadying themselves for the verbal lashing they expected.

For his part, the captain settled back against the chipped headboard, breathing fast, face flushed, fingers digging into the mattress as if he hoped to claw the straw out, his eyes still on the door.

It felt as if we were frozen in a frieze, time passed so slowly. I expected someone to clear his throat or announce something, but the silence seemed to have been almost spell-woven, it was so resolute and powerful.

Finally, Braylar said, to everyone and no one, "You have doomed me. You know this, yes?"

Hewspear looked at both of us before saying, "Captain, we were simply out of options. You had sunk too deep. That was doom, doom we couldn't afford. So—"

"Do you suspect my sister will simply forget this happened? What she discovered? She is a Memoridon. Bloodsounder. Memory magic. Memoridon. And one who seethes to see me undone. But this is larger than me. If Skeelana has divined our secondary purpose in this region, and reports it to my sweet sister, that, too will be cut short. Everything we've accomplished here, and hope to, undone." He released the mattress, flexed his fingers.

"Got to say, Cap," Mulldoos replied, "Borderline ungrateful, really. We disobeyed you, aye, but Skeelana saved your—"

"Larger. It is larger. Out. The lot of you. And send someone up with some ale. Any ale will do. Just so long as the man who brings it isn't one of you. Or I will be in need of my sister's help again. And that I simply can't stomach."

Though his words lacked the usual volume and venom, there was no mistaking the absolute truth in them.

Everyone filed out without another word. I was the last, and stopped at the door, turned around to ask whether he wanted it closed or not. Braylar was staring at Bloodsounder, the chains spread on the bed next to him, one of the heads of the Deserter Gods tipped so it appeared to be staring back at him. Or would have been, if it hadn't had spikes extending in place of eyes.

I closed the door quickly, shivering, as if I had just seen an apparition. Though it was hard to say whether the man or the weapon seemed more haunted, saved or no.

I crept down the stairs as quietly as possible. The ground floor was dark except for a few tapers here or there still barely glowing, and most of the men had claimed rooms from the looks of it, or left to bunk down in one of the nearby houses, but there were still some forms on the common room floor. Hewspear and Mulldoos were nowhere to be seen, so I assumed they must have left already. Which was all for the best. Bumping into Mulldoos in the dark was only marginally better than being crept up on by Soffjian.

The stairs were worn smooth and indented where traffic over the years had been heaviest, but even stepping elsewhere, the boards creaked and groaned as if they were designed to wake everyone sleeping within one hundred feet. Still, I managed to get to the bottom without disturbing anyone, but I wasn't ready to go to sleep. I navigated through the room without too much trouble, though I did nearly trip over someone's foot before finally making it out the door.

Outside, the night air was cold, and I clutched the writing case tight, hunched my shoulders, shivered, and started walking, unsure what my plan was. There were some blankets in the wagon in the barn and I briefly considered heading there, if not for the night, at least until I cleared my head. But my last visit there hadn't gone all that well, so I kept going.

Even with the moon and its ring flaring brightly in the mostly cloudless sky, and the stars out in force, the village and the world around was as close to complete darkness as you could imagine. The fact that it was utterly deserted except for our small troop made it all the stranger. Lost in the Green Sea, there was a sense of desolation, hopelessness I never imagined I could repeat in any remotely populated area. But here, with all of the trappings of civilization but none of the population, it was somehow even lonelier.

I was feeling forlorn and frankly sorry for myself when I thought I saw a silhouetted figure standing in a small lane between two houses. It took my eyes a moment to adjust, but there was no mistaking it—I wasn't alone. There was a figure there, still as a scarecrow, where no scarecrow could possibly be. My heart started beating like a rabbit's, and I cursed myself for leaving Lloi's sword in the wagon, even if I was just as likely to hurt myself with it as anyone else. An assailant might not know that.

The voice almost made me unleash my bladder. "You were right. About the vomit. And I'm glad I didn't have any wine. I think. Though that might have dulled the sensations a little, it wouldn't have improved the taste at all."

I breathed easier and started to walk forward, but then thought better of it. Perhaps Skeelana wanted to be alone. "How are you? I mean, I know you're not well. Based on seeing someone do what you did before. What they did before. Not you. Since you hadn't. Done it before, that is." Mulldoos was right—I was a charmer. "How are you?"

"Aside from spewing my guts out, you mean?" She laughed, though I suspected at least partially forced. "Well. Thank you. And you're right—I've never done anything like that before. And hope never to again. Finding those memories, of the men he killed with that thing? That took the most time, but was the easiest part of it really. Taking them into myself though, ridding him of them. That. . . " I couldn't see her face. She paused, and possibly shuddered, though it could have been a trick of the night. "That was painful. And difficult. Every part of me rebelled against doing it. I've taken memories from someone before, but they were always his own. Completely different. These. . . the woman in your company described it as poison, right? And that is accurate, to a point, but. . . "

It hung there for a bit, and then I did approach closer and lowered my voice. "But?"

"But, it was more than that. Worse than that."

I almost didn't want to know. "How so?"

After pausing again, Skeelana said, "Poison is dangerous, deadly even, but natural. It isn't malicious. But those memories? They were unnatural, but more than that. And not just the fact they were foreign, and didn't belong, though that accounted for some of it. But some residue of some-thing. . . worse. A taint of some kind."

I was confused. "A taint? Of what?"

"Bloodsounder. The captain didn't steal those memories. The weapon did. And there was some malice, or maybe worse, involved. It's hard to describe, and even saying it out loud. . . "

She searched for the right words and shook her head. "Preposterous. It sounds preposterous, I know." Skeelana sounded tired, and somewhat spellbound as well, as if she'd been walking up the stairs of an incredibly tall tower, trapped in a dizzying spiral, exerting herself to the fullest, only to reach a landing and look out over an expansive, and perhaps terrifying, landscape. "Being bombarded by those memories, incredibly intimate reminders from the men he killed. It was like talking with ghosts. But even that isn't quite right. There was something about each memory I absorbed from Killcoin, took on myself. It was as if I could feel Bloodsounder behind me. And it was. . ." She shook her head. "I know how ridiculous it sounds. But there was rage, a silent rage there. The flail didn't want me to drain those memories from him. It would have fought me off if it could have. It wanted to."

She looked at me, the rings in her nose and ears catching the moonlight, and I could feel her searching, measuring my reaction, tense, as if expecting me to laugh or call her a fool. Instead, I was trying to decide which questions I could ask while I had the chance, without taxing her too much. "Soffjian didn't look as. . . surprised as I would have guessed. When Hewspear and the others described what had befallen or bedeviled the captain. In fact, and this might not be generous, she seemed as if the words confirmed something she already knew or suspected. This isn't the first time Memoridons have encountered something like this, is it?"

Skeelana didn't reply right away, and I was afraid I'd overstepped, but she didn't curse me or so many of the things everyone else seemed inclined to do when I started asking questions, so I took that as a good sign. Finally, after looking around to be sure no one had crept up on us in the dark, she said, "Not like this. Not exactly. But we have discovered weapons of a similar nature before. Only they didn't quite. . . work."

"Work? You mean, they weren't cursed?"

"I'm not sure cursed is the right word. My sense—and I fully admit, I could be wrong—but I think Bloodsounder does exactly what it was intended to. Only we don't understand what that is. But I'm not sure inflicting damage on the wielder, or punishing him, or cursing him, is any part of it. I just think we don't know exactly what it does, or why.

But it does function. It does work. And that we haven't seen before. Not like this."

I recalled the edge in Soffjian's voice as she asked her questions, quickly, but precisely too. It wasn't anxiety. It was excitement. "She wants to study it, doesn't she?"

"Of course she does. Why wouldn't she? This is the first weapon we've seen that actually bonded."

"Well," I replied, framing my words carefully, "I can see that, from your perspective, this would be a find of some kind. But I suspect the captain doesn't particularly welcome the idea of being studied or experimented on."

Skeelana seemed genuinely surprised. "Perhaps not. But cursed or not, it grieves him, and might be doing far worse. I went in to do one thing, which I did. Mulldoos looked really eager to chop someone in half with that cleaver of his. So I got in and out. But if we can unravel how it works, we can probably show him how to use Bloodsounder, rather than the other way around. At least, there's a chance we could. But we would need to study it."

"And him."

"And him. The bond. Yes."

I leaned against a gate that seemed unlikely to support my weight for long. "You mentioned Bloodsounder had awareness of a kind. And hostility. You said it would have rebuffed you if it could. What if *it* doesn't particularly welcome any attempts at unraveling?"

She gave that thought and replied, "Aware or not, it is an object. And it can be manipulated. All objects can be manipulated. This might just be trickier, is all."

"Perhaps. But the captain? He is not likely to sit still for any manipulation, no matter what kind of rhetoric you couch it in."

She nodded slowly. Then, either tired or sad or both, she replied, "He might not have much choice."

I thought about that. And the night suddenly got much colder.

Skeelana seemed to feel it as well, and hugged herself. "You should get some rest, Arki. We'll be leaving early, I imagine. Captain Killcoin might begrudge us helping him, but I'd wager he feels better now than he has since he first picked Bloodsounder up. Night."

She turned and headed back toward the house I assumed she was sharing with Soffjian. I wanted to call out something as well, but the moment was past, and she was swallowed up in the night.

I headed back toward the inn, wondering at the wisdom of mentioning Soffjian to Braylar's men, encouraging them to solicit her aid. Skeelana had doubtless helped him, maybe even saved him. And probably more cleanly than Lloi had ever managed.

But calculating the cost was something else altogether.

As Skeelana predicted, Braylar didn't waste any time the next morning rousing his troops before dawn. It felt like I'd barely closed my eyes, and every muscle seemed stiff. Even the bowed and beaten beds in most road inns were preferable to the cold ground. But I wasn't about to stumble about in the dark and check rooms for occupants. And there was something that just seemed more. . . plaguish. . . about a bed in this village. So uncomfortable floor it was.

I rinsed my face in water, rubbed my eyes, grabbed the nuts and dried fruit that was offered, and followed the other Syldoon out, noting that they were grumbling a bit as well, even as inured to such things as they were. That helped. A little.

The wagons had already been brought out of the barns, and no one risked a sharp rebuke from a commanding officer by dawdling. Horses were saddled immediately, and it didn't take long before our small company was on the move again, me sitting in the wagon, Braylar on the bench at the front, and the rest of the Syldoon riding.

I lifted the canvas flap and looked out the back as the village behind us was suddenly completely deserted again. While I'd never considered myself bound to one spot, I'd done more traveling in the last two tendays than I had in most of my life prior. Even leaving a plague-ridden dead village gave me a slight pang.

As the wagon jostled over the rutted and uneven road, pots and pans and tools and every other thing that could possibly swing from a hook oscillating wildly, I was about to find the spot where I was least likely to get banged in the head from something when Braylar called me to the front of the wagon.

I made my way forward, arms up to ward off blows, and still managed to slam my shin into a crate as I pulled the canvas flap back and awkwardly dropped myself onto the front bench.

The captain didn't speak right away. I wondered if one of his men had told him I suggested Soffjian tend to him, or that I met her in private (well, got cornered with no one around at least), and fully expected him to verbally or physically assault me in either case. Hazarding a look in his direction, I was almost shocked to see just how calm he was. And not like he had been as he receded from himself in the steppe, growing more and more distant, a forced placidity that left him essentially a husk. This was something else. I'd seen him appear bitter, angry, measuring, enraged, witnessed him issue hard orders and biting rejoinders, and sarcastic assessments, all with an excess of vigor and indulgence. But now, he looked. . . thoughtful. I'd only met one or two men who might have been smarter in my life—instructors at university—but while Braylar did a great deal of thinking, it still always seemed to be pulsing with intense and critical energy, calculation just preceding violence of some kind. Or crafty consideration before delivering a charade any playhouse actor would be proud of.

But not meditative thought. And certainly not after returning to the land of the living the night before to discover that a Memoridon had been walking in his skull. The unwound quiet was more disturbing than any tempestuous rampage would have been.

I broke the silence. "Are you feeling well, Captain?"

He didn't respond immediately. I was about to ask again, wondering if maybe I'd been wrong and he was in danger of slipping into himself when he said, "I've had another person moving about inside me, who I didn't trust in the slightest, in league with the person I might trust the least, and with no permission granted from me, either expressly or even obliquely. How do you imagine I feel?"

The tone didn't dovetail with the language at all. Any other time, this would have been delivered with a hint of rancor and ridicule. But it was still eerily calm.

"I can't even begin to imagine how you feel, Captain. I suppose that's why I asked."

I cursed myself the moment the words were out. But he turned his head my way and replied, "You do have the right of it. You couldn't fathom it. Betrayed and violated, not only with my men's knowledge, but their provocation and approval. And yours, of course. Don't think for a moment I'm not aware of the part you played."

The urge to look away was strong—at the horses' asses, my feet, the woods on either side of the track—anywhere or at anything besides my accuser's face. But that would only compound whatever guilt he was assigning. "Captain, it was the only recourse we—"

"No, no. There are always options, Arki. Sometimes the choice is between two equally detestable options, but there is never only one recourse."

"Very well. In that case, there wasn't enough time to find another Lloi. The choice was let you rot or invite your sister into the room."

"It was not simply my life hanging in the balance, scribe." Braylar lifted his hand, and drummed one finger on his temple as he looked at me. "There is information here—that I don't expect you to be aware of—that could damn not only me and my men should it fall into the wrong hands, but our entire Tower. And more besides. There is more at stake than my sanity or even life." He looked back to the road. Well, the Syldoon riding on it ahead of us, more precisely. "Never fear, I don't blame you. Much. As I said, you couldn't be expected to know just what a terribly incriminating and costly move it could be inviting a Memoridon to tromp around in my memories, yes? But Mulldoos? Hewspear? Vendurro?" Still very calm, he shook his head. "They put everything at risk. Everything we hold dear and fight for, at least."

I tried to find a compelling rebuttal and opted for the most direct one. "They saved your life."

"Yes. Yes, they did. For the moment. But they could have signed all of our death decrees in the process."

"Would you rather we'd let you wither and die?"

I expected masterful obfuscating or an abrupt change in topics, but instead he replied, "No. Far too much was risked, and very possibly for naught if we are all hung without reprieve when we return to the capital. But in truth, I am not ready to die yet. A coward's confession, but there it is." He still possessed the strange calm. Which was nearly as disquieting as his bald honesty.

Figuring I had only a moment or two before he recovered and assumed his normal slippery mantle, I asked, "After Skeelana was done, and your sister confronted you, what was she talking about?"

He didn't respond right away and I sat there mute as we rolled along. But he still seemed placid, which was peculiar, and the silence wasn't as oppressive as it had been in the past. I thought about a different line of questioning, but waited. Braylar looked up and watched some squirrels chittering on the branches above us, not happy to have whatever squirrelly business they were on interrupted by a small caravan. Braylar pointed out a black squirrel. "My tribe. The Vorlu. They put a great deal of stock in omens, believing the natural world will give you signs if you are smart enough to pay attention. Observing a black squirrel, for instance, was supposed to portend good luck. And like most superstitious primitives, they were sorely mistaken."

Braylar paused, and I thought maybe that was designed to dry up conversation, but then he sighed deep and long and said, "I was a boy, and had seen twelve winters. Ice cracked, spring rains came, and with spring, the Syldoon returned to the tribelands. Every three years, they came to our islands, and the tribes sent some of their children willingly with the Syldoon. Hewspear has gone on at interminable length about this Syldoon tradition, yes?"

I nodded and he continued, "On our island, the Syldoon arrived in the spring, a few weeks after thaw. They sent word to our tribe, as well as the Zundovu, the Bandovar, and others in the area, and we were invited to Sanctuary."

"Hewspear mentioned this. What is that exactly?"

"A very pedestrian and unoriginal name for the meeting between the Syldoon and the tribes. Any hostilities between the tribes—and there was always some, as we were constantly raiding each other's lands—the hostilities were called off with a temporary truce. The meeting took place at a camp in neutral territory, where everyone would consort, trade goods, reintroduce themselves."

I said, "Something of a fair, then?"

"On a very modest scale, yes. The site was between villages, so nothing like the festivals you see in places like Alespell. No jugglers or stilt-walkers, menageries or rippers. No huge crowds. Mostly, Sanctuary was designed to foster good relations between the Syldoon and the tribals. Which it did, for the most part."

I thought back about the piecemeal information I'd gleaned when they were talking the night before—really, all I knew was that his father was murdered somehow. "So, even though the tribes you mentioned fought constantly—"

"Frequently."

"Frequently, then. Even with the warring going on, or raiding, they honored the truce? Did fighting ever break out at Sanctuary?"

Braylar was still looking up at the trees. "On rare occasion. While we would steal each other's sheep and murder anyone who tried to stop us, there was still some etiquette observed. Sanctuary was sanctuary."

"So," I tried to imagine all these barbarians agreeing not to massacre each other for a day, "did all the tribes attend unarmed then? I'm assuming the Syldoon didn't?"

"Tribal warriors were allowed to bear one weapon only—we would sooner cut our cocks off than be completely disarmed—but they had to be bound by a peace cord."

"A what?"

He glanced at me and smiled, devoid of derision and remarkably free of twitches. "I do forget sometimes where you come from. It is a leather thong on a scabbard that was looped around the hilt. A peace cord hinders the drawing of a blade, especially in a moment of anger. It was used during tribal weddings, funerals, treaties, surrenders. And Sanctuary. That was my first one. My father took us. Soff and me. It would be my last as well."

I hesitated to ask the next question, but seeing how generous he was with information, I pressed on. "So your father was a warrior?"

"Ha! No. Not even reluctantly." Braylar took a deep breath, released it out his nose. He looked pensive, but still not as irritated as I expected. "I don't know if any of us know our fathers well. We often see them as less or more than they really are. I knew he was fat. I knew he was soft in our discipline, often deferring to our mother. He liked bees and honey. He was a good breeder of sheep, and could play the flute with moderate success. He brewed very fine mead, but rarely drank, despite the often-flushed face and broken blood vessels in his nose.

"And I knew he would rather do anything but fight. This last colored everything else in my eyes. The Vorlu is a warrior culture. A man is judged on how well he wields a sword or a spear, how many raids he has been on. A man who does these things well is glorified in song and poem, his exploits recorded to be celebrated, and a man who does them exceptionally well is remembered in exceptional songs that are sung for eternity. A man who fights poorly might still be valued in the tribe for his husbandry, craftsmanship, knowledge of the law, what have you. But he'll never be glorified, and even if he's gifted beyond measure at what he strives at, he'll be forgotten. Quickly."

"Your father, then?" I asked.

"In my eyes, my father was a weak man, a frightened man. I didn't value him. He taught us how to swing a sword or strike with a spear, but with little enthusiasm and less skill. I was embarrassed for my father. And for myself. And so, being a foolish boy who failed to appreciate what he had, I routinely mocked him, and did everything to incur his wrath, which rarely showed, despite my best efforts.

"Still," he said, with a sweep of his hand, as if wiping away an unpleasant memory, "I was excited to be going to a Sanctuary with him. And when I saw a black squirrel on the way there and pointed it out, my father laughed and said the day promised good things indeed. The morning was cold, the ground colder, but the sun was out, and many of the Vorlu attended, eager to see what goods the foreigners brought this year, glad to be able to venture out after huddling around fires for so many months. The camp was small—several pavilions, a few wagons, little else. But it wasn't the size that made an impression, it was the inhabitants. For most tribals, their birthplace is their death place, their lives lived and lost in a ten mile radius. But at Sanctuary, we were exposed to grand foreigners, soldiers who had once been as we were, tribals, but who now traveled across seas, roamed over continents, conquering and trading and exerting their influence in countries far and wide in ways we could not possibly imagine."

"Were they so very different in appearance?"

"Oh, yes. Some fair skinned, with ruddy cheeks and beards like bird nests, who shaved their heads from the crown back but braided the front down along their ears. Men with skin like dark clay who pierced their faces and carved runes into their cheeks. A few who shaved their entire bodies, arms, head, eyebrows, and dyed their ears yellow."

I thought about the Syldoon in his company, a mixed group to be sure, but without any wild flourishes. "But your own crew—?"

"Ahh, yes, picked in part to appear innocuous, yes? These Syldoon at Sanctuary were chosen to awe with the wild diversity."

"You'd seen them before though? The Syldoon?"

"As I said, they came every three years. But they never failed to impress. Many of the Syldoon were similar to my own people, swarthy and dark-haired like the Vorlu, but others clearly hailed from distant lands and climes, with a wild variety of skin tones, physiques, and features. In that respect, it was the greatest menagerie in the world. And my first Sanctuary was the first opportunity to see them up close.

"Our father pointed out the Syldoon commander, a small man with gray eyes and cropped hair. He was squatting in front of a map and glanced up as the tribes filed into the encampment, but made no other sign of recognition.

"Tables and benches were laid out with Syldoon wares on top of them. Wineskins and fantastic bottles made of colored glass—blue, brown, green, red. I had never seen the like before. Bolts of cloth as strange and foreign as the races that wove them. Stirrups. Sharp fruit that looked like misshapen purple stars. Pungent spices in tiny bleached boxes. All things from lands we had never seen before, designed to awe and amaze. Which they did, provincial barbarians that we were."

I asked, "Did the tribes bring their own wares?"

"Yes. We had nothing the Syldoon hadn't seen before, of course, but tradition is tradition. Scabbards and belts, boots lined with marten fur. Sealskin cloaks. Jugs of mead. Combs carved from bone. Torcs of silver and gold. Harps, flutes. Quivers decorated with shells and antler. And my father with his honey."

He said this last bit with an edge, but it slipped away as he continued.

"The Syldoon and the tribes greeted each other as dogs do, warily, unsure what the relationship might be. The tribes eyed each other suspiciously, the Syldoon looked on with closed expressions. A few greetings were spoken, without warmth. But slowly the haggling began. And with each bid and counter bid, even those requiring an interpreter, the tension seemed to disappear. Our father approached a man with large ears who he seemed to know. There were reserved smiles on both parts. The man exchanged a few words with our father and then lifted a crate of lemons, which I had never seen before. My father pulled a clay jar of honey out of his satchel, and both began examining the other's wares, chatting like morning birds. I had no interest in fruit, odd or no, and still less in honeycombs, so I turned away to see what else I could see."

He took his eyes off the branches overhead, no longer interested in squirrels of any color.

"I walked toward a table crowded with colored bottles. Soff moved off to inspect some of the rich cloth. I was holding a small vial the color of swamp water in my hand when I heard something in my father's voice that caused me to turn around."

While his eyes were open, it still felt as if the captain were almost narrating one of the stolen memories, living or reliving it in excruciating detail, even though this day must have happened decades ago.

"There was a young Syldoon," he said, "standing between my father and Lemonman—short, patchwork stubble on his face, dark of hair and eye. The young Syldoon looked angry, my father looked confused. The Syldoon swore, stepped closer to my father and knocked the clay jar out of his hands. It hit the dead grass and didn't break. Lemonman yelled the younger Syldoon's name—Slinger—and said something else I couldn't make out. My father bent over to pick the jar up. The young Syldoon kicked the jar away before my father could reclaim it, and this time it hit a rock and cracked. Honey began oozing into the dirt. My father looked up at the Syldoon, shook his head sadly, and took a step to grab the jar. The Syldoon grabbed my father's sleeve and pulled on it hard enough that my father almost lost his balance.

"Lemonman cursed the younger Syldoon, pointed toward their encampment, yelled something else, and my father straightened up, red-faced. The Syldoon flipped his cloak back and reached for his sword, and my father's eyes grew wide and then he fumbled for his. Not being a martial man, he would have been doomed even had he drawn his blade, even against a clearly drunken opponent, but he never got the chance. My father grabbed the hilt and pulled, but the peace cord was still tied and the sword didn't move. But the young Syldoon had no such problems."

"He didn't have his cord tied?" I asked, and silently cursed myself, afraid any interruption would still him.

"No," he replied. "He did not. The bastard's blade slid free clean, flashed in the morning sun, and disappeared in my father's belly. My father stared down in disbelief.

"It's said that when some events occur, time stops. This moment was such a moment for me. Every detail—the mud on the hem of the Syldoon's cloak, the stitching on my father's satchel, the stillness of the air, the skeletal bareness of the trees in the distance, the yellow grass at their feet—all in my mind now as if I saw it this morning. In this way, the moment does last forever. But on that day, it didn't, and time eventually returned, and chaos with it.

"I screamed, the Lemonman stepped back, his crate upended on the ground next to the broken jar, his hands waving in the air in front of him as if he could ward off what he was witnessing, I heard Soff wail, though I didn't see from where. I wanted to grab a bottle off a table, to smash it and grind it in the Syldoon's face, I wanted to run to my father, I wanted to run away, to do something, anything. But I couldn't. I stood there, watched as the Syldoon pulled his sword out of my father's belly, transfixed as my father dropped to his knees and fell forward, hand still on the hilt of his sword. I listened to the screaming, absently wondering if it was mine. And then my uncle Sirk moved past me, sword in hand, walking slowly, deliberately, heading toward the boy who had just stabbed his brother. And he looked like he belonged on a frieze himself—his face and eyes were stone."

"He was a warrior, I take it."

"You apprehend well. A vicious bastard in most ways, but a warrior of the highest order, to be certain. Another Syldoon soldier saw him coming, unlooped his sword and stepped in his path. Neither said a word. Sirk appraised the man, and then threw a blow from the high guard position, but it was a feint, and the blade whipped back down and to the right, cutting deep into the man's exposed left leg. Before the Syldoon could even cry out the sword reversed directions, up and to the left again, slashing across the inside of the sword arm, cutting cloth, flesh, bone.

"The Syldoon dropped his sword and fell to the ground, unsure which wound to hold, and my uncle walked past him. Another Syldoon with a two-handed axe moved forward to intercept. He told Sirk to sheathe his sword but my uncle ignored him. Seeing his comrade dispatched so quickly, the soldier didn't wait for Sirk to act. He closed in and delivered a blow straight down that, had it connected, would have split my uncle in two. But it didn't. My uncle stepped to left and as the axe cleaved air, then moved forward."

He tapped me on the lower stomach and made me jump. "The point of Sirk's sword entered just above the man's right hip and came out the other side. The soldier screamed and looked at his side dumbly. Sirk planted his left palm on the Syldoon's chest and pushed him off his sword as he pulled it free. The man collapsed and curled into a ball and Sirk stepped over him as if he were a pile of steaming shit he didn't want to risk soiling his shoes on, eyes focused on the man who had slain his brother. I had never witnessed my uncle in battle before, only having heard stories, but they had utterly failed to capture exactly how efficient, purposeful, and economical he was."

He said this as if he wasn't aware how neatly this assessment applied to himself.

"A trebuchet was no less awesome to behold in its controlled fury and mechanical purpose. My uncle imparted little to me, but he told me once that many men rage and scream during combat in the hopes of bolstering their abilities or devastating their foes' courage, but the finest warriors were those who reined in emotion, who acted only with clean technique and clear purpose. So, in my mind, in that brief moment when he continued on so coldly as if he were walking alone in the woods, I imagined the entire Syldoon army advancing on Sirk, one man at a time, each of them dispatched with as little wasted movement as possible as he made his way casually to his revenge, and I laughed, laughed out loud like a man bereft of sense. And while I had several reasons to hate the man, for that single moment, I loved him.

"But then four more Syldoon moved to impede my uncle, swords raised, and the spell was broken. They demanded he disarm but he continued forward as if deaf. I saw two Vorlu run over to help him, and some Zundovu untied their peace cords to join the fray as well, although who they were going to attack I couldn't guess. I grabbed a blue bottle then, too late, and ran to help my uncle and my father if I could."

Quietly, I said, "But you didn't make it."

"But I didn't make it," he agreed. "I heard a bowstring hum and an arrow sprouted from the back of my uncle's leg. He made a sound that I can only call a growl and spun around, still holding his bloody sword. I looked back to where the arrow had come from. The Syldoon commander was standing on a table, five archers beneath him, composite bows drawn, arrows nocked.

"The commander shouted, 'Drop your weapons. All of you.' All around the encampment tribals and Syldoon were armed and ready to kill each other. Sirk looked at the commander, looked at the archers, spat, and turned to face the Syldoon in front of him again. He took another step, dragging his wounded leg, and another arrow appeared in his lower back. He started to fall forward, planted his sword in the dirt and laid his weight on the pommel, holding the hilt with both hands. The sword bent but didn't break.

"Soffjian ran over and stood between Sirk and the archers, covering his body with her own. The commander called out again, 'I won't say it a third time. Anyone who doesn't obey will be shot. Drop your weapons.'"

"And did they?"

"It would have resulted in a bloodbath that cut my life short otherwise. Slowly people lowered their blades, slid them into scabbards. Sirk's sword bent under him and snapped. Soff tried to grab him as he fell, but she wasn't strong enough and he slumped over onto the ground. I ran over to them, realizing only after I got there that I still held the glass bottle stupidly in my hand. I dropped it and knelt next to them. His breathing was labored. There was a growing circle of blood around each arrow. Soff cradled his head in her lap and cried.

"I heard the commander again. 'Vorlu, Zundovu, Bandovar. Return home. Return to your homes now. This Sanctuary is over.' I looked over at my father, started to rise to go to him. He was motionless on his belly, head turned sideways. It's often said that a gut wound is the worst kind. A man stabbed or shot by a bolt or arrow in the belly could linger for hours, even days, experiencing the most awful suffering imaginable, overtaken by fever, begging for death to claim him or his comrades to finish him off. But there are rare exceptions. Men who survive. Men who die quick. My father might not have been dead when he hit the ground, but something inside was cut deep, and he died fast, his eyes still very much open. And I sat down and wept harder than I have in my entire life as my dead father stared at me."

He stopped for a moment, hitch-laughed, and said, "So much for black squirrels, eh?"

I didn't know how to respond, or if he even expected one. So after sitting silently for a while, I asked "So the vow, the first one Soffjian mentioned, that was—"

"Made later."

It seemed curt and succinct was returning to claim its seat. "Did you vow. . . to avenge your father? That's what it sounded like she was talking about."

"My people have five categories of death. Muli: The accidental death. A child eating poison mushrooms, a man mistaking his foot for firewood and bleeding out in snow. Droos: The natural death. A man dying under the weight of his years, a woman dying in childbirth. Nince: The elemental death. Drowning. Fire. Lightning. Vali: The glory death. Men dying in raids, in personal combat, defending their cattle. And Buntu: Murder. My father being stabbed."

"But. . . " I stopped myself.

He looked over at me, the familiar irritated expression also finding its way home. "Yes?"

"Well, perhaps there's some nuance there I'm not familiar with, but wouldn't your father be 'vali,' as it was personal combat?" His expression darkened, and I unhelpfully added, "Of sorts?"

Braylar gave me a look that could have skinned pelts from flesh. "Personal combat is a duel, or a fight on a battlefield, or even the madness of a raid, between two armed men who know the stakes and willingly enter into the melee or pursue a foe. When one man draws a weapon attempting to kill the other, and the other, inept and hopeless, tries unsuccessfully to defend himself, it is not combat. But murder. Buntu.

"And it's said that of the five deaths, only Buntu isn't tolerated by the gods, for it's the only one they haven't foreseen. The father, brother, or son of a man murdered must avenge this kind of death, or they're almost as guilty as the man who murdered. Murder unavenged is called the Twice Murder—Bunturu—as it's considered twice as heinous and appalling to ancestors and gods alike, and so to the living.

"My uncle tried and was cut down. My sister was forbidden from trying. And while I was considered too young, not yet a man, I was the only one to stand between Buntu and Bunturu. That is why my sister goaded me into making my vow."

"She also said—"

He slapped the bench. "Enough. You have a job to do, it is high time you set to it."

I nodded, thinking he meant for me to record the most recent events, and started to rise when he asked, "At the worst possible moment, no questions?"

I froze, uncertain.

"Are you not going to ask what job I am referring to?"

I sat back down, unsure what he was playing at. "Uh, what job are you referring to?"

"There is a reason why you are in the wagon with me. And why the crates of mysterious parchments have been moved here as well."

Comprehension was sometimes the slowest dawn of all. "The crates?"

"You have done an admirable job recording thus far, but that, as you now know, is only half your job. Translation is the other and unquestionably more vital and valuable half." He pulled a small brass key from a belt pouch. "You are familiar with the first crate, I believe?"

I felt a surge of excitement and nodded quickly, taking the key.

"Very good. We have a day's ride before we arrive at Henlester's little lodge in the Forest of Deadmoss. I suggest you begin."

Finally, a chance to do what I was trained for. "Do you want me to transcribe all of it word for word, or as many as I can work out? Or just the sections that seem germane to—"

"All. I hired you for your education and skill, not your judgment in using them. Leave the judgment to me."

"But you're really hoping for information about the Deserters, or early records of Memoridons, or whatever they called them before they were called Memoridons, right?"

"And anything to do with peculiar weapons or artifacts that behave like this one." He drummed two fingers along Bloodsounder's haft. "You will likely encounter a great deal of information that relates to none of those things. I don't particularly care. Transcribe every bit of it you can. Let me worry about divining the meaning, yes?"

Even while I was eager to begin, I'd never considered the prospect of trying to do the translation in a wagon on the way to capture or kill (I never could be sure which) one of the highest ranking clerics in the land. "It will be difficult enough parsing things out. This is a language that isn't even spoken anymore. At least as far as I know. So it will take time. But even more challenging doing it in a moving wagon and—"

"I don't recall—did I say this wouldn't be odious or arduous? If so, I grossly misspoke. But it is the task before you, and if you happen to uncover some sparkling gem of knowledge that proves useful to me, your own utility will increase tenfold. So begin translating. Now."

And just like that, the steel and command was back. Or perhaps it was always there, a sword in a soft leather scabbard, and I'd somehow gotten distracted by the delicate tooling on the surface and forgot that a bloodied blade was inside the whole time, just waiting to be drawn and used.

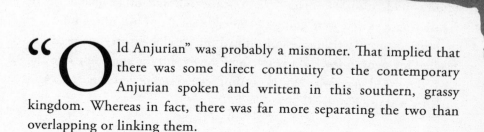

"**O**ld Anjurian" was probably a misnomer. That implied that there was some direct continuity to the contemporary Anjurian spoken and written in this southern, grassy kingdom. Whereas in fact, there was far more separating the two than overlapping or linking them.

The task was going to be time-consuming and incredibly difficult—I hadn't had cause to translate it for years, and like any language, if you do not exercise your use of it, it grows fuzzy, distant, and foreign again.

So, as I pulled the canvas flap shut in back and fastened the tie tight, and took the key in hand, excited despite knowing I would probably wade through miles of tedium and frustration before uncovering anything remarkable, if the latter happened at all, it occurred to me that I couldn't simply unlock the crate and start in. I had to have a system for cataloguing, tracking so as to work through it methodically and systematically.

I popped my head back through the flap at the front, earning a disgusted sigh. "I don't want to include commentary or marginalia on the source material, but can I at least tick off my spot on the pages, or mark which ones I've completed?"

"You've never heard of piles?"

"Piles fall. Especially on a moving wagon on a rutted road that is probably worse than traveling across virgin landscape."

I saw only his profile, so couldn't work out his expression, but after a pause he replied, "A small mark and one only per page. Do not sully these pages, archivist. Do you understand?"

"Yes," I said, returning to my place beneath a swinging pot.

I found myself simultaneously delighted and dreading what would happen after clicking the lock open. Delighted because as exciting as it was to be doing something I was good at again, exercising some skills that had been dormant for some time, it was even more invigorating to know I was going to be exploring material that had been moldering in some vault or tomb for centuries, perhaps longer. And dread because the long spells of unpleasantness that accompany any stretch of translation were going to be trebled as I struggled to find my footing with such dusty content, and to parse out the original intention of the words, allowing for peculiar idioms, odd cultural context I wasn't aware of, and other challenges of translating text that were going to be heightened and magnified now.

Retrieving my writing desk, I pinned the parchment to the raised lid, readied my pens, uncorked my ink, and slowly slid the small key into the lock. It popped open with a rather unimpressive and pedestrian click. And then I got started.

The first few hours were no less bumpy than the road. It had been so long since I'd seen script like this, it almost seemed like a language I had no familiarity with at all. I stumbled, and backtracked, and generally stared at the scribbled words, befuddled.

I was beginning to despair of ever making sense of the words on the page. But very slowly, with each passing mile and hour, it began to come back to me. Slowly. When we stopped at midday, I was shaking, sweaty from being confined in the stuffy wagon, frustrated, and glad when Braylar bid me lock it all up and take a small break.

Vendurro tried to initiate some conversation, but after offering only a few stilted replies, and realizing I was directing my irritation his way for no good reason, I excused myself and took a walk through an untilled field.

When we finally started forward again, I took my spot, a little more relaxed and grounded than I had been. Wine helped. Though it was closing in on vinegar.

Throughout the afternoon, things haltingly started to come easier, as I immersed myself in the source material fully without worrying overmuch about how precise of a translation it was, or how long it seemed to be taking to regain any fluency in the language. As the day wore on, I felt myself becoming engrossed. Not in the material itself, which proved to be a lay subsidy roll in the first instance (as dusty a topic as the scroll itself) and the first three codices in a twelve-part series dealing with early religious and secular Anjurian law that outlined the intersection but more often the tensions and gulfs, going into voluminous detail about defining the castes and how they ought to be represented in local courts, rights of inheritance, and other equally riveting analysis of ancient jurisprudence. But engrossed in the process itself, the puzzling it out.

When the wagon stopped abruptly, I'd almost forgotten I was actually riding in one, or that we had a very unpleasant destination before us. Until Braylar pulled the flap aside and called back, "You've spilled enough ink for the day, archivist. Get your wits about you." He looked at the stains on my fingers and then my face, where I must have touched myself while penning. "You have spilled more than enough, in fact. I gave you a directive not to sully the pages. Clearly I should have told you to protect yourself from them as well."

I nearly touched my face again where he was staring and stopped myself. "Are we at the lodge?"

"Yes, Arki. Henlester is just outside. He invited your personally to sup with him and discuss ink preferences."

The flap fell closed again. For a moment, I couldn't tell what felt worse—stopping when I felt as if I was finally building some momentum, or stopping because we might actually be near a site where more blood was going to stain the grass and leaves.

I stowed my gear and clambered down from the wagon, joints aching, muscles sore from assuming the same bent posture for so long. No sooner were my feet on the ground than the Syldoon pushed the wagon into the deeper brush and trees on one side of the road. Working quickly and methodically, they had it covered so well that you would have had to pass within arm's length or bump your shin on it before even noticing the wagon was there. When it came to matters of subterfuge, they really did have unparalleled skills.

The woods had closed in considerably, furry ferns bent low, gnarled armored oaks with their purple-black serrated leaves crowding together, hulking thick-trunked elms ringed in reddish-orange moss peculiar to this region, hoary larch, the towering and narrow spear pines jutting up so high they seemed intent on piercing the clouds. Even though we were still on a road, of sorts, it was narrow, and the foliage was dense and almost obtrusive, the tall trees blocking out most of the sun, the shrubs and bushes seeming to lock limbs in an effort to prevent anyone from even thinking of leaving the open path.

Braylar walked my slow but trusty and generally benign horse over to me as the others finished climbing back into their saddles. They had the horses that had been pulling the wagon drawn up behind them.

The captain handed me the reins. "Climb aboard, scribe. This boat won't steer itself."

I looked at my horse and hesitated. "I could stay with the wagon. To watch over it, that is. Alert you if anyone investigates. Make sure no one breaks into—"

"Your concern for my property, while commendable, in unwarranted. Two of my men remain behind. The saddle, Arki."

I reluctantly hoisted myself up, threw my leg over, wincing as sensitive sores that hadn't had any time to heal were immediately being chafed raw again. But really, it wasn't the discomfort or the anxiety about the woods that gave me pause, it was leaving the translation now that I finally had a chance to dig into it.

All the Syldoon were on horseback, and the Memoridons were as well. Soffjian rode up to Braylar, posture as rigid and perfect as his own.

"Sister," he said, leaving it at that.

"Brother," she replied, but not content to stop there. "How are you feeling today? Less burdened, I hope?"

"Do you now?"

"Not personally, of course. Personally, I prefer you anguished. Tormented even. Which you obviously manage surprisingly well without any help from me. But I have a professional interest in you now." Soffjian looked down at Bloodsounder, which Braylar pointedly ignored.

"Ever the professional."

"Skeelana seemed to think there was quite a bit of residual. . . matter spattered inside you. Quite the cleanup job, from the sounds of it. So, do you feel sufficiently scoured now? Ready again to proceed recklessly into the wild for no good reason?"

Braylar ignored her and Soffjian turned to the trees and rolling hills, as if she could see Henlester somewhere out there in the hidden distance. "I'm curious, though. Are you more in a rush to be overcome by stolen memories again, or to risk the wrath of the Emperor, who did not expressly give you leave to go priest hunting in the wilderness?"

"The Emperor did not expressly deny it, either. He issued a command to return, and we will do so, never fear."

Soffjian gave him a long look that seemed blank and composed but I suspected masked a good many broiling emotions. "The command is yours, for the moment, Captain. But I must go on record as—"

"Objection duly noted, duly considered, and duly rejected and forgotten. Anything else, Memoridon, or are you done meddling? For the moment, of course."

She smiled in return and pointed toward the woods. "Lead on, oh puissant warrior. By all means."

He didn't respond and started riding into the trees, though whether or not on some path remained to be seen. Mulldoos, Hewspear, and Vendurro followed immediately after, and the rest of the Syldoon filed in behind. I hesitated, and so missed my chance to ride amongst the captain and his lieutenants, but I wasn't looking forward to riding next to any of the other Syldoon, who tolerated me only slightly better than they did the Memoridons in the company. So that left me to ride next to the unwelcome women.

Soffjian ignored me, eyes still tracking her brother, again with the disquieting blank expression, and she moved ahead as Skeelana fell in alongside me. She waited until Soffjian had put a little distance between us, then leaned closer to me. "So. You've been sequestered away."

There was no rise at the end to indicate it being an actual question, but it clearly hung there like one, or at least an invitation for me to elaborate. "I was feeling a bit off. That rabbit we had didn't really agree with my stomach. Most wild game doesn't. How are you doing? Better I hope?" I suddenly felt guilty that I'd been so absorbed with translating I hadn't stopped to ask her earlier in the day.

Skeelana nodded. "It was violent enough—my insides rebelled worse than any time I can remember—but it passed almost immediately after. I was dizzy for a bit, when I spoke with you, but otherwise fine, and even that didn't last all that long."

"I should have stayed with you." She glanced at me, one pierced eyebrow raised. Quickly, I added, "Outside, I mean. Last night. To be sure you were well. I shouldn't have left you out there by yourself."

"If you recall, I told you to." She smiled. "And besides, while that fumbling gallantry of yours is endearing, I can fend for myself just fine. If you recall."

I did recall, all too well. That Hornman blinded, swinging wildly after she stole his sight. While she might not have been able to cripple or kill like Soffjian, I had no doubt she could defend herself well enough, at least long enough to escape an assailant. Which of course there were none of in a dead and deserted plague village. "But if that spell hadn't passed quickly, or had stolen your wits or laid you low? No one but me knew where you were."

"Less fumbling, no less endearing." She ducked a low-hanging branch and I did as well. "The other woman, the nomad in your party—Lloi, was it?"

I nodded.

"Was she ever overwhelmed? Or so sick she couldn't recover?"

"I only saw her treat the captain one time, and she wasn't then, but from what I heard she didn't fare so well the first time. And I can't speak to how long it took her to manage what she did. To not pass out or avoid choking on her vomit or whatever."

"Gallant and charming."

My cheeks flushed hot at the sarcasm, but she was still smiling and continued before I floundered over any more words. "But she wasn't a trained Memoridon. While I'd never attempted anything quite like that, I know what I can do and can't do, and what's more, how to monitor and control myself while doing it. Still, thank you for the misplaced concern."

We rode along in quiet, winding down a brambly trail into thicker foliage, the birch and poplars growing more crowded, the leaves rustling in the breeze above. "Are we in the Forest of Deadmoss now?"

She looked around, the ring in her nose glinting. "Looks mossy enough to me—I think so. I saw a low stone wall on the outer edge of the woods, near a meadow. I'm pretty sure that marked the beginning of the priestwood."

Even though it was daylight, and there was no threat to be seen, who knew if Henlester had men patrolling the woods, or if Brunesmen were circling the area as well. Quiet seemed prudent. And still, my train of thought led me to a question I couldn't put aside.

I tried for a whisper, but it still seemed obscenely loud in the forest. "Is Sunwrack near any part of the Godveil?"

That almost-but-not-quite-mocking grin. "Is anything? No one intentionally lives near it, do they?"

"But I imagine you've seen it?"

"Of course. It marks the eastern border of Urglovia."

"Some say you—the Memoridons, I mean—that the original ones, they inherited their powers from the Deserter Gods. Do you think that's true?"

Skeelana's grin got bigger. "A bit presumptuous. But I have heard that rumor."

I tried to phrase it as if I was only making idle conversation, not actively looking for any information. "Do you think there's any truth to it?"

"I wasn't there, Arki. It was a loooooong time ago. When those Gods left, they did a pretty good job of not leaving many clues behind. So no one can say with any certainty."

"Maybe not. But do you think it's possible? What your kind can do, it's obviously. . . "

"Yes?" Again, the quizzical look. It was actually growing on me.

"Well, except for the Syldoon, the entire world would rather see you dead than exercising those powers. They're obviously potent. And alarming. So when you're first trained, do your masters tell you their theory about the origins?"

"They do indeed."

I waited, and when she stopped there, toying with me no doubt, I asked, "Aaaaand? What did they tell you?"

"That we were trained as the high priests of the Deserters. Before they deserted of course."

I resisted the urge to yank on the reins. "What? You just said you didn't know. And that it was presumptuous."

"I did. And I did."

"But—"

"I didn't say I believed it. But that is what we are taught, yes."

"But you don't believe it?"

"I didn't say that either, now did I?" She started to laugh and then stifled it, looking ahead to Soffjian to see if she overheard. More quietly, she said, "I think skepticism is healthy. And that we can't ever know. I'm more concerned with the here and now than what happened over a millennium ago, anyway." She gave me a pointed look. "Why are you so curious?" She was still smiling. But not as large.

"It's my nature. And my training. I ask questions. Look for answers."

"I see. Even when they are impossible to know or find?"

My horse clomped along, leaves mulching underhoof as we started up a rise. "There are always answers. If you are stubborn enough to keep looking."

She shrugged. "Or convince yourself of them. Why did you ask about the Godveil?"

I leaned forward slightly to compensate as the ground sloped a bit more. "They erected that behind them. I was just thinking, there must be answers to a great deal of questions on the other side."

When I stopped there, she waited and then said, "Aaaaaaaaand?"

It was my turn to bite down on a laugh. "I was also thinking that if the Deserters had really gifted some of their powers and knowledge to the Memoridons, even ages ago—if that were true, than perhaps you possessed the key to parting the Veil. Really parting it, passing through."

She nodded very slowly. "Well, given no one knows for sure where those lovely gifts came from—despite seeming awfully, zealously certain, and wanting desperately to believe they were handed down from on high, because wouldn't that be a wonderful boost to self-esteem—then the odds of us discovering a means of overcoming something erected by the Gods themselves seems pretty thin to me. And no amount of wishing otherwise or hunting is going to—"

We heard a low whistle and stopped. Ahead of us, Soffjian had one arm raised, the back of her hand to us. The Syldoon had stopped not too much further in front of her as well, and they were climbing down off their horses.

Soffjian did as well, and Skeelana took that as our cue. As always, I was the last one to catch up. Skeelana and I walked our horses up to the rest of the company. Braylar lashed Scorn to a tree, and everyone knew that wherever else we might be going it was on foot, and they did the same.

Then the captain faced our small company and pointed to the top of the hill. "We're nearing a small ridge. We walk until we get close to the top. Then we slither the rest of the way. The hunting lodge is in a cleared-out space on the other side. We aren't the first ones here, but that's no surprise. Foss reports our dear friend, Captain Gurdinn, has led a Brunesmen expedition here as well. So, we take up position near the top—" He glared at me and the Memoridons for emphasis—"Silent position, it should go without saying, but I am forced to, lest someone alert the entire valley to the fact that we've joined this little party as well—and then we will see what we see, yes?"

I heard "Aye, Captain" several times from those closest, and the rest nodded, and he looked directly at me and the Memoridons to be sure interpretation wasn't an issue.

The Syldoon crouched down, their armor covered by tunics again, their shields obscured by leather covers, helmets blackened by soot, though not the mail drapes the captain and lieutenants had on theirs. Still, it was clear they had opted for stealth again as much as possible.

I slung the belt and crossbow on my back and the quiver around my waist, and grabbed the trunks of trees to help keep my balance as we ascended the rest of the way. Lloi's curved sword was belted around my waist as well, though I knew if things were dire enough that I had to draw it, it mostly meant we were done for.

Skeelana was just in front of me, and I found myself watching the way her hips shifted back and forth. Even on level ground, she had a bit of an involuntary sashay that was hard to turn away from, but watching her take the incline was almost hypnotic. I shook my head as I tripped over a root and forced myself to watch where I was going.

There was a part of me that hoped Foss had been wrong—maybe the lodge was in the next small valley, or maybe an entirely different forest altogether. The sweat started to come, even with the air growing chillier, and I breathed faster, despite the small climb not being the most exerting. Witnessing more combat was a bad enough prospect, but I'd sampled what it was like to actually participate, and was in no hurry at all to try it again.

I glanced at Skeelana, forcing myself to look above her waist as I wondered how she was faring. Was she as nervous as I was, given that she was somehow even less experienced and equipped? Or was she secure in knowing that her powers—bestowed by deities, stumbled upon by chance, discovered by peculiar accident—would be enough to see her through?

Nearing the top, everyone crouched down, making their way more slowly toward the crest of the hill, and then we all lowered ourselves to our bellies for the final distance, crawling through leaves and twigs and other detritus of the forest. I passed a large patch of strange mushrooms, with the heads inverted rather than domed, as if designed to capture the water that fell rather than repel it, and nearly bumped into Skeelana.

Even before I could see anything, I heard sounds from somewhere far on the other side, voices carrying through the woods, a hammer pounding something, a whinnying horse. I smelled smoke, too, and then right near the top of the ridge, got a whiff of meat that must have been on a spit. My mouth started watering as I imagined the skin crackling and blackening. Which was an odd sensation, given that at any moment we could be shooting our enemies, or maybe being skewered by them ourselves.

I wasn't the only one suddenly feeling hunger pangs—I saw Vendurro lick his lips.

Braylar ordered the bulk of his men and the Memoridons to hold here. He kept moving up the remainder of the rise with Hewpsear and Mulldoos flanking him. I was crawling on my hands and knees, when I felt a slap on the back of my legs. Vendurro whispered, "Ass down, Quills. Cap said slither, not crawl like a plaguing possum."

I did as instructed the rest of the way. When I finally peered over the edge, I wished I hadn't. On the other side, in a shallow depressed stretch of land that wasn't really large enough to count as a valley, the priest's hunting lodge dominated the scene below us. I had expected a manor house mostly of wood, but the central building was built almost entirely of stone, three stories tall, with a rectangular tower on one corner. And the compound was surrounded by a thick, high wall that any smaller castle would have been jealous of, and beyond that, a deep dry moat. The drawbridge was up and surely locked tight.

This wasn't a lodge. Or like any lodge I'd ever seen, anyway, and I'd visited my share while serving minor puffed-up nobles who treasured hunting almost as much as their wives and mistresses. No, this was a fortified keep.

And it was under siege. Just out of arrow shot, along a glade edged by thick trees, Baron Brune's soldiers had made camp, with several pavilions and smaller wedge tents near the picketed horses. There were a lot of Brunesmen there.

High Priest Henlester had attracted quite a gathering.

Vendurro whistled, though it was more of a half whistle, more for effect than anything. "Plague me. Baron wants that buggering priest something awful, don't he?"

Hewspear and Mulldoos seemed to still be assessing everything before them—likely counting the men they could make out in the lodge, or the number of cook fires, or something else that would help them sort out the best course of proceeding.

Braylar was still surveying as well, though the sweep of his eyes always seemed to hint that his calculations would continue long after anyone else's stopped, as he considered every angle and played out a multitude of scenarios.

Mulldoos shaded his eyes against the setting sun. "I'll say this. High Priest might be a cheating, murdering bastard with a queer taste for damaged whores, but he knows how to pick a good spot to take a stand. Dug in good there."

Hewspear agreed. "Stout walls, a fair number of guards to patrol them or man them if they have to fight off an assault."

"How many men, you reckon?"

"With the priest?"

"No, how many men does it take to milk a cow." Mulldoos said. "Of course with the priest, you old whoreson. How many men in his outfit?"

Hewspear ignored the jab and studied the hunting lodge. "Hard to say, but judging by the size of the quarters and stables, could be thirty. Perhaps more."

Mulldoos shifted and looked at Vendurro. "And you, with your beady little eyes, how many men there flying Brune's colors, do you figure?"

Vendurro ran a finger back and forth under his nose, mouth parting and closing as he did a quick count.

"Hard to say for a certainty."

"Not asking for certainty. Asking for your assessment, you skinny prick. Give me a figure."

Vendurro kept counting. "Five pavilions, a bunch of horse picketed there near the woods, two wagons. Fourteen—", he stopped himself, finger tapping the air in front of him as if he was flicking the canvas itself. "No, fifteen small tent. I'd say forty Brunesmen. Fifty maybe."

Mulldoos looked over at Braylar. "So that's one real fortified lodge, and rough on seventy or eighty men down there with sharp pointy things milling about, none going to be real glad to see us. Can't say that you look real fazed by the numbers. Guessing a scout confirmed that for you already, huh?"

Braylar replied, "That is why we employ them. I do so hate surprises."

Mulldoos looked at Hewspear again. "Got a well, don't he, the priest? Right there, real close to center of the compound. Not hurting for fresh water, is he?"

Hewspear shifted uneasily, the hard ground doing his injured ribs no favors. "No. No, he is not hurting for fresh water. And unless I miss my guess, that lodge has a well-stocked larder as well."

Mulldoos nodded, the pale head bobbing on that monstrous neck. "We're agreeing entirely too much here, but seems like the priest boys can hold out here for a good long while. Especially with that fish pond on the far side there. Maybe not provisions like a castle proper, but I'm thinking at least a few weeks. Maybe more. You reckon?"

Hewspear inched away from the ridge and sat up, breathing easier. A little. "Not having been inside, or knowing if the seneschal is competent or a horrible drunk, it is difficult to gauge. But unless they were foolish in preparations, you are probably right. At least two weeks, possibly more."

Mulldoos moved back from the edge of the ridge as well, having seen enough. "Uh huh. Agreeing entirely too much. But there's one thing I'm still awful confused about."

He stopped, looking at the captain, waiting for him to prompt him with the question. When Braylar didn't, Mulldoos said, "Just wondering why we aren't back in our saddles riding to Sunwrack right about now."

Braylar didn't look at him as he replied. "The answer is simple. Our quarry is down there."

Mulldoos leaned on his elbows, looking back and forth between his captain and the edge of the ravine. "Ayyup, Sure enough. Surrounded by a whole lot of stone and a whole lot of men who got no love for us at all."

"You're more right than you know."

Mulldoos worked on that for a moment, then said, "Right, am I? So I'm more confused. If it were me hearing me say we should head on out, and I agreed with what I had to say top to bottom, then the pair of us would hold hands and march down this hill and ride hard to put some miles between before night came on strong. But not you. You hear me out, tell me I got the right of it—which, I got to say, Cap, I get so seldom, just not sure how to take it—but then you seem more dug in than ever. Real, real confused."

Braylar pulled Bloodsounder off the hook on his belt, the chains rattling against each other like an animal giving a warning signal just before the attack, and then he picked up one of the Deserter heads, staring at the agonized face. "Gurdinn is down there."

Mulldoos said, "OK, you seen him. And? Still not sure how that ties one thing to the next. Might even be more reason to leave. Seemed a competent commander on the whole. If even more bullheaded than you."

Braylar brought the flail head closer to his own. "I haven't seen him."

"Then, why—" Mulldoos stopped himself and nodded slowly, the pale stubble on his face like flecks of gossamer. "Ahhhh, should have guessed. Bloodsounder whispering secrets in your ear again."

We all waited for Braylar to say more, and when he didn't, Mulldoos asked what we were all thinking. "So, you want us to beg for scraps? What did you see, Cap, that's got you so willing to dismiss real sound advice to do the opposite of what we're actually doing?"

Braylar moved away from the ridge and slowly stood, joints popping in his knees, and slipped the flail back on his belt. "I can't say for a certainty. Bloodsounder was not especially forthcoming, and the images were far from clear. But this much I can say—if the flashes foretold anything, an opportunity to steal the High Priest might present itself without me ordering us in a futile charge to our doom."

Hewspear spoke up, "Captain, while I've learned to put great stock in your warnings and premonitions, as they've turned the tide of a battle on more than one occasion, I have to say, even if what you saw is accurate, we don't have the luxury of time. And the Brunesmen and the priest are locked in a stalemate—neither will engage the other anytime soon. Henlester isn't sallying out to meet his foe, not with the strategic benefit of a solid defensive position. And Gurdinn has little choice but to try to starve out the garrison, as he brought no siege engines, and likely no engineers to build them. Either way—"

"Nobody's moving," Mulldoos finished. "They're going to stare at each other just out of bow range and dream up real nasty ways of killing the other, but no one's making a move just now. And if we sit here too long, that bitch of a sister of yours will be sure to make our lives hell when we get back to Sunwrack. So we aren't getting any kind of opportunity anytime—"

It was Braylar's turn to interrupt, and his tone suggested the discussion was no longer a discussion of any kind, but a prelude to a mandate. "I expected more imagination. Both of you have been involved in enough sieges and studied countless more to know better. While the majority are prolonged, and eventually end with one side starving or diseased enough to surrender or quit the field, with only a few requiring an all-out assault, there are also numerous occasions when something quick or unexpected decides men's fates. A poisoned well. Treachery within the stronghold, a sally port unbarred. A daring raid by an elite squad. The arrival of rescuing forces that drive off the besiegers. The arrival of more besiegers that tip the balance. And while I can't say which of these things is going to occur, I do know that there is a strong likelihood we will have our opportunity, and have it soon. Bloodsounder is sometimes wrong, or my interpretation faulty, but I feel strongly this is not one of those times."

We all scooted back from the ridge top and then Braylar looked at Hewspear. "We watch and wait. A day at least, possibly two. If nothing happens in that time, we leave without our quarry, and with no blood spilled. Assign two men to haunt this ridge and monitor the incredibly hostile multitude down there."

Mulldoos had a sour look, but Braylar didn't give him a chance to object. "Have the men alternate watch. I believe the Brunesmen are fully occupied, but as you say, Gurdinn might not be an absolute fool—it's possible he'll have a patrol in these woods. Counter that with our own. Understood?"

Mulldoos couldn't have liked the orders any at all, but he knew he had pushed as far as he dared. "Aye, Cap."

Braylar nodded to all of us. "Cold rations, voices silent, armor covered, weapons at the ready. We might need to move fast when the time comes. And you can be sure it will." He marched down the hill without another word.

Mulldoos got up and slapped the dust and dead leaves off his legs. "Well, that's that, then. You heard the Cap. Let's go find a bush and get some rest. Vendurro, hold the ridge until you're relieved. Won't be long."

He started down as well.

Hewspear pulled himself up to his full height, again moving gingerly. I was about to offer him a hand but didn't want to insult him. "Shall we, Arki? There is banquet of dried goat, dried dates, and stale water waiting for us below."

He dug the butt spike of his slashing spear into the dark earth with each step, using it as a staff to make sure he didn't lose his footing. I gave

Vendurro a quick look—he was crawling on his belly back up to the edge of the ravine. He looked back at me and gave me a smile before returning his attention to the lodge and camp below.

I never had any cause to know soldiers particularly well before riding with the Syldoon, I'd overheard enough of them and in enough places to know the majority were exceptionally gifted grumblers, with no shortage of things to complain about. While the Syldoon were no less human than the rest, and certainly must have detested some of their duties, assignments, or discomforts, they took a queer pride in braving the worst of them, as if simply by being Syldoon they had developed a much higher tolerance for all things nasty, cold, and loathsome, and seemed to take any piling on as just another challenge to surmount.

I hurried to catch up to Hewspear, and it was him who actually reached out and caught me as I stumbled, tripping over an unseen hole in the ground. My jostling must have sent his ribs grinding, as he winced with the effort of stopping my fall, but it came and went before he assumed stoicism again.

Yes, they were a peculiar breed of men.

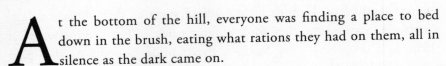

At the bottom of the hill, everyone was finding a place to bed down in the brush, eating what rations they had on them, all in silence as the dark came on.

I was scouting out the best spot myself, which was to say the least worst spot with the fewest roots or rotten foliage, when I spotted Braylar and the recently relieved Vendurro standing together apart from the rest.

I approached slowly, reluctant to interrupt if they were deep in conversation, and when it was obvious they weren't, cleared my throat.

Both men looked at me, and Braylar said, "One thing you will learn traveling among soldiers—always bed down or close your eyes when you have opportunity, as sometimes it can be quite hard to come by."

"Well," I replied, smiling, "Being soldiers yourself, you aren't doing a very good job of leading by example."

"Ha! True enough. A failure of leadership on my part. Do you have something on your mind?"

I wasn't certain this was the time or place to raise the question, and hesitated.

"Don't be coy, archivist. I cannot abide it, and we have less time than you might think. Speak directly or not at all."

"Well, the death of your father," I began slowly, fully expecting him to cut me off. When he didn't, I continued, "That seems a seminal moment. A defining moment, if you don't mind my saying,"

"I believe I do. What of it?" he said, short, but not hostile. Yet.

I glanced at Vendurro, who was watching me carefully, curiosity on his freckled face, though whether to see how wildly I was about to misstep or how much the captain would reveal, I couldn't say. "What happened after?"

"The vows, do you mean? The broken pledge I made before the eyes of gods and men to avenge my father? Or the other, to protect our people from the Syldoon scourge many years later, equally fractured?"

232

I nodded slowly.

"Those," the captain said, "I will not tell you about just now." I nodded again, a bit disappointed but not surprised, and at least glad to have escaped a verbal beating. But then he went on. "But I will tell you of what immediately happened after my father died." He added quietly, almost to himself. "I am not entirely sure why. Who wishes to relive a moment of both grief and shame? I have never spoken of it, and only two others know what occurred. One, my wretch of a sister. So it might be good you get the account from me. Or perhaps I am merely melancholy. Or maybe we will all die on the morrow, so what difference does it make. Who can say?"

Vendurro said, "Aww, Cap, if it's something you'd rather not. . . " But it was half-hearted at best, as it was obvious he wanted to hear it as badly as I did.

Braylar waved him off. "Days passed after my father was murdered. I don't know how many. I'm sure I ate and shat and slept, but again, I have no recollection to support this. The first thing I remember is my mother touching my shoulder as I lay on my pallet, staring at the wall. I turned and looked at her. Expressionless, she told me Grubarr was there to see me."

"Grubarr?" Vendurro asked, and I silently cursed myself for asking the captain to speak with a member of his company around, even one I liked. My questions were usually enough to dissolve the captain's resolve to reveal.

"Ahh, of course—you would not know. My tribe had three priests, Earth, Sun, and Moon. Lawkeepers, among other things. Grubarr was the Earth Priest, and the kindest of the three. So when my mother roused me, I stared at her, not seeing her face, not understanding what she said. Her words were wind, a meaningless sound that provoked no response or reaction in me whatsoever. I've seen old men in my village, whose age outraced their minds, who no longer responded to human speech, who didn't respond to much at all. The only thing they registered was light and dark. At night they slept. During the day, they stared. I often wondered what they were thinking about, trapped so deep inside themselves. Now I know. Nothing. They think of nothing."

Once he started speaking about it, he didn't slow or stop himself. "I seem to remember her shaking me, helping me stand. One of us dressed me, most likely her. And then I was outside, standing in front of Grubarr, standing alongside my sister. He looked at us, looked at my mother. I remember that. The look on his face. True sadness. But on a face that has seen much of it. And then he told me the first thing I remember with clarity. He told us that we were to prepare our father for burial. These words I understood as words, they drew me out of myself, but they still made no sense to me. Soff didn't respond either. Grubarr looked at our mother and back to us and tried again. I remember his words that day clearly, which is surprising, given the fog I was in. He said, 'I would it were different, truly, but you must assist today. With the burial preparations. So. Follow me, please. I will spare you the worst. But you must attend me. And we can't wait any longer.' And then he asked if we understood.

"Soff nodded slowly, although she looked as if she were nodding off to sleep rather than affirming anything, eyes half-closed, chin almost on her chest. I didn't nod. Or respond. Grubarr put his hand on my shoulder then, squeezed once. 'Braylar,' he said, 'I'm sorry. There are no choices here. You have suffered, I know. I will do my best to be quick. That, I swear. But we must go. Yes?'

"He was wrong, of course. Up until that point I hadn't suffered at all. But I was beginning to, that morning, and I realized, some part of me anyway, I realized I was about to suffer immeasurably, and indefinitely, and I wanted nothing so badly as to climb back to that spot where words were wind and nothing meant anything. But it was too late. I was among the living again, and the truth of his words struck home—none of us had a choice.

"I looked at my mother. She said nothing. She just looked tired, very tired. And so, not knowing what else to do, I turned to Grubarr and nodded. And followed, walking across the patchy yellow grass, through the village. Several villagers saw us, but averted their eyes quickly, returned to their tasks."

As much as I begrudged Vendurro's interruption, I could not stop from asking, "Why did you have to help in the preparations? Was it customary for children to—"

"It was a punishment. For grave robbing. Soff and I had been caught during the winter."

Vendurro said, "I told you Cap had some kind of experience with such things. Just figured it was, well, more successful."

Braylar ignored him.. "So my sister and I had been assigned to Grubarr to assist with burying our dead. All. I knew I wasn't prepared for what we were about to see and do. That winter we had tended to a handful of dead, and being a small village, we knew all of them. But they were not relatives. They were not my father."

"Plague me," Vendurro said. "They couldn't make a plaguing exception? For your da?"

Even in the dark I caught Braylar's twitch-smile. "My people are not big on exceptions." Then he continued. "Grubarr led us to his longhouse. It was larger than most, with several rooms, each separated from the others by a doorway and a thick flap of felt. The deadroom was the last. It was here that the preparations took place.

"Before we entered, Grubarr stopped us, touching our arms. He looked back and forth between us and said, 'Words I give you, they cannot stem the pain. This I know. But I will tell you one thing, and that's all. When I was nearly your age, Soffjian, my mother, she died. Droos. One day, strong, healthy, young; the next, stricken, ill for many moons. And then gone. The priests, they examined, they inspected, but they didn't know. There was no knowing to be known.

"The Earth Priest went on, 'I won't lie. This wrenched my heart. I had no brother, no sister, and my father, he was—well, this isn't about my father. No. It's enough to tell you, I suffered. Truly. Deeply. Alone. I wanted to die. And this idea, this dying notion, it didn't frighten, it didn't pain. It was almost a comfort. I played with the idea, carried it with me, every day. Until one day, I lost it. I didn't lose the grief, but I lost the dying wish. I don't know who found it. Perhaps you.' He looked closely at us, measuring, and then said, 'Perhaps not. But if you did find it, it's a thing that prefers to be lost. You'll live. You'll endure. And one day, you'll recover. I did. All do in time. You will as well. No one told me this when my mother died. But had they, I wouldn't have believed them. It's no different with you, I'm thinking. But one day, many years from now, I'm also thinking you'll give this same speech to another, and it will be their turn to be disbelieving.'

"I didn't know whether to cry or scream or hit him or fall into his arms. So I did nothing. Soff opened her mouth as if she was about to say something, but it got lost before it came out. He said one other thing, telling us that if we ever wanted to talk he would listen, and then he dropped his hands. He reached into a wooden bucket and pulled out three damp strips of cloth. He handed each of us one and then wrapped the last around his head a few times, covering his mouth and nose."

"For the smell?" Vendurro asked. And then added, "Sorry, Cap."

"Yes. The strips were saturated in fresh horse piss. There are numerous ways a man can stink, but never so powerfully as when he has decided to die. Even after a few days they begin to rot inside, to liquefy, and the stink is like the worst sulfur and swamp gas, enough to make the strongest stomach turn and the strongest man gag. Horse piss is a preferable alternative.

"We tied the strips around our mouths and noses, Grubarr pulled the flap aside, and in we went. Our father was laying on a table near the middle of the room. His chest was bare but otherwise he was dressed as he had been the morning he was stabbed. His skin had changed color and was now an odd greenish-blue tint. His body bloated, but not uniformly, some parts more swollen than others. There was some fluid collecting beneath his nose and at the corner of his mouth. And even with the cloth around my face I felt my gorge rise."

He looked closely at me and said, "Perhaps it was a blessing you never knew your father, and your mother gave you away for a bag of coins. You never had to see them dead."

It wasn't said with cruelty, but stung just the same. I wondered if my mother was still alive.

Braylar said, "Soff and I stood next to each other, staring. Neither of us cried. Not just then. I had cried myself into a stupor just after his murder, and I wasn't quite ready to begin again. I simply stood there, feeling empty, small, lost, exhausted. And as Grubarr had said, unbelieving. Despite the evidence in front of me, I refused to believe this was happening. Soff reached over, took my hand in her own." He stopped and added, "I see your skepticism. Do recall, this was before broken vows, yes? At one point, there was some rough tenderness betwixt us."

Neither of us responded and he went on. "There were no windows in the room—no one else in the village wanted to smell death and Grubarr didn't want perversely fascinated children disturbing his work—but there was a hole in the roof, like a smoke hole, although there would be no large fires in this room. It was overcast that day, ready to rain, and the deadroom was very dark, lit only by a few candles in the far corners and what weak light came through the hole above. Flowers and herbs hung upside down from the support beams, drying, so many that it seemed there was an inverted field suspended above us. There were many, many shelves, all of them lined with bowls and vials, lidded jars and small boxes, all manner of things. I'd become familiar with some of them over the winter. Crushed flowers, tooth and nail from a hundred different animals, a multitude of dyes, mushrooms, small pelts, oils, dried milk, chalk, charcoal, and on and on and on."

"What plaguing for?" Vendurro asked.

"Grubarr had told us once that there were those in our tribe who didn't understand the old ways, the elaborate treatments of the dead, or the living for that matter. Some argued, although never loudly, and certainly never in the presence of their priests, that the dead should be burned, their ashes scattered, or simply buried, and be done with it."

"Aye," Vendurro said. "That's how my people went about it."

Braylar nodded. "I remember Grubarr had been smiling as he told us that, his heavy hands busy grinding holly with a stone pestle. And saying, 'Old men keep old ways. Were I a youth, I might argue for change. But I'm old, and I do only what I can do. Someday you and your ways will grow old too, and you'll cling to them, moss to a stone.'

"I tried to imagine another day, any day other than the one I was in, but it was no good. The stench was too strong and my imagination too weak. Grubarr stepped past us and approached my father. He rolled up his sleeves—his forearms were thick and the gray hair that covered them thick as well, almost fur really. Any other day this struck me as funny and put me at ease in this place, but it didn't that day.

"He took a damp cloth out of a wooden bowl and began cleaning the dried blood off our father's belly. There was a lot of it, belly and blood. Soff and I released hands and stepped forward as well. As we got close my breath stopped in my chest. Having prepared four bodies for burial over the winter, we knew what to expect—the stiff, unyielding muscles, the cold skin, the blood that had congealed—but those experiences did nothing to prepare us for this."

Maybe Braylar was right about my parents. Some things were better left unseen and unknown.

"I stopped at my father's feet, afraid to move closer. His boots and the front of his pants were still covered with the reddish mud, the mud that clung to him when he fell forward. It was difficult to tell where mud ended and blood began.

"Soff was braver than I was, but only a little. She stopped at his waist, opposite Grubarr. The cloth on her face was rising and falling quickly. Grubarr continued working as if neither of us were there, wiping, wringing, wiping, wringing. Soff, said, very quietly, 'He. . . are we going to bury him?'

"Grubarr didn't look up, continued cleaning. 'A simple grave, yes.'

"Soff reached out to touch our father but pulled her hand away. 'And what will we bury with him? We will bury something, won't we?'

"'Yes,'" Grubarr said, wringing out the cloth. "'All of us go with something, smallest to largest, youngest to oldest. Your mother, she'll decide. She will include honeycomb, yes?' He smiled at Soff but she didn't return it. 'If you have other suggestions, she'll want to be aware of them, I think.'

"Soff nodded but said nothing else. A short time after, she asked, so quietly I could barely hear her, 'What will we do. . . what will we do once you've cleaned him?'

"'Hmmm. Nothing. Something. I'm unsure. The wound, it will be filled with paste, dill and ash, but I will do this. I'll do most of what needs done. If there's something I need from across the room, you'll fetch this something, and if I need mixing, you'll do this mixing. But little more. It's enough that you are here. And here you be. So.'"

His ability to recall conversations so many years gone by was just short of wondrous. Was his memory simply that astute? Had the gravity of the occasion imprinted the words in him somewhere? Was he simply filling in missing pieces? Had Bloodsounder somehow brought his own memories into sharper relief?

I asked none of these though as he went on. "Grubarr finished wiping my father's belly and dropped the cloth in the bowl of bloody water. I looked at the wound then and I couldn't take my eyes off it. So small, so narrow, only two inches long. It was hard to believe this was enough to kill a man. And yet it had. So quickly. So very quickly.

"I remember thinking it was amazing that my father's fat belly hadn't stalled the blade, hadn't saved him, and then I felt ashamed, bitterly ashamed. It seemed even in death I couldn't respect him. And that was when I began to cry again. Feeling it come, I tried so hard to stop. I wanted so badly to be strong, to at least appear strong. But I could feel it slipping, all my strength washed away with the blood. I stared at the bottom of my father's old boots, at the dried mud, tried to focus on that, to block the rest out, to think only of the mud, and how it was so close to raining, it might start any moment, and as soon as it did, there would be more mud, new mud, everywhere, the rain would turn the whole village, the whole world to mud. But it was no good. The tears fell, my nose began to run. I stepped back, began to shake. I bit my tongue and clenched my fists, my nails digging into my palms. But having found my tears again I couldn't get rid of them."

He recited this distantly, not quite like when he was narrating stolen memories of dead men, but not far off, either. If this was a confessional of sorts, it was devoid of passion or pain, as if it had happened to someone else.

"Soff saw me," Braylar said, "and she started toward me, and then I began to sob. I fell forward on my knees, just as my father had a few days before, and I wished there was mud, mud I could swallow, drown myself in, but there was only dirt, and I grabbed handfuls of it, smashed it into my hair, my face, my eyes. Soff tried to pull my hands away, to hold me. And I could take no more of it. I climbed to my feet and burst out of the room, and the next, and the next, out of the longhouse. I ran into the woods, away from the village, ran until my lungs felt like they might split open in my chest, and then I continued to run, hoping they would, hoping they would rip and tear, and I would be the next one Grubarr would have to work on. But they didn't, they only gave out. I fell over, and still my body wanted to cry, but there was no breath for it, so I lay there, wracked with silent sobs, wanting to die, feeling like I was, pounding the dirt because I couldn't scream.

"It was only then that I realized where I'd run to. The grove of dying birch near our village. I had not gone nearly as far as I'd guessed. Having gotten some of my breath back, I stood there in the rain, suddenly angry. No, furious. At my father for getting killed, at the gods for allowing it, at my ancestors for creating him and me. I screamed at all of it, as new tears watered my face, and then I screamed at the futility of screaming at all."

It was difficult to imagine the captain so overcome, but even more difficult imaging having to endure all this.

"I ran over to the closest standing birch, and kicked that, pushed it. The rotting tree groaned but didn't fall. And so I retreated, ran at it again, hit it with my shoulder, with my head, and fell off it, bounced truly. Fell into the wet grass and looked up at it. But it was moving just then, albeit very slowly. It creaked, and groaned, and made all of the noise it could with its treeish voice, and then, with one last, wet crack, it fell. The rotten tree fell away from me, colliding with another as it went and taking that down too.

"My shoulder ached, snot bubbled out of my nose as my head pounded like a great drum, and I felt all the world like a gaping, pulsating tear, exposing all the tissues beneath, tissues that would die if they were open too long. I couldn't have put it into those words then, but I was a wound that knew it must be cauterized, burnt until the blood stops flowing and the tissues blacken and close in on themselves. I didn't have the words, but I knew—sensed perhaps—that that was what I must do.

"And so I got to my feet, ran to the next standing tree. I found a log alongside it, one of sturdier stuff than dead birch. I lifted the small log and clubbed the dying birch in front of me. I hit it, bits of peely white bark flying, again and again, until my hands blistered and split open and blood ran sticky across my palms, and then this tree fell as well. And it went on like this. I pushed and struck and screamed and cried, killing these dying trees, one after the other, killing them and cursing everything I could think to curse, over and over, clearing the already sparse glade like a maddened druid. And this went on, for how long I don't know. But it continued until I could continue no more, until the wound was seared shut and a dozen more trees littered the ground around me."

Braylar stopped for a moment, looking back and forth between us as if he had nearly forgotten there was an audience at all. Then he said, "Rather than help prepare my father for his funeral, I fled to the forest to knock down trees and rip my hands bloody."

Vendurro clearly wasn't accustomed to being in a position to soothe his captain at all, but he tried just the same. "You weren't but a boy, Cap. And it was wrong, you having to prepare your father like that. Sorry if you feel the opposite, but got to say, that's rough, even for a no-exception making kind of people. You weren't nothing but a boy."

"True enough. I was but a boy. But I was also the only relative capable of avenging my father, and I was off to a miserable and shameful start. I vowed then that the moment of weakness in the deadroom would be my last. Vowed that I would punish the man who killed my father, who prevented me from having even the chance to grow to appreciate the man he was, instead of recoiling from the one I thought I knew. I made these vows and several more, not knowing that they were but the first I would likely break." He blew on his hands, shook his head, and said, "Rest while you are able." Then he disappeared behind some trees.

Vendurro looked at me and said, "Revealing a cowardly deed is about the bravest thing a man can do. Not saying it's cowardly, what he done, running like that. Sure I would have done the same, or bawled like a babe before even getting to that deadhouse, had to be dragged there kicking and screaming. But in his eyes it is. And. . .well, plague me, but I never heard him go off like that in all my years. Can't say it don't make me a wee bit nervous."

I couldn't disagree.

Vendurro moved off to find his own spot to sleep in and I looked around at our company. With Syldoon on the ridge, out in the woods to spot any incoming patrols, and back with the wagon, it really did seem a meager force. I pulled my thin blanket around me, vowing not to think about the likelihood of us all dying in this forest, and tried to find any stretch of earth that wouldn't prove miserable. Even after clearing out every pine cone, pebble, and stick I could find, my chosen patch of ground still seemed just as bumpy and intent on keeping sleep at bay.

I tossed and turned for some time, and each movement only served to make things worse. Still trying to get over my amazement that Braylar not only spoke at great length with little reticence at all, but chose to reveal something so intimate and painful, I wrapped my blanket on my shoulders and walked out of our small glade, careful not to kick any of the bodies on my way. They were easy enough to avoid, even in the dark, as the Syldoon were breathing deeply or rumbling away in a mixed cadence of snores.

I climbed over a log, ducked under a tree, and was looking to find a good place to relieve myself. It was the woods, after all, so there wasn't a really bad place, but I'd been told to walk far enough way that I didn't piss on anyone's head, but not so far I got lost in the woods.

Satisfying those requirements, I was about to pull my trousers down when I felt, rather than saw, someone nearby. I froze, hoping it was another Syldoon, and not a Brunesman sneaking through the brush, or an animal, or better still that I was merely imagining things.

I looked around. With the horned moon high in the sky, it didn't take long to see Skeelana's silhouette. I took a few steps closer, approaching from the side, watching the details of her profile materialize in the dark—the large lips, the puckish nose, the hair seemingly trying to flee her head in as many directions as possible. I was about to say her name softly when I noticed her eyes were closed. She stayed like that, standing perfectly straight, eyelids shut but fluttering gently, for a long time. As she wasn't a horse, the only other thing I could imagine was that she was one of those people afflicted with nightwalking. There was a man like that in my wing of the university. He could wake up almost anywhere at any time of night. The headmaster had warned us to leave him be, under threat of the cane, so we had. I'd never seen them wake him or try.

But that was a contained building and complex—this was the wild, with a camp full of enemies half a mile away. I was debating whether to try to rouse her, or to possibly try to direct her back to wherever Soffjian had bedded down, when Skeelana's eyes suddenly sprang open.

She didn't look disoriented, which was odd, and she turned to head back to our small camp and saw me standing there watching, she jumped back, hands coming up, either to defend herself or to work some awful Memoridon magic on me.

I said, "Skeelana, it's me! It's Arki!" in something between a hiss and a whisper—a hissper.

She lowered her hands, though slowly, as if she wasn't sure whether to believe me, or was possibly still considering working some invisible spell. "Damn you! What are you doing out here?"

Skeelana sounded flustered, or embarrassed, or both.

"I'm sorry, I needed to, uh, empty. . . anyway, what are you doing out here?"

Skeelana crossed her arms in front of her chest, though whether to ward off the chill or because she was adopting that staunchly offended posture only women have mastered, I couldn't say. "That's actually no business of yours."

Well, that answered the arms question. "I didn't mean to startle you, or, uh. . . I'm sorry."

"You didn't startle me. You—" she snapped. But after a moment, forced herself to soften the edge, if only a little. "You did, actually. A little. I'm mostly mad at myself for not being more careful. You did nothing wrong. In fact, you've been nothing but kind, actually. Which I find a little unnerving, to be frank." She looked around, hearing something small rustling in the brush nearby. "We really do need to stop meeting in the dark alone like this. It might set people to talking."

She was making light, but there was actually some truth to that. I tried imagining what Mulldoos would say if he caught me out here with a Memoridon. It wouldn't be pretty.

I wanted to excuse myself, in part because my bladder was full to bursting, in part, because it was the smart thing to do, but I stayed. "You said it was no business of mine, and I respect that. I do."

"Do you?" There was some amusement there, though whether it was tinged with flirtation or irritation, it was impossible to say.

"I do indeed. But tell me this one thing, please. You weren't nightwalking, were you? Or meditating? And you obviously weren't relieving yourself. What were you doing, exactly?"

"For someone allegedly respectful of boundaries, and wanting to know one thing only, you do ask far too many questions."

I expected that, and nodded. "That's fair. Well, then, I should—"

"I was sending a message," she said quickly, as if she was revealing far more than she should have. "If you must know."

I pulled the blanket tighter to ward off a cold breeze, and then wondered if not offering it to her was rude, or if offering it would be impudent and rude for different reasons. I opted for the second rudeness. When she declined the blanket, I couldn't help asking, "A message? To another Memoridon, I take it."

"Exceptionally clever." I wasn't sure, but it seemed like she was smiling.

"You can. . . what? Pass thoughts to each other? Read minds?" The question didn't sound as ridiculous as I expected it to. Hearing of such things before meeting Lloi and now the Memoridons, I dismissed them as uneducated superstition or at least exaggeration. Now, I was almost prepared to believe everything.

"No," she replied. "Not exactly. Not like you think, anyway. We can't pass along long complex thoughts, or communicate the way you and I are now, rapid exchanges and questions and nuance and so forth. We transfer memories to each other."

"Memories? I don't understand. Memories of what? What you've seen recently? Heard?"

Skeelana shook her head. "No. That is, the most gifted and experienced can do something like that, provided they are much closer to each other. But at this distance, the only thing we can reliably pass to one another are small bits of image and sound that we've all memorized before."

That sounded incredible, but again, having seen what I had, not entirely improbable. "Like a code, you mean? What kind of memories?"

She replied, "Something like that. A code, that is. Small, short, simple memories are the easiest. A fish swimming in circles in clear water means one thing. A hawk diving for its prey another. Something active, distinct, but still brief. String them together, and you can convey a great deal."

It was foreign, and sounded marvelous, really. But everything she said led to more questions. "Why not just memorize an alphabet then? Transmit one letter after another, like writing, with your mind? Wouldn't that be the simplest way?"

"It might. Well, it would. But there are two things that prohibit that from working. Again, when we are separated by great distances, even the most talented can only convey a few images at any one time. No one I've ever met could maintain the focus and concentration long enough to make. . . mind-writing like you described work. Or effectively anyway."

"And the second thing?"

She took a step closer and said, "I will take that blanket, now."

It took me a moment to comprehend, but after I handed it to her, she wrapped it around her shoulders. "The other is, something lively, colorful, dynamic—that's easier to recall, receive, pass along. I can't tell you why, precisely. But all of the memories in our language, our code, are meaningful. They are rarely static, and they are the kind of thing you would attach emotion to. That's what makes a memory powerful. Here. Let me show you."

Before I had a chance to decline, she closed her eyes and then I suddenly smelled an unexpected and potent odor: ginger. It bit at the nostrils so hard I could nearly taste it, and my stomach grumbled. The smell grew more powerful, and then faded away immediately as if it never existed at all. Immediately, another odor hit, equally out of place in the forest—bananas, overripe but not having spoiled completely. I'd only smelled them a few times, as they weren't native to Anjuria, but there was no confusing the smell with anything else.

This disappeared as quickly as it came, though, replaced by a pungent perfume that swirled with vanilla and lavender and hints of some other cloying thing I couldn't place. Followed immediately by the stinging brine and dead fish of the sea.

I would have suspected I was losing my mind if I hadn't known it was merely being played with.

When the final odor disappeared, leaving the night air somehow flat and almost destitute, I said, "That's amazing. Those are all yours? Memories of smells?"

"No. Those are shared memories. From early training, actually. Memories of smells are easier to transfer than images for some reason. I suppose emotions get caught up in them more? Not sure. Anyway, those are some of the first we learn to pick up and pass on."

Now that I had her talking, I figured it was time to circle back to my original question. "So, what was the message?"

"Hmm?"

"The message you sent to someone back at Sunwrack."

She suddenly handed the blanket back. "I've already blathered more than I should. And your bladder will pop soon. Get some rest, Arki."

And just as she had the night before, she melted into the darkness and was gone, leaving me standing there, cursing myself for being so clumsy. And also a bit in awe.

Sleep would be even more difficult prey now, but I knew I had to try.

A hand shook my shoulder, and it was rough enough that I guessed I must have fallen into a deep sleep, despite the cold, the damp, and the uneven ground only slightly more comfortable than sleeping on broken glass.

I tried to orient myself. It was still dark, and the hand was still shaking me. I sat up and told whoever it was I was awake.

The hand withdrew. "Thought you might have died or something," Vendurro said. "Weren't even snoring, just curled up like some stone gargoyle."

I looked around. Nearly everyone else was moving, gathering their sleeping rolls, packing any loose items, though we were all pretty light in that department, most of the supplies being back in the wagon or on the pack horses.

Vendurro stood, and I got to my feet as well, stiff all over, the blanket still wrapped tight. Everywhere I looked, breath was ghosting in the air. We were moving somewhere in a hurry. "What's happening?"

"Can't say for a certainty. Cap seemed real intent on getting the crew going. But whatever it is, it's happening big and happening soon. Let's hoof it."

Almost with alarm, I realized the last thing I'd been thinking about before falling into that deep sleep was Skeelana, and that I was looking around at our party, trying to spot her.

I shook my head and focused on keeping up with Vendurro as we made our way through brambles and brush and onto the base of the hill that led up to the ridge. Though it took me long enough to recognize it, having been woken from the depths, it struck me suddenly that in addition to the lamellar on full display, weapons buckled and strapped on, shields slung over backs or bucklers clipped to belts, everyone was carrying loaded crossbows as well.

Vendurro must have read my thoughts. "Might get ugly right quick. Fighting in the dark is worse than fighting in full-on day. Can't see the carnage or bloodletting, true enough, which is something of a blessing, but you also can't make out friend from foe. Leads to bad decisions, bloody mistakes, even panic, you don't have a steady hand running the crew. Lucky for us, we got Cap. He'll see us through, even if we need to start loosing bolts before sunup. Buckle that quiver, ready that bolter." I couldn't be sure, but I think he smiled.

The small company was gathered together, looking to Captain Killcoin and his lieutenants who were standing a little further apart, arguing with Soffjian from the looks of it. The captain might have rankled at her being involved at all in this operation, but she did have the habit of turning him and his chief advisors into a unified front. Hewspear and Mulldoos might have had leave to question their captain's decisions in private, at least to a point, but they never failed to support him in front of the troops, and never more so than when she was aligned on one side, and the three of them on the other.

I saw Skeelana then, holding herself apart from the rest, observing either everyone or no one. She was even less equipped for a confrontation than I was. Well, except for her ability to warp men's minds of course. There was that.

Soffjian shook her head, rather violently, and then walked away, joining Skeelana, speaking quickly and quietly, clearly unhappy with the situation.

Captain Killcoin saw Vendurro and summoned him over with a quick wave of his arm, and when I didn't immediately follow, he waved faster. I ran to catch up, ignoring the glances from the soldiers around me. Some were likely indifferent to my presence or my proximity to their captain, but I frequently sensed that others were none too pleased, even if being a part of Braylar's inner circle meant increased likelihood of receiving a tongue lashing.

There was another Syldoon, one of the pair on watch at the ridge, I gathered, who had been waiting for Soffjian to move off but now joined the group as well. I approached the five men as Hewspear asked the soldier, "Has there been any movement? Anything unusual?"

The soldier had bloated lips and small eyes that could charitably have been described as beady. "No, sir. We alternated, just like you and Cap ordered. Been a fresh eye on the site the whole night. Torches on the wall, dying camp fires among the Brunesmen, so hard to make too much out. But nothing real peculiar."

Mulldoos drummed his hand on the buckler on his hip as he faced Braylar. "What do you want us to do, Cap? Everybody got all dressed to scrap, but seems like we might be a mite early to the party yet."

Captain Killcoin was looking up the hill, one hand on the top of Bloodsounder's haft. I wondered if maybe he needed the elaborate whirling to capture the least muddied images and sensations, as he'd done in the grass. But even some of his men were familiar with the odd divinations, the two women in the group surely weren't, and I knew he was in no hurry to reveal anything to them unless it was bled out of him.

I thought he was going to have to admit that Mulldoos was right, and order everyone to unclench the nerves and cool the bloodlust, but then I saw movement further up the hill, and heard metal and gear gently rattling as the other solider who'd been manning the ridge jogged down to us, stones and rotting leaves kicked ahead of him.

The Syldoon came to a stop in front of the group and saluted.

"Report, soldier."

"Got some activity, Cap."

Braylar stepped forward. "I gathered as much, since you nearly broke your neck racing down here to tell us as much. A few more details would be welcome."

The soldier replied, "Aye, Cap. Sorry. Baron's men, seems like they're breaking camp."

I couldn't tell if Braylar was relieved or disappointed. "Pulling out?"

"Can't say for sure, Cap. They're pulling the pavilions down, alright, and some of the small tents too. But the command tent is still standing. And given that the commanders generally don't like to choke on dust or step in shit, seems plenty queer that they haven't broken that down yet. Plus, a lot of coming and going in the night the last few hours."

Braylar turned to the beady-eyed Syldoon. "And that didn't strike you as peculiar? Excessive traffic to Gurdinn's tent?"

The soldier looked both red-faced and a bit confused. "Gurdinn, sir?"

"The man in the tent receiving so many midnight missives. In the future, please remember this moment the next time I ask you if anything unusual is afoot and be prepared to hurt your neck nodding furiously if you've encountered the same level of activity. In addition to preferring to keep their boots clean, commanders only like to be woken repeatedly or kept awake half the night for a phenomenally good reason." He turned to the rest of our small assembly. "Come. Let's see what to make of these camp happenings."

The captain started up the hill as quickly as he could and still maintain his footing in the dark. The two soldiers loped after him and fell in on either side.

Mulldoos looked at Hewspear. "Devils take him, but he's right too plaguing much." Then the pair ascended as well.

Vendurro wasn't struggling as much as the lieutenants—in fact, he seemed pretty adroit at avoiding injuries—but he chose to stay at my side as we followed. I wondered if he feared I'd stumble and roll back down to the bottom, or turn an ankle in the dark. Or possibly he just wanted some company. I imagine if Glesswik had been there, they would have kept pace with the rest.

He elbowed me in the side and nearly sent me toppling, so my safety clearly wasn't paramount. "Mulldoos ain't never found a comfort level of no kind with Bloodsounder. Distrusts the thing something fierce, even when it proves itself over and over. Can't say I blame him—mighty unnatural. But it's saved us more than once."

I tried not to let my labored breathing show. "But it's been mistaken before, hasn't it? Led him astray."

Vendurro pointed further up the hill, presumably at the soldiers and the captain ahead. "No more or less than anything else. Either way, he gets it more right than wrong. Lieutenant ought to quit fighting that fact so plaguing hard, no matter how plaguing queer the thing is."

There might have been something to that. But just then, I was happy not to be wearing armor, despite my earlier misgivings. Trudging uphill in full Syldoon gear didn't look like much fun, even if Vendurro had the youth and energy and training to show no ill effects.

When we got near the top of the incline, I saw the others had already gone prone and inched up to the edge, helmets off so as not to reflect any moonlight. I dropped to my belly and did the same, creeping forward until I could look down on the hunting lodge and surrounding area.

There were torches on the walls of the compound, and in the tall wooden towers along the wall, and while it was impossible to make out much in the way of detail, the shapes of the priestguards were hard not to miss, and the light glinting off mail or helms.

The besiegers' small camp had plenty of torches too, away from the tents, and some in the hands of soldiers moving about, so it was even more difficult to discern much, except that there was plenty of activity, and while some figures didn't catch the light, wearing gambesons, most were in hauberks.

Mulldoos shook his head. "If Gurdinn is down there—"

"He is," Captain Killcoin countered emphatically, pointing out a figure striding between his men. He had a full hauberk as well with a coat of plates over the top, the rivets winking on and off as they caught the light, and his spaulders, steel vambraces, and finger gauntlets reflecting the fire and moon as well. There was no mistaking him for anyone other than the commander of the forces.

"Fine. That's him," Mulldoos said. "But what's he plaguing playing at? That might not be a castle, but it's a lot more fortified than any lodge has a right to be."

Vendurro asked, "He can't be thinking of attacking, can he? He'd be a fool to, right?"

Hewspear grunted as his ribs pressed against cold ground. "He is a stubborn man, but you're right—it would be foolish to attack an enemy dug in like that. Especially since he doesn't have siege engines. This is our first night—perhaps he's ordered feinted attacks like this the last few nights and evenings."

Mulldoos mulled that over. "Wear the holy bastards down, you think? Gurdinn's got more men, for certain. Keeping watch on a wall tweaks your nerves tight as it is, but especially if you think an attack might be coming."

"Or maybe," Vendurro offered, "he feints a few nights in a row, until the priest's guard is either so tired, or right sure it's nothing but another fake, lets their guard down some."

"Nah. He ain't attacking. Like the wizened windmill said, he's stubborn, but not stupid. Not that stupid, anyway."

We watched and waited as the pearl light crept over the horizon to the east. The dawn suffused the thin clouds above the treeline. I rubbed my hands together, looking forward to the warmth the sun would bring, and wondered just how long we planned on laying in the dirt waiting for something to happen. I leaned close to Vendurro and tried to ask only so loud for him to hear, "Why would it be so foolish to attack? If it's not as sound defensively as a castle, that is?"

But Hewspear overheard. "Not a castle, true. But they'd still have to make a break over open ground, arrows raining down, and then try to scale the wall. The defenders, even at a numerical disadvantage, are in a stronger position."

"What're you babbling on about?" Mulldoos asked.

Hewspear repeated my question, and Mulldoos looked over at me. I expected some hostility, but he was remarkably restrained. "Gurdinn's got more men, twice as many, maybe. But he'd lose big numbers charging that wall. Not worth it. No commander orders a siege, even on a fortified hunting lodge. Not unless he's got to."

"You mean, if his men are starving or freezing?"

"Don't go laying siege in the winter, scribbler. But starving, yeah, losing men to desertion, disease. None of which are in play here. Only been here a few days. No call to waste men on the walls at all."

Hewspear, ever eager to contest his comrade's opinion, said, "Unless there were other reasons the commander had little choice."

"Such as?"

Vendurro piped up, "Maybe the commander don't want to pay a visit to that table in the baron's playroom you all told me about."

Braylar said, "No, the Baron might be impatient, even impulsive, but he's no fool—he would have no wish to see his men's lives thrown away."

"Even to capture a man who tried to kill him?"

Braylar shook his head. "Suspects attempted to kill him. That is the key. Suspects. That, and he values Captain Honeycock too highly."

I watched the torches moving in Gurdinn's camp. While the men wielding them seemed to be moving almost randomly before, several appeared to be forming up roughly into a square now.

"What if," I asked carefully, "the High Priest is expecting reinforcements?"

Mulldoos turned and spit against a nearby tree. "Nah. They got their household guard, and some troops on hand. But no army to speak of.

Gurdinn might not have one gathered here either, but he's got a sizable enough force. Henny's got no reinforcements."

"Sellswords maybe?" Vendurro asked.

Mulldoos shot the younger man a look. "You been kicked in the head by your horse recently? Nowhere near enough time to hire help of that kind. Telling you, Gurdinn's just playing games here. He. . . "

Mulldoos trailed off as the torches and dark figures indicated more Brunesmen had formed up into another sizable square, thick with shields held above their heads and in the front line.

Both squares started forward as the first light of dawn broke over the horizon.

"Nahhhh, he ain't plaguing doing it. Feint, nothing but a feint." But Mulldoos didn't sound entirely convinced.

The priestguard in the towers started shooting arrows. I couldn't make them out really, but I heard the twang of the bowstrings, and then saw a few strike the ground in front of the Brunesmen.

The two squares suddenly surged forward, breaking into a trot as they rushed the wall. Once in range, the arrows started to come fast, but the initial barrage thunked into the shields held overhead.

Vendurro slapped the cold ground. "Plague me, but they're doing it. Mad bastards are rushing the wall!"

If there had been more men on the walls with bows, they might have whittled the Brunesmen down quickly with a withering hail, but there only seemed to be a handful of bows shooting at them, and the locked shields did their job for the most part—only two soldiers were struck, neither fatally.

The two squares reached the wall and Brunesmen stepped out to throw torches. One was struck in the shoulder by an arrow and his torch fell harmlessly to the ground, but the other launched his up into the wooden tower as an arrow whizzed above his head and forced him to step back under cover of the shields. The squares parted a little, and the Brunesmen positioned ladders in the base of the dry moat as best they could and leaned them up against the wall. It didn't look easy, but Henlester hadn't thought to fill the dry moat with any kind of spikes or impediment, so it didn't slow down the besiegers overmuch. A concentrated rain of arrows came fast and heavy, and a few more Brunesmen were hit, their armor sparing some the worst wounds, but still, men fell in the dry moat, some certainly never to rise again.

I found myself leaning forward to watch, and saw the others doing the same. Suddenly I heard a scream, and thought one of the Brunesmen dead or dying, but it was an archer on the wall. He had an arrow in his neck and toppled backwards, disappearing from view.

Gurdinn had brought some bows, and the archers were out there in the dark between the torchlit camp and the torchlit wall, loosing arrows with little risk of being hit themselves.

Mulldoos actually whooped. "He might be a plaguing horsecunt, Cap, and a fool besides, but he's got guts! Got to give the bastard that."

The torch that had been thrown up into the tower must have been stamped out or kicked back behind the wall, but the archers weren't showing themselves as much, given that their silhouettes made them targets and arrows continued to plunk into the wood or ricochet off the stone every time they stood to take aim at the men scaling the walls.

Gurdinn's men climbed the ladders, shields held above them with one arm to offer some protection from the archers above. Though the walls were shorter than those around a castle, they were constructed in similar fashion—there was a parapet for the priestguard to man the wall, though simple and wooden. Two of the priestguard flung one ladder back before a Brunesman could get purchase, but when two more tried to throw off the other ladder, a priestguard was struck twice and dove or fell, and the other ducked, giving two of Gurdinn's men time to climb over. The first was cut down as an axe struck him in the face, and he tumbled backwards into the dry moat, but the other held off two more priestguards long enough for more Brunesmen to gain purchase and start battling the priestguard on top of the wall.

Three more ladders went up, and while two more were knocked back, the third held long enough for more Brunesmen to rush over the top and take the wall. The priestguard fought hard, and several Brunesmen were thrown or knocked off the wall.

It was difficult to make out much except shadowy movements, and flashes of torchlight off bits of armor and weapons and the edge of shields. But the ring and clamor of battle carried loud enough that felt like it was taking place right in front of me.

Mulldoos was right. Gaining and holding the spots on the wall was proving costly. Even with Gurdinn's archers in the dark shooting at what must have been close range and taking out some of the priestguard, I saw several Brunesmen fall, either wounded badly enough to be out of the fight or dead. And a fair number who had been near the tops of ladders when they were repulsed must have sustained grievous injuries as well hitting the stones or packed earth below.

Vendurro pointed to the opposite side of the compound. Fire suddenly bloomed in two of the wooden towers there.

Braylar nodded in appreciation. "He drew most of the defenders to the north wall with the showy assault. The priestguard didn't have enough men to hold the entire perimeter, or they were undisciplined and left the southern stretch. Either way, a clever stratagem."

The priestguard saw the flames as well, as several went running across the courtyard to put them out and fight off any invaders inside the compound.

I saw one fall, dropping his shield and clutching the arrow in his thigh. It looked to have been shot from somewhere near the fires.

"Very clever," Braylar said. "Captain Honeycock has lost men, but it won't prove nearly as costly as it should."

The defenders fought for every inch of the north wall as they tried to repel Gurdinn's soldiers—some more ladders were pushed away, some more Brunesmen were cut down or pinned with arrows, but Braylar was right. With their forces split between the walls, the priestguard were overwhelmed, their bodies thrown from the wall or littering the courtyard.

When the balance shifted, it tipped quickly. Several Brunesmen that had managed to secure a spot on the courtyard formed up in a half-ring, fending off the priestguard while one of their comrades unbarred the large wooden gate and let the remainder in.

Near the wooden tower closest to us, three Brunesmen raced up the stairs. The archer in the tower had been shooting at other Brunesmen coming through the gate and hadn't seen those nearest him until it was too late. He dropped his bow and tried to draw his sword, but a spear took him in the throat before he got it out of the scabbard.

Another pair of the priestguard started falling back to the lodge itself, shields and swords still up, as four Brunesmen advanced on them. I couldn't tell if the Brunesmen ordered them to surrender or not, but if they did, the priest's soldiers ignored them.

Two of Gurdinn's men in the center kept the priestguard occupied, swords flashing, shields blocking the blows, but the other two quickly flanked the priest's soldiers and cut them down, hammered them from all angles until the swords found a spot not protected by mail and pummeled or shattered the bones and flesh underneath. The four Brunesmen moved off quickly in a group, attacking another knot of the priest's soldiers from the rear who were trying to retreat from the wall.

Several of Henlester's men ran for the entrance to the lodge, but Gurdinn's men cut them off. Looking around, and seeing themselves badly outnumbered, they started throwing their shields and weapons in the dirt.

I thought with their blood up, the Brunesmen might not be in the prisoner-taking mood. Gaining the courtyard hadn't been easy, even with the diversion, and they'd seen several of their own wounded or cut down. But Brune's soldiers were disciplined enough not to murder unarmed men. Or feared punishment from Gurdinn. Or more likely the Baron himself. Either way, they kicked weapons away, ordered Henlester's soldiers on their knees, and bound their arms behind their backs.

A few more priestguard fought on in small pockets, but soon the clang of battle died down, and it wasn't long before the remaining priestguard saw that the engagement was decided and threw down their weapons as well.

I saw Gurdinn in the middle of the courtyard, his sword edged in blood that looked black. He took stock as the priestguard were trussed and guarded, as the Brunesmen dead and wounded were tended to, cleaned his blade and slowly slid it back in the scabbard. Like Braylar, he led from the front.

Mulldoos said, "Lost some men, but that old bastard pulled it off. Stubborn prick, but seems to be smarter when the fight's on than when it ain't."

Hewspear agreed. "Smart plan, sound execution. He lost fewer men than he really should have, all things considered."

"Then again, Henlester might have a former soldier or two in his employ, but if so, judging by that fiasco, they're either green as hell or ain't seen any proper fighting in a long time. No cohesion at all. Lost their advantage, responded too slow or too fast."

With the gate open, most of the Brunesmen had moved into the lodge compound, some to guard the prisoners and lead them back to their camp, some to aid their wounded, but most gathered around Gurdinn as he called out something in the direction of the stone lodge. I noticed he hadn't slung his shield on his back yet.

Vendurro asked, "How long, you figure?"

"Before what?" Mulldoos replied. "Henlester comes out or I take a shit?"

"The surrender, I was thinking."

Braylar didn't give Mulldoos time to respond. "The High Priest stood a fair chance of holding Honeycock at bay, provided he held the wall. But the lodge proper isn't designed to really withstand a serious attack. Too many doors and windows. Two or three accessible from the top of the stables, there." He pointed, presumably for my benefit, as if I might not have been able to identify stables or windows. "I'm guessing there are only a handful of priestguard inside—he committed them all to the defense of the wall. As he should have. Now that he's lost that, and unless I misjudge and Henlester is a tremendous fool, he will come out shortly. He has little choice."

"Head held real high, though." Mulldoos laughed. "Like Gurdinn ought to be grateful he deigned to surrender to the likes of him and his lot. Ought to kiss the hem of his tunic, thank him for being such a holy horsecunt of a powerful prisoner."

Hewspear added, "Which is exactly why he might keep Gurdinn waiting all morning. While he has nothing to truly gain by it, inconveniencing someone he considers a lesser shouldn't be discounted."

We waited, and watched Gurdinn waiting, and I broke the silence by asking, "What if he's holding out for a rescue?"

Mulldoos snorted. "Rescue? You know something we don't, scribbler?"

"You said yourself that Gurdinn wouldn't attack a fortified position unless there was a compelling reason to do it. So Henlester has no more troops, as you said. But what about some of the other priests? This lodge belongs to High Priest Vustinios, correct?"

"That it does. But offering sanctuary is one thing. Sending in a relief force and inviting war from a big-britches baron is something altogether different. High Priest Vustinios might have given Henlester the keys to the lodge, but he ain't risking his neck more than that. No rescue party coming."

"Well, why did Gurdinn attack in the night then? He took the compound, but he lost men, even with his ploy. Something pressed him to act."

"Can't say. Because he's an impatient prick?" Mulldoos tried to make that sound as dismissive as he could—and did a very credible job—but I sensed a note there. As if the question were niggling him more than he was giving me credit for. Particularly as time dragged on.

Gurdinn wasn't content to sit and wait too long, though. He bellowed out something, an ultimatum no doubt, and when the doors didn't swing open and he was answered only with silence, he ordered some men with axes into position while the rest of his men readied their shields and weapons again.

But before the first blade struck wood, the door slowly swung out over the landing. The Brunesmen stepped back, and a man emerged who had to be High Priest Henlester. As predicted, he did carry himself with a degree of haughtiness, but no more or less than most influential fieflords or clerics. High Priest Henlester looked around at the armed men facing him, his white hair hanging wild about his shoulders, face clean shaven, and then he hiked his tunic in his hand and walked down the stairs, looking every inch like someone in command of the situation and not someone about to be a bound in chains.

He marched up to Gurdinn, and they had a lengthy exchange. Then Henlester turned and summoned some of his acolytes who had been hiding inside the hunting lodge. They filed out, looking nervous and staying close together like a flock of chickens. They didn't appear nearly as confident that the gods would protect them from angry men with bloodied swords. Which was wise, although now that Gurdinn had Henlester in hand, he didn't seem all that interested in the minions. He finally slung his shield across his back and started across the yard toward the gate, his men ushering Henlester forward. Other Brunesmen guided the remaining acolytes, though "herded" would be closer to the truth, and a few went into the lodge, I imagined to search the grounds for any priestguard or holy men attempting to hide behind.

As we watched the Brunesmen directing their prisoners to the wagons and tents of the besiegers-turned-conquerors, Mulldoos scooted back from the ridge and sat up. "Stupid, lucky, skilled, maybe some mix of the three, but Gurdinn's got Henfucker by the nose. Now what?"

Braylar didn't reply immediately, but then he suddenly seemed to make a decision. He moved back as well, and when he was far enough away not to be sighted from the other side, stood, shaking the small stones and leaves from his hands. "Now, we get him."

The other Syldoon all edged back and got to their feet as well, and Mulldoos said, "Gurdinn lost some men down there, for sure, but still has us outnumbered pretty good. Guessing you got yourself a plan then, Cap?"

Braylar looked at his men and smiled. "I have myself a plan." Then he started down the hill.

"Worried he was going to say that." Mulldoos followed, with Vendurro, Hewspear, and myself a few steps back.

For once, I shared Mulldoos's sentiment exactly.

Braylar got his troops moving quickly and it wasn't long before we were back in the saddle. If the Syldoon were curious what we were up to, they kept it to themselves as far as I could see. Braylar ordered two men to ride on and reclaim the wagons and to meet us several miles ahead on the road east toward Marty's Fork.

Everyone seemed glad to be riding again, and heading in the direction of home. All save Soffjian, and to a lesser extent, or at least by proxy, Skeelana. I overheard Soffjian asking her brother what had happened so quickly to convince him to quit the area and return home. In true Braylarian fashion, he ignored her the first time, and hedged when she repeated her inquiry the second.

It was clear he was less than forthcoming, but aside from a small uneven smile that radiated condescension, she did and said nothing else and fell back from him as our company rode through the woods, choosing instead to wait it out and ride alongside Skeelana.

I rode past the pair, and Skeelana looked over at me. As ever, there was a peculiar amusement there, playing on her lips and skittering across her eyes, that I couldn't quite fathom. It was as if she found the sibling squabbles amusing, even if our lives might be hanging in the balance or outcome. Or maybe it was the entire enterprise she found funny. Or me. That last possibility bothered me the most. And the fact that it bothered me at all bothered me even more.

We wound our way around the broad twisted trunks of the bronze trees. Braylar was maintaining as quick a pace as we could manage through the forest, short of blindly galloping and getting whipped in the face with passing branches.

When I finally passed the rank and file Syldoon and approached the captain and his closest retinue, I wondered what Braylar's plan consisted of that was going to throw his much smaller company against a larger one that proved itself eminently capable in matters of bloodletting. Though I had no idea about specifics, I didn't need Bloodsounder to tell me that violence was coming. There was no mistaking that.

We rode up and down the hills throughout the morning, with two Syldoon scouts somewhere ahead, one periodically falling back long enough to report. The company broke once to give the horses a rest, but not for very long. The captain pushed hard, and that resonated with his men, even if he hadn't shared his plans. Their mood seemed to change as we pressed on, more stern and serious, as if they intuited their leader was bringing them to combat.

The group stopped and cared for the horses again early afternoon, as our smaller dirt path grew together with a wider and grassier route, the tall blades blowing in the breeze. It was much too early to make camp, so something else was afoot. After receiving another report from a soldier and sending him back on his horse, Braylar summoned his company together. They all looked at him expectantly. I seemed to be the only one with obvious nerves.

Captain Killcoin pointed at the broader trail and said, "Captain Gurdinn is going to be leading his Brunesmen down this path sometime in the next few hours. He has several wagons in his little caravan, so the going will be slow. I expect him to round the bend in the trail near dusk. He has more men in his company. A fair amount more. But as you no doubt heard, they attacked the hunting lodge this morning, and they will only be eager to find a suitable place to collapse for the night.

"They won't have that opportunity."

A few men chuckled, and others leaned in to hear more. All save Soffjian, who stood against a tree, no less stiff than the trunk. Maybe more.

Braylar continued. "They are bearing a fair number of wounded soldiers, with priestly prisoners in tow as well. Chief among them, High Priest Henlester. Which must be quite the burden. I would very much like to relieve Gurdinn of some of it, yes? So, half of you will cross to the opposite side of the trail and wait for my signal there. Benk reports that the wounded and prisoners are near the rear of the caravan. So after a third of the procession passes, you will lay into them with the crossbows.

"As I said, they are fairly well-trained, and no fools. But fairly rigid. They will do what we'd expect Anjurians to do when ambushed by a barrage of bolts. The forest is crowded. No good for horses. So they will dismount and form up. Shield wall, most likely. And after they have withstood another volley, they will advance on you. And that is when we will attack from the rear."

I saw some Syldoon nodding, and a couple smiling as Braylar said, "The objective is to capture Henlester. Or see him dead, if capture proves untenable. No needless risks. We are not trying to wipe this caravan out, or even drive it to flight. We capture Henlester, and then we melt into the woods. Reconvene heading to Martyr's Fork. Do not underestimate these Anjurians. We are superior soldiers, but they outnumber us greatly even after suffering losses at the lodge, and they aren't fools. We engage them only long enough to achieve our goal and disappear. One objective, and done." He looked around slowly at the assembled crew, taking each in turn before asking, "Are there any questions then?"

No one replied right away, and right when I thought the captain about to send his troops off, Mulldoos said, "Alright. I got one. They got numbers, like you said. Even with a good ambush—and I'm going on record here and saying this sounds as good as they come—we still only have the one objective, like you said. But I know how you hate to leave an enemy at your back or hightail from a fight of any kind. So, I'm thinking we got a chance to wipe them out here. If the Memoridons lend a hand, that is. So that's my question. Will the Memoridons be lending a hand?" He looked at Soffjian then.

Braylar said, "I would never presume to answer for my sweet sister, but I suspect the answer is a resounding no."

Soffjian replied directly to Mulldoos. "As you well know, I answer to Commander Darzaak. Not my brother, and certainly not his surly and dim lieutenant. We're here to ensure you make it back to Sunwrack safely and in a timely fashion, neither of which involves me fighting your fights for you. So let me be clear: I will not assist in actions I consider unnecessary, and frankly in violation of the spirit of the command. Which is to return promptly. So, finish playing your war games in the woods, and let's get on with it. We have a road to ride."

Mulldoos spat in the grass. "Figured as much. You were a man, I'd call you coward instead of just a woman who meddles where she shouldn't and don't help out where she should."

Soffjian showed her teeth, though it was clearly vulpine. "And if you were any kind of man, I'd take offense."

Mulldoos stood, laid his hand on the large pommel of his falchion. "You might be a witch, bitch. But you still bleed, don't you?"

"With every moon. But seldom else, Syldoon. Seldom else."

The two of them stared each other down before Hewspear cleared his throat. "Well. That answers that question pretty soundly, I'd say."

Braylar looked around the rest of the company. "Any others then? Preferably those not destined to end in bloodshed and memorycraft among our own?" Braylar waited for only a moment, clearly not in the mood to entertain more discussion. "Very good. Hewspear, lead a handful of men across the trail. When the Brunesmen are ripe for plucking, you loose first, yes?"

Hewspear nodded and picked out some Syldoon to accompany him. They led their horses out across the path, and then disappeared into the thick woods on the other side.

I looked at Braylar. "What if the horses whinny? Won't they give away Hewspear's position?"

Braylar watched Soffjian and Skeelana walk off in the woods as he replied, "Hewspear has been involved in an ambush or two in his time, Arki. He will tether the horses far enough away not to alert the Brunesmen, but not so distant they can't reach them in a hurry."

He looked at Vendurro. "Sergeant?"

Vendurro stood at attention. "Aye, Cap?"

"When we have word that their little convoy is coming, Mulldoos and I will lead some men back to get in position to hit the wagons and get our priest. You'll remain here, opposite Hew. Just after the lead horses pass, he'll send the first volley. As I said, I expect them to dismount and form up. If so, wait until you have their backs to you to loose from this side. If they opt to try to ride into the woods, shoot immediately. Understood?"

"Aye, Cap. Fast or slow, pulling triggers once I get their backsides. Got it."

Braylar twitched or smiled—it happened so quickly it was hard to be sure which or if it was a combination. "I can always count on you to parse out the essence of a thing. Take five and Arki will stay with your group."

Vendurro moved off and picked his men, relaying the directive they had, and they began spanning their crossbows, flipping the fur-covered flaps off their quivers.

Braylar pulled the remaining Syldoon aside and made sure they were clear on their role in the engagement. And just like that, Mulldoos and I were standing a few paces apart. He wasn't paying me much attention though as he sat on a log, checking the buckles on his splinted greaves and vambraces, sliding the falchion free of the scabbard three times, inspecting the steel edge of his shield. I had no armor, and only Lloi's sword, and though I was tempted to slide it free from my own scabbard, I knew that would only end in mockery, so I looked up through the trees, watching as a group of perfectly aligned geese flew overhead, flashing through the spaces between the branches.

After the disappeared from view, I listened to their honking grow fainter as well, wondering if they were a good omen or bad.

When I looked back down, Mulldoos was staring at me. I forced myself not to look away, and did the only manly thing I could think of, giving the small quick nod I'd seen so many soldiers share that somehow conveyed respect and acknowledgement and absolutely nothing at all.

Mulldoos continued staring for a minute, shook his head, and returned his attention to his gear.

Vendurro made me jump as he somehow moved alongside without me hearing or noticing. "Always been curious about something, Mulldoos."

Mulldoos didn't look up again as he ran his fingers over the straps of his shield, feeling for something. Excessive wear? A tear? Something else. "Oh yeah? This ought to be good. What you curious about, Ven?"

"Well, when you call someone a horsecunt, are you calling them the lady bits of a whore, or a filly's pink business? Could go either way, couldn't it?"

Mulldoos stopped and did look up, fixing his pale eyes on the younger man. "You're some kind of something, you are. This is what you think about right before shooting yourself some Brunesmen?"

Vendurro shrugged, the lamellar plates clacking a bit as he did. "Like to keep my mind moving. Instead of fixating on the bloodletting. Plenty of time to think about that after. Before, I like to keep it moving. So which is it?"

"I ain't called anybody a horsecunt in, shit, not sure how long."

"Matter of minutes, most like. So, is it a whore or a horse you're talking about?"

"Does it plaguing matter?"

"Neither's much of a compliment, that's for certain. But the meaning of something always matters."

Mulldoos looked up at the foliage, miming as if he was seriously mulling the question over. "Well then, I suppose it all depends, don't it?"

"On?"

"On what I happened to be thinking of right before the dumb horse-cunt asked me a fool question right before a battle instead of inspecting his gear like he ought to. See now, right this second, I'm wishing we had more room to maneuver. Never liked fighting in a forest, if it could be helped. So I got horse on the brain. So when I say to that dumb bastard that bothered me when I was doing what I ought to be doing, "Hey, you whopping dumb horsecunt, maybe you ought to be picking out the straightest quarrel to loose first, or making sure you ain't busted a lace on your armor there, instead of letting your mind wander all over the world and bringing back the stupidest question you could think to utter, I suppose I'd have a horse in mind. You are the slit of a horse. Clear it up any?"

Vendurro didn't look insulted in the slightest. "See now. That's all I needed to know."

"You've been kicked in the head by your horse. More than once. I swear it's true. Not—"

Braylar returned, his lamellar and mail clattering and slithering, so there was no mistaking his approach. "Vendurro has the right of this. The meaning of a thing always matters. Always."

"Oh yeah? How do you figure?" Mulldoos asked.

"There would probably be far fewer conflicts in the world if we all made more efforts for clarity of communication."

"Nahh. We'd just understand why the other bastard hated us a little bit better, is all." Mulldoos plucked a mushroom off the log and threw it out of the shadows of the woods, watching it spin fat end over thin as it flew through the sun.

Braylar said, "Disregard etymology at your peril, Lieutenant."

Mulldoos stood, armor clinking. "Sometimes I swear I'm the only one in the outfit that ain't been kicked in the head by his horse."

Vendurro watched Mulldoos go and laughed, shaking his head. "Bristliest bastard ever been born, that one."

Braylar was watching the trail. "And yet, perfectly suited to his station."

"No argument there."

"The Brunesmen should be along shortly. Stand ready." The captain led his horse through the trees.

Vendurro shook his head and then punched my shoulder. "Come on. Cap's right on that count, got to stand ready. Span that crossbow, Arki. Unless you plan on throwing quills at the baron's boys."

I wanted to protest I didn't intend on shooting bolts at anyone if I could help it. But it would be better to have a loaded crossbow in my hands and not loose it than to have a Brunesmen attacking us and be stuck with quills and ink bottles. I nodded and followed Vendurro to the other group of ambushers.

I sat in our pocket of woods with Vendurro and the other Syldoon in our group and waited. In my brief experience, that seemed to happen a lot more in soldiering than the songs and tales would have you believe. Rather than brave assaults, stirring duels, colossal clashes of armies, and heroic last stands that everyone so often heard about, it was largely proving to be cramped muscles, stiff backs, long stretches of boredom and inactivity or unremarkable travel, punctuated by brief episodes of horrific bloodshed.

A short Syldoon next to me with a weak chin and watery eyes swore and swatted at an insect at his neck, his hand leaving behind a small red smear.

Vendurro hissed at him. "Hey, I got an idea, Morrud. So long as you're flailing around and making your cuirass jingle jangle, maybe you could sing a little ditty or two, knock out a nice beat on the log there, something the other troopers can dance to. What do you say?"

Morrud replied, "Bloody tar fly bit me. Right there on the neck, it did. What—"

"Worst bunch of ambushers I ever laid eyes on. You shut your yap now, keep it shut. This gets spoiled on account of your plaguing mouth, you can be sure Cap ain't going to be any kind of pleased."

He didn't have the natural bluster of threat of doling out damage that Mulldoos did, or the stately carriage of Hewspear, and was only a sergeant rather than a lieutenant, but Morrud shut his yap just the same. While he might not have feared Vendurro directly, he clearly wasn't inclined to incur the captain's wrath if he could help it. Smart move.

Vendurro looked relieved. More responsibility fell to him now with Glesswik gone, and while he was bearing the weight of it well enough, he clearly wore it like a poor-fitting cuirass.

We waited as the sun slowly slid behind the treeline, sending stark dappled shadows across everything that seemed to undulate as the breeze caught the branches high above us and gently shifted the boughs to and fro. It was strangely idyllic, the sound of the trees swaying, the woods peaceful, serene. It was hard to believe it might all erupt into chaos at any moment. I wished Gurdinn had chosen to lead his convoy along a different route through the forest, knowing that he hadn't.

And then I heard it. The jingle of harness, the soft clomp of hooves on the packed earth. I watched the bend in the path a hundred yards away, hoping my ears played tricks on me, sure they didn't, and then the first horseman rounded the bend, looking ahead wearily, helm and hauberk and spear head flashing as shafts of the last day's sun filtered through the trees and danced across the steel. And then more horsemen appeared in a column behind him.

Captain Killcoin had been right to hold off the ambush until now. The remainder of the sun was directed right into the Brunesmen's eyes, and whatever hostile energy they had after the attack on the hunting lodge had fallen aside by now, replaced only by weariness and a desire to get out of the woods and return to the road back home. The Syldoon around me had their crossbows loaded and ready and I held mine, very careful to keep my hands, branches, and anything else away from the long metal trigger, terrified I would accidentally loose it and give away our position and the attack.

The Syldoon around me were crouched behind trees, and I mirrored them as much as I could. The rest of Gurdinn's convoy came into view, what view I allowed myself around a trunk, as the lead soldiers continued riding, spears at rest, shields slung on the saddles or their backs, shoulders a bit slumped. After ten horsemen, I saw the first wagon, pulled by four oxen, moving slow. It had a flat wooden roof, iron bars all around behind the driver's seat, and a locked gate to the rear. The prisoners were sitting inside, backs against the bars, the wagon rocking as it rolled over the uneven ground, axle creaking, with the driver goading the oxen on to keep them moving. Other horseman followed, another caged wagon full of prisoners pulled by horses this time, more horseman, and a final supply wagon with no bars, with the remaining prisoners tethered behind, arms bound, walking. There were four or five more horsemen in the rear.

I knew the Syldoon would have the element of surprise and didn't intend to fight them toe to toe, but seeing the convoy approach, even with the circumstances in the Syldoon favor, I imagined a hundred ways it could all go horribly wrong. And only a few of them due to me bungling anything.

But I held my breath, listening to the branches blown by the breeze, counting the seconds off, looking off to the west as the setting sun was turning a lurid, deep red.

Several horses rode past our position, and no signal was given. I wondered if Braylar had called the ambush off when I suddenly heard a trilling whistle.

And then. . . chaos. I heard the twang of crossbows followed immediately by screams. I peeked around the trunk, face pressed to the bark, and looked through the bushes and smaller trunks ahead.

Two horses were now riderless, and several other soldiers had stout bolts sticking out of their hauberks, though it was impossible to tell how deep they had penetrated. The Brunesmen were reaching for shields, pulling weapons to the ready, looking around the woods for someone to fight. I heard orders being called up and down the line, though I couldn't make out the words, and saw Gurdinn riding among his men to where they had been hit first, shouting at them. A few of the horsemen rode toward the edge of the woods, but Gurdinn screamed at them to form up. Another volley of bolts flew out of the trees on the other side of the trail, and I thought I saw Syldoon, but only for a moment before they were hidden by trunks again. A horse went down, a quarrel sticking out of its muscular neck, and the rider was trapped underneath, flailing as he tried to pull his leg out from under the beast. The other Brunesmen jumped off their mounts, lining up together facing the woods, overlapping the edges of their shields, dropping their spears and drawing their swords.

More bolts came out of the trees, close enough together to be a volley, but most slammed into shield faces or skidded off the tops of helms or the greaves beneath the shields. One or two struck hauberks, but none of the injuries dropped anyone from the shieldwall. The line of Brunesmen started forward on foot, heading toward the woods, and most of the others between wagons were forming up as well.

I gripped my crossbow tight, wondering if Braylar's plan was already unraveling, when Vendurro gave a hand signal to the Syldoon around me. They darted forward, found good spots aiming between trees, lined up their shots, and loosed at the backs of the Brunesmen advancing in the opposite direction.

Every single bolt struck a target, most square in the back of a foe. With mail and padded gambesons, the Brunesmen were well protected—those shots would have killed every less-armored foe on the spot—but they weren't invulnerable, either. One stumbled and fell, and another dropped to his knees, groping at the man next to him as he tried to rise, but his legs didn't seem to be working.

When the Brunesmen realized they were caught between crossbows on either side, someone else shouted orders and they stopped advancing and reformed, creating two smaller shield walls facing the woods on either side, with the wounded or dead in the middle. This group in the front of the wagons was pinned down, especially as another volley hit from the opposite side, thunking into shields. And there was a moment of disarray, with horses screaming and some running off, the lead wagon driver struck twice by bolts and falling into the dirt, the drivers behind diving for cover, and it looked like the Brunesmen were immobile, paralyzed by uncertainty and maybe fear.

But if the rest of them were, Gurdinn was not. He rode up the line, calling out commands, no doubt calculating by the number of bolts that his attackers were smallish in number, even with them reloading so quickly with the devil's claws and loosing faster than any normal crossbowmen could. The group of soldiers in front stayed put, the wounded crying out or falling still in between what remained of both lines. But other lines had formed up facing either side of the trail and with Gurdinn bellowing, they started toward the trees in a hurry, keeping the shields close as they could as they moved at a jog to close the distance and meet their attackers.

Vendurro and his men loosed another volley and then moved back away from the trail, darting between trees. I was frozen, watching the shield faces bob as the line advanced on us, angry, wounded, scared men no doubt filled with rage and eager to spill the blood of the attackers who had struck them so unexpectedly. Unable to move, I watched the red sun flash on the helm tops, and then Vendurro grabbed my tunic and pulled me hard. "No time for spectating, Arki!"

I jumped up and ran after him through the woods until we came to our horses. I didn't have time to ask questions, just climbed into the saddle as quickly as I could, careful not to shoot my horse or any of the men by accident, fumbling with the crossbow, my foot slipping in the stirrup, my heart hammering in my chest, blood pounding in my ears, breath coming faster, as I heard shouting in the woods behind me, so close I thought I might feel a sword slash across me at any moment.

But then I was up, and kicked my heels into the horse's side harder than I meant to, and he jumped forward as we moved around and between the thick tree trunks as quickly as we dared. I was tempted to look back, but I was afraid that as soon as I turned I'd be struck in the face by a low-hanging branch and knocked out of the saddle, easy target for slaughter.

Common sense won out, as I realized that if they hadn't reached me yet, they weren't about to on foot—even if we couldn't move fast, Braylar had chosen the perfect spot, largely clear of brambles or brush to slow our escape, so no one on foot could have caught up.

We made our way through the woods, and they were thinning out as we moved closer to the edge of the tract of hunting forest and approached the open ground beyond. I had no idea if this was part of the plan, and if so, if it was working as expected or not. All I could do was keep my head down, stay in the saddle, and try not to fall far behind the superior horsemen in front of me.

And then, suddenly, we broke free from the trees. The rolling plain beyond was almost overwhelming in its openness, especially lit by a brilliant, almost awful sunset, the sky never redder, every cloud seemingly blazing from within, suffused with fire and vengeance, roiling, churning, nothing but fury in every direction. Some poets spoke of red sunsets as things of sublime beauty, prefacing good fortune or romance, but they always seemed to be foretelling some bloodletting, murder, or tragedy writ large for all the world to see, and never more so than now.

The Syldoon rode out fifteen paces and then halted, turning their horses to face the trail, all spanning their crossbows, one or two looking back in the direction we's come from as they worked the levers and fitted new quarrels in place, checking for pursuit.

Another group of Syldoon cantered out of the treeline on the opposite side of the trail, Hewspear raising an arm and hailing us as his men reloaded their weapons as well. I wondered what we were going to do—ride hard and regroup somewhere else? Race back down the road and into the fray? I hoped no one meant to enter the woods again and fight the Brunesmen there. I was a scribe, not a soldier—if I accompanied them, I was sure to either get myself killed or accidentally kill one of my comrades, and if I refused, I was sure to incur the wrath of Mulldoos.

Then I heard more horses galloping our way. The Syldoon raised their crossbows, almost in unison, to take aim, assuming as I did that it was Gurdinn and his men rushing to meet us. But instead it was a wagon riding out of control, the horses spooked and running of their own volition with an empty bench behind them and prisoners tumbling around inside the cage, struggling to grab the bars and stay upright, most failing and falling as the runaway wagon veered wildly.

Syldoon on both sides of the trail raced forward to intercept the wagon. The horses pulling the wagon were in full panic and gallop though, and more horses racing alongside them didn't seem to be doing much to calm them down. While the Syldoon were able to force the course in the general direction of the stone wall marking the edge of the forest, it wasn't until one Syldoon riding alongside managed to grab the reins that it looked like they had it under control.

That's when things went horribly wrong.

One second the wagon was slowing as the Syldoon guided it toward the wall. The next, it must have hit a rut or a sudden incline in the ground, as it lurched onto two wheels, holding there far longer than I would have imagined possible as all the prisoners inside screamed and tried to grab the bars. And that shift finally caused the wagon to topple over. With a horrendous crack, it fell on its side in a cloud of dust and skidded and bounced on the earth, the two closest horses pulled down by the harness as well, the Syldoon barely riding clear of the wreck.

The two wheels up in the air still spun, one smooth, the other wobbling on the damaged hub, squeaking loudly. The prisoners were such a shifting tangle of limbs it was hard to tell how injured they were, or who had been broken or even killed. I imagined the high priest buried underneath them, his neck or back snapped, his lungs crushed, his lifeblood seeping into the grass beneath the bent iron bars that now served as the floor.

All of the Syldoon dismounted. Hewspear pointed to the wagon. "See what's worked loose, lad. We need to find out if Henlester lives."

Vendurro nodded and ordered a few of his men to join him as he inspected the wagon. The gate was still locked, so they started testing the bars. Several of the prisoners got uneasily to their feet, while others still lay in a heap, shifting and moaning. Some of them were in the stiff robes of Truth, and several appeared to be soldiers, obvious from their bearing, even without the arms and armor.

But one prisoner stepped clear of the rest, moving gingerly, as if favoring some wound or afraid to accidentally bump one of the injured men around him. His white hair was in greater disarray than before, tufts sticking this way and that in a halo around his bald pate, and his face was as lined as parchment that had been dampened, crushed into a ball, and unfolded to dry, lines criss-crossing each other apparently at random. The blue veins in his forehead were alarmingly prominent, which together with his age should have given him a look of frailty, weakness. But there was an undeniable air about High Priest Henlester, and not simply because the others moved away deferentially.

He exuded an authority, a power, made even more impressive given his status and situation. Henlester was coldly appraising the Syldoon outside who were arguing amongst themselves about the best way to get the prisoners out.

None of the bars had broken free, even with Syldoon pulling hard on them. Vendurro pushed a Syldoon aside. "Ain't coming loose, Benk. And you ain't so mighty you'll be bending iron. Plaguing idiot. Someone get me an axe!"

Benk took a step back. "You going to cut the iron then?" And when Hewspear glared at him he added a belated "Sergeant?"

"Wagon's made of wood. I sort of had my mind set on cutting that, you dumb fuck." It didn't earn the immediate looks of respect and fear it would have delivered by the pale boar, but it was passable. "Now, you know what an axe looks like? Big metal end, long wooden end?" Benk nodded. "Fetch one. Quick like." He looked at the men around him. "Rest of you, get those shields on your arms and hoist your weapons. Got company."

I looked back down the trail toward the woods and saw Braylar, Mulldoos, and two other Syldoon riding hard, pursued by five mounted Brunesmen. A moment before I'd been thinking it looked like Braylar's plan had worked—we had stolen the wagon containing Henlester and would win free with the awful cleric. Now, with Brunesmen appearing and more certainly on the way, I wondered if we wouldn't be slaughtered against the stone wall.

The Syldoon around me readied their weapons. I wondered why they didn't mount back up, but I guessed they meant to stay with the wagon, at least until they got the high priest free, but I remained in my saddle—I was a terrible fighter on foot or horse, but at least mounted I stood some chance of riding clear if necessary.

I looked back to the trail—a Brunesman just behind Braylar closed the gap and slashed at Braylar's shoulder, the sword skidding across the lamellar plates as the Brunesman hadn't gotten close enough when striking. Braylar slowed a touch, caught the next blow with his shield, and delivered one of his own, the twin chains whirling above the back of his helm, the Deserter heads striking the Brunesman's forearm, just above the gauntlet. The hauberk prevented the spikes from biting deep, but the Brunesmen dropped his sword as Braylar whirled the flail around and brought the heads colliding back into the man, striking the side of the helm.

The Brunesman started to ride off, teetered, and then slumped forward, jostled off his horse's neck, and fell from the saddle.

Benk ran around the back of the wagon. "Nobody got no axe, Sarge. None of the boys here favor one in battle, and nobody thought to be chopping wood during an ambush."

Vendurro kicked the wooden bed of the wagon. "Plague me! Plague me tooth to toenail! Use your damn sword then! Gosswin, give him a hand, you two, smash some boards loose and—"

"A word, if you would." Henlester stepped over an injured prisoner with a bloody scalp, stooping beneath the bars, his hands a breeding ground of brown spots, and face more deeply lined than the most gnarled tree. And yet his eyes were still sharp and commanding. "Would you be rescuers or new captors?"

Vendurro looked over at him. "What's that?"

Henlester sighed. "I'm not sure it matters. A cage is a cage, out is better than in. I believe I saw a toolbox along the bottom of the wagon. No doubt full of tools. No doubt including a hatchet or axe or some such thing."

Vendurro gave Benk an evil look and jerked his head toward the other side of the wagon. Benk ran the other side and then cursed. He poked his head around the corner. "Locked. Need an axe to get in to get the axe."

"Plaguing idiot!" Vendurro drew his sword, and for an instant I thought he meant to cut down his man, but he raced around to the other side. I moved the horse far enough so I could see what he was doing—he knelt and drove his pommel into the lock several times before it fell free. He opened the lid and several tools spilled into the grass, among them a mallet and a small axe. "Benk! Get over here! Now!"

They each grabbed a tool and looked ready to assault the wagon bed. That seemed the strongest part, so I yelled, "The roof!"

The pair of them looked at me like I was mad. "The roof is thinner!"

Hewspear said, "The lad's right. Set to, and be quick about it!"

Glancing back toward the woods, I saw Mulldoos and another Brunesman exchanging blows as they rode—though the racing horses made it difficult to land anything substantial for either man, as the slashes either missed completely or slid off shields, and Mulldoos was at a disadvantage, as the Brunesman was on his left, so he had to deliver blows across his body. But then Mulldoos jerked the reins and moved so close the pair of horsemen could have embraced. He knocked the Brunesman's sword arm out of the way and struck the man in the helm with the shield edge, rocking his head back. Mulldoos slammed his shield boss into the Brunesman's nose, spraying blood and nearly knocking the other man out of the saddle. Then Mulldoos brought his falchion down in a vicious arc.

The broad blade struck him on the neck, and while it didn't shred the mail, the man dropped his sword and his shield arm fell limp to his side. The falchion came down again in the same spot and the Brunesman toppled from the saddle, his foot twisting and catching in the stirrup as he was dragged through the grass.

Vendurro and Benk continued hammering and chopping the wooden roof as the prisoners moved back or pulled their comrades away from the splinters and wood chips that immediately started flying inside the wagon.

Hewspear and his men loosed a volley, and another Brunesman fell. The remaining two had seen enough and turned, trying to head back to the woods. But the other mounted Syldoon still had their crossbows out, and the Syldoon around me had spanned again, and another volley was loosed. The bolts struck their targets, and both had gambesons rather than hauberks, so they fell from the saddle before making it halfway back to the trees.

Braylar and his men rode hard for our position. When the captain reined in, he threw his leg over his horse's neck and vaulted to the ground. As ever, his eyes took everything in quickly—his soldiers armed and ready, the overturned wagon, the dead horses still in their harness. He addressed Vendurro and Benk. "Well, I am no wainwright, but it seems you've run into some difficulties here." He looked at Henlester, who was leaning against the bars, shading his eyes to avoid stray wood chips. "At least the good cleric is alive and well. That is something."

Vendurro kept chopping, sweat pouring down his face. "Have him free in a sec, Cap." Two more blows and he dropped the axe, and Benk threw the mallet in the grass as well as the pair pulled planks away from the crater they made in the roof. Nails screamed in protest, but two boards finally came loose. "Plague me," Vendurro said, wiping his brow, "but they built this thing good." After pulling unsuccessfully on another board, he bent down and retrieved the hatchet.

Braylar looked back to the woods, clear of Brunesmen for the moment. I saw Henlester's eyes fix on Bloodsounder, first widening in surprise, and then narrowing in what I would have wagered was avarice. This wasn't lost on the captain who watched the man as he said, "Best get our holy captive free, Sergeant. Double time, if you would." He called out to the other Syldoon. "We will have unwelcome visitors any moment. Half of you, mount up, hop that wall there, and take cover on the other side, horses down. Wait on my signal, crossbows ready. I would like the Brunesmen to think they have easy prey."

His soldiers obeyed instantly, climbing back in the saddle, riding off a bit to get some room, turning, and then racing for the low wall. I held my breath, sure someone would be unhorsed or break a neck, but only one of the horses clipped the top of the wall with its hooves, sending small stones flying, but not enough to cause an injury that I could tell.

After they dismounted, I expected the Syldoon to jerk on the bridles or bits to compel the beasts down, but they proved just how little I knew about horsemanship. To a man, they spoke quietly and soothingly to the horses, and with a firm but gentle touch on the thick necks, they encouraged them to lie down, disappearing on the other side of the wall.

Vendurro, Benk and two other Syldoon worked at the boards and had created a hole nearly large enough for a man to climb through when a large group of Brunesmen rode out of the forest. Gurdinn was at their head, the setting red sun glinting on the contours of his helm, spaulders, and mail. He briefly surveyed the scene—the Brunesmen horses wandering riderless, the overturned wagon surrounded by a handful of Syldoon— and then Gurdinn spurred his horse forward with his men on his heels.

Mulldoos noticed me and swung his shield in my direction. "Got a real good view from up there, do you?"

I realized I was the only one in our company still mounted and imme- diately climbed down as Mulldoos shook his head, chuckling behind the mail drape on his helm. It was completely incongruous, his mockery as a larger enemy was getting ready to trample us, and yet made sense at the same time.

Luckily, with the wagon for cover and the stone wall immediately behind, the Brunesmen couldn't simply ride over us. So they slowed their charge as they came on, no doubt preparing to simply overwhelm the small group with superior numbers. But when they were fifty feet out, Braylar called out, "Loose!" and the Syldoon hiding behind the wall sprang up, crossbows ready, and let fly. The sudden barrage of bolts disrupted the Brunesmen charge, dropping several from the saddle and sending others reeling off in various directions, many with quarrels sticking out of their gambesons and hauberks.

But Gurdinn regained control of his men quickly enough, bellowing orders. He leapt from the saddle, shield and sword ready, and those closest did the same, dismounting and forming up quickly, having already seen how fast the Syldoon could reload back in the forest. Those who had broken from the wedge were turning their horses, coming back as well when the second volley was loosed.

This time, expecting the attack and with shields locked together, few Brunesmen were hit, with only one more mounted soldier falling, catch- ing a bolt in the armpit as he dismounted. Then they were all on foot, running full on. The Syldoon on the other side of the wall dropped their crossbows, drew their sidearms, and started climbing over to join their comrades. Even with their neatly executed ambush and Gurdinn's men thinned, the Syldoon were still outnumbered.

I held my ground, crossbow up, sighting down the length at the foes closing fast as they shouted some sort of warcry, just as they'd done in the copse when we fought alongside them only a few days prior.

One soldier on the end of the line dropped his shield a bit to look over the top, and I aimed as best as I could and squeezed the trigger, expecting it to sail high or thunk into a shield. I was shocked as it struck him in the face and the soldier dropped to the ground.

I had no time to think on it as the Syldoon readied their weapons— swords, falchions, slashing spears, maces, shields up, and stood around the wagon to meet the Brunesmen. I looked up from trying to span the crossbow as quickly as I could and saw the final instant before the two sides clashed under a blood red sky.

There were no more tricks or maneuvers, no more ambushes, and un- like the fight in the copse, no cover besides the overturned wagon still full of terrified prisoners. With clangor and clang, the two sides met as men tried to beat, slash, or bludgeon each other to death.

Two Syldoon shouldered past me to meet the Brunesmen, and I nearly discharged the crossbow as I was jostled. They rushed past and it was mayhem everywhere in front of me. No sooner had I sighted a Brunes- man to try to shoot then the battle shifted, the bodies moved, and there was suddenly a Syldoon in between. Afraid to pull the trigger again, sure I would strike down one of Braylar's men, I considered drawing Lloi's blade, but knew I would only get myself killed if I waded into the melee.

The Syldoon tried holding a line, but it wasn't a shield wall, and as they were outnumbered, it flexed and broke up, smaller groups of men fighting together to keep the Brunesmen from flanking them. The wall behind us might have prevented any retreat, but it served to keep the Brunesmen largely in front of us as well.

Two Brunesmen worked in tandem near the edge, trying to take out the Syldoon before them. They were turning him, keeping him on the defen- sive as he blocked and avoided blows, unable to throw any of this own. It seemed any instant they would down him, and I nearly shot the crossbow, but then Hewspear moved in front of me, his long slashing spear coming down in a high arc. The Brunesmen hadn't seen him approach either, and the closest barely got his shield up in time, expecting to block the blow. But Hewspear had anticipated the block, maybe even counted on it, and drew the spear back before it struck the shield, recocked the weapon, and sent a thrust out—it was aimed perfectly, striking the Brunesman's thigh just beneath the hauberk and above the greave, biting deep into the flesh.

The Brunesman took a step back with one leg, and nearly toppled putting weight on the other. Seeing him off balance, Hewspear swung again—the Brunesman blocked it easily enough with the edge of his shield, but then Hewspear jerked his weapon back, hooking the shield edge with the lugs and pulling it back, and then thrusting forward, driving the point into the soldier's stomach. I couldn't see if it pierced the mail or not, but it doubled him over, and Hewspear finished him off with another downward stroke to the back of the neck and then began working on the lone Brunesman in tandem with the other Syldoon.

This played itself out everywhere I looked, advantages turning quickly for one small group or another, impossible to gauge who was actually winning the fight. A retreating Syldoon took a step back from a pair of advancing Brunesmen, ran into the stone wall, tried to slip away from it, and took a blade across the arm, right above the splinted vambrace. He screamed as blood covered the iron, dropped his sword, fended off two more blows as he turned and tried to get away from the wall and draw his suroka. Another blade struck him in the side, across the lamellar, doing little if any harm to him, but the next cut caught him across the back of the thigh. The Syldoon dropped to one knee, and I was sure he was dead. A Brunesman advanced, kicking the shield aside to deliver the fatal blow, and jerked back as the Syldoon drove his suroka up the inside of the hauberk, either into the soldier's crotch or deep inner thigh.

The other Brunesman slashed twice across the Syldoon's face and neck, felling him. But his comrade fell backwards on the grass, dropping his own sword as he clutched between his legs, trying to staunch the blood that was flowing far faster than I would have imagined possible. He was looking up at his comrade, leaning back on his shield, shaking his head over and over, and then Mulldoos came up behind the standing Brunesman, the wide blade of his falchion coming down hard. The Brunesman must have sensed him there or registered alarm on the other Brunesman's face, as he tried turning, shield coming up, but it was far too late, as the falchion struck the soldier across the back of the neck. He would have been decapitated on the spot except the falchion hit some mail as well. The Brunesman fell, the gushing blood making the other man's leg wound seem inconsequential.

Mulldoos took two more strides as the wounded soldier tried reaching for his sword, kicked the blade away, pressed the bottom edge of his shield on the Brunesman's stomach, and then nearly cleaved his face in two with the falchion.

I turned away, feeling my gorge rise, and saw a Brunesman five paces away striding toward me, no doubt glad to see an unarmored opponent. I froze, nearly forgetting I was holding a crossbow before bringing it up fast and squeezing the long trigger. The bolt ricocheted off the top of his helm. The Brunesman shook it off, taking the last steps to finish me. I threw the crossbow at him as I reached for Lloi's curved blade, missing the hilt on the first grab and only feeling my fingers close around it as I stared at the blade coming up from behind the shield. I knew I was dead for certain when the soldier stumbled and stopped.

Soffjian was suddenly there, her scale corselet blazing like fire, her cloak, hair, and the tassel of her weapon looking even more red than usual in the last day's light, clouds roiling at her back. She was like some sublimely beautiful and horrible spirit the dying sun had set loose upon the world. The middle tine of her polearm was covered in blood, and as the Brunesman turned to face her, I saw a large blood spot in his lower back where the weapon had penetrated his gambeson.

He took a few steps toward her, moving slowly, but having forgotten about me completely. I considered running to get the crossbow back and reloading it, but having come so close to being cut down by the man, the urge to hurt him physically, personally, was stronger than any restraint or fear. For the first time in my life I felt rage—hot, coursing, powerful rage. I drew Lloi's curved blade and started toward him, not sure what I meant to do, not caring.

Soffjian thrust several times in quick succession: high, low, a feint back high, low again. The Brunesman managed to block each one, if just barely, but she completely occupied his attention. So I took the sword in both hands and slashed across his back as hard as I could. It wasn't a falchion, and I wasn't Mulldoos, but Lloi's blade cut through part of the filthy gambeson, tearing the weave and batting and leaving a gash across his back.

He screamed, wheeling around, and I saw over his shoulder that Soffjian was spinning to face another soldier, her hand splayed out as it had been in Alespell. She would be no more help.

The Brunesman had two wounds to the back, but neither incapacitated him. He came at me, shield up, sword hand hidden behind it, the blade angled over his shoulder. I swung at him wildly, the curved blade skidding off the surface of the shield, and started backing up, swinging again. He blocked the second blow easily and threw one of his own, his sword coming out fast, so fast. I managed to get Lloi's blade in front of it, just barely, and felt the reverberations up my arm, stepping back quickly.

Realizing I didn't pose much of a threat, the Brunesman came at me in a rush, not worrying overmuch about defense. He battered me with his shield, knocking me reeling into the wall behind me, the jutting stones digging into my back. The sword came down, and I managed to deflect it just enough with the curved blade and tried to move away, but he pinned me there with the shield, his face behind it, the nasal on his helm crooked, sweaty brown hair nearly in his eyes, lips curled away from teeth the color of ear wax. The face of my killer.

He pulled his sword arm back and thrust it forward. I managed to wriggle aside, but felt it slice into my side and yelped. He pushed harder with the shield as I started kicking and trying to shove him far enough off to escape or at least free Lloi's sword.

The Brunesman's arm went back again, but before he could drive it into me, his eyes went wide, and suddenly the point of Soffjian's polearm burst out of his throat. I pushed away at the shield, now slack, trying to get away from him and the blood spraying out of him, and slipped to the side. He dropped his sword, fell to his knees, convulsed, and then Soffjian kicked him in the back as she wrenched her ranseur out of him and he fell forward, face smashing into the wall.

She stood there, a vision of sunset and death, and I shivered. I hadn't even seen her come out of the forest. I didn't remember her arriving on the scene at all. No doubt exactly as she intended.

Soffjian glanced at my side, and I looked down as well. There was some blood on my tunic, but not nearly so much as I imagined, and while the wound burned, my guts weren't exactly spilling down my trousers.

"Look at you," Soffjian said, lips almost caught smiling. "You have a lucky rib." Then she turned and jogged off to another pocket of combat.

My hands were shaking as I slid Lloi's sword in my belt and retrieved my crossbow, looking up repeatedly to be sure no one was moving in to kill me. Steadying myself as best I could and trying not to think about how close I'd come to being skewered, I fitted the bolt in the slot. I scanned the fighting around me, and that's when I saw Captain Killcoin surrounded by three Brunesmen nearby, two with gambesons and swords and oval shields, the third as heavily armored as Gurdinn with the coat of plates over the mail, and various bits of steel or iron everywhere else. I thought it was Gurdinn, but he lacked the gray beard, and wielded a vicious-looking axe of some kind in both hands, the long crescent-shaped blade attached to the thick haft on two socketed spots, with a nasty point on top and a slightly curved point on the back end.

The two with swords were closest, and trying to spread out to flank Braylar. He slowly retreated, shield up, the arm with Bloodsounder cocked behind it, the flail heads falling just behind his shoulder. The Brunesman on the right made a quick move as if he would engage and Braylar pivoted to him, but it was a feint; the other Brunesman came in fast and the captain must have either anticipated it or felt it through Bloodsounder, as the flail shot out without him turning to face the opponent directly, snapping straight out across his body, whipping over his shield edge. The Brunesman didn't get his shield up in time, and as he was springing forward, had no chance to dodge—the Deserter heads struck him just below the rim of his helm. If he had a nasal, it might have protected him from some of the damage, but he didn't, and he had to have lost one eye, possibly both, but the fountain of blood prevented me from telling which. He screamed and dropped his sword, stumbled and fell, gloved hand spread over his eyes and face.

The other Brunesman had already been moving in as well, hoping their staggered attack would have forced the captain into a mistake, but Braylar reeled the flail heads back and had them arcing out again, with minimal movement from the wrist or hand. The Brunesman blocked the strike as he stepped in, deflecting the heads slightly, but losing sight of Braylar for an instant. That was all it took—Braylar sprang forward and tripped the Brunesman, redirecting the flail heads as he did, and bringing them down hard across the back of the soldier's helm as he fell past. The Brunesman tried to break his stumble with the shield but Braylar was relentless, closing right behind him, striking again before the soldier could regain his balance and bearings, the Deserter heads coming down directly on the crown of the helm. The Brunesman went down on his face and didn't move again.

Captain Killcoin spun around just as the heavily armored Brunesman with the big axe closed in, but held off attacking as he sized Braylar up, and there was something about the way he moved that suggested he would prove a tougher opponent, even without a shield. Not frantic or even hurried, but alert, poised. He moved like Captain Killcoin.

The axeman had the benefit of range with the longer weapon, and one that looked like it could dole out horrendous damage with a single blow. I didn't imagine many weapons looking as dangerous as Bloodsounder, but this axe certainly matched it.

Advancing, the Brunesman changed his guard, raising his weapon above his head, and Braylar shifted his shield slightly as he started sliding to his right. The Brunesman altered the angle, moving with Braylar, and then came in fast, the axe rising a bit higher before coming straight down. Braylar had already stepped back out of range, but the Brunesman slowed the descent and then thrust the long weapon more quickly than I expected possible.

Braylar's shield snapped down, pushed the tip aside, and I thought he might advance as well, try to close the distance in order to bloody Bloodsounder again. But the Brunesman had his axe up as he took another step in. Braylar was attempting to move out of range but couldn't avoid the blow entirely—he had to block it with his shield, though he didn't take the weapon on directly, but deflected it and then stepped back and to his right.

I took aim, seeing a brief opportunity, but as the combatants shifted I jerked the crossbow up as I squeezed the long trigger, fearing I would hit the captain, and the bolt flew harmlessly off into the distance.

Braylar continued to circle, just outside the Brunesman's range, but also well outside his own range of being able to deliver any kind of blow. I wondered why he didn't try to close the space—was it respect for the weapon, or the man wielding it? Was he simply measuring his opponent, pacing the blows and movement and looking for the right opening to exploit?

The Brunesman came in again, guard high, feinted a blow coming left to right, then changed course, cutting the opposite way as he stepped in. Braylar knocked it aside, stepped out of range and avoided the next blow completely, and then came forward fast. The Brunesman attacked, Braylar blocked, but the Brunesman turned his weapon and caught the back of Braylar's shield with the curved point at the rear of the axehead, jerked it hard, pulling Braylar off balance slightly.

The captain slipped on the grass and fell to his knee.

He was scrambling to get back to his feet, but the Brunesman didn't miss his opportunity. With surprising speed, the large blade rose and fell, and this time, being half on the ground, Braylar wasn't able to slip the blow or merely turn it. The axe head came down and sent wood chips flying as it nearly shattered Braylar's shield.

The Brunesman attacked again, axe blade quickly rising up and down, ready to cleave the captain in twain. Braylar rolled to his right, barely dodging the weapon as the axe bit into the earth like a plow head. The Brunesman brought it up to strike again, grass and dirt flying from the blade as Braylar got to his feet, retreating a few steps to shake the ruined shield off his arm and draw his suroka.

He crouched, Bloodsounder in one hand, suroka in the other. Neither seemed like they would do a very good job stopping the axe, especially if the arm holding the suroka was injured at all. The Brunesman started forward again, and while I'd seen the captain in trouble on the battlefield before, he suddenly seemed to be in more danger than ever. I looked around—the other Syldoon were fighting off Brunesmen of their own and no help at all, and Soffjian was squaring off with one as well.

I finished reloading and started running to try to get in a position to shoot my crossbow again, hoping I could find a good angle before Braylar got chopped into bloody bits.

The Brunesman swung the axe, thrust again, kept pressing forward, moving from one attack to the next smoothly, almost casually, as Braylar was on the defensive, stepping out of range or dodging the large but surprisingly fast weapon until he found himself losing room to maneuver as he nearly backed into the wall.

I thought I had a shot, raised the crossbow, sighted, and then it was gone. Cursing myself for hesitating, I ran closer.

The Brunesman stepped to his left, trying to keep the captain pinned, and then came in again, the axe moving in a blur. But Braylar rushed forward as well, getting just inside the axe's reach—the Brunesman struck him in the side with the haft, clanking on the lamellar, and knocking the captain hard to his right. Braylar managed to break his fall by sticking Bloodsounder's haft onto the ground, the flail heads trailing in the grass behind him, and looked up to see the axe at its height.

I was lining up another shot, sure it would be too late, when Braylar launched himself under the axe blow, rolling into the Brunesman's knees, knocking the larger man backwards and bowling him over. The Brunesman's helm bounced off the ground, and Braylar scrambled on top of him, knocking his arm aside, striking him in the face with the splinted vambrace three times, then pulling the coif aside just enough to drive the long suroka blade into the man's throat.

He climbed off and was getting to his feet when another heavily armored Brunesman with a great helm and an oval shield and spear was there, thrusting. Braylar managed to knock the spear point aside with his suroka so it skidded off the lamellar cuirass, but the Brunesman pulled it back, and the spear head lashed out again and again, each time just knocked off line and missing the mark as the Brunesman advanced and Braylar scooted back into the wall.

I was raising my crossbow when I saw a blur behind the Brunesman and heard metal on metal. A throwing axe fell to the ground behind him and the Brunesman spun to face the threat, not knowing that his attacker was Mulldoos, ten paces away.

Not worrying about a perfect shot this time, I simply brought the crossbow up and loosed. The bolt struck the Brunesman in the shoulder, in the hauberk just outside the coat of plates, and stuck—the soldier jerked once right before Braylar jumped on his back, snapping the flail around the Brunesman's neck and grabbing the chains on the other side.

The Brunesman was a head taller than Braylar, practically lifting the captain off his feet as he whirled and tried to shake him off, then let go of his spear with one hand and started elbowing Braylar.

Braylar crossed the chains and the flail haft at the back of the Brunesman's neck, pressed his knee in the small of Brunesman's back and drove the larger man forward, shaking off the elbows that struck lamellar and did little good. Braylar yanked on the haft and chains as hard as he could, trying to finish him off. The Brunesman reached back, tried to grab Captain Killcoin's forearm, head, anything, before snatching a handful of mail sleeve and pulling, trying to get purchase.

Pulling the chains and haft, Braylar used his knee for leverage, choking with everything he had until the Brunesman suddenly struggled less. He clenched the mail sleeve one more time until he went limp, falling to his knees, great helm slumped onto his chest.

The captain tugged another time to be certain, then released the chains and let the body fall sideways to the earth. He shook his left arm, bent over for a moment as he looked over at Mulldoos, now right in front of him, and then back over his shoulder at me as I worked the devil's claw.

Braylar shook his head once, straightened, and stepped back to retrieve his suroka from the grass.

We heard a piercing whistle blast, followed immediately by a second, and then the few Brunesmen who weren't immediately engaged began running back to reclaim their horses.

The balance had tipped.

Mulldoos picked up his throwing axe, slid it back into the leather strap at the back of the belt. "Got to say, Cap, never seen you choke a man to death with that thing. Real original. Inspired even."

While his face was obscured by the mail, there was no mistaking the grim smile he had behind it. Then Mulldoos asked, "Letting Gurdinn ride free?"

Braylar kicked his shattered shield as he watched the few Brunesmen mount up. "They left a portion of their force back in the forest. We don't have the men to run them to ground. We have what we came for." He looked at both of us again. "I do hope you aren't waiting for gratitude." He looked at me. "Either of you. I had things in hand."

Mulldoos nodded slowly. "Aye. Fooled that big bastard into thinking he had you and was about to pin you to the wall, when it was you working him the whole time."

Captain Killcoin ignored his lieutenant and kept his eyes on me. "And while I grudgingly admit you helped save my life once, you nearly killed me just now."

I was about to protest, but then thought better of it and clamped my jaw closed. But Mulldoos had no such reservations, and shockingly defended me. A bit.

"You should count yourself lucky you got a scribbler dumb enough to run into combat. The last couple would have been cowering behind a wagon wheel. Expected it of this one, too. Life is full of surprises." He looked at the last Brunesmen riding back down the trail into the forest. "What now, Cap?"

"Now we see if this was all worth it." And he started toward the wagon again.

The Syldoon had been outnumbered, more lightly armored, with a stone wall at their backs.

But they'd prevailed. Somehow. They'd felled their foes or driven them from the field. And while the relationship with Baron Brune was now irreparably severed, the Syldoon had their prisoner.

They won. Bloodied, injured, and fewer in number now, but they won.

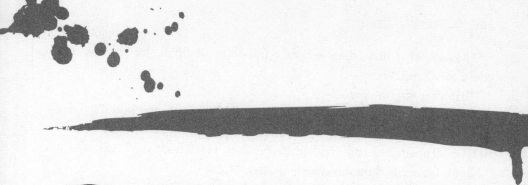

Captain Killcoin looked around at our battered and bruised company. With the Brunesmen fled and combat over, it was oddly quiet, save for the odd moan or grunt, several coming from the overturned wagon. Braylar walked toward it, his byrnie and lamellar cuirass rustling metallic as he went.

All of the prisoners huddled as far from the bars as they could. Some of their wounded cried out as the men around them shifted, jostling whatever bone was broken. The captain unfastened his helm strap and pulled it up and off his head, the mail aventail tinkling as he did. His hair was drenched in sweat, and there was a red band across his forehead where the helm padding had pressed tight. And faint bruising around the noose tattoo around his neck.

Henlester locked eyes with Braylar, saw the noose, and said, "Ahh, so it's the mighty Syldoon, is it? Now, this is a surprise. It was too much to dare hope for a rescue, and yet I allowed myself to, if only briefly. But it's clear I simply only have new captors. Will you unlock my cage only to herd me into another, Syldoon?"

Braylar twitch-smiled and turned to Vendurro. "The men do appear uncomfortable, Sergeant. Let's remedy that, yes? Finish cracking this wagon open. Immediately. Let it never be said that the Syldoon are uncharitable hosts. Even as captors."

Vendurro said, "Aye, Cap." He walked over to the group of soldiers and relayed the order to Benk and the other Syldoon who had been hammering and chopping at the wagon previously.

Benk replied, "Be a lot easier if we had two axes. Or a bigger one. Didn't some Bruneboy have a big old axe, in the grass somewheres around here?"

Vendurro spat. "Cap said immediately. Know what that means? It means right here and now. Shut your yap and get to it."

"I know what immediate means, Sarge. Not a halfwit. Just saying, we could finish quicker if—"

"Rip that wagon apart. Now."

Benk gave a weak half-hearted salute, rolled his eyes, and said, "Come on, then," to the other soldier. They were moving toward the wagon when Braylar stepped over and grabbed Benk's arm. Hard from the looks of it.

Benk faced his superior, clearly uneasy. "Cap?"

"If I ever hear you disrespect an officer again, I will strip you of arms, armor, and horse, and leave you for the enemy to deal with. Do you understand?"

Benk colored up and the gulp was unmistakable. "Aye, Cap."

"Very good." Braylar released him and Benk all but ran over to the wagon and reclaimed the small hatchet and returned to chopping as the other Syldoon started pulling at a board.

It seemed a harsh reprimand, given how much latitude Braylar allowed his own retinue, but perhaps it was the public nature of the disrespect that rankled the captain so.

When the Syldoon finally ripped enough planks free, the captives filed out, Henlester first, followed by the priestguard and those uninjured underpriests who assisted with the wounded last.

Captain Killcoin ordered a man to ride ahead, then he faced Vendurro. "Get the good priest there on a horse. We ride out." He turned to Benk and added, "You stay behind. Alert us if another Brunesmen force pursues. I expect they will. Captain Gurdinn will rage for a few minutes, but he will have them after us before we know it."

Benk saluted much more smartly than before, rotating his arm in that odd fashion they had after pumping his fist on his chest.

The Syldoon were either mounting up on this side of the wall, or vaulting to the other to reclaim their mounts. Vendurro had Henlester up in a saddle, but the High Priest called out, "Syldoon!"

It was clear from the tone that he wasn't speaking to anyone but Captain Killcoin.

I was spinning my horse in a circle, trying unsuccessfully to climb into the saddle, when I heard Braylar reply, "How may I help you, my esteemed cleric? Would you prefer some refreshment before the ride? Some honey cakes and tea, perhaps?"

As I settled in, sliding my foot into the stirrup, Henlester said, "What of my men? You don't intend to leave them here, do you?"

Braylar looked at the small sad group. "That is precisely what I intend. As you so astutely pointed out, you have merely changed captors. They would be no better off in our company. In fact, they might not fare so well at all. We are cruel to the point of savagery, I'm afraid, and in quite a hurry besides."

Henlester's thin lips thinned further, and barely seemed to move at all as he said, "The Brunesmen might slaughter them."

Braylar smiled. "Nothing would please me more, as the Brunesmen would have to catch them first. Recapturing prisoners, even those on foot, takes time. We could do with some time." He looked at Vendurro. "He is in your charge. If he attempts to flee, bludgeon him into submission. If he attempts it twice, slit his throat. He is not so valuable that we can afford to waste time recapturing." And then back to Henlester. "There—you see how this works now?"

The captain addressed the underpriests and priestguard, all of them staring at their high priest. "You are free men again. I suggest you run and run fast. For those too injured to flee. . . hide well. I suspect the Brunesmen will be too busy pursuing us to pursue you. But then you can never be certain, can you?"

Then Braylar's horse was off, and our party followed his lead, leaving the overturned wagon, dead horses, huddled prisoners, and slaughtered men in our wake, as the last of the sun's light still curved over the horizon and lit the clouds and the world for a few more brief moments.

I looked over my shoulder. Henlester's group was unsure what to do, one guard pointing back toward the woods, another toward the stone wall. At least the captain hadn't killed them outright. That was something.

We rode in silence, picking up pace as darkness came on. I moved up to the front, just behind the captain and his lieutenants. They were arguing, though it was difficult to make out all of it over the clap and clomp of hooves on the earth.

Mulldoos said, "You think Gurdinn leaves the convoy behind and tries to ride ahead and run us down?"

Hewspear said something I couldn't hear and I caught the last part of Braylar's response, "—rigid bastard. Follows orders to the letter. So, I'd guess Brune told him the prime objective was the old cleric. He'll ride hard. So we'll ride harder."

Mulldoos replied, "What of our own wagons? Maybe ought to stow them and circle back. Seems like—"

"No. We can't risk that. You know this, yes?"

"I know Gurdinn leaves his own wagons, he'll run us to ground, sure as spit."

"And if he does, we'll make him deeply regret doing so. We have the priest. We have our treasure." He jerked a thumb over his shoulder at me, though I hadn't even known he was aware I was there. "And we have the scholar to unriddle them, yes? So. We return with all of it, or we do not return. That is all. You are expert tacticians. I suggest you craft tactics to make sure it happens."

Mulldoos grumbled something to Hewspear, who nodded slowly. They talked, or argued—it was difficult to tell one from the other with them—with barely any space between them or their mounts as they nearly knocked helms together.

I moved up along the other side of Captain Killcoin. He didn't turn my way or address me, content to simply ride into darkness as quickly as was safe to manage. Braylar seemed to sense my unease, or at least my shoddy horsemanship. "Do not worry, Arki. They have good eyes for the night. Better than ours, I believe. Riding along a beaten trail like this, we are fairly safe. Provided no one thrusts a torch in their faces. And we don't have to gallop or jump any walls."

"Will we need to? Gallop or jump, that is?"

Braylar turned in my direction, his eyes lost in the shadows of his helm, face covered by the mail drape. It was a visage that did nothing at all to calm the nerves. "Hard to say. If we do, I expect we will be light one archivist when we are done." His humor was difficult to read most of the time, but more so with only a little moonlight flashing on his eyes to indicate there was a man in the helm at all.

I supressed a shiver as best I could and we rode in silence, but I couldn't resist staring at him.

Braylar glanced at me and said, "Out with it. Your unspoken questions are more often annoying than the ones you insist on jabbering, as they hang there invisible, fraught with portent and nervous energy. Speak."

I looked over my shoulder briefly, spotting Soffjian and Skeelana near the rear of the company, far from listening distance. "Are you feeling. . . well?"

"I am alive. Beyond that, wellness is a luxury."

"What I mean to ask is—"

"I know precisely what it is you mean to ask. I suspected as much before you asked it. As to how I feel, I will tell you this—the memories have not begun invading as yet, but I sense their scouts. Tentatively exploring, moving hidden and malicious. If I had a way to trap and destroy them I would. But even Lloi could never manage that."

I stole another quick glance behind us. "Perhaps a Memoridon could. They already know you will be bombarded, so maybe you could—"

Braylar's breath came out diffused, broken by the mail mesh. "They know far more than they should already. I will give them no more opportunity than that."

I framed the next question carefully, turning it over in my mind and asking it a few different ways silently before settling on the one I gave voice to. "Would you be so reluctant if your sister wasn't involved?"

"No. I would be more so. Far better to have a known enemy than an unknown one."

"But how are Memoridons enemies? I still don't understand this relationship. They answer to your Tower Commander as well, don't they?"

"To him and only to him, Arki. Their agendas are frequently not syn-onymous with the rank and file soldier. And when it comes to matters of memory magic—with Bloodsounder and my own peculiar affliction clearly falling within that purview—that is their jurisdiction. I have no wish to be their pet, or their experiment, or part of some obscene research. Skeelana has been in me once already. I would not invite her there again unless I have exhausted all other options. And what is more, unlike the Syldoon soldier, they had no choice in their tenure in the Empire. They obey the Commander only because they have to. Coerced fealty is not loyalty. " He turned, and it was as baleful a look as could be cloaked in so much metal. "You would do well to remember that."

I nodded quickly and he said, "Very good. Now be silent. I will simply have to endure your unasked questions harassing me. It will be a long night and a long ride." And then he nudged his horse further ahead, plagued by whatever unseen devils assaulted him.

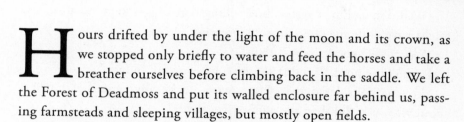

Hours drifted by under the light of the moon and its crown, as we stopped only briefly to water and feed the horses and take a breather ourselves before climbing back in the saddle. We left the Forest of Deadmoss and put its walled enclosure far behind us, passing farmsteads and sleeping villages, but mostly open fields.

My body was stiff and sore, but aside from the small wound on my side that burned abominably, I was not in horrible shape. I wondered how well the other Syldoon were holding up. And more importantly, how long their old captive would be able to continue. I'm sure he was far more accustomed to perfumed pillows than midnight flights. Still, he seemed to sit the saddle much better than I did, his posture and bearing erect, his white hair lit like snow in the moonlight. You would have thought we were stealing a king.

Falling back slightly, I found a place in the line mostly to myself, not speaking with anyone, and doing my best to stay out of the way.

I'd never ridden in the middle of the night before, and while I wouldn't have guessed I could fall asleep bouncing and jostling so much, I had to pinch my wrist to keep myself from sliding out of the saddle. But after a while even that failed, and for long stretches I felt myself dozing, starting awake every time my chin dropped toward my chest, and then almost immediately after shutting my eyes again.

After one such start, I heard a voice next to me. "So, you've pulled the trigger twice now. How do you feel?"

I nearly jumped out of the saddle. Even though she kept her voice low, I had been dozing deeply enough to miss Skeelana riding up alongside me.

"What? What did you—"

She smiled. "To be accurate, you've probably pulled it countless times now. The trigger, that is. But only a handful in battle, by your own admission. And only twice that ended someone's life. So, sympathetically, I can't help wondering—was it easier the second time? Or do you feel worse?"

I looked at her. Several pins in her hair glinted before winking out as some clouds draped the moon completely. "Well, perhaps next time we are stuck in battle, you might lend a hand. Find out for yourself."

She shrugged. "Like I told you, I'm no war Memoridon. I wouldn't even wear this stupid suroka, except it's mandated. Far more likely to stab myself with it than anyone else."

"Well, I'm a clumsy scribe, but pulling that trigger kept me alive, and might have done the same for someone else."

"So you feel good about it then?"

I shook my head. "I didn't say that. I feel awful, in fact."

Skeelana considered that. "But better to be alive and feel horrible about what you did than the alternative, right?"

"Back in Alespell, you defended yourself when you had no choice. Maybe you didn't draw blood with steel, but you defended yourself, and took a life. How do you feel?"

It looked like she had a small smile on her face. "Awful, in fact. I'd say that speaks well of us, really. We should feel awful. Killing another person, no matter the circumstance, well, it's no walk on rose petals, is it? But what I'm asking is, now that you've done it twice, was it easier? The second time?"

I pulled a flask off my belt, uncorked the bottle, and drank some stale water before answering. Skeelana declined my offer and I slipped the stopper back in, thinking about the best way to put it, to capture some part of my feelings. "The man—the men, now—the men I killed or helped dispatch, they weren't just alive. They had *lives*. Friends, families, dreams, fears, secrets. Things they hoped to do and never would have the chance now, things they wished they hadn't done and lost the opportunity to atone for. I'm grateful I am not afflicted like Captain Killcoin. Thanks to Bloodsounder, he knows more about the men he killed then some of those in his own company, maybe even his personal retinue.

"But even without being privy to all those awful personal details of the men killed, it's still impossible not to think of everything you ended. All with a simple blow, or worse, the squeeze of a long steel trigger. So much obliterated by such a simple act."

"And yet they donned the armor. They picked up the weapons. They knew they were taking the risks, these men. It's not as if you senselessly murdered someone in the street."

"No," I replied. "That's so. And while knowing that should make it easier to deal with, to bundle any guilt in a box and bury it somewhere, the truth is it doesn't. You asked me how I feel, Skeelana? I feel worse. Happy?"

Her smile turned slightly sad, and then disappeared altogether as the moon was cloaked again. "No. I'd hoped to hear it was easier and less terrible, truly."

"Why? You'll stay out of the fray, won't you? You said as much."

"I will try, Arki. I will certainly try. I did witness it, all of it, from the trees. And when I saw you shoot that soldier, shoot him dead, I imagined it was me, and imagined how I'd feel. I'm sorry to say I guessed right."

We rode in silence for a while, and then Skeelana asked, "Speaking of Bloodsounder, how is your captain faring? As you said, unlike anyone else here, he has more than his own ghosts or demons to contend with, doesn't he?"

"That he does." I nodded slowly, remembering what Braylar had said about the Memoridons, and considered what I could or should share with her. For better or worse, I was aligned with Captain Killcoin and his men. He clearly didn't trust these women, his sister least of all, but it obviously extended to any in their order. And yet, Skeelana already knew his secret, and having already drawn out the poisonous memories once, knew it better than anyone else, really. There was little point in dissembling now, or even withholding information. And yet. . . "The captain doesn't confide in me a great deal. Much at all, truly. So you would need to speak to him to better gauge his condition. And I wouldn't suggest it. He is. . . prickly."

"Truly? I hadn't noticed." She chuckled to herself, and as usual, I felt myself drawn to her, against my better judgment and admonishment from the captain.

There was some silence after that, and I yawned, and she did immediately after. I looked up the line at the soldiers half asleep on their horses, and back, seeing the next rider several yards behind, bobbing in the saddle. Lowering my voice, I said, "When you were. . . inside the captain, scouring out those foreign memories, you had orders to stop there."

"Yes. That is true."

"But was that even possible? Surely you must have encountered his memories."

She hesitated before replying, "Not intentionally. But I did have to sift around inside your captain to discover those memories infecting him. And it wasn't a pleasure barge down a languid river, that's for sure."

"So. . . then—"

"Are you asking me what I saw, or felt, that I shouldn't have?"

"I suppose I am."

She rolled her shoulders and stretched. "Never fear. I obeyed Mulldoos—I didn't want to spend any longer in the man than I had to, and I had a job to do. I saw snippets here, quick flashes there, nothing substantial, more impressions really. I worked fast. I will say this. While he might not consider you his closest companion, and barks at you frequently, he does bear a certain fondness for you. I think it even troubles him that he does, but there it is."

"But sometimes you enter someone like that, hunting for the truth of something, right? Intent on unveiling what someone knows or recalls?"

"Sadly, interrogation like that is sometimes necessary. Though it's not always even what a person actively recalls. Some memories get locked away, buried, and those can be the greatest finds of all. But yes, sometimes we have to explore anything and everything. Why?"

I kept my gaze straight ahead. There was something frightening about the prospect of a Memoridon slipping inside you, about such a power, about being so vulnerable to it. But something else, as well? A thrill perhaps? The idea of such a connection, such intimacy, was unnerving to be sure, but also exciting. With Skeelana at least. The thought of Soffjian invading was beyond terrifying.

"Well," I began slowly, "do memories ever break apart or get lost forever? Painful ones? Early ones?"

"Yes, memories can erode. Or rot. Like food left too long in the undercroft. Some memories are definitely more impermanent or perishable than others. Smart Memoridons have cast theories about for ages, but no one truly knows why. Not really." She looked closely at me. "Why do you ask?"

Before I could answer, the riders ahead of us slowed and then reined in completely, so we did as well. I squinted into the dark and watched another single rider slowly materialize far ahead of our company, coming down the road toward us. He stopped as he reached Braylar. They spoke for a few moments and then Mulldoos rode down the line, calling out, "Almost to the wagons, you whoresons. Then you'll get out of the saddle for a couple of hours. Quicker we get there, quicker you get some relief."

I sighed. A few miles weren't a huge ordeal after riding most of the night, but the wagons weren't over the very next hill either. I turned to say as much to Skeelana but she was gone.

When we rejoined our wagons, it was everything I could do not to collapse on the spot. But the horses needed to be taken care of. I understood now why all my Anjurian patrons had employed grooms and stable hands. While I was grudgingly coming to appreciate the bond a man and a horse could have, and the opportunities to deepen in it the quiet moments of unsaddling the beast, brushing it, caring for it, I wanted nothing more than to let it ride off into the fields and disappear forever if it meant I could finally rest.

But I forced myself not to rush, to do it all properly, no matter how tired, or how much I felt like I might be sacrificing crucial minutes of my own sleep. I'd heard the Syldoon talk about the importance of horse care enough to realize that if I skimped, even a little, I increased the chances of my mount coming up lame or sick, and therefore my own chances to lose my mount and to be left behind.

When I was finally finished, I didn't ask Braylar if I could use the interior of the wagon for sleep—that might have played in the Green Sea, when it had just been the two of us and very occasionally Lloi, but no one was sleeping in there now, and I knew it would appear presumptuous, weak, or both to ask for special accommodations. The Syldoon who had been with the wagons took watch. I unrolled my bedroll, set my crossbow next to me on the grass, with the quiver in easy reach, and pulled a blanket up to my chin, curling my body in a ball to ward off the chill.

Even though I was cold, sore, exhausted, hungry, and uncomfortable on the unforgiving ground, I still fell into inky slumber before I had a chance to tally a single one of those complaints.

I was shaken awake and it felt like I'd only just closed my eyes, despite the sun having risen for quite some time, judging by its height. Vendurro looked down at me, big toothy smile on his face. "Climb the ladder and empty the bladder, Arki! Time to move."

Sitting up, I wished I had another half day to sleep. Everywhere around me, men were moving, armored and saddling up. I would have been more amazed I'd been able to sleep through all the activity at all if I hadn't spent most of the night riding away from an enemy who might catch up to us at any time. The Syldoon always seemed to have one enemy or another chasing us.

Vendurro handed me a flask. "Cap says you're to ride with him, you lucky bastard. Got your horses tethered to that wagon already."

I accepted the flask and he offered me his arm, which I took as well, clasping his forearm as he clasped mine, and he hauled me to my feet. After thanking him I took a swig. It was warm wine, and tasted of leather, but still a welcome change from brackish water. Vendurro slapped me on the back and almost made me piss myself as I walked off into the grass, looking over my shoulder to be sure neither of the women were nearby.

Done, I walked over to the lead wagon. Braylar was sitting on the seat already, in armor but without the helm, and alternating tugging on one leather glove and then the other. I reached up and held my hand there, and when he merely looked at it rather than helping me up, I wondered if riding in the wagon was so preferable after all.

Braylar said, "There are some nuts in a small sack, just behind the bench. Some dried meat of mysterious nature, though I'd recommend chewing it for an inordinate amount of time before attempting to swallow. It will transform into a horrible ball of meat-cud, but at least you won't choke on it."

He always had a way of making every meal with him seem so appealing. I settled onto the bench, looking at the road ahead of us, resisting the urge to look behind. But I couldn't resist asking, "Has Benk reported anything from the rear?"

Captain Killcoin started the team of horses. "No. So you can be sure that when he does, you'll hear about it the very moment I do. That is if you aren't absorbed in writing or translating." He turned in my direction, and gave a hitching smile. "Your writing table is just inside the wagon. I'm sure you two have missed each other. Once you have brought the record current," he handed me the small key, "continue translating the documents. As hastily as you can manage while still being accurate, yes?"

I looked at him and he looked back to the road as he got the team of horses moving. "You didn't think you were suddenly relieved of your obligations or duties, did you?"

"No, it's just, what if we are attacked? Gurdinn is out there somewhere, and—"

"And if and when he catches us, I will give the order to put the pen away, yes? But we have a respite, however brief, so use it. The wily cleric is unlikely to voluntarily reveal much, but if you can uncover anything translating related to his order, and its association with the hedge witches, that would be more useful than you know."

Even as tired as I was, almost to my bones, I felt a surge of energy. I was finally about to get back to the one thing that I had some talent at. And it wouldn't involve any bloodshed whatsoever.

After settling in and retrieving my supplies, I opened the writing desk the captain had gifted me with and set my small knives and inks in front of me, glad to be wielding something that had little chance to kill or maim anyone. At least in my hands. I'm sure Mulldoos could find a way to sever or impale someone with every instrument I had, or to force someone to drink ink until dead. Shuddering at the thought, I tried not to think overmuch of death. Which of course was impossible, as I had to record quite a bit that had happened recently, much of it violent in the extreme.

When I was finished, it was time to turn my mind to something that was admittedly mundane and laborious, but which I still found riveting and fascinating. Sifting through all the onerous records and difficult passages with nothing more interesting than ledgers of grain purchased and sold, or an inventory of stock in a larder was tedious, but so long as it promised even the possibility of something evocative or useful, it was worth it.

I started in where I left off, forcing myself not to rush for fear of missing some vital snippet of information or a subtle reference buried in the text. While subsidy rolls and a catalogue of blazonry were unlikely to have anything worthy of excitement, there were poems that were difficult to decipher but might provide some obscure hint or connection to some layered truth. And even if not, there were some fabulous illuminated bestiaries that were a wonder, and there, I had to force myself not to dawdle.

After several hours, my eyes grew heavy, as most of the translation involved records of taxes some fieflord or other paid a bigger fieflord, hundreds of years ago, payments by bailiffs or reeves in some village that ceased to exist, the running record of construction costs and challenges for a castle or temple that took twenty-five years to complete, the revenue from a fishpond, a wonderfully illustrated calendar, contract and coroner's rolls, customs and manifests, ancestral rolls and theological disputations, and every other possible document that might have been penned.

The wagon jumped and tilted as we rolled over rough, uneven ground, and I frequently had to reread passages again and again, having lost my place, and this also contributed to heavy eyelids.

We stopped and rested at midday, and progress was so slow I was reluctant to leave the covered wagon, especially since it had ceased moving. Vendurro brought me some stale oatcakes, a few wrinkled carrots, and some ale that tasted like yak piss (or what I imagined it tasted like, never having sampled it).

Much of the afternoon was the same. Aside from occasionally shifting to stretch my muscles and avoid cramping, I sat absorbed in my work, reading, puzzling over dense passages that didn't avail themselves very easily, scratching my notes out on separate sheets of parchment, and translating well into the afternoon.

So, eyes weary, back sore, mouth dry, and dusk only a short time off, I was nearly ready to take a break when I opened an ancient book with a wooden cover that was embossed in peculiar copper designs, whorls within whorls. It was the personal account of a high priest of Truth. The initial passages weren't especially intriguing, but there was something about it, a feeling I couldn't shake, that if it didn't contain something momentous, it would at least reveal something that Braylar was hoping to find. I couldn't say precisely what it was, and as I slowly made my way through it, page after page, I began to think it was merely wishful thinking.

And then I encountered a section that stopped me cold. I reread portions of it carefully, working out as much as I possibly could. When I was convinced I wasn't misinterpreting, I went over it again just to be sure. Then I grabbed the book and my notes and nearly fell off the wagon entirely as I ripped the flap aside and climbed over the bench, hitting Captain Killcoin in the shoulder.

He turned, scowling, ready to berate me, but I was so excited I didn't even apologize, just sat down hard on the bench and said, much too quickly, "There's something here."

His irritation slipped free. "Is there now?"

"And," I looked around to be sure the Memoridons weren't riding nearby, or anyone else really, "it relates to what you inquired about."

He stared at me, no doubt waiting for me to continue, the glint of anticipation there, and then said, impatiently, "A guessing game, is it? How wonderful. We can while away the remainder of our trip as I try to divine what you might have found in those delicate yellowed pages. I only wish we had thought of this sooner. So, what clue shall you offer up first?"

I opened the book and thumbed through carefully until I found the section where things got interesting, stuck my index finger on the page, tapping it several times. "Translation is a difficult thing. Full of vagaries. Gaps in interpretation. Often you have several potential readings, and simply need to go with the one that seems to make the most sense, given what's preceding. And following."

"I do know what context is," he snapped.

"I haven't worked out all the nuances yet, as I only came across this today, but—"

"Out with it!"

I glanced around again and lowered my voice so it could barely be heard above the creak of the wagon and horse's hooves. "This book makes reference to Bloodsounder."

He looked at me closely, no doubt to make sure he heard me correctly. "Are you certain of that?" It was a raspy whisper.

"No. It's translation. I'm certain of almost nothing. And I don't mean the flail by name."

His eyes narrowed to gray-green slits. "You are very bad at this game."

"What I mean to say is, it doesn't mention the name 'Bloodsounder,' but it references named weapons, and. . ."

He looked like he wanted to use Bloodsounder just then, or at least hit me with the book. "You waste my time. This is a practice that stretches back centuries, millennia. The first bog-man who climbed out of the pulsing muck probably named his club something before smashing someone over the head with it."

I tapped the page again, scanned, and read, ". . . *and the man who wields the Sentries*—or guardians, maybe, but likely sentries, there is a subtle distinction in Old Anjurian—*the man who wields the Sentries shall be a sentry himself, in defense of the temple, in defense of the Gods*—and this is important, as the name here is one I've seen in several other places. They refer to the Deserter Gods, I'm positive. *And the weapon bequeathed by the Gods and taken up by the man shall be the same henceforth, so that all shall see that sentries of Sentries serve the Gods who made them, and are called one thing.*"

"Yes, so some holy warriors had weapons and they shared names. A peculiar custom, it's true. But this has something to do with Bloodsounder, how, exactly?"

"I think that was their way of conveying the bond the man and weapon had, that they shared something. A connection. And the weapons are described as sentries. What do sentries do? They warn—of trouble, of danger. What does Bloodsounder do? It warns you of violence, approaching violence. I think Bloodsounder is one of these sentries."

"And I think you grossly overestimate your translation skills."

"It goes on for a few pages, describing the temple guardians, the sentries they bear, and how man and weapon protect the temples—"

"That is what men with weapons generally do, archivist."

I shook my head and continued reading a few pages later, a bit haltingly, correcting myself a few times, "It goes on for a bit, nothing of consequence or related, and then . . . *the Grand Sentry of Sentries in our temple is Grieftongue, wielding Grieftongue. He has been with us for several years now, and performed goodly. . .* or godly, it is a bit fuzzy here, the usage, and it might even be more like 'exceptional' or—" I saw the dark look he gave me and continued, "*goodly (or godly) work, defending the temple and all who set foot inside it. And his great service has always been costly. One cannot wield weapons bequeathed by the divine without grave toll. Our priests have always healed him, cleansed him—*" I gave Captain Killcoin a pointed look, eyebrows raised. "Cleansed. Him."

He was unimpressed so I pressed on, "*Cleansed him, made him whole again. But now that the Gods have abdicated—*or departed, but I believe—" He glared and I continued, "*...abdicated, they have left only their absence behind, and none of their powers. The priests struggle more and more to cleanse Grieftongue. I fear they can no longer make him pure. I overheard High Priest Movellent tell. . . instruct. . . him to lay his weapon down, before it killed him. And Grieftongue's eyes lit with such wrath, I feared he would strike his*

superior down and end him. . . kill, kill him. . . but instead Grieftongue has
quit the temple. It was said he walked toward the Godveil, and though he was
expecting to perish, he did not. And yet, he left this world behind.

"I fear he will not be the last to abandon us. Not only have the gods forsaken
us, but our temporal protectors are beginning to as well, taking their Sentries
with them. All will be lost soon. Everything holy stripped from the world. This
is our judgment. We must be deserving of this. It is the only explanation. We
have failed somehow. All of us have failed. And now we must suffer."

I closed the book and looked at Braylar. "You asked me to translate
because you were hoping to find evidence, anything to do with Bloodsounder, or the Memoridons, or the Temple of Truth. Any connections.
I've seen other obscure references to temple protectors before, and other
texts mention the Sentries in passing. But this is the first that provides so
much information."

The captain looked at the book, at the copper wires that ran in intricate patterns on the fragile wood. "I will grant you, it could be something.
But it could just as easily be nothing. When you have corroborated, or
compiled more, then we—"

He stopped and looked up, tugging on the reins to stop the team, his
other hand dropping to Bloodsounder's haft. His lips were pressed tight,
and the skin all over his face suddenly seemed tighter as well, as if he were
suffering a strain of some kind. I didn't hear anything, or see anything
either. "Captain, is—"

"Be silent!" He ran his fingers down the chains and toward the Deserter
Gods hanging at his hip.

I looked at the blackened steel flail heads, their spikes sharp and the
metal dull, almost deflecting light, and wondered if Bloodsounder was
truly a Sentry. Had something so horrible actually been gifted from the
Deserter Gods? It didn't seem possible. Not unless it had corrupted over
time. Or the Gods themselves were malevolent. Neither prospect was very
comforting.

Braylar stood up suddenly and flicked the haft up with his left hand,
snatching Bloodsounder off the hook at his belt with his right, holding it
out in front of him. While he didn't twirl it overhead, he wore the same
expression he had in the Green Sea, the muscles in his face rigid, eyes
vacant, and I knew he was feeling something. The coming violence. Real,

or a false impression, he was sensing something, but I hoped Bloodsounder was deceiving him again.

Mulldoos and Hewspear rode up on either side of the wagon, curious why we stopped. Mulldoos took one look at his captain and ran his meaty hand through his pale stubbly hair, turned, and spit angrily into the grass. "Plague me."

Hewspear shaded his eyes and scanned the road behind. "Is it Brunesmen, Captain?"

Captain Killcoin sat down slowly and slid Bloodsounder back on his belt. "A very large host is coming, Lieutenants. And I don't believe it is Brunesmen. Though if I am right, it will hardly matter. They are certainly no friends of ours."

For someone who didn't like riddles, he did favor the cryptic.

"Hornfuckers, Cap?"

"Fuckers of horn is a very good guess. Though we'll know soon enough." He pointed down the road. A few moments later, a single horseman appeared, riding hard, a dust plume trailing behind.

We all waited until the Syldoon reined up and saluted. Sweat was pouring down his face, and the dust that followed him stuck to it. He coughed and covered his mouth and then said, "Got a problem, captain. Big one. Fifty or sixty riders heading our way, if there's one."

Mulldoos whistled through his teeth. "Fuck, but you pissed those boys off something fierce."

"How long?" Braylar asked.

The rider replied, "Few miles ahead. Got a little time. But not much. Not much at all."

Captain Braylar turned to Hewspear. "How many fighting men do we have left?"

Mulldoos interjected, "All of us banged up, Cap. Any who ain't ain't here. Any who can ride can fight."

Eyes still on Hewspear, Braylar said, through exceptionally tight lips, "How many still in the saddle, Lieutenant?"

Without calculating, Hewspear replied, "Twenty, Captain. Though Benk and Jotty are riding rear, keeping a keen eye for Brunesmen."

Braylar shook his head and replied, "Those are not good odds," just as Soffjian and Skeelana rode up.

"What odds are those, Bray?" No one answered right away as Soffjian looked at all of us, at the dust still settling in the ground, and then up the road. "Are we expecting company? The only time men speak of odds is gambling with coins or gambling with lives. Please tell me you are going to roll dice."

Still no one answered, and Soffjian fixed her gaze on all of us in slow turn. Finally, Braylar said, "There is a large party of Hornmen heading our way. I suspect they do not have cards."

Soffjian scowled as Skeelana said, "So just how bad are these odds, then?"

"Bad enough that wasting time talking about them now will get us killed."

Mulldoos asked, "How about the quarry?"

"We *are* the quarry, Lieutenant."

Mulldoos pressed on. "Passed a deserted one, several miles back. We could—"

"Even if we could make it back there in time and manage to hide ourselves, which I doubt, I'm entirely certain the Hornmen are looking for us. They would likely send men to investigate the site, and then we would be trapped and surrounded. And while we haven't sighted them yet, the Brunesmen are behind us somewhere as well."

Soffjian said, "I know you, brother—your notion of 'bad odds' is 'certain doom' to anyone else. If we can't hide, we ride then. You have what you dragged us off into the wilderness for," she jerked a thumb toward the rest of the retinue behind us. "You have your prize. Let's run. All the way to Sunwrack if we have to."

Braylar slapped the side of the wagon. "The priest is no encumbrance. But the wagons would slow us down. The Hornmen would overtake us, for certain." He looked at Hewspear and Mulldoos. "Our only choice is to take them on. Rolling gear formations. Whittle them down."

Mulldoos soured immediately, and while he was biting his tongue to avoid openly questioning his captain in front of the Memoridons, he clearly was trying to find words to disagree without being insubordinate, and it was a visible struggle.

But Soffjian saved him the trouble. "And what cargo is so precious that you'd throw all your lives away rather than leaving it for the Hornmen? I respect technique and skill more than anyone, and know all too well what your men are capable of, but even with crossbows and evasive maneuvers, you won't be able to fight off a far superior force. Which it must be, for you to admit the lousy odds. How many men are coming? Forty?" No one replied. "Fifty?" Still no one. "Gods, more? You better have the King of Anjuria stuffed in a box back there, brother. And even then, doom is doom. So what is it? What are you carting along?"

Hewspear interjected, "Captain, none here are cowards. If you issue the order to fight, we all will, to the last if necessary. But these odds are. . . long indeed. Perhaps we—"

"We do not leave what we have sacrificed so much already to gain." The captain got off the bench and jumped down to the grass and walked back to untether Scorn.

Soffjian called after him, "You've been a fool most of your life, brother. Rash, brazen, irreverent, and at times treating your own life with less value than a pile of shit. But not so with your men. Run. Before it's too late. You cannot defeat fifty or sixty men. You might make their victory costly, but you cannot win. My abhorrent charge is to see you home, and I mean to do it. But I have fought for you twice against my better judgment already, and will not do so again. Run. I implore you."

Captain Killcoin mounted his horse and rode back to the front of the wagon, one of the harnessed horses shying away from Scorn.

Mulldoos said, "Pains me something fierce to agree even halfway with a witch, Cap, but I think your sister might have the right of it. We got Henlester. The rest of it, well. . . the hard part was finding it all in the first place. We lose it now, ain't near as lost as it were before. We can get it back from the Hornmen. But not if we're all dead."

Braylar seemed genuinely torn. While he was as hard a man as I've ever met, Soffjian was absolutely right on one count—he did not throw away his men's lives willingly. But he shook his head, pulled his crossbow up and began spanning it. "The land is hilly, but not overly so. Not enough to appreciably reduce our range. The Hornmen will not be as well armored as the Brunesmen. They never are, and especially a host this size. We circle and loose and drop their numbers until the odds are not so dire." He slid a bolt in place, devil's claw slapped back down on the stock, looked up, and gave a feral grin. "It's a good day for crossbows. Ready the men."

Soffjian shook her head and started turning her horse, clearly not intending to stay, when Skeelana offered, "Perhaps a trade would be in order."

Everyone looked at her, having forgotten she was even there. She continued, "A war Memoridon could come in quite handy right about now. She could probably tip the odds considerably. Maybe even make counting heads irrelevant, assuming she could meet the foe on ground of her choosing."

A wrinkle bridged Soffjian's dark brows, "And why exactly would I want to do that? This fight is ridiculous. An unnecessary waste of lives."

Skeelana said, "If the good captain here were to indulge us, reveal what the terribly secretive cargo is, perhaps a resident war Memoridon might be inclined to put aside past rancor, save the company, and help everyone get back to Sunwrack with no more lives lost. Speaking hypothetically, of course, not being a war Memoridon myself." Her half-smile tilted this way and that. She seemed entirely too pleased with herself, given that we were minutes away from being overwhelmed by a small army and utterly destroyed.

I expected Braylar or Soffjian to immediately dismiss the idea, singly or in unison, but it hung there between them, seeming to gain strength the longer it went unchallenged.

Mulldoos said, "Hate the idea of needing help from the likes of her, Cap. But might be she could turn this one."

"*She* is right here," Soffjian said, "and given how rigidly I disagree with this engagement in the first place, my uppity comrade might have overstepped herself. I wouldn't spill tears to leave you here to be ridden into the ground. But the Tower Commander wants you back. As does the Emperor." She paused before adding, "Comply with Skeelana's suggestion, and I—"

"They are scrolls," Braylar said. Soffjian waited and then he elaborated, "Books. Stray pages. Any ancient recording I could find. Chests of them. Three years of hunting them, obtaining them." He pointed a gloved finger at me. "To be translated in full now that we have a competent scribe."

Soffjian looked intrigued, but not entirely convinced. "You would risk your entire company over some documents?"

"They are in Old Anjurian, some in Middle, so it is impossible to adequately gauge their value. But I hope very much to find the secret to severing the bond I have with this black thing that plagues me." He hefted the flail heads and let them fall back to his thigh. "These records were purchased from collectors, stolen from temples, plundered from dusty crypts. You of all people should appreciate the irony of that." The captain gave his sister a wicked grin. "Bloodsounder grieves me, wracks me, in ways I cannot possibly explain to you. So yes, I would risk almost anything to be rid of it. Or at least control it. Add 'selfish bastard' to the list."

She smiled back, though no less wolfish than his own. "It is near the top already. And if I didn't have an imperial mandate hanging over my head, and a witness," her eyes flicked over to Skeelana long enough to register anger, "I would likely applaud your selfish death spiral. But I realize the admission must have cost you, pained you even, which brings me a little pleasure."

Soffjian looked down the road and nodded once. "I will do what I can. I can't promise it will be enough, and do it reluctantly, but—"

"Duly noted," Braylar replied. "Duly." He looked at Hewspear and Mulldoos. "Ready the men. And lay out some caltrops, will you. There are some in the other wagon." He started to turn away and stopped himself. "Oh. And keep Henlester chained inside. We had one priest escape us already. Do not let it happen again."

Hewspear and Mulldoos nodded and rode back to alert the men. Soffjian gave her shorter comrade a look that could have melted steel and then rode ahead to survey the road, the land, or something else. Or maybe simply to wait and prepare herself in silence.

Braylar gave Skeelana an appraising look, as if taking her in for the first time. "Well done, small adept. I do sometimes forget just how adroit you Memoridons can be."

She gave a mock bow and replied, "Some of us don't possess the ability to level armies at a look, my lord, but we all have our uses."

I had a number of questions swirling, so many it was hard to fix on one. So I blurted out the first that came to mind. "What is a caltrop?"

The answer came from over my left shoulder—Vendurro rode up, holding a large sack, and slipped his hand in. "Nasty little bit of business, that." He pulled out a sharp iron object that had been painted a dull brown and tossed it to me—it was basically four long spikes forged together. It jabbed my thumb and I nearly dropped it at least three times as he said, "No matter how it falls, one of them spikes is always pointing to the sky. Might not always cripple a horse, but enough to hurt them plenty good, throw a rider, break up a charge, slow an advance."

I held it up and looked at it, wincing as I imagine that in a horse's hoof. "Why brown?"

"On account of most roads and earth being brown-like. Doesn't do much good if you can see the sun glinting off it from a hundred yards out."

Braylar said, "Spread them out, about seventy-five yards from our position, ahead of Soffjian. I want the Hornmen to see us, see our numbers, and salivate. They are little better than a local militia—they lack discipline and I suspect when they see their huge advantage, they will come in hard. They'll expect to flank us, so they'll likely ride at us spread out, so make sure you get those caltrops on a lot of ground."

Vendurro nodded and he called out to another two Syldoon bearing bags and the three of them rode ahead, passing Soffjian. Only Vendurro acknowledged her with a nod.

I asked, "What is she going to do, captain? Is she going to kill a large number, or drive them mad? Like she did in Alespell?"

Braylar grabbed his helm, overturned it on the saddle in front of him, and pulled the mail out to make room for his head. "I do not know for certain what she intends. Not all war Memoridons have the same. . . skills. But—and the short Memoridon can correct me if I am wrong—killing a man with memorycraft requires intense focus. It can only be done singly, and it is draining, yes?" Skeelana nodded, and Braylar said, "So I expect she has something else in mind. If you will pardon the expression. A host of fifty-five is little better than a host of fifty-eight."

He pulled his helm on, secured it, and said, "Stay with the wagon. Keep a crossbow at the ready. But if you are forced to loose it, it probably means Soffjian failed, we failed, and we are all doomed already. If the worst happens, I'd suggest getting on a horse and running. Only you wouldn't make it very far." He looked at Skeelana. "And you? Do whatever it is you do when not delighting me by tweaking my sister's nose."

Skeelana smiled and gave another small mock bow. "Each of us our talents."

Hewspear and Mulldoos and the remaining Syldoon rode up on either side, crossbows loaded, lamellar and helms on, sidearms at the ready.

Captain Killcoin turned Scorn about to better address them. Scorn took that as a sign to piss a steamy stream into the dirt. "Our Hornmen friends have come calling. Quite a few of them, as it happens. Seems they didn't appreciate being cut down in Alespell or losing a border tower.

"My sister is going to run interference and do what she can to slow them down. I'm assuming a fair number will still come for us, too many to close and fight hand to hand. Rolling gears, soldiers. Rolling gears. Do not engage until we have whittled them down sufficiently to turn the battle in our favor."

There were nods as several spanned their crossbows, and Braylar continued. "Hornmen might be good at scaring travelers and collecting taxes, but they are barely better than a bandit militia. Once we tip things to our advantage, I expect them to break and flee. If they do, run them down if you can, but don't pursue overlong. Regroup here, and we ride hard for Sunwrack. Understood?"

The Syldoon called out "aye" or saluted or both and started spreading out in a line.

I recalled our encounter with the Hornmen in the Green Sea, and thought Braylar might have been overselling things—even if young, green, with several boys in their company, they were a much larger host, and I didn't imagine they were going to simply break to pieces against the Syldoon like a listing ship on the reefs, no matter what Soffjian did.

fter grabbing a crossbow and quiver, I returned to my seat. Vendurro and the other two horsemen returned from spreading the caltrops in the grass and across the road and rejoined their comrades in the line ahead of our wagon, waiting. Soffjian remained on her horse on the road, fixed to the same spot she had been in, staring straight ahead.

I finished checking the small steel sight on the crossbow, careful to keep it pointed out into the fields, made sure the fur-covered flap on the quarrel case was folded back, and tried not to count the seconds until the Hornmen arrived. But I wouldn't have counted all that high, even if I had. Unlike the Syldoon, they didn't employ scouts, apparently safe in their numbers and the privilege of being the protectors of the road. A large number of them rode over the small hill far ahead of us, six or seven at a time. It was hard to make out details at that distance, but while they all had armor caps or helms of some kind, the sun only lit on metal armor here and there—most must have been wearing gambesons or boiled leather. There were spear points aplenty, however.

As more Hornmen appeared, the sheer number of them was enough to make me catch my breath, even if they were a mish-mash force. They might not have been an army, but near sixty men on horse, armed and angry, intent on vengeance, was still an intimidating sight. I couldn't imagine the bravery it must take to watch a huge enemy host fill the field in anticipation of a true pitched battle. I longed to jump on a horse and ride in the opposite direction.

And yet there Soffjian stood alone, ranseur in the leather sheathe alongside the saddle, watching them slowly arrive until their leader must have called a halt to evaluate. A single woman in scale armor, holding no obvious weapon, and a small force and some wagons in the distance behind her as if to parley—not exactly the stuff to induce fear or hesitation.

I saw two or three Hornmen at the front huddling as close together as they could while still on horseback, talking animatedly. There was some pointing, some gesturing, and then, exactly as Braylar had expected, they fanned out along the top of the hill.

Skeelana's horse whinnied and I looked over, not even noticing that she hadn't moved back to the rear wagon. "I will never understand men," she said. "But especially those that play at war."

She saw my questioning look and qualified, "I would think it odd that a much smaller group would stand their ground. Wouldn't you? You're a man, but not a martial one. That's a compliment, by the way. But wouldn't you suspect something?"

I watched as Soffjian slowly raised her arms and spread them wide. "We killed a small number of them in the Green Sea, with a few survivors. One recognized me in Alespell, and we killed a larger number when they tried to trap us there. Then we slaughtered them in their own watchtower and burned it to ground. The only thing we didn't do was rape their wives or kill their dogs. I expect they're pretty angry, so maybe not thinking all that clearly."

Skeelana nodded slowly. "That does make a mannish sort of sense. Though the Syldoon wouldn't rush into a battle unless they had examined every angle first."

"Well, they are no Syldoon, that's for certain."

"Well, neither are you." I felt Skeelana staring at me, and looked away from the Hornmen long enough to see the intensity in her blue eyes. "Does your captain know that one of the Hornmen from the steppe saw you? That you are the cause for all this mischief?"

I tried to keep my face blank, and as usual, utterly failed.

Skeelana winked. "Don't worry. Your secret's safe with me."

And then the Hornmen charged.

They galloped down the small incline, those on the road kicking up dust, those who had spread into the grass on either side, clumps of earth and sod. While no army, it was a huge group of horsemen, and no matter what tricks or traps were laid, I couldn't see how we would survive or avoid capture.

Yet, the Syldoon waited, not raising their crossbows or moving their mounts yet. Ahead of them, Soffjian was still in the saddle, arms outstretched and angled slightly toward the Hornmen as if to welcome the oncoming horde.

Having seen what happened in Alespell, I knew there would be no pyrotechnics. But at that distance, I wouldn't be able to even see the slight telltale shimmer that she emitted in Alespell. I was wondering how I would know she had done anything at all when I saw the splay her fingers on both hands and tilt her head back as if she were merely enjoying the warmth of the sun on her face.

Then a number of chaotic and awful things happened very quickly.

Several of the Hornmen jerked on their reins, some falling from the saddle. Others seemed to have lost complete control of their mounts, as they rode into each other, again with several riders falling to the dirt. Some Hornmen were shaking their heads back and forth, a few slapping their helms, or clawing at the air in front of their faces. What had been a charging line of horses was now in complete disarray, with many racing off in every direction except for the one they had been heading in.

The rest still came on, though it was impossible to tell if they'd suffered whatever had befallen their comrades. Soffjian wheeled her horse around and raced back toward the Syldoon line with roughly half of the Hornmen host pursuing her, some slower than others.

The Hornmen hit the patch of ground where Vendurro and the others had hidden the caltrops, and while some made it through unscathed, a large number of horses screamed as they seized up, a horrible, nearly human sound, and then threw their riders, or became uncontrollable in their pain.

It was terrible to behold. The whole scene. And it got worse.

The Syldoon raised their crossbows, took aim, and loosed almost in unison, with only a few shots coming late. Not nearly as well armored as the Brunesmen, a half dozen or more Hornmen were struck and wounded or killed on the first volley. Their shields offered some protection, but not nearly enough.

The Syldoon reloaded, working efficiently, and then rode to meet their foes, and I got to see what "rolling gears" meant. Braylar's men sighted their targets as they cantered, loosed again, and then curled off to the right and left as they reloaded, and the Syldoon who had been behind them did the same.

More horses screamed and Hornmen fell from the saddle, but the remainder kept coming, probably not having realized how swiftly their overwhelming advantage was disappearing.

The Syldoon rode in circles, loading and shooting, taking down their foes, staying outside of javelin range, not letting the Hornmen close. The Hornmen dropped and continued to drop. If they had a commander who would have recognized that things had tipped abruptly and inexplicably out of their favor, he was dead or he'd ridden off already.

Thanks to whatever Soffjian had done, some sneaky tactics, and discipline, the Hornmen were routed and destroyed. It was shocking how quickly it happened.

When a handful of Hornmen realized that everything had gone wrong, they turned and tried to flee, and were summarily shot in the back. Some Syldoon pursued those who fled, careful to stay away from the grass that hid caltrops. One or two Hornmen weren't that observant or lucky, more concerned with escaping than anything else, and went over the same sabotaged ground again. One horse fell on its side, crushing the Hornman underneath, and another was so hobbled it didn't take long for two Syldoon to catch up and fill him with bolts.

There were around ten Hornmen who had slowed their mounts further up the hill, and appeared to be riding aimlessly in no singular direction, holding their heads, shaking their helms, hunched over. Not knowing that their force, so formidable only moments before, had been wiped out.

"What. . ." I found myself whispering, in awe, and raised my voice. "What did she *do*?"

As Skeelana leaned forward on her horse, watching the Syldoon take out the remaining Hornmen, she replied, "Unless I misjudge, she has blinded them."

I looked back to the field, and all of the behavior suddenly made sense, but I still found myself amazed. And a little horrified. "Blinded them?"

For once, Skeelana didn't seem bemused. "You recall, I told you that everyone has internal screens, or veils, that protect them from the constant bombardment of sensations."

"I do. Though that still seems incredible."

Skeelana pointed at the scene ahead. "More incredible than this?"

I conceded the point as another downed horse or man screamed, it was difficult to tell which. She said, "Well, tearing them asunder will drive a person mad, or kill him. As it did in Alespell. But Killcoin has the right of it—that requires tremendous focus. Here, she spread her attack wide, to strike as many of them as possible. So, she didn't destroy the veils entirely, only tore holes in them. I've seen her do it once before."

I watched the wandering Hornmen on the fringes of the battlefield, still drifting. "Is it permanent?"

"For some, yes. Those probably directly in front of her. The further away, the less severe. Some will be blind for a few hours, or days. But it doesn't really matter, does it?" She sounded sad.

"Why is that?"

"Because death is permanent."

My stomach clenched as I looked where she did, and saw the Syldoon riding down those blind men, some of whom tried to run, a few who turned their horses madly about, jabbing out with spears before being shot out of the saddle.

The Syldoon caught up to them, herded them, and butchered them.

I stood up, wanting to rush out to somehow stop them. While it was one thing to kill a man who was fighting back, this was cold savagery. Unjust. Unconscionable. The foes might as well have been disarmed.

I was about to jump down and get on my horse tethered to the rear, ride out to plead with the captain to show some clemency, when I remembered that all of this was traced back to that moment of ill-given mercy in the tall, wave-like grass. Somehow I had talked Braylar out of killing an unarmed man then, despite his misgivings for doing so, and it had ultimately led to the battle in Alespell when I didn't confess seeing the spared man in time, and from there to the killing and destruction at the watchtower, and finally, to this bloody moment.

All back to me.

There would be no dissuading him this time. Not now. Certainly nothing from my mouth could alter the course of this action. I slowly sat back down, and though I wanted desperately to look away, I could not.

Mercy was lauded as a virtue by priests, by kings, by parents. And yet, the choice not to slaughter a man in cold blood had led to countless other men being killed.

Skeelana seemed to sense my thoughts. "There is no kindness in war, Arki. But at least you didn't have to kill anyone else today. That's something."

Nodding slowly, I felt numb, watching Syldoon finish the Hornmen off one by one. I finally looked down at my feet and sighed, then pushed the crossbow away from me, on the vacated seat on the bench.

When I looked up again, Soffjian was nearing the wagon, dismounted and walking her horse. Her face was exceptionally pale, eyes nearly closed, a vein like a lightning bolt prominent on her forehead, and she moved past without acknowledging either of us.

Skeelana got off her horse and tried to give me a wan smile, gave up, then turned and disappeared as she followed the spent Memoridon.

I looked out at the field and was somewhat shocked to see Braylar and Mulldoos leading a handful of prisoners toward us. Blind prisoners. Stumbling, falling over each other and every odd clump on the ground, holding each other's arms and belts to try to stay on their feet, heads jerking in the direction of every sound.

Why had he spared them? It certainly wasn't an unexpected outpouring of compassion. As Lloi had once said, the man didn't do anything without calculating really hard on it first. So why then, if not mercy for mercy's sake? The Syldoon clearly weren't taking on more prisoners, not with the Brunesmen somewhere behind us, and sparing men that might turn around and join the enemy again later flew in the face of everything Braylar had shown me at the watchtower. The captain had, against his better judgment, allowed me to haggle for a man's life in the Green Sea, and he would never let me live down how that had turned out. So why now?

The captain took his helm off. He was sweaty, but otherwise hadn't exerted himself overmuch. This must have been the most lopsided victory he'd ever been part of. Except for one Syldoon who had been sliced on the bicep by a javelin, and another who had foolishly come too close to a blind Hornman and been struck by a wild blow, I don't think they had suffered any casualties at all. And certainly no fatalities, unless one of those minor wounds festered. At the beginning of the battle, I'd been sure we would all likely be killed, and the very opposite had occurred. It was staggering really, and certainly more so for the blind and vanquished Hornmen in tow. Why were they alive?

As Braylar halted near the wagon, he must have read the question on my face as clearly as ink on parchment. "Am I such a monster that it's inconceivable that I might let a fallen foe live?"

I spoke carefully, especially with his other men reining in close enough to hear. "No, but you are somewhat of an. . . uncompromising man."

Mulldoos looked around the field, and then at the newly blinded men, who flinched at every sound, unlike those who had been born to the condition or grown accustomed over the years. "Got to say, Cap, sort of wondering the same thing myself. Why herd them like crippled calves? Could have let them herky-jerky themselves over the horizon and saved some time. Why bother with the round-up?"

Captain Killcoin ignored him and looked at the small group of cowed and shocked prisoners. "Who among you has some rank and can speak for the remainder here?"

Most of the Hornmen were in stained gambesons or mismatched bits of boiled leather, but there were two in byrnies. The closest, a balding man of middling height, gray stubble across his face, called out, "Bull here? Or Corrviss?" After a pause. "No? How about Seddwin or Nails?" He sighed, straightened up a little taller, reached out to touch the shoulders of the men just in front of him, pushed them aside, and took a couple of hesitant steps forward. "That be me, looks like. Name of Rozvert. Men call me Rose. Who am I speaking to, then?"

It struck me how much courage it must have taken for him to accept that he was what amounted to the commanding officer present. Blinded, trounced, and likely fearing execution, he acquitted himself far better than I would have.

Braylar replied, "I am Captain Braylar Killcoin, commanding officer of the Outriders of the Jackal Tower, Fifth Tower of the Syldoon Empire. And while your commission might prove to be a short one, I am encouraged to see a man of some salt in front of me."

Rose's eyes darted around, tracking the captain's voice and every shift in the saddle or cleared throat in the vicinity. I would have panicked, but he seemed to steady his eyes, though they were locked in on Scorn's forelocks, so it was clear he still wasn't seeing anything. "You the ones that did for the watchtower a few days back? And our brothers in Alespell before that? Hate to think we got what we got here going after the wrong men."

I wondered if Braylar would spin a lie of one color or another, but he dealt with the question head on. "We were indeed. Though to be fair, we tried to pass by the watchtower without incident. And in Alespell, it was your brethren who attacked us."

There was murmuring behind Rose and he turned and spit into the grass. "Well then, I got to say, Syldoon, really wishing we was in opposite positions right now. Because I'd be looking for the highest branch to hang you from."

"You would hang blinded men? How delightfully savage of you. Then I am very fortunate we are in the current positions we are in. And you are as well. Despite the urging of some of my more merciless men here, I do not intend to hang you, or otherwise bring an end to your miserable lives."

Rose brought his sleeve up to rub it across his sweaty pate, stopped short to be sure he didn't hit himself in the face, then finished wiping his brow. "What did you plaguing do to us, you Syldoon bastard?"

Braylar replied, "You would do well to remember that the roles are *not* reversed, Hornman. And as to the answer, it wasn't me. I am but a humble soldier, like yourself. Though clearly better at it. No, that was the handiwork of a Memoridon. And not an especially nice one."

"The blindness? Is it. . . " he licked his lips, then forced himself to continue, "for good?" It was clear the prospect terrified him more than being executed.

Braylar looked for Vendurro, and finding him, said, "Clean up those caltrops. We will be back on the road shortly." Vendurro nodded, and Braylar looked at Rose again. "As to the duration, not being a Memoridon I can't say for certain, and as she has retired for the afternoon, I would only be hazarding guesses."

The Hornman's face hardened, and I found myself saying, "Only those closest to Soff—. . . to the Memoridon are likely to have permanent or long-term blindness. The rest will recover in time." Immediately, I regretted letting the words out of my mouth. Braylar was looking at me curiously, Mulldoos with a face flushed with anger, the rest of the Syldoon with equal parts surprise or hostility. Only Hewspear seemed bemused.

Even Rose cocked his head, trying to locate the new person addressing him, and then said, "That's a boy. Unless you done started doing things real different over there in the Empire, none of your witches got cocks. What does this plaguing boy know about it?"

Braylar didn't look away from me as he replied, "That is an excellent question. Which I will ascertain the answer to another time." He looked back to the Hornmen. "But for now, the only thing that concerns you is the very immediate future."

Rose looked ready to spit again, then thought better of it. "What of it, you prick? Can't imagine it's any better than what you gave the boys at the watchtower."

"I have spared your lives, but can snatch them away just as quickly. I do not expect gratitude, but a little humility and politeness is in order, even feigned. You might have a future yet, if you can manage to still your prideful tongue and do as you're told. Do you think you can manage that, Hornman?"

Rose didn't look like he could manage that at all, but after a long pause, he unlocked his jaw. "You best not be speaking about me only. What happens to me happens to the rest of my boys here. Good or ill."

Braylar smiled an unpleasant smile, though the chilling effect was lost on the man in front of him. "Their well-being is in your hands, blind man. Do not test me."

Rose stared ahead, lips pulled tight, veins bulging in his temples.

Braylar continued, "As it happens, you are not the only party that is pursuing me just now. So—"

"Ain't surprised at that. Only thing that's surprising at all is it ain't more of us—"

The crossbow bolt in the throat stopped him short. The Hornman reached up to grab it, spitting blood all over his chin, sightless eyes darting in all directions, and then he dropped to his knees and then fell over on his side. Most of the other Hornmen stepped back in horror. Only the other man in a byrnie crept forward, kneeling alongside Rose, reaching out tentatively to steady the dying man as his body jerked in the grass.

Braylar spanned his crossbow again as he said, "Now then, for those in attendance who might not be able to tell from the gurgling noise you heard just now, your lippy self-proclaimed leader is bleeding his last at your feet. I have no wish to kill unarmed blind men—it is hardly sporting, and brings me no pleasure—but we are running out of time. You there, the only other Hornman in mail. Stand."

The Hornman did so, slowly, his palms out in front of him as if expecting a crossbow quarrel to rip into him at any moment.

"What is your name, Hornman?"

The man reluctantly stuttered out, "Crowder."

"Very good, Crowder. And do you think you can be a good soldier, follow orders, and not get yourself or any in your small band killed? Because

I tell you now, I am out of patience, but not bolts. So if you cannot manage this task, we are done playing choose the leader. You all die now."

Crowder looked down as he heard Rose wheeze his last, cough, sputter, and die.

"Hornman!" Braylar yelled.

The man snapped his head back up.

"I will not ask again. Can you follow orders and save what remains of your sorry troop here?"

Crowder nodded slowly, still tensed, and then belatedly added, "Aye. Yes. Yes, tell us what you want of us."

After hearing no further retorts, Braylar continued, "Very good. A sensible man at last. Now then, heed me closely. Baron Brune's men are on the road behind us, led by a gruff man named Captain Gurdinn. They will likely be here in half a day, possibly less. When they come across your stumbling crew, you will convey a simple message. Something of a warning, really. Following me so far?"

Crowder nodded fast, several times.

"Good. You will tell them, as your condition bears out, that we destroyed a full company of Hornmen after our resident war Memoridon blinded near on sixty men, including your sad crew. Let the Brunesmen know we only allowed you to live to provide evidence of this. If they choose to pursue us, we will have ample time and opportunity to cripple their much smaller party, and you can be sure I will not be so charitable in leaving prisoners a second time."

Crowder made sure nothing more was forthcoming before asking, "Is that it, then?"

Braylar started to nod and stopped himself. "That's it. Stay on this road and deliver this warning as instructed, and you and your men live. Even a group of blind men can manage this, I am thinking."

Crowder was staring at the grass in the distance between them, nodded quickly, and then added, reluctantly, "And after?"

"After?" Braylar asked. "Well, Gurdinn is no monster. I assume he will take you in, or see you provided for. But even if he leaves you at the road-side, you will be alive. And that is surely finer than the alternative, yes?"

He didn't wait for an answer and called out to another Syldoon. "See to it they have some food and water. And give them their weapons. I am a hard man, but not cruel top to bottom."

Riding alongside the wagon, Mulldoos muttered, "Waste of decent steel. Better to give them some walking sticks."

Braylar leaned back on the bench next to me and said, "Now, Mulldoos, I did give my word."

"Also shot one in the face."

"It was the throat. And I warned him, did I not?"

"You should have shot them all in the face, you ask me. They'll probably run for the woods the second we're out of sight."

"In a manner of speaking," I said and then regretted my joke immediately.

Braylar laughed. "Delightful. But I am thinking this Crowder is too cowed to disobey, even after we ride off. He will deliver the message."

Mulldoos shook his head as our procession rolled on, leaving the stunned Hornmen on the side of the road—it was difficult to tell if they were more relieved to be alive, or terrified of being stranded without sight in the middle of nowhere. "You wanted to leave one to warn Brune's bastards, one would have done it. All I'm saying. No need to leave a handful of them. And their weapons? What the hells will they do with those besides cut themselves up? Probably hurt themselves with spoons right now."

Braylar laughed. "A single blind man signifies nothing. Eight—"

"Seven," I amended.

"Seven blind men make for a more compelling warning. Much harder to ignore. And as to their weapons, well, if brigands happen along, at least the sightless Hornmen can kill themselves first."

Mulldoos shook his head again. "Got a right peculiar sense of fair play, Cap. Right peculiar."

"So I've been told."

Mulldoos turned and rode back to either join the men or check on something, leaving the captain and me alone again. For once, I was actually sorry to see Mulldoos leave.

Braylar didn't look my way or say anything, but the silence was filled with palpable unease, though it was hard to tell if it was more on my part or the captain's. He hadn't struck down anyone else with Bloodsounder—I don't think the Syldoon had even raised a melee weapon, except to use the flats of their blades to beat down a few blind prisoners—but his disquieting quiet was almost worse than an energetic rebuking.

"Are you—"

"If you say 'well,' I will throw you off the wagon and leave you to shepherd the blind bastards behind us."

Well. That was at least familiar.

I tried a different tack. "I was wondering something."

"Of course you were."

"I don't generally find myself agreeing with Mulldoos, but I am curious why you left any of the Hornmen back there."

We passed a dead horse and some blood stains in the grass on our left. "I'm rather surprised at you, Arki, exceptionally tender soul that you are. I imagined you would have been thrilled."

"I'm glad you spared them. Well, most of them anyway."

"Ahhh. . . so that's what is troubling you, yes? That I shot a blind man?"

"A blind prisoner."

Braylar looked at me and forced a smile, thin but surprisingly unwobbly. "It was clear Rose was not going to be cooperative. The whole point of sparing them was to have them be blind witness and keep Gurdinn from pursuing, and Rose would have led them into the woods the moment we rolled off. Or blindly attacked me if I gave him a blade. He has no one to blame but himself."

I chose not to argue the point. "Let's assume Crowder does as you commanded. I still don't quite understand, why the necessity for a warning at all? Don't misunderstand—I am happy you let them live. But with Soffjian in the company, couldn't you simply do the same thing to the Brunesmen?"

Braylar replied, "I would have thought you could tutor me on that score. Given your newfound expertise in all things Memoridon."

And order on the wagon was restored. I felt my cheeks flush, even if I'd been wondering when he might comment on that. Perhaps I should have chosen to talk about caltrops or rolling gears instead. "I chatted with Skeelana briefly. She mentioned that the blindness might pass. Or not."

"Well, then clearly she neglected to mention that Soffjian is not all-powerful. Blinding dozens of men on a field of battle is not so easily done as all that. Frankly, I am surprised she is still sitting in the saddle. I imagine your short confidant is propping her up just now and tending to her needs. Even if she was inclined, which she is not, my sister won't be of any use to us or even herself for some time. For everything, a cost, archivist. And some things are less cheaply purchased than others, yes?"

Memory magic did seem to exact a toll on the user. Though Braylar was an unwitting user, at best. I was tempted to ask again how he was faring before recalling the warning. "Are there many like her? Among the Syldoon Towers?"

"War Memoridons? No. Which is likely a good thing."

"Why is that?"

He swatted at a cloud of gnats. "It is true, if we had more with Soffjian's very dangerous talents, we would be all but unstoppable. Anjuria never would have opposed us, or if they had, turned into a kingdom of the blind and mad if we allowed any to survive. But the Syldoon have kept the Memoridons in check in part because they are so few in number, and even then, those who can wipe out battalions like my sister are fewer still. There are rigid limits on both counts that all Towers must abide by. Mutually agreed upon limits. Any found violating them risk severe penalties."

"Such as?"

Braylar looked at me and twitch-smiled—I was finally growing accustomed to it. "The Fifth Man."

I waited for him to explain, and he must have enjoyed my waiting as he waited until I finally opened my mouth to ask for elaboration before saying, "Any Tower found violating the Memoridon limit must choose one fifth of its forces—nomination, lottery, volunteers, what have you—and summarily slaughter them. This includes the Tower's Memoridons, so they don't have incentive to try to swell their numbers on the sly."

"One fifth. That is a severe penalty. Have many Towers risked such a punishment?"

Braylar replied, "That depends how you define 'many.' Four Towers have suffered the Fifth Man, but over the course of several centuries, that isn't so very many. The largest of these was the Stag Tower—they were a prominent faction, nearly forty thousand strong. It took several days."

"The Emperor executed eight thousand men?"

The twitching lip froze. "You misunderstand. The Stag Tower had to carry out the punishment themselves."

"What if they hadn't? Complied? Has that ever happened?"

Braylar nodded, slowly. "Once. Ten years ago. The Broken Tower."

"Did you. . . so you saw it happen, then? Were you in Sunwrack?"

Braylar closed his eyes. "I was. The Broken Tower—well, that's what they're called now. Before the incident, they were the Fox Tower. The Broken Tower refused to strike down their own men. They were a smaller Tower—ten thousand strong. And they refused. So, it fell to the other Towers."

"You and the others executed the thousand men?"

"No. We executed all of the men. Every last one. Most Towers that are commanded to enact the Fifth Man resist, stall, appeal. But none absolutely refused before. We didn't have all ten thousand locked away. The Fox Tower repudiated, all but daring us to carry the sentence out. Perhaps thinking we wouldn't. It was unprecedented, as I said."

"But. . . "

"But the Emperor ordered it done. The law is the law. And so the other Towers attacked. Some from Fox escaped into the Torchfield and took to the streets. We hunted them down, district by district, house by house. Until every last one of the ten thousand was dead. Along with countless Thurvacians and casualties aplenty among the other Towers. Even Sunwrack, Capital of Coups, in all its bloody history, had never seen carnage in its streets as it did that day."

We lapsed into silence for some time before I finally asked, "So, what now?"

"Now, we return to Sunwrack, hopefully without encountering any more large groups of armed men that would like to see me dead. And you return to your translation. You said you needed opportunity? Well, unless assaulted again, you shall have it. We have many, many miles before we reach Sunwrack. Surely enough for you to make considerable progress."

While the prospect of doing something useful that did not require wielding a crossbow made me excited, I paused to ask, "And what of Henlester?"

"What of him?"

"Well, you mentioned you wanted him for political reasons, and because he might have knowledge about Memoridons. Or at least the early versions of them, before the Syldoon used them. Are you going to, uh, interrogate him?"

The wagon bounced over a rut and nearly sent me off the bench. "I do hope the High Priest proves worth the risk. I will not press him with Memoridons around, not until I have something of substance to talk to him about. If there was something that occurred deep in the history of his order, he would likely be aware though, and it would be better to have something concrete to assail him with. So, put your skills to use, Arki, and stop dawdling."

Even with the rising temperatures inside the wagon, it was a welcome distraction to seclude myself in there and being poring over pages again. The passages in Middle Anjurian, while not easy, weren't entirely unfamiliar, and tended to go more quickly. Not quick. But more quickly. In some instances, I had to force myself to slow a bit, to be sure I wasn't missing anything or performing the gravest of translator missteps, seeing what I wanted to.

Still, hours came and went, and there was very little of interest in the remainder of the first chest. Well, of interest to Braylar—I found the entire contents absorbing. But while there were a number of references to the Deserter Gods here and there, none were especially illuminating or revealing anything new or noteworthy. And there were a few more oblique references to weapons like Bloodsounder, with one more corroborating the notion that wielder and weapon shared a name and were somehow bonded in both a physical and metaphysical sense (which was noteworthy, and certainly worth pointing out to the captain), but again, nothing entirely new for the remainder of that day.

We made camp in some woods alongside the road, hiding the wagons as best we could.

The next day passed, and I was so buried in the work I nearly forgot that the Brunesmen might still be out there hunting us until one of the scouts returned and reported that they were no longer even within a day's ride of us. They had slowed or turned away. Or at least intended to give that impression. Braylar, suspecting a possible ploy and not one to deviate from protocol, especially as it involved gathering intelligence, ordered the scouts to remain vigilant. But it appeared that the blind men had indeed served as a warning.

Even though the Hornmen had been attempting to kill us, I hoped the blindness proved to be temporary. It might have been more merciful to kill them otherwise. No one had an easy path through life, but cripples least of all.

With the most recent threat having been averted and no new ones presenting themselves, we fell into a familiar rhythm over the next two days—breaking to rest the horses and feed and water them at almost the same time of day. I spent every hour of sunlight in the wagon, sweating and sifting through old or ancient documents, jotting notes, compiling and cataloguing what I discovered. Braylar even surprised me by allowing me to light a lantern each night to continue working.

We hit Martyr's Fork and started our journey on the north road, and aside from some subtle changes in the landscape, with slopes and hills beginning to become more pronounced, and forest and woods less frequent (or at least broken up by more patches of stony ground), little changed. My rolling scriptorium continued rolling, Syldoon recovered from wounds and tended their armor and weapons, and I found myself listening to pieces of their conversations, jokes, and songs, happy to be doing something I enjoyed, but again feeling alienated, as Braylar had commanded the soldiers to leave me to it. Vendurro stopped in a few times, or entreated me to take a meal with the men, which I sometimes accepted, but for the most part I was immersed in my work and content it was me and my pages.

Aside from me, there were three other people who also rode with the company without being a part of it. Henlester was always either chained inside the other wagon, or guarded by one or two Syldoon a fair distance from wherever we stopped or rested. I rarely saw him, which was just as well. I might not have been familiar with the man, but what I did know made my skin crawl. And even beyond his taste for damaged whores and the likelihood that he killed them, his disloyalty to the Baron, and the fact that he had tried to trap and kill us at the ruined temple (never mind that we had intended the same for his underpriest), there was the churning arrogance. Though he was clearly a prisoner, he comported himself like the jailer.

And Soffjian, of course, who stayed distant from the Syldoon, ate her meals separately, and didn't engage the Syldoon any more than absolutely necessary. Though she did seem more at ease now that we were finally on Lord's Highway heading north, she was still bristly and clearly made anyone within twenty yards nervous, especially after her display against the Hornmen.

While Skeelana often joined her, she did occasionally attempt to joke with the men. Conversation seemed to wither and die quickly, however. While she wasn't nearly as aloof (or dangerous) as Braylar's sister, she was still a Memoridon. A creature apart.

I found myself sometimes hoping we would have more opportunities to chat, but aside from a few brief exchanges, she gave me space. Which irritated me, whether done to protect me or comply with an order by Braylar or some mysterious whim. And I was irritated with myself for being irritated.

But I needed to focus, not get distracted by ridiculous conversations with impossible women. Still, I found myself thinking of those exchanges we had had, and hoping we could have more once I had translated through the contents of all the crates and chests the Syldoon had gathered. Foolish beyond foolish, but there it was.

And then it happened. Finally.

While I'd been happy enough just to be using my talents, and the captain didn't overtly pressure me to deliver any result, I could tell by his looks and short questions about progress that he was impatient. And frustrated, even as I assured him that it was better to be as deliberate and accurate as possibly, rather than risk missing something or getting it wrong.

In truth, after those original bits of text regarding mystical weapons, I was beginning to despair of finding anything related to any topic Braylar had put me on alert for. So when I came across a section written by what must have been one of the original priests serving the Temple of Truth, I was relieved, intrigued, and excited again.

A great deal of it dealt with confusing clerical politics, their order's somewhat antagonistic relationship with the secular rulers of the day (some things never changed!), and the day-to-day operations—all tithes and meal preparation and logistics and records of visits from visiting clerics, stretching over years. My initial enthusiasm waned.

So when I finally came across a passage that dealt with what could only have been the forerunners to the Memoridons, I was elated. It was extremely difficult not to plow ahead, to try to find out what I discovered. I desperately wanted to simply be done, to share the translating success with Captain Killcoin.

But I forced myself to proceed slowly, setting an agonizing pace, working with the source material for several hours, toying with various choices of interpretation, trying to stay as authentic to the original verbiage and intent as possible. And then I revisited again, and still again to be sure I had a handle on the language, the content, the meaning of the words, resisting the urge to scramble and rush, finally having something significant, substantial, and exciting to work through.

After scribbling my final notes, I realized we had actually stopped at some point, and I'd been so occupied I hadn't noticed. I grabbed the parchment, blew on the last of the ink to dry it, and then made my way out of the wagon, fighting off a dry breeze to avoid losing all my pages.

From the looks of it, I must have been lost in translation for quite some time—saddles were off, most of the horses groomed and fed already, some men were preparing a fire. Mulldoos and Hewspear were closest to the lead wagon, both leaning against their saddles, Mulldoos with his arms crossed behind his head, Hewspear more upright and looking less comfortable, his ribs still giving him trouble, no doubt. I wondered how long it took bruised or broken ribs to heal. I'd had a toe broken by a large wine barrel before, and that had been a minor misery. And I didn't have to keep riding and fighting every day.

They were both watching two of the younger Syldoon sparring with shields and blunted blades. Not seeing Braylar anywhere, I walked over to his lieutenants and stood a few feet away and then asked where I could find the captain.

Hewspear started to reply when Mulldoos slapped his meaty thigh. "Fusko, you dumb whoreson. You used the same feint six times running—you really think he's falling for it again?"

Fusko, short and thin-framed but incongruously having a moon-face, now red with exertion, called out over his shoulder, "Fell for it twice already. Didn't you, Welt?"

The other soldier was breathing heavily as he circled his opponent. "Once, you prick. And quit calling me Welt!"

"Twice, and quit getting hit and I will!" Fusko feinted a blow to his opponent's head, and when "Welt" shifted his shield just a hair, the real blow snapped down toward the opposite leg. But Welt dropped his shield in time and knocked the blunt away.

Welt called out, "Once, you dumb prick!" and kept circling.

Hewspear started to answer me again when Mulldoos yelled, "I'm inclined to side with Welt on this one. You are a dumb prick. And while you might be fast, most experienced fighters ain't falling for your feint anyway. Best come up with a different tack, boy. And another thing, you're stopping anytime he blocks or avoids the blow, resetting. Got to keep after it, more blows, change it up, keep his shield and legs moving. String more combinations together, one blow flowing into the next."

"Even if I struck him?"

"Ain't struck him the last few times, have you, quick prick?"

Fusko couldn't really argue that point. He kept pivoting and circling as Mulldoos leaned back against the saddle again. "Been a free soldier, what, five years now? Shouldn't have to be reminding you of this shit, boy."

Fusko stepped in, threw a shot at Welt's helm, blocked by the shield, and another blow to the opposite side, blocked by the shield, but he slid the edge of his own shield around his opponent's, ripped it out of the way, and thrust, blade perpendicular to the ground.

But Welt had anticipated it, sidestepped it, so the rounded tip of the blade slid past his gambeson.

Mulldoos shook his head. "Miserable display, boy. Miserable. And your thrust wasn't parallel anyway. Bad form. Now switch up—Welt's got the active sword now. If you defend half as poorly as you strike, it'll be you covered in bruises, you plaguing bastard. What are you waiting for, Welt? Get after it!"

Welt seemed only happy to do so—he began a barrage of blows, using his length, reach, and excellent footwork to good effect until he had Fusko almost spinning and tripping over himself. He landed a blow on Fusko's exposed thigh, and the smaller man, thinking the engagement was over, started to lower his defense when Welt struck him again on the shoulder.

"You dumb prick! It's to one! Can't you plaguing count? One!"

Mulldoos laughed and said, "Now that's how you string together a combination! And Fusko—anytime you lower your guard, you deserve to get hit again."

Fusko gritted his teeth, shook his arm out, and got back in position, swallowing whatever retort he had in mind.

Hewspear looked up at me. "I believe the captain is stretching his legs."

"Is he. . . ?"

"I cannot say. He did not look especially afflicted."

I nodded, watching as Welt circled the shorter Fusko, moving well for a bigger man, confidently, smoothly. I said, "I would have thought, just coming from a battle and not sure if another might be around the next bend, that you'd all take the break to, well, not train. To let wounds heal."

Mulldoos glanced up at me as if seeing me for the first time, despite the fact I'd spoken twice and Hewspear had responded. "Notice only the young stupid pups are out there getting sweaty and dusty." It wasn't nearly as much of a rebuke as I expected.

"When you got on Fusko about his thrust, what was that all about? Why does the sword positioning matter?"

Mulldoos curled his index finger and invited me closer. I suddenly felt like I'd lowered my guard and hesitated. He said, "Ain't going to hurt you, scribbler. Too much exertion. But I ain't getting up to show you neither. Come here."

I fought the urge to look at Hewspear and bent over. Mulldoos reached up and grabbed my shoulder firmly with one big hand, and kept the fingers straight and tight together with the other hand, simulating a blade. He turned the hand so it was perpendicular to the ground. "Now see, you thrust like this—" the fingertips shot out, and though they only went a short distance, his hand still almost knocked the wind out of me, "—and a real bad thing could happen. Might be you get it lodged on the edge of a rib, or worse, stuck between a pair. Get caught like that, blade's not likely to go in far, the man you're stabbing is going to stab or slash you back."

He pulled his hand back, turned it flat to the ground, and out it shot, thumping into my stomach, again nearly sending all the air out. The scary thing was, I don't think he was actually trying to hurt me at all. "Do it like this though, and might be you still hit a rib, but if you do, point only, quicker to withdraw. Not likely to get you killed. And if you miss the ribs, get a clean thrust, no chance of catching it on anything going in or coming out."

Mulldoos released my shoulder, and I nodded and stepped back, trying not to sputter as I said, "Makes sense."

"Course it does." Mulldoos looked at Hewspear and kicked his leg. "Remember Ultonis? That's how he went out, wasn't it? Stuck on a rib?"

Hewspear pulled his leg out of Mulldoos's reach. "It is. Though all this talk of ribs is making mine ache."

"Only thing worse than an old goat is a whiny old goat, bleating on about how his ribs are hurting."

"We still have nothing on gimpy pale boars."

Mulldoos kicked out at him again but Hewspear had moved just out of reach. Then he looked back at me and I was afraid he was going to offer another demonstration again. Instead he said, "Ultonis jabbed an Anjurian something fierce, but the blade was at a bad angle. Got in there, punctured some organ or other, but he couldn't pull it free, the edge was lodged on a rib, just like I said. Anjurian had time for one blow of his own. Ultonis died with an Anjurian sword in his gullet, the Anjurian with a Syldoon blade lodged in his gut. Looked like dance partners."

Then he laughed, and Hewspear smiled.

Every time I felt like I was just beginning to understand the Syldoon...

I saw the captain round the end of the wagon at the rear of our small camp, heading in our direction. Turning to Mulldoos, I said, "Many thanks for the thrusting lesson. But I have something I need to speak to the captain about just now."

Mulldoos glanced at the pages in my arm. "Got something good, do you?"

I tried not to smile and failed. "I think so."

Mulldoos got to his feet. "And I'm thinking I'll want to hear this, too. Cap told us about the Bloodsounder bit. Like to hear what you got for us now."

I didn't welcome explaining everything with him as part of the audience—he always seemed to unsettle me, even when he wasn't jabbing me hard enough to leave bruises.

He reached down and offered his forearm to Hewspear. "Come on, you mummified bastard. Ain't planning on running through the whole thing later at your leisure."

Hewspear accepted his help as they each clasped the other's forearm and the shorter man hoisted him to his feet. "Your kindness is effervescent at times, Mulldoos. Truly."

"Your sarcasm stinks worse than ox piss." He called over to the sparring Syldoon. "Fusko—go fetch Vendurro. Quick. And make sure you sight the witches. If you can't spot them, you tell me quick as spit, you hear?"

Fusko saluted, laid his waster and shield on a blanket on the grass, and ran back toward the other wagon.

The lieutenants and I approached Captain Killcoin. He stood there, arms behind his back. "Three unlikely allies, yes? This can only be very good or very bad. I just saw Henlester, so I know he hasn't escaped or been killed. Has Scorn died then?"

Mulldoos slapped me on the back, and I nearly fell over. "Scribbler's unriddled something in the dusty pages, he says. Figured we'd save some time and go through it all on the once. Ven's on the way."

"Well. Even if it proves less than gripping or convincing, it is better than a dead horse." The captain turned and started walking away from the wagons and the camp, over the stones and stubbly grass. Vendurro saw us and ran to catch up.

When we were a suitable distance from the other men and any Memoridons (that I could see anyway—if Fusko hadn't located them, he would have reported it already), Braylar stopped and said, "Very well, archivist. I am prepared to be regaled, mystified, and awed. Or at least reasonably distracted. Tell us what you've uncovered."

I hadn't been prepared to share it in front of his retinue. It was difficult enough to discuss these things with the captain alone. But there was no getting out of it now.

After clearing my throat, I began prefacing with the caveat about the perils of translating, and that it could be rife with errors if rushed, and sometimes even when not.

"So," Mulldoos said, "What you're saying is you're guessing here. You really don't know shit?"

Hewspear answered before I had a chance to. "I believe what he's saying—correct me if I'm wrong, Arki—is that it is an imperfect endeavor, so we will need to bear that in mind as we listen."

"Sounds like he doesn't know horseshit. But go on, scribbler. Tell us all what you don't know."

I was going to ignore the jab, slide out of its path, but instead chose to address it. "With any translation, there is always the question of felicity, or synonymous choices that don't overly muddy the original text. Yes, there is doubt that despite your best efforts, you have missed something, or distorted it, that you've somehow lost the essence of what had original been put to paper. Pure, perfect translation is only a dream. That much is true. Especially when you are talking about a culture that existed nearly a thousand years ago and taking into account how much has changed. Even with two live languages used in the here and now, you can't have perfect translation. I don't deny any of that."

Mulldoos looked at Braylar, "See, Cap, told you from the beginning, this was a waste—"

"But I am as well equipped as any scholar you could have chosen to read these texts, and while perfect felicity isn't possible, I am reasonably confident that I have translated them well, and done them no injustice. I simply wanted you to understand that there will be some minor gaps, or variance in interpretation. It can't be perfect. But I have translated them and translated them well. And I'm positive that what I've found, if not wholly complete, is exactly the sort of thing you were hoping might be in these pages."

I heard Vendurro whistle behind me. No one else made a sound as Mulldoos looked at me a long time, pale eyes hard and unblinking, nostrils flaring a little. "Well then, why didn't you just say as much from the get-go? Enough with the hemming and hawing, scribbler! What did you plaguing find?"

Braylar couldn't fight off a small smile, and I held my notes and the original pages in front of me, summing up that this was the personal record of an ambitious underpriest of Truth who was somewhat obsessed with the memory witches he had been hearing so much about. And as it would turn out, he would have quite a bit of experience with them.

Mulldoos interrupted, "See? That's what you should have led with."

"When was this, Arki?" Hewspear asked. "Roughly?"

"Judging by other references in the text, this had to be fairly early in the order's history, as quite a bit of what preceded all the memory witch passages was dealing with the temples establishing their protocols and infrastructure, what they had adopted from other religions that were springing up, and practices they intended to avoid and not repeat. So, though the underpriest never says as much, I'd guess somewhere in the vicinity of eight hundred years or so."

Mulldoos looked ready to ridicule again, but held his tongue. So I pressed on, "Anroviak spent a lot of time writing about problems his order was facing, both bureaucratic and simply in terms of attracting followers. He laments the recent plague and—"

Vendurro said, "A thousand years, and they plaguing had the plague."

"Shut it," Mulldoos said.

"He catalogued all the things that were proving problematic," I continued, "but finally arrives at the one that seemed to be troubling his order the most, as it was apparently a recent, and unprecedented phenomenon."

I looked up, feeling a little awkward that all eyes were on me, but also pleased to see that they were, if not rapt and hanging on every word, at least locked in and waiting. But Braylar anticipated where I was going. "Memoridons. Or their forerunners at least, as the Syldoon coined that phrase."

"That's right. Memory witches. The populace at large was understandably in an uproar any time there was even a hint of a possible witch being in their midst, stealing their dreams, invading their memories, slithering through their minds."

Mulldoos said, "You'd think they would have been knocking the temple doors down. Anytime there's plagues or famines or folks find themselves knee deep in a rising shit river, people look to the gods for help."

Hewspear replied, "Ahh, but you're forgetting one thing. This was in the immediate aftermath of the most powerful gods fleeing the world, not only turning their backs on us, but damning us as well. I can see where the people would have been reluctant to place their faith in higher powers again. A thousand years, and the wounds still haven't healed—I'm sure just then they were gaping and raw."

"You mouth is gaping and raw. Go on, scribbler."

I forced myself not to smile, with effort. "Despite the outcry from all corners, Anroviak seemed somewhat sympathetic, at least initially—he didn't blame the witches directly, but seemed to consider that they might only have been a residual effect of the Deserter Gods, unfortunate souls who had merely been somehow blighted or contaminated in the wake of the gods taking their leave of the world." I read from my notes: "*While I hesitate to grant them any kind of special status or elevate them too far above rabid animals or trees struck by lightning—miserable creatures or things simply in the wrong place at the wrong time, rather than the beneficiaries of any conscious gifts or talents by the gods, old or new—I believe it is a mistake to*

see them destroyed altogether. This will prove an unpopular position with my
brothers, I'm certain, but perhaps there is something to be learned from them."

Mulldoos laughed-hooted, it was hard to be certain which. "Unpopular? I'd say. Wish to gods here and gone everyone had just stuck to hanging
or burning them. Us included."

Vendurro looked around, no doubt to be sure Soffjian and Skeelana weren't
nearby, though even not seeing them didn't guarantee they weren't there.

I explained that some of the next passages were a little murky, quick
to point out for Mulldoos's sake that this was largely due to stained pages
and faded ink rather than any limitations of mine as a translator. "As far as
I could tell, Anroviak was going into detail describing some of the heated
debates he had with other members of his order as he advocated studying
the witches rather than simply killing them off. He was met by quite
a bit of opposition from his temple brothers, but for reasons he didn't
delve into, it seemed he had the ear of one of the higher priests—at least
as far as his own estimation of his importance and worth went, and was
allegedly thought of as a reasonable legate in the order."

"Don't they all?" Mulldoos said, smirking.

I didn't point out that the same charge of overestimating our talents
or position could be leveled at almost any of us, mostly because it would
call my own skills into question again. So I ignored the point and moved
on. "Anroviak's arguments didn't win over the bulk of his order, but he
convinced enough of the important minorities who had clout and sway.
While he was charged with destroying any other sorcerers he came across,
Anroviak was granted the opportunity to capture and study the memory
mages as he saw fit, provided he relayed all his findings."

"Wait, other sorcerers?" Vendurro asked. "What kinds of other sorcerers are we talking about here?"

Mulldoos said, "The kind that turn dumb people asking dumb questions into slugs or ash."

Braylar elaborated a little further. "While memory witches have been
the prime subject of hatred, fear, and oppression over the centuries, you
will on occasion see someone else accused of other forms of witchcraft and
nailed to a wall."

I continued, "The next several chapters in the memoir detailed his
mostly failed efforts to track down the dream thieves/memory witches.

His soldiers always seemed to arrive too late to rescue the witches before villages or lords killed them, or when they did managed to capture one, they either didn't possess the powers they were accused of or failed to cooperate."

"Huh," Mulldoos said, looking at Braylar. "Fancy that. Never saw that coming in a thousand years."

Braylar replied, "Ignore the jabbering apes and continue, archivist."

"Well, Anroviak didn't give up. He kept capturing, kept experimenting with reluctant witches, challenged them, and when they insisted they couldn't do what was asked," I looked at Mulldoos, "the underpriest ordered them cut open, sometimes after he killed them, sometimes when they were still alive. There was mention of skull saws, ribs being extracted and pulled free, and organs poked and prodded and removed. Again, sometimes while the poor wretch still lived."

Vendurro gave a long, low whistle. "Really took his job all kinds of serious, didn't he?"

"He considered it his holy duty. And while it's difficult enough to gauge tone in something written in your own language, let alone something written a millennium ago, Anroviak sounded awfully arrogant to me. He was sure he would be the one to unravel the mystery of the memory witches. That it would be his means of rising high in the order." I left out that I was tempted to skim those gruesome details, but forced myself to read every disgusting and detailed word, and was glad of it when I failed to make out some of the language.

"Anroviak's disappointments were perfectly clear, as he went on at great length describing his failed attempts to produce any demonstrative or persuasive results and increasing frustration. He even admitted he briefly considered falsifying records and testimonies, but wouldn't allow himself to do so."

"Course not," Mulldoos said. "Real man of principle. Good to know holy bastards were still holy bastards a hundred hundred years gone. Kind of a comfort."

Vendurro replied, "I don't get you. You hate Memoridons, or witches, or whatever you want to call them. Why do you care what he did?"

"Couldn't give a shit and a half, Ven. And while I got nothing against seeing them hang, experimenting on the poor bastards is something else altogether. Especially when some of them probably couldn't walk into another man's dreams any better than I could. . ."

He sought the right expression, and Hewspear offered, "Keep your lips pressed tightly together while our archivist regales us with a fascinating story that has been buried in the dust for a thousand years?"

Mulldoos grabbed his crotch. "Bite my rod."

"I would rather not, though thank you for the invitation."

Mulldoos started to reply when Braylar said, "Enough, the both of you. Go on, Arki. I would have you finish this before another millennium comes and goes."

I flipped over a page and continued. "After a number of failures and setbacks, Anroviak finally rescued a witch who was not only cooperative, but actually possessed some of the skills she was accused of. Her name was Ruenzina."

Vendurro asked, "How come witches are always women folk? Why can't a man—" but he stopped himself when he saw Braylar glaring at him. "Sorry, Cap. Just curious, is all. Seems awful—" and then stopped himself a second time as the glare became glarier. "Right, Cap. Another time, then. Go on, Arki."

"Ruenzina was a willing subject, apparently recognizing that her usefulness would determine exactly how long she stayed alive. They conducted a number of tests in front of countless clerical witnesses, where she demonstrated that she did in fact have the ability to walk in other men's minds. Underpriest Anroviak was afraid of being branded a charlatan, so from what I gathered, he went overboard. The details of the tests, their results, and their meaning, were delineated in excruciating specificity, chapter after chapter."

"Like this report," Mulldoos said.

"Be glad I'm not reciting the translation word for word. In any event, Anroviak wasn't content to simply prove that the memory magic was in fact real—he wanted to control the person wielding it. That was easy enough with one witch surrounded by countless guards, who didn't possess the training to fight her way free, as Soffjian would have now. No, Anroviak wanted to bind Ruenzina to him somehow, so experiments continued, even as he instructed his men to continue following up on reports of more witchery, and sparing the lives of the accused if they happened to arrive in time. Which seldom occurred.

"But Anroviak wasn't able to effectively bind her to him at all, and only succeeded in compiling more failure to do so. And when Ruenzina attempted to escape, no doubt sensing that her usefulness was quickly going to come to an end, she was cut down."

"That it, then?" Mulldoos asked.

Braylar looked at my notes and saw that I hadn't gotten to the end. "I'm assuming not."

I nodded and said, "Anroviak presented his findings to the order, but he cursed himself for taking too long to present the actual witch. Without her to substantiate his claims, the order was skeptical at best, even with all the notarized witnesses. They ordered him to discontinue his experiments—it was a waste of resources, they said. Witches were to be hunted and killed, and if he performed admirably in that regard, his obsession would be forgiven. But he wasn't to waste any more time on the pursuit."

Hewspear gave a wry smile. "I'm guessing that didn't sit too well with our ambitious, fixated underpriest."

"No," I replied. "It did not. He stormed out of the temple, furious at being publicly snubbed and humiliated. Called his superiors myopic fools and a number of other things that were difficult to make out entirely, but clearly weren't flattering." I looked at Braylar. "He obviously didn't intend for them or anyone else to read any of this account. Where did you find it?"

Braylar twitch-smiled. "It is amazing the things people leave behind. Continue."

"Well," I flipped the page, scanning and summarizing, "Anroviak documented his efforts to continue hunting, in direct violation of his orders and overwhelming lack of support now. And he managed to capture more witches in secret, here and there, over a long stretch, though it was some time before he found another who could actually do what she was accused of and was willing to help. But when he did, she did everything he asked, completely pliant."

"You should show this to Soffjian," Mulldoos suggested. "She could learn a thing or three about being agreeable."

Braylar glared him into silence and I continued. "Well, Mulldoos, you'll probably appreciate this—this witch, Vella, was the daughter of Grass Dog immigrants."

"Horseshit," he said.

"No horseshit," I replied. "And apparently, Vella's parents knew about her talent, or taint, or whatever you want to call it."

"Taint's too pretty a word," Mulldoos said.

"And since the Grass Dogs were already an ostracized and marginalized people in Anjuria, they attempted to keep her abilities secret rather than risk being killed along with her, as sometimes happened."

Vendurro shook his head slowly, a little ruefully. "Good thing Lloi ain't here to hear this. She would have been mighty jealous."

Braylar said, "She also would have told you all to shut your mouths and let our scholar speak."

No one else said anything, so I did. "Vella's tribe had been annihilated by a neighboring tribe, but before they fled, they heard of a witch who had managed to moderate her powers by somehow communing with the Godveil. Her parents wanted to keep her alive and her secret safe, so once they were in Anjuria, they visited the Godveil.

"Anroviak was pretty incredulous here. While the Godveil hadn't been around for that long yet, he'd heard only stories of men's minds being destroyed whenever they approached, or them being killed outright. It's clear in his account he initially thought Vella was lying, mistaken, or mad, and told her as much. But Vella swore to him that was the only thing that kept her safe for so many years, her visiting the Godveil, and somehow purging herself, or stilling the ability somehow. The text is a little unclear here."

"Or maybe it's you who's not getting it right," Mulldoos suggested.

"It's true, I am translating a man's words a thousand years distant, and he is transcribing or even translating hers. It sounded as if there was quite a communication gap even between them, and it took some time for Anroviak to parse out this much. So these passages are trickier than the rest. I'd need more time to work out the nuances here, but I also know I have the deeper essence right. He was skeptical, and Vella was equally insistent that approaching the Godveil was curing her, at least temporarily."

Hewspear was chewing on a piece of straw, slowly, thoughtfully. "Does our good underpriest give more specifics? What exactly happened to the young Grass Dog witch when she ventured near the Godveil? How was she able to purge herself?"

Braylar didn't scold his tall lieutenant, as all three Syldoon looked at me expectantly. Quite a reversal to be the one possessing some knowledge they didn't, however small, and to be looked to for the answers for once. It was difficult to suppress a grin. The only thing that helped was that I didn't have an adequate answer. "Whenever Anroviak describes her account, he uses the phrase *en bozwek,* repeatedly. Which can be interpreted to mean 'awakening' or 'emptying.' Which is odd, because both could be accurate. Apparently Vella had a difficult time describing what happened—she referred to it as having an awful dream that seemed to go on forever. Walking toward the Godveil was like waking up for her. The terrible dream ended. At least for a while. And when it felt like it was beginning again, she'd make another pilgrimage.

"In any event, her family was driven further west, the remnants of her tribe herded out of the Green Sea and further away from the Godveil. A forced migration. And once they were deep in Anjuria, they couldn't continue the visits. So her pilgrimages became less frequent. And without a way to relieve herself, or wake up, or whatever we want to call it, she was discovered."

Mulldoos looked around to be sure no one was approaching, then turned to Braylar. "That's twice now."

"What? That you made a cryptic declaration? I assure you, it is far more than that."

"Two mentions of approaching the Veil." Mulldoos looked at me. "The other thing you told Cap already, about the warrior with a cursed weapon like Bloodsounder—he walked into the Veil, too, that right?"

I started to answer in the affirmative, but Braylar cut me off. "No, that is a supposition. The text said only that he did not die but left the world behind. That could be poetic license, or a heroic tale, or many things. But the most likely is a ridiculous fabrication." He turned to me. "So, did this underpriest of Truth put her story to the test?"

"He did. Anroviak escorted her there under guard, and watched as she approached, sure that her parents were ignorant savages and she'd only have her mind and soul blasted into oblivion, exactly like every other person who made the critical mistake of venturing too close. Or she was lying, and would confess before she got too close. But he also vowed to explore and exhaust every possibility, no matter how unlikely. So he and his small group of loyal soldiers watched as Vella walked toward the Veil, and were amazed when she was not struck down, but stood directly in front of the pulsating wall, completely unharmed."

Mulldoos started to say something, but Braylar hissed him into silence and I pressed on. "She was still lucid as she returned, and exactly as she promised, she was unable to move into another's dreams or mind. So she alleged. Somehow, she had channeled her power and offered it to the Godveil and managed to walk away. Anroviak had never heard of such a thing, so he immediately instructed some of his underpriests to begin furiously researching, trying to uncover any other evidence, apocryphal, anecdotal, or otherwise of anything else quite like that.

"But before he made any notable progress or at least had a chance to record it, the triumvirate discovered that he had been disobeying them. His last entries, bitter and vitriolic, indicated he was heading to trial to defend himself. But the final lines, scribbled rather hastily from the looks of it, stated that he believed he'd discovered something. *If we capture the Godveil, we capture the witches. The Godveil is the key.* He jotted down something about 'frames.' It could be 'fence' or even 'prison'—I'll need to reexamine. But he seemed to suggest there was a way to syphon off some of the Veil, some portion that wouldn't prove deadly. And with that, control the witch. But that was it."

I looked up from my notes to see everyone staring at me. Vendurro was the first to speak. "That can't be it. Got to be more, doesn't there?"

I shook my head. "Not in his account. Nor the remainder of that chest, either. I scourged the other scrolls and books and whatnot, hoping that somehow he had continued recording somewhere else. But that was it. At least so far. I still have a great deal to go through. But it's pretty evocative, or tantalizing at least. This is the kind of thing you were looking for."

Hewspear pulled the straw out of his mouth and said, "It is a shame there isn't more. Much more. It could very well be that this underpriest was mad or grossly mistaken, or taken in by a charlatan. There are a number of possibilities here, and without being able to corroborate. . . it is a fascinating account, to be sure, and encouraging, but. . ."

"It is not proof of anything," Braylar finished. "Just as the other record of someone wielding another weapon like Bloodsounder does nothing more than establish that such a story existed." He tapped the chains. "Still.

It is tantalizing, I will grant you that. That is the right word. Frustrating allusions, but tantalizing just the same. I hadn't truly expected to find anything even auspicious."

I replied, "While there have been a large number of allusions to witches, the Godveil, and even a few mentions of cursed weapons, they were always brief and sporadic. These two accounts were the only ones to delve into things at all. I had to sift through a lot of dusty immaterial documents."

Braylar laid his hand on my shoulder. "You have done excellent work here, Arki." Then he looked at his men. "I believe a conversation with our tight-lipped cleric is overdue. Vendurro, fetch him please."

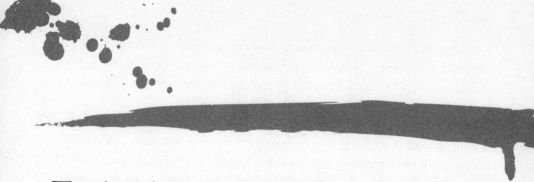

I wasn't sure if I was supposed to leave or not, but I assumed Braylar would instruct me to if that was the case, at least as soon as he recognized that I hadn't left. He seemed distant, lost in a thought thicket somewhere as he looked off into the woods, his left hand idly drumming fingers on Bloodsounder's chains.

Mulldoos and Hewspear had walked a short distance away as we waited, talking quietly amongst themselves.

I felt a bit awkward standing there with my pages in my arms, essentially alone in the middle of the Syldoon, but also filled with a sense of true purpose and usefulness for the first time. While translating in a moving, hot, foul-smelling wagon was far from pleasant, it was exhilarating to do it at all, and to have these hardened soldiers hanging on my every word was strange but wondrous as well.

Hewspear and Mulldoos walked back when they saw Vendurro return with Henlester. The High Priest looked tired, his eyes a little sunken in his sallow cheeks, the lines in his face even deeper and crinklier than before. And yet he still maintained a rigid posture that belied his years and his portly belly, and he seemed just as haughty as ever. "Well, this is a murder of crows, if I've ever seen one. What do you have need of me for, Syldoon?" He looked back at the small camp and his dark eyes narrowed further. "And why pull me from the luxurious surroundings of my rolling prison? It does my old bones no good at all."

Braylar swept his arm lazily, indicating the countryside. "Perhaps not, but fresh air is excellent for the constitution. And I thought it was high time we had a little chat."

"Did you now? And what would you like to chat about, Black Noose? My favorite herbs? Whether I prefer a high boot or low? With my frail ankles, it is high, if you must know."

The captain smiled. "I suspect there is nothing frail about you, holy man, no matter how many years you have stalked the world."

Henlester looked at our small group, taking us all in slowly. "And you would be mistaken. But since you haven't been thoughtful enough to bring a bench or chair, I would prefer we end the fecund pleasantries. What is it you want of me? I find this air stifling."

"My Emperor likely has a good many things to speak to you about, and I won't presume to know what all of them are. But just now, I wanted to ask you about something else entirely." Henlester's wrinkled face seemed to somehow rumple up further. The captain let him chew on that for a moment and then said, "I am quite the student of history, your eminently Eminence. Oh, I can see it on your face, you find this surprising. It runs counter to all your dear-held beliefs that the Syldoon are naught but barbarians and beasts—even considering such a thing is like to upset your entire opinion of us, I am quite sure. But there it is. And of late, I have taken quite an interest in the history of your own esteemed order. Fascinating tales. Almas the Deliverer, one of the first to spread the word of your faith, bringing hope to the hopeless masses. Jendor of Farmoss, called the Unwashed, as he apparently vowed never to bathe until every soul on soil had converted to Truth. Which seems a convenient excuse for poor cleanliness, if you ask me."

"No one did," Henlester spat.

Vendurro nodded. "He has you there, Cap."

"Be that as it may. The stories of those first priests, even the self-proclaimed filthy ones, well, one can hardly help but be inspired, yes? Your forefathers stood against the despair and malaise, the utter devastation of spirit visited upon the world as the Old Gods, the Great Gods, the only gods we'd ever known, in fact, left us high and dry." He raised a fist. "And they said, 'Hope is not lost! The world is not lost!'"

"Did you drag me out here only to mock me, Black Noose?"

Braylar clicked his tongue on the roof of his mouth. "You mistake me, Your Eminence. I find all the accounts of the origins of your order truly remarkable. But while the miracles and marvels, the triumph in the face of the overwhelming, are all infinitely compelling, being a military man who lives and dies by logistics, I was far more enthralled by the accounts of the men, and in a few small instances, women, who did more than preach and proselytize."

Henlester looked suspicious, even more than he had even moments earlier, which hadn't seemed possible, as Braylar continued. "I am speaking of the ones who organized, collected the coins, built the temples, created the hierarchy, and a thousand other things required to transform a humble and modest movement into the rich and powerful order we see today."

Hewspear nodded and said, "All odds were against it, and yet you prevailed. It is a captivating bit of history."

"Yes," Braylar said. "All the minor gods who had flickered and faded while the Old Gods held sway, little more than shadows or chattel, flourished as the founders of Truth and other devout zealots took advantage of the absence of the Deserters. Those small gods hadn't been powerful enough to usurp the celestial throne, but they were clever enough to seize the opportunity."

Henlester's pale eyes were drawn into slits. "Your words and tone are an ill match, Syldoon. And my bones ache. What's more, the gods do not abide mocking. So are you through with false admiration? Am I free to return to my wheeled dungeon now? Or would you torment an old vanquished man still more?"

Braylar raised both hands, palms out. "You mistake me, High Priest. I truly do respect the work your forebears did. Particularly the will to create something out of nothing, as I said. But while your annals are full of stories of those who strove to bring order and structure out of the void, there are also tales of those who were driven by passions and impulses that the order did not condone. Where there are rules, there will always be rule breakers, yes?"

Henlester looked at each of the Syldoon in turn, as if trying to discern what trap was being laid for him. "I mislike your insolence, your irreverence, and your lack of faith or respect. But most of all, I mislike your babbling. If you have some point, come to it."

Braylar continued as if the high priest hadn't spoken at all. "I am drawn in by the histories of your most pious, but being a black-hearted, black-noosed savage, I am far more intrigued by those in your order that were branded traitors or heretics. Such as Anroviak."

He let that name hang there, whether for dramatic effect, or to gauge Henlester's reaction, but if the latter, he must have been disappointed, as the high priest hadn't so much as shifted an eyebrow. "What of him? A heretic, as you say, who cavorted with demons and was decried for it. Nothing more interesting than that."

"Oh, he was insufferable and insolvent, from all reports. Qualities I admire. But it wasn't demons that I heard tell he trafficked with at all. No, it was witches. Have I been reading the wrong accounts, Your Eminence?"

The high priest waved a hand, "Demons, witches, what does it matter? He was a heretic and paid the penalty for it."

Braylar looked at Mulldoos, "Does it matter whether it was demons or witches, Lieutenant?"

"The holy prune says no, but I'm thinking it just might."

"As am I."

Henlester's face had gone the color of spoiled milk to, well, a prune. "You have insulted my god, the founders of our order, and now my person. Are you quite through, you insolent bastard?"

"No, not quite. You see, the tale I heard was that Anroviak hunted and studied witches, by leave of the triumvirate. His 'heresy,' as you call it, was only affixed to him after he refused their orders to cease."

A warm breeze blew, and Henlester's white hair billowed like a fine nimbus around his head, as his chin lifted and he assumed the air of authority and command that would have been most impressive. If he hadn't been a prisoner. "Lies. Damnable lies. Anroviak was a promising underpriest who was led astray by demons, and there's an end to it."

Braylar shook his head. "Again, not quite. You see, I have not only Anroviak's own personal account, which on its own would hardly be fully reliable, but I have seen documents, records from members of the triumvirate, that confirm his version of those events."

Henlester sneered, and while he still possessed all his teeth, they were a deep yellow. "And now you damn yourself with lying. I can see why you have an affinity for Anroviak."

"The truth is the truth, even if falls off the tongue of known liars." He pointed at me and said, "This scribe has examined the documents, translated them, and they bear out all I have said."

Henlester looked at me, as unimpressed as if I had been wearing a shift covered in shit. "Then you repeat his lies. Which brands you a fool. Worse, in my mind. The only records of Anroviak's misdeeds, trial, and punishment are housed in Sezwenna, holiest of holy cities."

"And where do you think we stole them from?"

For the first time, Henlester seemed at a loss for words, if only for a moment. But he recovered quickly enough. "You seem unable to string together two words without one being false."

Braylar turned to me. "The key."

"To the chest?"

"No, to a fair maiden's heart. Yes, the chest, you dolt, with Anroviak's account. Quickly now, lest his Eminence have cause to insult my integrity again. The book and scroll, they are in the chest just behind the barrel of dates, yes?" I nodded and handed him the key and he said, "Vendurro, be so kind as to fetch them both. Be quick about it. But careful as well. They are exceptionally brittle. Unlike our guest here, no matter how much he conveniently moans about his age."

"Aye, Cap. Though careful and quick ain't usually allies."

Henlester didn't spare Vendurro a second glance as the sergeant ran toward the wagons. "On the tongue or paper, a lie is a lie. Or forgery. Amounts to the same. What is this mummer's farce about, Black Noose?"

Braylar replied, "Regardless of how you might caw to the contrary, Anroviak was not simply a heretic or disobedient cleric. His actions were endorsed by the order. At least until they weren't. And he discovered something, didn't he, priest? About how to control witches, to collar and harness them? Whether for nefarious purposes or simply because the man had a devious curiosity, he found a way to bind memory witches to his will, did he not?"

The high priest was hardly awed. "You are mistaken or lying, but it hardly matters which. Either way, you are not speaking truths."

Braylar turned to Mulldoos. "I am beginning to suspect the good cleric does not believe me."

"Looks like. Most of the time he'd have good reason, too. But today he caught you in a real truthful mood."

"Wounded from all sides. But no matter. Our proof is running this way just now." Vendurro handed the captain the book and the scroll. "Now then, would you care to take a look, Your Eminence?"

His Eminence did not, sniffing instead. "Some dusty tomes prove nothing."

Braylar held the book out. "Ahh, I see. You can't read Old Anjurian."

Henlester did not rise to the bait. "If you knew anything about our order, as you say, you are aware that even our initiates read, write, and speak Old Anjurian."

Mulldoos said, "See now. You hadn't need for any scribbler at all, Cap. Should have just thrown the high priest in a sack years ago and made him translate."

"Somehow I think his Eminence would prove. . . reluctant. He does not seem to be in a cooperative mood. But no matter. The accounts are here, as I said. But I suspect you know that. You simply did not know that I happened to obtain them. That bit might be surprising, but not the contents. Not to a learned and literary man like yourself."

Henlester's thin lips were pressed together, and hardly parted as he replied, "Here is what I suspect—if the Anjurian lords had been less splintered, greedy, and factious, they would have defeated your kind long ago. Against a resolute foe, you are worthless. What I want to know is, why are Black Nooses getting their noses dusty in old tomes anyway? You are the only filth among civilized nations who have taken to taming memory witches, thereby soiling yourselves. I saw their black arts at work myself. Even if there were records out there in the world, what of it? What more could we teach you about deviltry that you have not mastered already?"

Braylar's playful mood seemed to vanish. "A cleric who fancies fucking and murdering crippled whores and cheating his liege lord giving advice on piety and manners. Ahh, irony. But you see, Your Eminence, I am not interested in the specifics of controlling memory witches. As you said, the Syldoon know the ways of this better than anyone. But I am very much interested in how Anroviak, and whoever he spilled his secrets to, devised a way to transfer the bonds once they had been established. Yes, that I am very much interested in."

Henlester laughed, a dry, rasping sound like leaves blowing together. "Even if I possessed such knowledge, which I do not, as I have told you I would never reveal anything to the likes of you. Unlike barons and kings, the priests of Truth are resolute."

Braylar stepped forward. "Sadly, I did not expect you would. Willingly. Now, we could interrogate you the time-honored way, with fire and steel. But we are humble soldiers, good at killing, less skilled at hurting a man but keeping him alive long enough to spill his secrets. And we have no interrogator in the company. However, we did have the foresight to bring two Memoridons with us. As you have noted, they are very good at blinding our overeager foes, but they have many other skills as well.

Chief among these—they are experts in the arts of discovery. Their talents make the finest Anjurian interrogators look like clumsy halfwits, and the veracity of the information is never in dispute. When a Memoridon slides inside a man and tears apart his memories, there is no dissembling, no subterfuge, no half-truths."

Henlester's pale lips pressed together so hard they nearly disappeared.

Braylar turned to Hewspear and said, "Yet, despite their prodigious abilities, they often have a decided lack of. . . sympathy for their subjects, do they not?"

Hewspear nodded slowly. "They do indeed. While they are able to slither into a man's mind and uncover any secrets hidden therein, it is an invasive, hostile act. In most cases, they cause unspeakable damage in the process. Many men," he sighed, "they do not die, but they never recover their wits at all, either. Husks, I believe the Memoridons like to call them. They have been hollowed out, turned in to simplest of simpletons, and often can't perform the most rudimentary of tasks and end up little better than beasts."

"Beasts at least know enough not to shit themselves," Vendurro added. "That there's as basic as basic gets, but I seen a man, after the Memoridons released him, he didn't know his name, couldn't speak at all in fact, kept clapping the air in front of him and gibbering nonsense. And he didn't remember not to shit himself, either. Someone likely got tired of the clean up or the stench and finally smothered the poor bastard with his own pillow. A babe or old man shits himself, well, that's half expected, so folks are willing to plug their noses and get on with it. But a man of middle years, an imbecile with shit running down his leg every day, well, not many willing to put up with that."

Mulldoos said, "And not just foreign bastards like yourself, Henfucker. Remember Weeze?"

Vendurro replied, "Of the Griffin Tower?"

"The very same. You see, he was suspected of treason. Tower Memoridons, they went in, ripped him apart from the inside out, got the truth of the matter. Turns out, the accusation hadn't been accurate at all. Only that didn't help good old Weeze none."

Hewspear said, "That poor bastard. Is he still living?"

"He is," Mulldoos replied. "The Griffin Tower commander had a pang of guilt once it was found out he was innocent. Didn't have the heart to put him down, though it would have been a mercy to. Holds his knees to his chest and rocks to and fro, mumbling naught but nonsense, 'the sheep in the deep do nothing but sleep' and the like. Don't think he shits himself. Might be the only thing that saved him so far. But still, a Memoridon ever rips into me, every man here knows to put me down rather than letting me half live like that."

Henlester had heard enough. "You fail to frighten, Black Noose," he said, for the first time not entirely convincingly. "You cannot afford to send me to your mind butchers. You need me for some vile scheme or another. Or you would have handed me over already."

Braylar held the book parallel to the ground and slid his fingertips over the worn leather cover and the tarnished brass fastenings. "You are not wrong about the schemes. If you would prove cooperative—something I am less and less sure of—then we might have some use for you yet. And while you would doubtless be a small piece on a large board, it is better than being swept off the board completely, yes? But weighed against that, I believe you possess the information I am seeking. And frankly, the need for that is more pressing. Ideally, we would have both, but if it can be only one, it will be the knowledge of Anroviak and his transfer of the binding. So, I ask you a final time, Your Eminence. How was it done? Tell me what I wish to know, and you not only escape the Memoridons, but prove your willingness to aid us. The Syldoon are cruel, it is true, but we can also be magnanimous on occasion, especially to those who further our goals. So, cruelty or magnanimity—which would you have us offer today, cleric?"

Henlester shook his head slowly, though it was clear he was shaken a bit. "I have nothing to tell you. Anroviak was a traitor to our order. Whatever he might or might not have known about binding witches has certainly seeped into the sands of time and been lost to the world forever. I have. . . nothing to tell you."

"So you have said." Braylar snatched a firebug out of the air, crushed it between his fingers, stepped forward, grabbed Henlester by the arm as he tried to step away, and then smeared the luminous leavings on the high priest's forehead. "But even if you do happen to be telling the truth, it could simply be that you no longer recall the details. You are incredibly old, as you say. You likely have forgotten more about your order's history than any living priest knows.

"But that is the terrible beauty about Memoridons—they can sift through every last thing a man has seen or done until they find what they are looking for. They will leave wreckage in their wake to be sure, but so be it, it can't be helped. I do not envy them the task, in truth—you have done awful things that would make a Syldoon blush, priest. I'm sure it will be an uncomfortable, gruesome slog for them, and they will need to cleanse themselves with copious amounts of lye when they are done. But we are out of time. And so are you."

The captain addressed Vendurro. "Take our cleric back to the wagon and fetch the Memoridons, Sergeant. We will have our answers now and be done with this."

"Aye, Cap."

Braylar waited as Vendurro grabbed the high priest by the arm an. "You heard Cap. Come on, your Gloriousness."

We watched the pair of them start toward the wagons. I waited until they were out of earshot and then whispered, "You do not intend to really ask Skeelana or—"

"Of course not," Braylar said.

"What will you do if, well, if—"

"If Henlester should call my bluff, I will simply say my persuasive lieutenants here convinced me to hold off until we have returned to Sunwrack. But I don't think it will come to that. Watch."

Henlester was taking small, shuffling steps, each more halting than the last. He was halfway to the wagons when he suddenly wrenched his arm free and spun, calling out to the captain. "Black Noose!"

The captain called back, "Your Eminence?"

Henlester hesitated. Then he nodded, and Vendurro led him back, trying to stifle a smile, and mostly failing. The high priest, a man who just a few days ago had been sitting in one of the largest seats in Anjuria, surrounded by wealth (more than his share, in fact), pulling the strings of lesser priests across the barony and beyond, and attended by faithful men who would procure him mutilated and crippled whores for his awful pleasure, suddenly looked defeated. And old. Being captured or imprisoned, you could always devise a means of escape or wait for your allies to ride to your rescue. So long as you lived, there was still a chance of some kind, especially for a powerful figure. But the prospect of having his towering intellect toppled, never to be rebuilt, of being husked by the witches he loathed even more than the Syldoon, well it was too much. That prospect was a fate worse than death, and the one thing that finally cowed the mighty and horrific cleric.

Henlester's eyes were full of hate, but also defeat. "I will tell you what I know. All of it."

And so he did.

The remainder of our trip, we were strangely unaccosted and free from danger. Gurdinn and his men had either gotten lost or heeded the warning, whatever other wandering bands of Hornmen there were out there had wandered down other trails, and the first and only ripper I saw was back in Alespell.

Skeelana's single ministrations must have cleaned the captain out thoroughly, as he didn't suffer as he had earlier, even after using Bloodsounder to claim lives.

We continued our gradual trek north, the familiar gentle valleys and pastures gradually giving way to rougher, rockier, hillier terrain as our progress was slowed by the pace of the wagons. We passed through farmsteads and villages, orchards and quarries, and a few ruined temples of the Deserter Gods. But with each day and another fifteen or twenty miles behind us, the changes to the landscape became more noticeable. The woods and dense forests thinned or were more broken up by fields, the towering fur pines and sky elms and champion oaks giving sway to stunted sycamores and dwarf spruce, and the further we went, to all manner of foliage I wasn't familiar with at all. There were groves of trees where the thick trunks twisted and wound around themselves, looking as if they had been bent and tied in knots by giants, and the branches were short and heavy with thorny, diamond-shaped leaves.

Apple trees gradually gave way to pear trees and fig. As we broke for camp one day, I saw a stand of trees that were queer—they peeled, like birch, only instead of being white, the bark was a ruddy orange color, and hanging from seemingly every limb were pods that gleamed like polished metal, flashing in the sun so brightly they were difficult to look upon.

I asked what they were, and Vendurro, pulling the saddle off his horse, replied, "Steel moths."

"On account of their chrysalises being so shiny."

355

"Nope," Mulldoos offered. "On account of them being full of moths with sharp steel wings. They come out of there, you best crawl under a wagon, as they're like to slice your throat or cut your eyes right out of your head."

I looked at him, and the uncertainty must have been stamped on my face.

"Gods be cruel, but you are a naïve bastard." He laughed and hauled his own harness down. "Get under the wagon, scribbler. And wear a leather bib. Plague me."

The land might have been slowly changing, but the translation gave only more of the same. Bawdy (and badly composed) poetry complete with erotic drawings in the marginalia (no translation needed there!) to ridiculous bestiaries full of manticores and long-limbed elephants, giant translucent bats, and something floating through the air that looked quite a bit like the boneless fringe fish.

But few extended references to memory witches, cursed weapons, or anything else Braylar had assigned me to catalogue. At least, nothing that added significantly to the findings we had already cobbled together with my previous efforts and Henlester's corroboration. Still, the infrequent allusions, even if brief, did seem to substantiate what we had gleaned already.

Just as it had with Alespell, traffic on the road increased the further we traveled into Thurvacia and the Syldoon Empire, though more due to the draw of the capital city than any famous fair. Cairns and carts, larger lumbering wagons, a woman driving goats with one of her small unruly children riding a burly one at the rear, men on donkeys or leading them along, a great many on foot, and a few wealthy enough to own horses. With the inked nooses bared to the world now, all of the native Thurvacians moved off the road to let us pass. They had lived the land for thousands of years, doubtless back to the age when the Deserter Gods were known and revered by name and the slaves, fief workers, and fief lords alike were the same people, the same race. But now there was no question who the held power. Anyone seeing a noose (or at least a sizable party of them) bowed or cleared the way, deferential.

And thankfully, no Hornmen or watchtowers in sight. They rode the roads in Anjuria and other kingdoms to the south, but fortunately they had no place in the north. In the Empire, with its standing army, there was no need for soldiers to patrol the routes, protecting (or preying) on travelers.

The road itself changed as well. Traveling through Anjuria it was usually dirt, or mud after a hard rain, and sometimes in a few baronies, cobblestones or bricks, at least in the areas immediately surrounding some of the larger villages or towns. But mostly rutted dirt or wheel-sucking, hoof-swallowing mud that seemed designed to slow travel and break ankles. But once we crossed over into Thurvacia, it was a different thing altogether.

Lord's Highway was far beyond the few stone-paved roads in Anjuria—a work of major construction and planning, broad and well-maintained, obviously designed to move both armies and civilians quickly and efficiently from one location to another. Cambered to aid drainage to the ditches alongside, flanked by footpaths and in some cases additional bridleways, they appeared close to uniform. Braylar assured me that while there were lesser roads, the main highways connected every major city or outpost in every Syldoon province, and most roads eventually led to Sunwrack.

Regardless of the terrain, whether rocky, broken by ravines or rivers, hilly, or mountainous, the roads were there, a triumph of surveying and engineering, a network unlike any other in the known world. Even in some of the marshlands to the east, I was told they were built on piled foundations or supported by stone piers.

Passing through Thurvacia, with the land growing hillier and rockier, we crossed a number of steep ravines over sturdy bridges, and as we approached the third or fourth such ravine, I saw something else coming down from the higher hills to the west. It looked like another bridge at first, but as we got closer I could see that there was no traffic on it. Then I realized that it must have been an aqueduct of some sort, bringing water down from the highlands. I had only read about them before—while Anjuria was home to hundreds or thousands of windmills, especially near the Green Sea, aqueducts were another construction peculiar to the Syldoon Empire.

I was sitting next to Braylar, watching the aqueduct further down in the valley as we crossed a bridge, and he must have seen the wonder on my face and smiled as if he had built the thing himself. "You will find that the further north we go, there are fewer large rivers and lakes and the land is more hilly and mountainous, so it is necessary to bring water from wherever it is found. The Empire would not persist without the aqueducts. They enabled growth and sustained it on a scale never seen before."

"It's large. Much larger than I imagined they might be, at least."

"Bah! This is nothing. If we ever have cause to visit the province of Urglovia, there you will see aqueducts of impressive size. They are famous for them, and some are so wide that boats can travel down them."

I stared at him, not sure if he was jesting or not. When he noticed, he said, "Truly. They are generally used for transport, and cross other bridges, ravines, or roads. The governor of the province, Munsellik, had a penchant for the dramatic, and he liked to sail a barge down the aqueduct, a floating manse. The aqueduct was broad enough for flatboats, but this barge was simply too much. Or the gods smote Munsellik for his vanity, as the arches gave way, the aqueduct collapsed, and down he and his entire gaudy party went, crashing to the bottom of the ravine below.

"The next governor took the lesson to heart, and after rebuilding the aqueduct, restricted movement on them to lighter and more humble transport. But the larger ones persist, in Urglovia especially. And you can still see the flatboats traveling down them."

"That's amazing."

"That is nothing. Manses might be forbidden, but in the heart of the province, they have aqueducts erected simply to serve as raised channels for sport skiffs to race on."

"But the water is precious, you said?"

Braylar replied, "So it is. And the Syldoon heart delights in ostentatious display and use of things. You will never meet a people more practical or vain in equal measure."

I shook my head, trying to imagine the wealth, time, and labor it must have required to build such things. And this was just the first of many sights and sounds that would amaze and shock me in Thurvacia, heartland of the Syldoon Empire.

After what felt like a tenmonth of journeying, we finally neared Sunwrack.

Braylar told me to leave off translation and called me to the front of the wagon. Which was just as well—the iron-shod hooves and iron-rimmed wheels of our party made a terrible racket as we clacked, clomped, and clattered over the stone highway, which was hardly conducive to concentration. But those could almost be tuned out, drifting into a loud, but repetitive cacophony. However, the closer we got to the capital, the more other noises joined our own as we passed traffic heading away from the city, or those who stopped to let us pass—a donkey braying, a child crying, horses whinnying, and a hundred other intermittent and brief sounds that made it all but impossible to focus. I kept reading the same lines over and over with no comprehension to speak of, and my head was pounding.

And the day was hot and dry as well—even with the front and rear flaps open, there was no breeze to speak of, so my tunic was sticking to my skin in every conceivable spot. I'd been in bathhouses where I sweated less.

So I was all too happy to move to the front of the wagon. I threw my leg over the bench and was about to crawl over when I looked up and felt my breath catch.

Sunwrack. In all its ancient, dirty, beautiful, and exotic splendor.

"Oh do sit down, Arki. You look an ass straddling the bench like that."

I did as he commanded and perched there, stunned. Until a short time ago, Rivermost had been the largest town I'd ever been in for much of my life. And then we journeyed to Alespell, baronial seat and home to one of the grandest fairs in Anjuria, and I'd been almost overwhelmed with the size and variety of sights and sounds. It was hard to imagine a more impressive city.

Clearly, I should have tried harder.

Alespell was a fortified city, to be certain, its defenses stout enough to withstand almost any assault—the walls, covered as they were in snails and plastered with gull droppings, were still impressive, tall and broken by towers every few hundred feet. But Sunwrack. . . its walls dwarfed those of Alespell, being at least fifty feet higher, maybe more, and there were so many massive towers they were impossible to count, each as large as most castle keeps, and flying a different banner at the top, incredibly varied in color and motif. While towers in Alespell typically had a silk standard on a pole on top to catch and snap in the breeze, these massive towers had the poles ringing the crown of the tower, with odd banners hanging down. The tops of the banners were embattled like the towers themselves, with the "merlons" of the banners being loops for the poles.

Hewspear was riding to the right of us and saw me inspecting the banners. "Pike Tower, Leopard Tower, Griffin Tower, Serpent Tower. Pretty much every charge you can imagine: eagle, elk, moon, fox, bear, crane, otter, falcon—"

"Goat, leopard, seastag, galley, stork, star wheel. . . " Vendurro offered, riding on the opposite side of the wagon with Mulldoos. "No dung tower though. Nor chicken come to think of it."

"Though there is a Cock Tower, with its crowing charge resplendent for all the world to see," Hewspear said, smiling all the while.

"I could really go for some chicken right about now. Or quail. Even a fried egg or five would do fine. Anything hot and greasy, so long as it ain't dung."

The smaller towers had normal crenellations, but the larger Towers that housed the Syldoon had fancifully carved merlons all along the embattlements, stylized representations of each Tower's sigil.

Mulldoos said, "Hard to believe we're home, eh, Cap? Haven't seen the rest of the Jackal bastards in, what, more than three years is it?" He actually sounded relieved, weary, and maybe a touch wistful. I would have thought someone else had spoken if I hadn't seen his lips move.

Braylar nodded, and for once, he looked almost at peace.

The whole exchange was so out of the ordinary, I had no idea what to make of it, before recalling what Vendurro had told me—this place was home to these men, in a way that I would never fully understand.

I was so amazed at the scale and immensity of Sunwrack and the countless number of great towers along its fortified walls, and our approach was on such level ground, that it wasn't until we were within a few hundred yards that I realized what I assumed was a simple dry moat turned into something much different.

First, it was at least over a bowshot wide. And it didn't appear to be a dry moat, or even a ravine. It was a chasm. A huge gulf in the earth separating the city of Sunwrack from all the surrounding land. I thought there must have been a bridge of some kind, and there was. Of sorts. The busy Lord's Highway led to a massive gatehouse on the edge of the chasm. But as the travelers heading toward the city were allowed through, and our group closed in on the first gatehouse, I could see that a lowered drawbridge served as the bridge proper, supported by a wide stone support column that disappeared into the darkness below, and on the other side of the platform, there was another rolling drawbridge and a second gatehouse on another huge stone column. This pattern continued, with four gatehouses spanning the chasm on their larger stone structure, for a total of six, as the final one that served as the entrance proper to the city was bigger than all the rest.

As we rumbled across the stone landings and wooden drawbridges, I saw why all traffic seemed to drift to the center of the bridge. Even with railings on the outside, the chasm was so deep that I couldn't see the bottom. I found myself craning to get a better look and glad that I wasn't walking along the railing. We crossed some deep ravines on our way to Sunwrack, but nothing so broad as this, nor deep. The bottom, wherever it was, was lost in shadow.

"I've never seen anything like this."

"No," Braylar replied, smiling. "You have not."

"Does this chasm go the entire way around the city?"

"It does. There are four entrances to Sunwrack, of identical construction."

"Was this a natural formation of some kind? Is that why the city founders chose the site?"

"Not being among their number, I could not say why the site was chosen. You are aware Sunwrack was not built a tenday ago, yes?"

"Yes. Of course." I stood slightly to look over the side of the next drawbridge. "But this. . . it's an island in stone."

"That is because it is not a natural formation."

"I knew it!"

"Then why did you ask?"

I barely heard him, looking at the chasm as it stretched around the border of the city and disappeared, another staggered bridge barely visible around the bend. "If this was dug by men, it must have taken. . . how long? How long did this take?"

Hewspear overheard me. "Twenty years," he said. "It would have taken much longer had they been using ordinary workers, but slaves do not have the luxury of complaining when worked beyond exhaustion. Countless lives in the making."

I reminded myself never to complain about my lot in life again. "Not Syldoon, then?"

He smiled. "No. Syldoon start out as slaves, but their lives are valuable and rarely thrown away, and certainly never in the construction of what amounted to a mass grave."

I tried to imagine blistered and brutalized men, digging out rock and dirt, hauling it out of the largest hole men had deigned to ever dig, deeper than any quarry, and broad, so very broad. Encircling a city that housed at least a quarter million residents, maybe more. And all for what? There were fortified cities in all lands, and none went to this extreme in creating such a defensible position. All those lives wasted. I wondered how many skeletons littered the unseen floor.

"Was it one of your Emperors who did this? Created this?"

Hewspear shook his head, coins jangling in the long braids of his beard. "No. This predated the Syldoon by a few centuries at least."

I saw something move on the rock wall on the other side of the chasm. At first, I thought it was my eyes playing tricks on me, too tired from scanning ancient documents. But as I shaded them and looked more closely, I saw there were several somethings. They scuttled down the rock face. And they were big.

Braylar was watching me and laughed. "Bull crabs."

I kept my eyes on them, the dark speckled chitin of their bodies nearly blending in with the stone. They had ten legs, the front two ending in large claws. And while it was difficult to tell from that distance, the bull crabs appeared to be bigger than large shields.

"Those things. . . " I started.

"Could kill you with one crunch," he finished. "They are vicious, but thankfully only fast in short bursts."

We passed through a gatetower, and I noticed the soldiers bearing those curious shields I knew were Syldoonian but had only seen before in illuminated manuscripts, as Braylar's company had adopted the round shields commonly seen in Anjuria. These shields had an embattled top to simulate the square crenellations of a tower, or in this case, Tower, and then tapered to a point at the bottom rather than the oval shape frequently seen elsewhere. They were all a deep green, with the repeated charge of white ram's heads strewn across them.

As we continued onto the next section of bridge, I looked at Hewspear and Mulldoos and Vendurro—it was obvious this chasm and its pecu- liarities were such a familiar sight they didn't even think twice about it. I asked Mulldoos, "And how would you assail Sunwrack if you had to?"

"Eh? What's that, scribbler?"

"Every time you and Hewspear enter a city, you like to debate how you would take it if you had to. Sunwrack seems about as impregnable a place as I can imagine. So, if you had to lay siege here, how would you do it?"

Mulldoos looked ready to say something snide or belittling, but then stopped himself. "I never gave it much thought, in truth. You, Hew?"

Hewspear shook his head again. "Strangely, no. We've entered this city hundreds of times, and we never stopped to consider it."

"Seems kind of disloyal, don't it?"

"Perhaps. But our young friend does have a point. Sunwrack is unassailable."

"You say that about every plaguing city we come into." He stroked his invisible beard and adopted passable Hewspear inflections, "'These fortifications are utterly impregnable.' Tighter than a priest's bunghole they are. Every plaguing time."

Hewspear laughed. "So, my siege-minded friend, how would you bring Sunwrack to ruin if you had the command? What would be your brilliant plan then?"

"Sunwrack's a tough nut, to be certain. Toughest I ever seen. No question." He pointed at the top of one of the huge towers. "Those trebuchets up there got range on engines any attacker might be dumb enough to line up on the other side of the Trench, on account of height."

"True."

"And once the bridges are pulled, no possible way to assault the walls."

"True as well. You are making my case for me," Hewspear said.

"Shut it, you old wrinkled prick."

"Wrinkled, aye, but wizened with wisdom."

Vendurro looked up at the red walls and slate great towers. "No way to assault it. How about starve them out?"

Mulldoos shook his head immediately. "This a plaguing city, you lippy pup. They got stores of food to last for years. No army could stay in the field long enough to outlast them."

Vendurro replied, "No frontal assault maybe, but what if a small group climbed down the trench in the dark of night, up the other side, managed to gain the wall? Open a gate from inside."

Mulldoos glared at the younger man. "And what if the besieging army had a platoon of horses with pretty wings and they could fly overhead, dropping fiery horseshit from the air." He pointed at the large gatehouse on the wall we were approaching. "That savvy group of mountain climbers would need to survive the bottom of the trench. Rats as big as weasels down there, feeding on the sewage. Bull crabs bigger than dogs feeding on them. Some say much worse lurking in the dark, feasting on both. So you're telling me a group survives the climb down in the pitch of night, fights through the nasty critters roaming the trench bottom, and somehow makes it back up the other side, with nobody sighting them and filling them with shafts. That what you're saying?"

"Might be they do. It could happen."

"Horseshit. Double horseshit. Ain't happening. Better luck finding them flying ponies."

I asked, "What about the aqueduct?"

Mulldoos gave me one of those looks that said he expected the next words out of my mouth to be worthless or worse. "What of it?"

"Well," I said, pointing at the aqueduct on the hill that fed into the city. "Perhaps scaling the trench wouldn't work. What if—"

"It wouldn't."

"Fine. It's impossible. But what if they chose to sneak into the city through the aqueduct instead?"

Vendurro pointed at me, "Aye, that's it! That could work!"

"Couldn't," Mulldoos said. "Like to drown or fall to their death more like. But even if they got into Sunwrack by waterway somehow, they got guards posted there, too. And you're both forgetting something anyway. Even if a group could somehow survive the trench or the aqueduct, which is next to impossible, but let's say they do." He pointed to the drawbridge ahead. "They make their midnight raid, and even manage to kill the guards on one gatehouse and lower one drawbridge from the inside. Also ain't likely, but maybe they're the toughest bastards who ever lived and they pull it off. Got another real big problem right quick then, don't they?"

Vendurro thought it through and looked back over this shoulder at the gatehouse we passed through. "Ayyup. Brave bastards would have to climb up from the trench bottom on those four as well, take all the gatehouses. Kill all the guards, roll out or lower all the bridges. All without raising an alarm. All at the same time."

"Ayyup," Mulldoos said, mocking only a little. "And if by some miracle they pulled this off, which they ain't doing, on account of it being impossible and all, but let's grant them that for a plaguing laugh. Let's say they secure all the gates, roll out or lower the bridge together at all points. Real hard to bring an army across one bridge in any kind of hurry—big enough for daily traffic, not designed for moving all your troops. Hew, how long did it take our Tower to cross last time we went out in force?"

Hewspear smiled. "More than half a day. Again, you have demonstrated my point most admirably."

Mulldoos ignored him, too intent on proving the young sergeant dead wrong even at the expense of his own argument. "Aye. And that was without the walls raining arrows and bolts down on our heads. Can't take a bridge, but even if you could, not taking the city that way."

"What's more," Hewspear added, "There are over fifty Towers housed inside Sunwrack. Let's say half of them were out in the field for our imaginary war here. That still leaves at least twenty-five to defend the city, plus all the auxiliaries and city watch. No, a direct assault would be a disaster and doomed from the start, and starvation isn't practical. I have to say, Mulldoos, that was the most backwards rhetoric I've ever witnessed."

"I'd spit at you, if you were closer."

Braylar had been silent, eyes roaming the faces leaving Sunwrack, man by man, and tracking the groups in front of us making it through the largest gatehouse and into the city proper. The captain never seemed to relax his guard, even when the rest of him was presumably at ease. He'd seemed to be ignoring the debate, so it surprised me when he said, "The water supply."

Everyone looked at him and waited for him to elaborate. "You can't take the city once it's locked up tight. That is evident enough. But if Sunwrack has a weakness, it is access to water. Yes, there are some wells that go deep, deep into the earth. But they are slow, and on their own, not enough to supply the city for long. Which is why there are vaults and cisterns and conduits. And the aqueduct. So if there were enough traitors in the city, and they were exceptionally well coordinated, they could conceivably poison the wells, and destroy the water vaults. While the besiegers took care of the aqueduct further up in the hills, either destroying that, or poisoning it as well." His eyes continued assessing and sweeping over everyone, as if looking for traitors.

Mulldoos laugh-snorted. "You got a devious mind, Cap. Right devious, you do. So there you go, old goat. Weren't my idea, but that could do it."

Hewspear wasn't entirely ready to relent. "Conceivably. But in addition to being legion, and exceptionally organized and working in perfect conjunction, these cagey saboteurs could also need to be exceptionally willing to die as well, as the vaults and wells are all well-guarded. Plus, they would really need to poison all the barrels of wine and beer besides. And this isn't a single castle we're talking about. That kind of coordination and execution, well. . . "

Braylar replied, "Likely to fail as not. Perhaps more so. But it seems the only gambit that might have any chance of success at all. Sunwrack might be next to impregnable, but no place is impervious to treachery from within. Least of all a city where factions are constantly conducting silent wars against one another, and a large chunk of the local populace would like nothing more than to feed its Syldoon overlords to the bull crabs."

And then we passed through the large gatehouse and put the massive walls behind us. We were in Sunwrack, Capital of Coups, center of the Empire and all the secrets, maneuvering, and treachery that went with it.

The Thurvacians weren't so very different from their Anjurian neighbors, at least physically. Perhaps a bit swarthier or more olive in complexion, with darker hair and darker eyes being more common. The capital was, after all, less than two hundred miles from the border of the kingdom of Anjuria. But with the Severed Sea and the Godveil an impassable border to the east, and the Moonvow Mountains and the Bonewash Sea marginally more passable obstacles to the west, there was only a small corridor between the kingdom and empire. But with hostilities for hundreds of years, it was no wonder that any exchange of ideas, invention, costume, and culture were stymied.

I watched Soffjian and Skeelana ride up. The Memoridons had to be factored in as well. While memory witches were persecuted or hunted in most lands, the Syldoon not only tolerated their presence but utilized them to the fullest. Even if all other conditions had been favorable, the Memoridon presence would have frightened off all but the most adventurous of Anjurians from entering the empire.

So, beyond some cosmetic similarities, the two peoples were noticeably disparate. Where Anjurians favored cotehardies and close-fitting tunics, tapered and designed to showcase the wearer's shape (with sometimes really unfortunate results), and hoods of various sizes, Thurvacians opted for flowing robes with broad voluminous sleeves, or trousers with large overcoats over their tunics, belted with broad sashes, and on their heads, small wool or felt caps trimmed with squirrel or fox fur or, in some cases, dyed feathers. The Anjurians preferred muted colors and dusky jewel tones, but Thurvacian dyers had achieved remarkable colors of nearly any shade imaginable, often bright and outlandish.

The differences extended to construction as well. The kingdom of Anjuria was filled with wattle and daub buildings, or timber, with stone reserved only for the wealthy. But in Sunwrack, the homes and dwellings frequently were red clay or brick, with a much larger number of stone buildings mixed in, utilizing arches for doors, windows, and support for terraced gardens. And most buildings were topped with sheets of copper or brass that had been polished to gleam, capturing every drop of sunlight and making it seem as if the city itself were nearly on fire.

But the Syldoon roaming the streets were more different still, and not simply because of the inked nooses or their pewter Tower badges. Captain Killcoin and his crew had tried to blend in with Anjurians, but here, I was confronted by appearances I had never encountered before. Tall, coppery-skinned men with faces that appeared scarred in ritual fashion; others who shaved the fronts of their heads and dyed the hair in back fantastic colors; more than once I saw two or three who had blue tattoos of ravens inked on their faces. The Syldoon were an eyeful.

Something struck me then. "All the Syldoon seem to travel in pairs, or even greater number. Is that a requirement?"

"If you are fond of your heart pumping blood, it is," Hewspear replied.

"I don't understand. This is the capital, and the Syldoon are the over-lords. Is it so unsafe to travel alone?"

Braylar replied, "You just hit upon your answer, archivist. We are over-lords. We rule over a much larger population of Thurvacians. While there have been very few uprisings, lone Syldoon have been murdered on occasion."

"I would expect murderers to suffer a pretty awful penalty. The mur-derers, I mean."

"When caught, they do suffer a very long, very public death. And when not caught, usually someone is taken in their place and executed as well. It does tend to ensure such violence against us is very rare. But one can never be too careful. And the other Towers are no friends of ours either."

Braylar turned down a street that led us through the middle of the city, which seemed to incense Soffjian. "The Avenue of Towers would be quicker."

"Yes," Braylar replied. "Yes it would."

She waited for him to say more, and when it was clear he didn't intend to, she grew more irritated. "So then, you are taking the slowest route because. . . ?"

"Because, sweet sister, while it does have the most traffic in general, it has the fewest Syldoon. And until we have spoken to our Tower Com-mander, I would rather not trumpet our arrival for every other Tower in

Sunwrack. You hastened us here. We are here. An extra hour or two will make no difference. Feel free to ride ahead or take whatever route you fancy, by all means."

She scowled. "My charge is to escort you the entire way, and—"

"You will not shirk in your duty. Not even in the capital city. Truly impressive diligence. Are you afraid I will whip the horses and drive them out of Sunwrack the second you disappear around a corner?"

Soffjian rode a little further ahead but not so far as to disappear around any corners.

We trekked through the center of the city. Where Alespell had been a confusing warren with streets running in every conceivable direction, and the buildings so crowded they blocked out most of the sky, most of the lanes and alleys in Sunwrack were orderly, running to the four points of the compass. And though there were several buildings that were taller than anything Alespell boasted, they weren't pressed up against each other nearly as close, as least not on the main streets.

Bells were tolling, heavy and leaden, too muted to actually be called "ringing." While I couldn't tell where they were coming from exactly, it was definitely somewhere ahead of us. Braylar's eyes lit up a little, and he stopped the wagon. The other Syldoon reined in their horses as well. A few men in rough tunics and trousers walked around us in the street and looked ready to complain about the holdup until they saw the nooses.

The captain looked at Hewspear. "When was the last time you saw a ceremony? Five, six years?"

"Seven, I believe."

"And you, Mulldoos?"

Mulldoos looked up at the unmoving clouds as the bells continued tolling. "About that. You thinking of taking a gander? Ain't our Tower. And your bitch sister won't be too keen." It didn't sound like he was too thrilled with the idea either, though.

"She wanted us to speed things up. Let us grant her wish and see what the other Tower is up to, shall we?"

We crossed several more side streets, the tolling growing louder with each one, and then Braylar called out to his sister once before turning and heading east. She spun her horse about and trotted back to catch up. Clearly not keen.

The street opened up into a square, and the first thing I saw was the large crowd gathered there, as if ready to watch a performance of some kind.

The second thing I saw was the gallows. A broad platform with ten nooses in the middle and ten men standing alongside them, and two armed men on either end

"Just in time," Braylar said, as we stopped near the edge of the square.

While the captain seemed to be at ease, the rest of the Syldoon were tensed up. Which struck me as odd, given the death they had doled out in the short time I'd known them. I had no wish to watch anyone hang—I'd seen it before a time or two, and it was nothing next to the messy, painful, and plentiful ways I'd seen men die while in their company.

Soffjian and Skeelana seemed to be indifferent, with Braylar's sister only saying, "I would have thought you'd seen this one time too much already, brother."

He ignored her and watched, as quiet as the crowd assembled before us. This was also unusual. Ghoulish as it was, hangings often drew an unruly audience, with rotten food and insults thrown in equal measure. But that was usually only with one condemned man choking at the end of a rope, or sometimes a pair. Did the fact that it was ten men somehow change things? I wouldn't think so. Or if it did, it was more likely to stir the crowd to greater depravity. Bloodlust was bloodlust, after all.

And then I noticed a few other oddities as well. None of the men next to the nooses were bound at all. Yet they all stood in attention, one step away, and they weren't dressed like the local militia I'd seen; they had no armor on at all in fact, and were garbed head to toe in layered black. Some with fair hair, others with locks and beards as dark as tar, a few with hair the color of rust or dried blood.

"Are those. . . are those Syldoon?"

"They are," Braylar replied.

"Why are they being hung? What crime did they commit?"

A man clothed all in gray stepped forward and began speaking to the men on the gallows, though I couldn't make out anything he said.

"No crime at all. This is their manumission, Arki. From this day forward, they will be free men, full Syldoon. Well, most of them, I assume. You never can tell."

The men on the platform replied as one to some question or directive they'd been given.

"Freed? But. . . they are about to be hung. Aren't they?"

"Indeed."

Hewspear said, "You are about to see Syldoon slaves leave off their bondage, transforming into Syldoon soldiers. They have been offered the chance to leave Sunwrack forever, or undergo the rite of manumission. These here have chosen to stay, to be bound forever to their Tower and barracks mates, but no longer as slaves. It is. . . something to behold."

I still didn't understand, and started to ask another question when Braylar silenced me. "Enough. Be still and watch, and you shall have your answers."

Somehow I doubted that, but I shut my mouth. The men on the gallows responded to a query or command in unison again, several times. Then they stepped to the edge of the platform and slipped the nooses around their own necks and pulled the knots tight.

Aside from a little murmuring, the crowd was still hushed, and there was a sense of expectation that was almost oppressive.

A figure appeared on either end of the gallows platform, both women, both with the standard surokas on their hips, but otherwise unarmed and unarmored. They wore the same outfit, turquoise jackets belted over brown trousers. The Memoridons were still as statues as the men stood on the edge of the platforms, ropes slack for the moment, and the crowd was dead silent now. You would have thought we were watching corpses being interred in a tomb rather than men about to have the life choked out of them.

The man in gray robes said something else, raised his arm up, and then all ten men willingly stepped off the platform and began to swing and dangle and choke, feet kicking several feet above the ground. The armed Syldoon drew their swords and watched from above.

I wanted to turn away—I didn't see how this would answer any question except how long it took for ten men to choke to death—when the Memoridons moved closer to the men at either end, raised their hands, touched the two men on the chest and the back, and dipped their heads.

Both men kicked more violently, thrashing as if being cut or burnt, and then they suddenly stopped, nearly at the same time. Their chins dropped onto the ropes that were strangling them, and the soldiers still on the platform cut them down in turn. Both men collapsed to the dirt in heaps and lay there, motionless, and the Memoridons moved to the next men in line and laid their hands on them as they had done with the first pair.

The Memoridon on the left took a little longer than the one on the right, but otherwise, it was nearly identical. And so it went down the line —the choking, the jerking as soon as the Memoridons touched them, the Syldoon being cut down once they had succumbed to whatever was being done to them.

But on the second to last pair, I heard Soffjian say, very quietly, "They are taking too long. Too long."

The Memoridon on the right finished with her man and he was cut down, and she moved to the final man on her side of the gallows and grabbed his chest and back. But her partner seemed to be struggling, as her man was twisting and turning so hard she was having difficulty keeping her hands on him. The man next in line was turning purple and already kicking his legs violently, so hard that he struck the Memoridon and knocked her away from the other Syldoon she was trying to save.

She finally finished, and the Syldoon on the platform cut her man down, but the remaining Syldoon was struggling so much she could barely get her hands on him, mouth open, tongue out, eyes rolling back into his skull, the veins and muscles popping out on his neck as he fought for breath that wasn't coming. The other Memoridon completed her ritual with the final man on her side of the gallows and rushed over to try to steady the hanging man enough for her partner to finish, but he suddenly went slack. She placed her hands on him, tried to perform whatever it was she needed to do, but it was too late.

The Memoridon looked up to the Syldoon on the platform, slowly shook her head, and he cut the man down. The other nine on the ground were all beginning to move again, pulling the cut nooses from around their necks, gasping for air, slowly sitting up with dazed expressions on their faces.

But the tenth did not stir. Would never stir again.

Still, a cheer went up from the Syldoon who made up the bulk of the audience, and several ran forward to pull their comrades out of the dirt and embrace them. Two Syldoon carried the dead body away from the platform, and I realized that when I first started watching, I expected them all to die, and when they were cut down in turn, I had assumed that they would all be spared. Somehow, seeing the tenth strangle to death was just as awful as if I had seen the lot of them.

Soffjian shook her head sadly, though I suspected she was more upset about the Memoridon's failure than the man dying. "Too plaguing slow." She turned her horse and said, "Seen enough, brother? I'm sure your commander will be delighted to welcome you home, and the Emperor will doubtless be thrilled to hear that the final operatives in the field have returned as bidden. Albeit much tardier than expected." Both Memoridons rode off. I was both thrilled and irritated that Skeelana looked over her shoulder at me before disappearing around the corner of a building.

The captain got the team moving again, the wagon creaking back into motion, and the other riders and the wagon behind us as well, as he took a side street toward the Avenue of Towers.

I waited, on the off chance that someone would volunteer the explanation, and when it was clear I would keep waiting until I ran out of breath myself, I asked, loudly enough for anyone to hear, to improve my chances of actually receiving an answer. "What did the Memoridons do? And why is that called the rite of manumission?"

Everyone seemed pensive and lost in their thoughts, but Hewspear was the quickest to respond. "When a Syldoon slave has completed his training, after a tenyear, he is given a choice—walk out of Sunwrack and all the lands of the empire, never to return again. Back to their original homelands, or go where they will, so long as they depart. Or stay and undergo the rite."

"How would anyone know that they didn't belong, that they were exiled?"

"Instead of receiving a tattoo, they would be branded on the side of their necks, and given a scroll that specified the allotted time that they could journey, depending on where they were headed."

"And if they lost the document?"

"Any branded former Syldoon without a document is hung or otherwise executed, this time without a reprieve."

I took one last look at the gallows before it disappeared behind us. "And if they choose to stay, to do the rite we just witnessed. What happens to them? What were the Memoridons doing to them?"

"Bonding with them," Hewspear replied.

"Bewitching them," Mulldoos countered. "Unless the bitches can't get the job done, and good men die for no plaguing good reason."

I opted to respond to Hewspear. "Bonding? How, and why?"

"A Memoridon can slide into nearly any man's mind, given enough time and opportunity, but never so easily as when he is at his most helpless. It's difficult to be more helpless than dangling at the end of a noose. The Memoridons take that moment to form an intimate bond, unlike any other."

"If by 'bond,'" Mulldoos said, "you mean getting raped in the ass, then yeah, the pair get bonded right good."

Hewspear ignored him. "As you saw, a man can only hang for so long, so the Memoridons have to be quick. Soffjian did have the right of it. And sometimes, men panic."

"Yeah," Mulldoos said, "Choking to death does queer things to some folks. Hard to figure."

Hewspear sounded a little irritated but pressed on. "Once the Memoridon establishes this bond, it is not easily broken. It can be strained with distance or time, so tenuous it is barely a vibration. But rarely sundered. Particularly if the Memoridon is skilled and strong. Unlike the skinny wretch who doomed the man on the gallows just now."

Mulldoos spit into the street.

"To what end? Why is it necessary to form such a bond?" I asked.

Braylar replied, "How do you think my sweet sister was able to track us to the Grieving Dog in Alespell?"

"Soffjian was one of a pair that, uh, bonded with you? While you hung?"

"Not our whole party, but most, yes. You see, a Memoridon can only maintain so many such bonds at any given time. But Soffjian can manage more than most. She is a viciously talented girl."

"So how does a Memoridon track you? Another Syldoon. Whoever."

"Ordinarily, a Memoridon can only sift through someone's memories if she is in very close proximity. But once she has formed the intense bond of the manumission rite, she can follow the memories, or at least what passes as the residue of them, and identify who they belong to."

We were approaching the tall outer wall and the Avenue of Towers at its base. "Wait, I don't understand. How is that possible? Memories are contained in a person. Aren't they?"

"For the most part, you are correct. And not being a memory mage, I cannot pretend to understand how it works exactly. But I asked the same question you did. And the explanation I received was, when you walk through the world, you leave indentations. So, too, you do the same with your experiences and your memories of them. A Memoridon who shows talent at hounding is trained to sense them, identify them.

"The difference is, when you leave tracks in the earth, sand, snow, they eventually disappear. Sometimes immediately, washed away by the next wave or snowfall, and sometimes after time passes. But with the memory 'divots' or impressions, they last much, much longer. There are so many, in fact, that the bonding ceremony is necessary. To establish a connection so that the Memoridon can separate the trail from the thousands of other invisible impressions we all leave behind."

I thought about that, and while it would have seemed the stuff of overheated story or overly wrought exaggeration only a short time ago, having seen Soffjian kill, drive someone mad, and blind a battalion of soldiers, it wasn't so very difficult to believe. "But why go to such lengths at all? Why risk Syldoon lives to establish that connection?"

Braylar was turning the wagon onto the Avenue, and Hewspear took the opportunity to respond. "A Tower Commander always has a way of locating his soldiers. There are many occasions this proves useful. During conflicts, when war Memoridons are dispatched and need to find their unit. When Syldoon are captured by the enemy."

Mulldoos finished the list. "And a big, fat deterrent. You see, a fool Syldoon gets the idea in his head he's had enough, time to run for the hills. Well, no hills far enough. The Deserter Gods might have been able to throw up the Veil and keep people from following, but Syldoon deserters ain't got such the same sorry luxury. They run, the Empire unleashes the hounds, and they'll hunt them to the ends of the world and back."

I wondered if that was why Mulldoos detested Soffjian so much, or if there was more to it. But I didn't have long to consider, and wouldn't have asked him even if I had.

The Memoridons were waiting in front of some stables, which were alongside some other two-story buildings at the foot of one of the massive octagonal great towers. I looked up and saw one of the banners unfurl a bit in the dry breeze. Three black jackal heads on a white band on top, with the lower half a deep red.

Soffjian said, "Consider yourselves delivered. At last. I imagine you have your reports to make, and I know we have ours." And with that curt farewell, she disappeared inside the gloom of the stable, Skeelana following just behind.

Captain Killcoin's lips seemed torn between a scowl, a twitch-smile, and something else, and his eyes were hard as he watched his sister go, but he forced a jovial tone as he said, "Lads. . . we are home."

He hopped down off the wagon, stretched his back with his arms above his head, twisting and turning. As the other Syldoon dismounted, Braylar cupped his hands in front of his mouth and yelled, "Grooms! Attend quickly and earn your keep! Attend slowly and earn some stripes!"

After the grooms raced out, received their tongue-lashing from the captain, and took the horses and wagons and whatever gear the Syldoon handed them, our party headed toward Jackal Tower. I looked up as we approached the stone stairs—the tower from base to crenellations had to be one hundred feet tall, or close to it, and the four turrets at the top were nearly as large as normal towers along any other curtain wall in Anjuria. It was somewhat staggering, and I was clutching my satchel and writing case tight to my chest as we started up the stairs. They wound around the outside of the Tower, slowly spiraling up, and with no railing, I moved closer to the stones of the Tower, even though the stairs were close to ten feet wide. But I was glad to see I wasn't the only one doing so. Even the Syldoon were being cautious, and High Priest Henlester was nearly pressed up against the stones and hugging himself besides. I wondered if he feared heights, and secretly hoped that he did. Very much.

The Tower entrance was about a quarter of the way up and next to the curtain wall. There were two guards posted, both in corselets with alternating red and white enameled scales, open helms with black horse-hair plumes draping down the back, and long spears and the peculiar shields with the embattled top and tapered bottom. One of them was young, not much older than me, and didn't appear to recognize Braylar or his retinue at all. He saw the nooses, but treated the company as strangers, and possibly hostile ones at that. "State your business," he said, mustering as much authority and gruffness as he could.

The older soldier elbowed him in the ribs. "You stupid whelp," he said, and it was hard to tell if it was good-natured or not. "That's Captain Killcoin you're speaking to."

After the younger guard looked at his elder blankly, the grizzled guard said, "Of *our* Tower."

"I ain't never seen him before," the younger replied, sounding as if he suspected he was being made sport of or tested.

"Course you hadn't. Captain's been in the field for a few years now. How long since you been hung?"

The younger guard tried to stand a little taller. "A year. Going on a year."

"Right. So quit flapping your yap then."

Braylar took the last few stairs until he was on a level with the guards. "He is merely doing his duty. I expect nothing less." He slapped the younger guard on the shoulder. "But the Commander is waiting on our arrival. And unless the years have softened him, I suspect impatiently."

Both guards quickly saluted and stepped aside, allowing the party through the entrance. We stepped into a long hall, Braylar leading the way with his lieutenants on either side, Vendurro having Henlester by the arm immediately behind, with me and the remainder of his diminished company trailing, four of the Syldoon carrying the chests full of the documents I had been translating near the back. I had the protective urge to walk with them, but resisted.

The walls were bare, with the occasional small window to let in some dusty light. We passed a number of rooms with doors closed, with one open that showed an office filled with desks and chairs and Syldoon clerks scribbling away. I felt a wistful pang—that was the kind of task I would have been set to if I had walked a different path and been a Syldoon.

Of course, I never would have been chosen, of if I had, would have died during training or the hanging. But still, I felt a weird affinity any time I saw someone else with a quill and ink jar.

One thin man saw our group and walked toward us, fingers stained with ink, a smudge on his smooth cheek. What hair he had left was the color of milk, and while his face was deeply lined, furrowed even, there was a youthful vigor and energy about him. "Well, I must say, Captain, I was beginning to despair we might never have the pleasure of your company again. Welcome home."

Braylar nodded. "It is good to be back, Vorris. Would you be so kind as to alert Commander Darzaak that we have returned?"

Vorris gave a wry smile. "I believe your sister did as much already, my lord."

"Why, of course she did. Very well. Good to be back, just the same."

The clerk smiled more broadly and headed back to the office or scriptorium.

We turned a corner, passed through another guarded door, and then down a hall I assumed was part of the barracks. I saw a room with bunks and low tables and benches, some chests, wooden lockers, and more Syldoon than I could count.

Here, all but the youngest of the men knew Braylar and his men instantly, and hailed them, clasping forearms, asking excited questions, making crude jokes, and each time it was left to Mulldoos or Braylar to close the conversation off and keep us moving. We were promised more drinks than any one tavern could possibly keep up with, and each time, after a few words we started forward again.

Out of earshot of the last group, Mulldoos said, "Told you the middle of the day was a mistake."

Just then, a mammoth man filled a doorway on our left, and he had to duck and sidle sideways a bit as he stepped through. He was at least a foot taller than Hewspear, maybe more, with arms and legs tree trunks would have been jealous of, and a dark beard that seemed intent on covering every inch of his face. Somehow, Braylar didn't see him, and for such a huge beast of a man, he moved quietly, and as he approached he lifted a finger the size of a bear sausage to his lips, or where I assumed his lips must have been under all that hair.

Then he wrapped his massive arms around Braylar and picked him up as if he were made of straw.

When he finally dropped him back on the floor, Braylar had gone red in the face. The huge man asked, "Not dead yet, eh?"

Braylar gave the most genuine (if tilted and cockeyed) smile I can remember seeing. "Not for lack of trying, but no, still living."

The huge man's beard parted just enough to reveal what looked suspiciously like a grin as well. "Pity. Still time. Glad you're back, though. Tired of hearing the same old war stories again and again. Be good to find out what's going on out there in the world."

"No war to speak of. Not yet, anyway."

"Pity there, too." Then he turned and walked back through the door, eclipsing the room beyond as he did.

We kept walking, and I tapped Vendurro on the shoulder. "Who was that?"

"Azmorgon. Some would add 'The Ogre,' 'The Giant,' 'The Owlbear' or some such thing after."

"He was imposing. What would you add?"

"'Azmorgon the Get-theFuck-Out-of-My-Way-or-I'll-Knock-You-Down-Running.' Did you see the size of that bastard? He could crush your skull with his thumb and forefinger if he had a mind."

We reached the end of the hall and started up some spiral stairs, passing a number of other floors on the way to the top—some closed off by large doors, others open to allow a glimpse of more barracks or supply rooms, a great hall, and other spaces I couldn't make sense of.

By the time we arrived at the Tower Commander's residence, my legs and lungs were burning, and there were spots like dark moths at the edges of my vision. There was a much larger arched door on a landing, with two guards on either side. They didn't move to stop us, so Vorris wasn't wrong—we were expected.

We stepped into Commander Darzaak's quarters. While hardly regal or extravagant, the main solar had far more flourishes than any room I had seen in the Tower so far. The ceilings were vaulted and painted with richly detailed scenes: a mounted hunting part pursuing a golden stag through a forest; two armies about to meet in a blighted battlefield under a large full silver moon; a griffin flying away from a farmstead with a large terrified cow in its claws, the farmer running after with pitchfork; and more besides.

There were small alcoves along the walls, each housing a different statue of filigreed metal sculpture.

A long wooden table occupied the center of the room, surrounded by several equally robust wood and leather chairs.

The commander himself was leaning against a windowsill, the horn shutters pushed out to let in the afternoon light. Shorter than Mulldoos and stockier besides, beyond middle years, a sharp widow's peak the color of ash, the remainder of his hair charcoal, with prominent sideburns that ran down his cheeks and across half his chin on either side. I wasn't sure what I expected of a Tower Commander, but he was something of a lord, so I expected brocades or rings or richly embroidered hems, but his clothing, though nice enough cloth, was plain and unadorned, the one flourish being a red sash that broke up his gray and blue tunic, overcoat, and trousers.

He turned and looked Braylar and his men over, hands clasped behind his back. "Captain. You look like shit."

Braylar saluted and replied, "I imagine I do, Commander. I would have chosen to bathe and to sleep for ten days, and I'm sure my men are of the same mind, but my sister was fairly insistent we report at once."

"Emperor's got a bee up his ass about something. You know he recalled the lot of you, and any other Tower operatives in the field?" Braylar nodded and Commander Darzaak said, "Poor maneuvering, if you ask me. Which no one did, of course, least of all that poncy bastard. But there it is. So, Soffjian said you met some trouble on the road."

It was clearly both statement and question.

"We did."

Clearly only statement and not an answer.

"I expect you have something to show for the dawdling then." His eyes were already on Henlester. "Is this the High Priest?"

"It is."

Commander Darzaak did not alter his stance, tone, or expression, but did switch to Anjurian that was near perfect. "And I expect you are wondering why my men hauled you from your homeland to have an audience with me. So am I."

High Priest Henlester replied in Syldoonian, though slowly and with an undeniable accent. "They were quite. . ." he glanced Braylar's way, "insistent."

"Course they were, Henlester. But we'll get to all that soon enough. For now, think of yourself as a very important guest, requiring many guards for protection and escort."

Henlester showed what could only be called a vulpine smile. "Spare me your pleasantries, Black Noose. Call it what it is and be done with this farce."

Darzaak said, "And spare me your haughty indignation, cleric. You want to spend the rest of your miserable life in a dark cell with moldy straw for a bed, eating pigshit? That can be arranged. You prefer to be put in a hole so deep you lose your wits and bite your wrists open to end it? We have plenty open at the moment. You like a quick hanging instead? Well, we do a lot of hanging hereabouts, so that's easy enough to arrange.

"Or, you play nice and behave yourself better than you've managed, and we can put you up in more luxurious accommodations than you deserve. Feed you figs and tea and tasty honey crepes, wear powdered slippers if you like, lay your head down on a fluffy pillow, or whatever pleasantries you think a man of your station should be afforded. Your treatment depends completely on you. So far, it's looking more likely you'll end up in a hole. But I like a good surprise. Think you can surprise me and rein in your mouth, High Priest?"

Henlester's smile slid off his face, and his lips pressed so tight the wrinkles surrounding his mouth seemed to quiver. But then he mustered a smallish bow. "I shall endeavor to be docile and demure, Commander Darzaak. It might take some practice, I am afraid, but I will try."

"And I will try not to clap you in irons or drop you in our Trench." Darzaak waved over some guards. "Escort our elite prisoner here to his quarters. See to it he wants for nothing. Except freedom, of course."

Henlester turned about quickly and strode ahead of his guards, as if he were familiar with the way and were leading them.

The Tower Commander watched the door shut before shaking his head and looking at Braylar. "You never seem to capture anyone pliable. Why is that?"

"Well," Braylar said, "that is likely due to the fact that most of my snares involve the puissant, and not millers and bakers."

Darzaak sat down at the large table and looked surprised he was the only one. "Oh, be seated."

Braylar and his men took chairs at the large table, and I grabbed an open seat next to Vendurro.

The Commander jerked a gray-haired thumb toward the door. "So. I got your note about playing the priests against the baron, and I seem to recall you mentioning that there was more to it than that. You suspected that puckered arse might actually be key to something bigger. I'm guessing you didn't haul him all the way back here on account of his pleasant demeanor. So what of it, Captain?"

Braylar said, "As to the first, when the good Emperor chose to pull us out of Anjuria with no notice, he likely undermined much of our good work there. I chose to kidnap the cleric in part to see what we can salvage there, if the goal is still to destabilize the barony."

"As far as I know, nothing's changed there. And as to the second. . ."

Braylar opened his mouth to respond but Darzaak cut him off. "Wait.

Before we get to that, we ought to make our introductions here." Darzaak fixed his eyes on me. "You know who I am. Can't say as I know you. And you look awful scribey. Would you be Arkamondos then, called Arki?"

Everyone at the table looked in my direction, and I swallowed hard. "I am." And then added, "Commander Darzaak. The scribe, that is. Arki."

"So, Arki, does it make you nervous that the two in line ahead of you died?"

Well. That was direct. I replied, "I can't speak to the others, Commander, never having met them at all. They must have been capable enough, or the captain would not have hired them in the first place. But I'm also confident there were good reasons they failed to hold the position for very long. So long as I perform admirably, I suspect my chances of survival are at least. . . better than awful."

That earned a chuckle from Hewspear and Vendurro, and smiles from Braylar and Mulldoos. The commander, however, wasn't especially moved to merriment. "Tell me, then, Arki, are you a trustworthy sort?"

"Yes, Commander—yes, sir. I believe so."

"Believe or would have me believe?"

"Both, if it please you."

Darzaak turned to Braylar. "So what of it, Captain? I'm assuming you would have killed the boy yourself if he troubled you overmuch. But let me hear it from you now. What makes you think the third will be any better than the previous traitors?"

Braylar replied, "Our young scribe nearly shot me. Twice, as it happens. But in both instances, he did so attempting to save my life. He has served admirably, translating the treasure we have collected. And he had opportunity to wander over to our enemy's camp, and chose not to.

"And as to trustworthiness, the first scribe's only lapse of honesty was exaggerating some of his skills. He wasn't as competent as I was led to believe, but he did not betray us—the simple sod happened to walk into the path of an arrow that was made for me. His crime was clumsiness. It was only the second who actually tried to sell us out. Arki did not fail such a test. He is loyal. Though clumsy as well, which does cause me some consternation, I must confess. But we could easily be on our fourth scribe by now. And we are not."

The Tower Commander looked at Hewspear and Mulldoos. "Are you of the same mind as your captain here?"

Hewspear said, "I have been wagering on his worth since I met him, and he has not disappointed yet. He even managed not to get himself killed in a few fights, which is somewhat miraculous when you consider his limitations on that score."

Mulldoos looked at me, pale eyes unreadable, but never comforting. After a long pause, he replied, "I trust my brothers in arms in the Jackal Tower. I trust Cap. That's where my trust begins and ends. Scribbler here ain't a Syldoon. Never could be one in a thousand years." I thought that was the end of it, until Mulldoos added, "But he does have more mettle and grit than you would suppose, just looking at the skinny bastard. And he's proved useful a time or two." He said this last grudgingly, but at least he said it. "Do I trust him? No, not a brother, like I said. Do I distrust him?" He shrugged his big shoulders. "Not as much as most."

"A ringing endorsement," Hewspear said.

"Considering he's only been in the company a short while, it's as like to be as ringy-dingy as he'll get. And if any of you halfwits was being square here, you'd admit the same."

Darzaak considered everything, staring at his hands on the table for a moment. "Fair enough. So, Arki, your good captain here managed to acquire quite a bit of old parchment by all accounts. Were you able to translate it then?"

"No. That is, yes, I translated a good amount of it, but not all. Not yet."

The Commander looked at Braylar. "Not used to doing debriefings, is he?"

Braylar gave the smallest of smiles. "He is smarter than he looks—I swear it. Arki, explain what you uncovered so far."

I had my writing case in my lap, but everything else had been carted off with the chests of documents. "Of course, Captain. But my notes—"

"Aren't necessary, just now. The Commander doesn't want every little detail. Only what you discovered about the Temple of Truth, and their efforts to control the memory witches of yesteryear. Broad strokes if you would, yes?"

I noted that he pointedly did not mention Bloodsounder, or what I assumed were related weapons that had been referenced, like the sword Grieftongue. And so after collecting my thoughts, I recapped as best I could.

When I was finished, Tower Commander Darzaak looked at Braylar again. "So. The puckered arse then. Was he able to elaborate at all?"

"He was indeed," Braylar replied. "According to him, the underpriest Anroviak was burned alive after his trial. Which should have dissuaded any from continuing that line of thinking or research. The Temple continued hunting and killing the witches. But there was another priest who discovered some of those early records. Likely the very same Anroviak memoir that survived to this day, and some other documents as well. And this priest, Untwik, carried on Anroviak's work on the sly. And apparently made some headway."

"Discovered the frames, didn't they?"

Hewspear said, "Well, the Syldoon have a long history of appropriating ideas from other cultures and improving on them. We simply didn't know it was this long."

Darzaak nodded. "So the Anjurians controlled themselves a few witches. We figured as much already, our own accounts hinted at it. But good to substantiate. Still leaves the real big question, though, the one I sent you boys prowling around there for in the first place. . . did they figure out how to siphon control, steal it from someone else? Break it, rebind it? Anything like that?"

"That's actually several questions, Commander," Braylar said.

"Same question in different clothes, more like."

"Fair enough. The answer to one and all is no, not that we discovered. Henlester professed no knowledge of anything like that, and though he is a slippery eel, everything he volunteered corroborated what Arki had already learned. So I am inclined to believe him. Though you could certainly put him to the Memoridons to test that theory. But either way, Arki still has at least one chest to go through. We might yet unearth what we're looking for."

The Tower Commander nodded slowly. "Aye. That we might." He didn't sound convinced. Then he said, "You've done good work. I've read the reports—you've suffered losses, and likely more besides since those were penned. The Emperor in his infinite wisdom might have fucked you in the ear some, but could be we still find a way to make something out of it."

Braylar leaned forward in his chair slightly, gripped the edge of the table. "So why did the Emperor recall us? What is happening here?"

"Wasn't just you. Cynead summoned back every operative in the plaguing field. You might have been the last, but if there is anybody else out there, it doesn't matter. The Emperor is short on patience and long on pomp. Called for a Caucus of the Towers, two days from now."

Mulldoos curled his hands into fists and the look on his face said he wished he could use them on someone. "Never a good thing, a Caucus. Always ends bad for somebody or other. What do you suppose he's planning?"

"Well, last time it was a bloody business, for certain," Darzaak replied. "No telling what his motive is now—long on pomp and secrecy, I should have said. But no, it's not like to be a good thing at all."

Vendurro asked, "Do you suppose he—" He stopped whatever question he had in mind and tried a different route. "Are you thinking it has to do with Thumaar? Should we be planning escape routes?"

Braylar shook his head. "No, he would have dealt with that in the dark, and only announced anything of the sort after he had rooted out the opposition and destroyed them. Not cause for a Caucus. He has another play in mind. He wouldn't recall every operative, summon the Towers like this, unless it was something bigger."

Darzaak agreed and added, "Most of what you boys have been doing was the continued work Thumaar started years ago. To be frank, I am surprised Cynead let you back into Anjuria after Thumaar was ousted. No, I suspect Captain Killcoin has the right of it. The Emperor recalling the lot of you is a bold move, but it serves a larger purpose. And that puts me at ease about as much as sticking my cock in a hornet's nest." He stopped and looked at me again. "Get yourself cleaned up, Arki. A bath if you like one. Some food, some rest. Then we need you back to it. Keep translating. Dismissed."

I stood awkwardly, nearly dropped my writing case, and nodded. "Yes, Commander Darzaak." I wasn't sure where to go, and was reluctant to ask.

Darzaak must have seen it on my face. "Ven, show him the way."

Vendurro stood up alongside me. "Aye, Commander."

"Oh, and lad?"

Vendurro had been starting toward the door, turned and stopped.

"I was might sorry to hear about Gless. He was a good soldier."

Vendurro straightened up, nodded. "Appreciate that, Commander. Appreciate that."

As we walked down the corridor, I said, "As always, I feel as if there are a hundred things I have no understanding of."

Vendurro laughed. "A hundred? Try a thousand. This is Sunwrack—even them of us who spent most of our lives here have no idea what's happening half the time, or like to happen two days from now. Place ain't called Capital of Coups on accident. Towers eliminate Towers, form alliances, break them just as quick, all positioning for power or to keep someone else from seizing it. It's actually worse when we ain't at war. Nothing brings the Syldoon together like a common enemy."

"Or a Caucus apparently. What is that exactly? I would have thought the Tower Commanders convened with the Emperor regularly. Or at least not so irregularly it would raise eyebrows when it happened. But this isn't that, is it? What's happening?"

"Towers operate real independent, most of the time. Twice a year they get together, regular like you said. But a Caucus is something else. Only the Emperor can call for one. All the Tower Commanders have to be present unless they're dead or dying. Them and their captains and chief officers. Failure to show is treason."

I understood Soffjian's urgency a little more in herding us here—clearly she knew or guessed what was going on. We started down the stairs. "So if we hadn't made it back in time. . . ?"

Vendurro was taking the stairs two at a time. "Awww, no. They wouldn't have hunted us down or nothing. Cap's a big man, for certain, but no Tower Commander. But it would have looked mighty queer, just the same. A Memoridon comes calling and cracking the whip, Syldoon best kick the spurs in. Especially if it smells like the summons is coming from the Emperor, not the Tower Commander hisself."

"Can I ask you something, Vendurro?"

He led me down a hall. "Course you can. If you don't mind much whether I answer or not."

"Are you worried about the Caucus? Sounds like something we should be worried about. Only you didn't seem particularly bothered."

"'We' is it?" He stopped and looked at me, gave a half-smile.

"Well, I might never be a Syldoon. As Mulldoos pointed out, clearly I am not cut out for it. But my lot is tied to the captain's, all of yours, as far as that goes. So, I suppose—"

"Only teasing you, bookmaster." I relaxed as he said, "Caucuses, Emperors, Tower Commanders, that's all above me. I'm just a soldier." He pointed up at the corbelled hall ceiling. "Leave all that for them to figure out. I just do my job, best as I can. I trust Cap and Hew and Mull to do right by me and the other boys."

We turned a corner, passing a Syldoon slave girl who gave me a queer look. "I've heard Thumaar's name a few times now. He was the deposed emperor, wasn't he?"

"Was indeed. Capital of Coups."

"But not killed?"

"Nope, Thumaar's alive and kicking. And like most that been on a throne and lost it, itching mighty fierce to reclaim it."

I supposed most deposed rulers would be, but still asked, "How do you know that for certain?"

"Oh, Jackal Tower is trying to help him do it."

He said it so nonchalantly, it took me a moment to register the enormity packed into such a small phrase. "You what?!" I nearly shouted, and then quieted myself and tried it again. "You're trying to reinstate him?"

"Ayyup. We're Thumaar's men. Some other Towers feel the same. Thumaar was twice the emperor Cynead is. Quick to a flask, a laugh, or revenge, he was. A hard man, but fair. We can get him back where he belongs, we will."

I looked up and down the hall, wondering if he should be proclaiming open treason so unabashedly.

"Oh, we're among Jackals here, Arki. Out there, we bite our tongues and smile pretty and salute proper, but every man here will piss on Cynead's corpse if we get half a chance."

"But. . . but aren't you worried about the Caucus and what it might mean, then? What if Cynead has gotten word that you are working against him?"

"Like I said—bigger problems for bigger men. We oust Cynead, or we die trying. It works out, or it doesn't. Truth be told, I'm a lot more bothered by what I got to do on the morrow than any Caucus the day after."

I thought about it, trying to puzzle out his meaning, when I recalled what the Tower Commander had said and remembered that losing a comrade wasn't the end of things. At least not for Vendurro. "So, you're going to see the widow tomorrow then?"

Vendurro looked at his feet, rubbed the back of his head vigorously. "I should go today. Still got a little sun yet. And tomorrow won't be no better. Might even be worse, when it comes to it. But I ain't seen my Towermates in a long time. Right now, I'm fixing to go see my brothers, drink too much, and lose more coin than I can afford." He looked up quickly. "Don't worry none, though. I'll keep the widowcoin in a separate purse. I might make a woman weep and slap me tomorrow, but I'll be thrice damned if I don't at least offer her her due. Knowing Mervulla, she'll throw it in my face. Before or after trying to rake my eyes out. Proud woman, and angry more often than not. Could be next time you see me, I'll have a patch. Maybe two, blinder than those poor Hornmen bastards."

He was trying to make light, but it was obviously forced.

"I can still come with you. If you like. If it makes it any less, well, if it makes it more bearable. Easier."

Vendurro stopped in front of a door, took a deep breath. "That's good of you, Arki. Mighty good. And it means a lot. But Commander Darzaak was cracking the whip on getting through the rest of those scrolls and whatnot. Wouldn't want to take you away from that."

I nodded, feeling relieved, as it was likely to be an intimate meeting and I would only be an intruder, but also guilty, as it was clear Vendurro was shouldering a burden. "I'm sure I can spare a little time. It's not like we have to travel back to Alespell to see her, right?"

Vendurro puffed out his cheeks, then exhaled slowly. "Wishing I could let you. But this is something I got to see through myself. My duty to do. Still, means more than I can say you offering like that." He checked the door, found it unlocked, and pushed it in. "Looks like the steward got here first. You'll be bunking in Cap's spare room. No telling if they dusted it or not, but other than being locked up for a few years, ought to be fine."

I stood there, satchel and writing case tucked in my arms. "What about you and the lieutenants?"

"Oh, Mull and Hew got their own quarters, being officers and all."

"But you're an officer too, aren't you?"

"Only difference between me and the other men is I got to suffer through more of their gripes and bellyaching. And occasionally repeat the Cap's orders if they're moving slow. Sergeant's a glorified grunt. I got my own room, true enough, but it's in the barracks with my brothers. All for the best. Easier to stumble in after swallowing a gallon or three of ale or sour wine. Fewer stairs."

He took a step back, looking ready to go. I glanced at the empty room ahead and had the uncomfortable sense that I was once again on a precipice. Every time I felt as if I had discovered the worst about what might happen accompanying the Syldoon, I learned some new horrible wrinkle—secretly supporting the deposed Emperor while plotting against the new one?

Vendurro must have seen my face and asked, "You wouldn't want to come with me, would you? Meet the mates, share some ale?"

I nearly said yes—it seemed a brighter prospect than being alone in a dusty room. But I was made for dusty rooms. And I didn't imagine the other Syldoon soldiers would be any more receptive to sharing a flagon with me than Braylar's immediate retinue would.

I shook my head, and Vendurro nodded. "Be seeing you then, Arki."

"Night."

I watched him head back down the hallway, not envying his task on the morrow, but jealous he would have old friends to take his mind off it tonight, and almost called out and asked him to wait for me to join him.

Almost.

Captain Killcoin's quarters were spacious, and he was lucky enough to have several arched windows along one wall. I looked out and saw all of Sunwrack spread out in front of me. Even several floors from the roof of the Tower, the view was amazing—the orderly grid-like streets and alleys running off in every direction; the vast plazas teeming with colorful crowds, shimmying, shifting; fountains filled with water from the aqueduct alongside gated gardens of fig and date and those peculiar trees that homed the steel moths; temples of every size, sometimes crowned with bulbous domes or topped with achingly thin minarets painted in black and white bands; crumbling facades and ancient arches everywhere; the brass roofs reflecting the last of the sunlight, the whole city ablaze. And of course the colossal walls and Towers surrounding the vast city—a ring of castles and keeps girding the heart of the Empire.

It really was astonishing. And a little dizzying, so I stepped away.

I walked through an open arched doorway to the adjacent smaller room. Being an interior apartment, this did not have windows but I was surprised to see a small rectangular light well that was lined with glazed brick, increasing the illumination. And there was a hook above the small desk and chair that had a lantern hanging from it.

It was not as pleasant as some rooms I occupied briefly in the houses of previous employers, but writing in here would be an absolute pleasure compared to tramping about in wagons, rumbling over ruts every ten feet, spilling ink and scratching marks on the page so sloppy I could barely make out what I intended when I looked back on them hours later.

Opposite the desk was a simple bed, but that too would be luxury after sleeping alongside a wagon wheel, stirring at every noise in the dark, wondering if Hornmen or Brunesmen or some other unknown enemy would come thundering through our encampment trying to kill us all.

I set my gear down and saw that someone, the steward or slaves who prepared the room for our arrival, had dragged in a copper tub as well. Or maybe the tub was always here, but one finger dip inside told me they had filled it recently—the water was lukewarm, but the copper held the heat nicely.

A bath. A warm bath. It felt like ages since I'd had one.

I pulled some new clothes out of my satchel and quickly stripped out of my filthy tunic and trousers, the wool caked in dirt and splotches of blood. After piling my smallclothes on top and unwinding the bandage around my waist, I stepped into the tub, actually relieved it wasn't boiling hot. I slid down, the water rising to the middle of my chest, the warmth luxurious, my itching wound finally forgotten.

A bristle brush was hanging from a hook on the side, and there was a small tray with a hunk of soap as rough as a millstone. I scrubbed and lathered and rinsed, then slid down as far as I could, my arms draped over the side, my eyes closed.

I only intended to rest, but must have fallen asleep for a few moments when I heard a voice. "Well. Don't you look cozy."

My eyes snapped open. A woman's voice. Skeelana.

I sat up straight and then started to cover myself.

She was sitting cross-legged on a chair behind the table. "Oh, the soap scum is like lily pads, and you've browned the water nicely. I didn't see anything."

"What. . . How did you get here?"

Skeelana pointed at the door. "Not exactly a challenge. Wasn't locked."

"What are you doing here?"

"Same as you. Relaxing a bit. You looked very comfortable before I startled you. I almost felt guilty." She didn't look it in the slightest. "Though now you don't look especially peaceful."

I had no idea what to do or say—I'd never been interrupted during a bath by a woman before, and certainly not one I was strangely attracted to. But she spoke to me as if we were strolling along a crowded street.

"Uh, what I meant to say was, is, I am glad to see you, but what are you doing here right now? The captain could return any moment, and I'm pretty sure he would have the same question, but asked much less nicely."

She didn't seem particularly bothered by that either. "Oh, I saw him earlier. Towermates he hadn't seen in years dragged him off to drink. I think we are quite safe."

The way she said that made me feel anything but. Though not at all in the same way my unexpected conversation with Soffjian had in the wagon in the dark. Here, I just felt off balance, flushed despite the tepid water, awkward, and uncertain. "I'm going to get out now."

Skeelana smiled. "By all means."

"That is, to get dressed. To—"

She stood up. "Oh, never fear, Arki. I'm only playing with you. I will avert my eyes."

True to her word, she turned away. I parted the dirty water as best I could, stepped out, shivering, even though the day was still warm. And slipped into my clean undertunic, tunic, and trousers as quickly as possible, stumbling as my wet foot caught in the pant leg and I nearly fell over.

Skeelana glanced over her shoulder and laughed. "You alright back there?"

"Yes," I said, trying to free my foot and work it through, again nearly toppling. "Just fine, thanks."

When I was finally dressed, she turned around and sat back down. "I'm sorry we didn't get to talk more on the final stretch back here. Soffjian felt it would be best if we maintained some distance. Especially after I treated Captain Killcoin. That did so unnerve his retinue, and certainly the man himself. I did miss our chats though."

I felt myself flush even more. "I did as well," I admitted, sitting on the bed.

We both sat quietly for a few moments, until she broke it with, "See, that's it, right there. Most people, this silence would be incredibly awkward. With you, it's only mildly awkward."

I laughed, and it felt good. Really good.

Skeelana looked at me, and while her blue eyes had a way of ensuring whatever I said next would be foolish or floundering, I still found myself enjoying looking back. "Aren't you worried? That you might have been seen coming in here? Is that. . . ?"

"What? Appropriate? No, probably not. Most Syldoon don't consort with us unless necessary. But we are *allowed* in the Tower, after all. We are a part of it, even if there is a divide. We can walk down the halls. And most anyone I saw ran off in the other direction as soon as possible, not especially caring where I was going. So no, not really worried. Though I don't intend on staying all that long. I mostly just wanted to find out what you think of Sunwrack so far."

I resisted the urge to walk over to the window and look out again. "It is. . . enormous. Staggering, really. I've never seen anything like it."

"It is big, that's for certain," Skeelana agreed. "After living here for so long, you tend to forget that the rest of the world isn't built like this place."

"You said mostly?"

"Hmmm?"

"'Mostly wanted.' Was there something else?" I tried to keep the nervousness and excitement out of my voice, chiding myself for being a stupid boy, for thinking an accomplished Memoridon was even remotely interested in me. For wanting her to be. It was foolishness of the worst sort.

She played with the jackal pin on her jacket. "You mentioned something, several days back now, that I've been wondering about."

I felt disappointment and relief. "Oh?"

"You asked me about memories. And how easy or hard it was to uncover those that had been lost or fractured. Something like that."

"You're a Memoridon—you don't remember?"

Skeelana tilted her head, smiling. "Oh, you witty boy. Yes, I do. And I got the sense that wasn't just idle curiosity. You were asking about yourself, weren't you?"

After a long telling pause, I went ahead and confessed. "No. That is, it wasn't idle curiosity." I considered changing the subject, ending the discussion entirely. But I found myself saying, "I never met my father. That I know of. I remember my childhood, of course. My mother. For whatever that's worth. But I was thinking, wondering, that is. . . "

She waited patiently. I pressed on. "Well, maybe I *had* seen him. Maybe he'd checked in on me and my mother when I was really young and I just don't remember. I met his retainer, but never my father. I don't think. And when you said sometimes memories get buried or broken, I was thinking. . . "

Hearing the plaintive tone, I regretted saying anything at all, but Skeelana gave me a smile without guile, mockery, or sarcasm. "It might be possible. Might."

"But, you could look. Inside me. Find it if it's there, maybe restore it." She opened her mouth, but I kept talking. "I know how ridiculous it sounds, or seems. I mean, even if a memory was there, even if I had seen him, knowing that, seeing it again, well, it wouldn't change my life. But still."

She nodded slowly. "I could look. Could."

I was about to nod myself, and stopped. "Is there danger? Could you. . . damage me?"

Skeelana shook her head. "Soffjian would peel you like an orange and break you into segments, but I have a delicate enough touch—I could flit around without causing any harm." But she stopped herself. "And still, I don't think this is a good idea."

"Why. . . why is that?"

"Well, when I searched Captain Killcoin for those stolen foreign memories, they were easy enough to find, really, and I could generally ignore his own. Generally. But what you are asking. . . it is too intimate, Arki. I would be sifting through yours, looking for this thing. And while I am as crafty at this as anyone, and have a talent for finding what I'm looking for, you would be exposing yourself. Without intending to, I might see things I shouldn't. Things you don't want seen. Embarrassing memories. The time you roped the unicorn thinking about your sister, or—"

"I don't have a sister, but if I did, I wouldn't!"

She stood up, walked toward me. "Well, be that as it may, we all have shameful memories. Horrible ones, sometimes. Painful ones. People don't invite me in voluntarily, after all. There is a reason for that. I wouldn't feel comfortable doing it. I'm sorry."

Skeelana was right. And I was a selfish fool for even thinking about it—I knew things about the captain that he would kill me for revealing to a Memoridon, even inadvertently. Still, she must have seen my face drop, even for a moment, and felt some pity.

Bending over, she ran her fingers across my cheek, and then her face was moving toward me, the dark skin closer and closer, and I felt my eyes lock on the stud on her round upturned nose, just before she placed her plump lips on mine.

My breath hitched in my chest, and I finally closed my eyes, turning my head slightly, kissing her back, her fingers moving across my cheek to the back of my head, and she pulled me in tight. She parted her lips a little, and I followed her lead—the only time I remember my heart racing faster was when the Brunesman stabbed me. Her tongue darted out, flicking across my teeth, teasing, curling, inviting me to let her in. I reached up and ran my fingers through her hair, jabbing my thumb on a pin, and she laughed and kissed me harder, placing her hand on my chest.

Skeelana smelled of valerian musk, and tasted like almonds, and I wanted to devour her, take her all in at once, feel her skin, her curves, her heat. I'd kissed a few girls before, but only truly been with one girl, and that was a fumbling, ridiculous encounter, elbows and heads knocking together, apologies aplenty, rushed and graceless and gawky. But here, now, I felt an arousal I had never experienced before, potent and fierce and primal. I desperately wanted to explore Skeelana, to please her.

And abruptly, it was done. She was moving away. I kept my eyes closed for a moment, not wanting to show the frustration, and when I opened them again, she was gone. Which was impossible—she hadn't had time to leave or hide. And then I remembered the Hornman in Alespell she had beguiled and looked closer.

I saw a shimmer along one wall, made out the shape of her, part of the outline, a faint rippling where I should have seen only stone and wood.

Skeelana laughed as the illusion rippled toward the door. "I was waiting for you to be clean. About time."

And then she was truly gone, leaving me breathing so heavily I was nearly panting, my head swimming, still tasting her, and hungering.

After Skeelana left, I lay back on the bed, waiting to cool down, revisiting what had happened over and over in my mind. And while it was completely unexpected, I fell into a deep slumber the dead would be jealous of.

Hours later, I woke, my pillow covered in sweat, the room dark, and saw a faint glow coming from Braylar's quarters. I climbed out of bed, body still feeling twice as heavy as it was, eyes weighted, and yet my stomach grumbling. I would have thought Skeelana's visit a dream, except I could still smell the valerian on my tunic.

I walked into his chambers, wondering what hour it was.

Braylar was sitting at the mosaic table near the window and the fireplace that must have rarely been used, a tallow candle burning low in front of him, his shadow dancing along the wall. His hair was disheveled, not nearly as slicked back as usual, and he was hunched over parchment sheets, most scattered on the table. There was a wooden plate in front of him, some small bones, a pool of congealed grease, a hunk of bread, and some olive pits.

And as ever, a pitcher of ale and a tall horn cup next to it.

I wondered if he was fighting off the effects of stolen memories, but it seemed he was just in the mood for drink.

My stomach rumbled so loudly he heard it. He must have known I was there already, as he didn't glance up from what he was reading, but indicated I should sit next to him.

I did, my stomach again protesting, unabashed.

Braylar looked over at me. "I was wondering when your basic needs would rouse you from your slumber. I heard you stirring and summoned another plate for you. Ale?" He picked up the pitcher, filling his own cup and stopping just short of doing the same with the other.

I had a bad head for drink even on a full stomach, but just then it did sound good, and it would at least fill my belly a bit before the food arrived.

Almost before I could nod he had filled the horn cup to the brim. After accepting it and taking a swallow—it was quite good, rich and heavy—I remembered Skeelana's words and said, "I would have guessed you'd be catching up with your Towermates below or in an alehouse somewhere?"

"I allowed myself a little of that, and there will be time enough for more. Or not, as it happens. But for now, there are a good many things I need to tend to first." He took several swallows of his own. "Still, one shouldn't be wanting."

There was a knock on the door, and Braylar said, "There, you see. Timing is everything." Then he shouted, "Enter!"

A young Syldoon, or Syldoon slave more likely, as the boy had not been hung or inked, came in carrying a tray with food. I clamped my hands on my stomach to try to stymie any more embarrassing grumbling from below.

The boy walked over, set the tray on the table and bowed low, avoiding eye contact with either of us. "Will there be anything else, my lord?"

"Captain is fine. Captain Killcoin, if you insist on formalities. And what shall we call you, boy?"

The youth, brown curly head still bowed low, thought about his answer before replying, "Whatever it please you, my lor—uh, Captain."

"And what did it please your parents to call you, my obsequious little man?"

He did look up then, but only for an instant before lowering his eyes again. "My parents? Captain?"

"Yes. I will insist on calling you Drizzleshit if you do not provide a suitable alternate."

The boy stammered but didn't provide an answer.

"Do you like 'Drizzleshit,' boy?"

The boy started to shake his head, stopped himself, and then shook it anyway. "No, Captain. Not especially."

"Then you best get out of my room and pull your head out of your ass before you set foot in here again. Do you understand me?"

"Yes, my—yes, Captain. Captain Killcrown."

"Killcoin, you dolt. Get out of here, Drizzleshit."

The boy backed away, still bowing, than turned and nearly ran into the door, fumbling with the tray as he shut it behind him.

Braylar shook his head. "And this is what we have to work with. If your raw material is shit, you can be sure the finished product will be little improved." He gestured at my plate. "Eat."

I picked up a large hunk of dark bread that was surprisingly dense and heavy. "I would think the raw material is always, well, raw."

"A wide difference between raw and impure. Ask any smith, Arki— when the iron ingots are poor quality, you might be able to hammer out a sickle, but you will never produce a fine fighting blade. It is the same with men. Which is why we only select the finest. Or used to." He glared at the door as if he might still be able to cause the boy running down the hall to trip over his feet. "Bah. Perhaps it is only me. Perhaps I have simply been gone too long and soured. Or perhaps things are as bleak as they appear and we are all sliding toward a cliff. It remains to be seen."

Braylar pushed his chair back and stood, steadily enough, but his red cheeks said he had been drinking for some time. "As you heard, we attend the Caucus in two days. Stay in this room until such time. Continue your translation, your recording, and enjoy the solitude."

He started toward his bedchamber and I asked, more loudly than I intended, "Do you have any suspicions about what will happen?"

"Today? Tomorrow? Eternally?"

"At the Caucus."

He looked over his shoulder, most of his face in shadow. "I always harbor suspicions, Arki. Always. You might think they would disappear back on familiar ground, among allies. And you would be an idiot for thinking so. The factions here revel in the opportunity to undermine and destroy one another, and alliances are forged of gossamer. The only thing you can depend on here is Tower. All else? The greatest suspicions imaginable. And never so legion as when an Emperor is pulling the strings. You can be sure he did not call a Caucus to hand out pretty doilies and candied eels."

The captain walked out of the room, and nearly took my appetite with him.

But Vendurro's logic suddenly seemed apt: do what you can do, and leave the rest to play itself out as it will.

I just wished I had his conviction in following it.

⊕

The next day I stayed sequestered in my room, happy to be translating in peace and quiet. But it was impossible not to be uneasy whenever I took a break or allowed my mind to drift. Braylar was correct—after reconciling myself to the fact that we were leaving Alespell and Anjuria, and surviving the various dangers on the road, I had made the mistake of thinking that Sunwrack would be a relatively safe, if alien, harbor. A respite from blood-letting and the threat of attack or ambush. But from everything I had heard, the thick stone walls, the thousands of loyal soldiers, the solidarity among them—they might as well have been paper and shadow for all the protection they seemed to afford. At least with the current emperor and Jackal Tower's affiliations with the deposed emperor. Our position seemed worse than precarious, with the politics here being brutal and bloody even on the best of days.

It was better to struggle through passages written by men long dead than to meditate on the possibility of joining them.

But the second day, the room felt smaller, stuffier, and I was having serious trouble concentrating—words swam, thoughts evaded, and time seemed frozen in amber.

So I was surprised but grateful when Vendurro stopped by. I expected he would have been carousing with his Towermates, or sleeping off the same, but then remembered the excursion he had to have taken already. I was reluctant to pry, but equally reluctant to say nothing at all, since he had confided in me. So after a short exchange where he asked me about the dates and figs on my plate, and if I had eaten their like anywhere else, as he seemed to think the figs in particular had a unique flavor in this region, there was a pause. So I inquired, rather clumsily, "You saw her then? The widow?"

He scratched the back of his head, looked around the room, as if he had entered and forgotten exactly why, and said, "Ayyup. Went about as expected."

"That well, eh?"

"Well, worse, truth be told. Mervulla went white the second she saw me. Alone, that is. Don't know that she ever had seen me alone before—it was either with Gless or not at all. So she seen me standing in her door after three years, alone, and she knew straight away before I opened my mouth at all, started saying, 'No, no' over and over. Stepped away from the door, nearly tripped over her child. Been so long since I seen her, hardly recognized the little bugger at all. But the kid being there just made something awful something worse.

"Right about then, I hoped Mervulla might come at me like I thought, flailing and scratching, maybe even draw a blade and try to stick it in me—that I could have handled. But she just sat there, mouthing 'no' and not really saying it at all, tears rolling down her cheeks, her little one holding her skirts and legs tight, looking at me accusing like, wondering what I done to upset their world so much for no good plaguing reason, not recognizing me at all.

"And that was just about the saddest thing I could think of."

"That she didn't recognize you?"

"Nah. That it meant she probably wouldn't have known her da, even if it had been him standing there at the door. And now she would never get the chance."

I almost said that at least the child had gotten to know her father in some small measure, but bit my tongue. And the alternate point, also thankfully unspoken, was that it was better to not know a father at all than to realize he was lousy at the job. But neither point was fair or just. Glesswik might not have been a good father, but it's said some grow into it. He might have.

Both comments were really more about me than this child I would never know, so I kept my mouth shut.

Vendurro spun a knife in a circle on the table, watching the blade catching the light. "I wanted to leave. Something fierce. Mervulla knew what had happened even without me uttering a word, and I figured anything I did say would only be sticking my thumb in the wound. But a man's got a foul job to do, whether it's shoveling shit or telling a woman her man got killed out in the middle of nowhere for no good plaguing reason anyone could put words to, well, best just to get to it and be done with it.

"We weren't what anyone would have called close, so I had no plans to hug her or even so much as touch her. But when she dropped to her knees, I put my hand on her shoulder. She was shaking, staring at the floor, sobbing real quiet like, not even bothering to whisper 'no' anymore, one arm real loose about her kid's waist, who was crying louder than she was, though couldn't have uttered why.

"I said, 'He went out fighting, just like you'd expect. Fought hard, to the end.' It was a lie, of course, or might as well have been, as I was the last to know he was dead. Well, second, next to the sobbing widow there on the floor in front of me. But it was a good lie, just the same. 'He wasn't here like you would have liked, I know. Won't pretend he was. But you ought to know, he was a good soldier. Did that as good as anybody I met.' Another lie, of course, but no worse than the first. But that was about all I knew to say.

"She wiped her eyes with the back of her hand, looked up at me. It was a long horsey face, and red-rimmed and snotty just then, but it struck me, like it had once or twice, that she was a handsome enough woman. No woman's a pretty crier, but I'd seen worse. And once she stopped crying, she was hardly a hag. She could find herself another husband. The widow-coin would keep her out of Beggar's Row or whorehouses, and she'd keep making some coin of her own out of their property. But I hoped she'd find someone else, not a Syldoon soldier. A man who wouldn't be riding off anywhere to die. But I figured that would be sour consolation, so didn't speak my mind on that count. That would have been the only true thing I said, but probably the worst of the lot."

"Probably a good choice to leave that unsaid."

"Aye. Instead, I fetched the bag of silver from my pouch, told her she could come by Jackal Tower every other month to collect more until it ran dry, or we could send a courier, if that was easier. Her eyes narrowed then, and the anger I had been steadied for finally showed itself—body tensed up, hands balled into fists, and she got off the floor, ignoring the whelp who was really starting to let loose now. Stared at me, looked at the bag as if it were full of scorpions, and I thought she was about to slap it into my face, or launch into an attack herself.

"But she reached out real slow, unballed a fist long enough to close it around the bag, and said, quiet like, 'Widowcoin, is it?'

"I nodded and replied, 'Captain Killcoin—you remember him, of course—he takes care of the fallen and those they leave behind. Glesswik's share—'

"She stopped me then. Said, 'That's the first you've called him by name. Since you rapped on my door. You know that, Ven?'

"I shook my head, though I knew she was right. And she pushed her child back behind her leg, stood a little taller, and said, 'That's the last time, too. Never going to hear another Syldoon bastard name him again. Anyone names him now, it will be me, on my terms. You had the best of him, the lot of you. Had the best years, the best Gless there was, left me with the rind. The rind and some coins. Now you get out of here, you son of a whore, and you step inside my door again, you better believe you won't be stepping out again.'"

"That is harsh."

"But true enough. I started to say something else, no idea what, as there weren't nothing else worth saying, but she stopped me anyway with a 'Go on. Get. Show me your backside, Syldoon, then never show me anything again.' She started crying again, but the controlled sort, jaw clenched, eyes as forgiving as wet stones.

"Never felt as low in my entire sorry life. Gless was like my big brother, and she had the right of it—I knew Gless better than her, would be like to mourn him harder, even. And that rankled her as bad as anything. She was right, we left her next to nothing, even with the coins.

"So I walked out. And if I ever see that horsey woman again, it will be too soon for both of us."

I wished there was something I could have said or done to lessen his load, but both of us knew there wasn't.

Vendurro seemed to sense what I was thinking, as he shrugged. "Anyway. Sorry for yammering on about it."

I suppose being a sympathetic ear while he unburdened himself was meager balm, but better than none at all. Unless talking about it made it worse. "I'm sorry you had to be the one to deliver the news, is all. But as you said, at least you put it behind you now. If you ever want to talk about it, or Glesswik, I'm always happy to listen."

He nodded and started to ask me something when Braylar, Hewspear, and Mulldoos came into the captain's quarters.

Braylar said, "It is time. Come."

I asked, "The Caucus?"

Mulldoos replied, "No. Time to dig a privy. I got your shovel, you skinny bastard."

I stood, and Vendurro and I followed them out. I suspected digging a privy might have actually been a preferable way to spend the afternoon.

We took the more circuitous circuit around the outer wall of Sunwrack, passing Towers large and small. Our own small company was the Tower Commander, three key captains, and a small number of lieutenants. I wondered if Soffjian or any of the other Memoridons would be attending, but then guessed the Caucus must have only been for the Syldoon soldiers. Which made me feel even stranger to be the only non-Syldoon in the group. Each of them had the same charcoal-colored tunic with a badge of the Jackal Tower on the left breast, and trousers, with a wide sash the shade of wine around their waists. And of course belts. With weapons. They never seemed to go anywhere without those.

I was a little surprised by that. In Anjuria and most any other civilized place in the world, men did not bear weapons in the presence of the highest lords, in particular kings and high priests, and I would have assumed this held true for emperors.

Mulldoos was the closest to me, and while I would have preferred posing the question to someone else, anyone else, I asked him.

He looked down as if surprised that he had forgotten actually buckling the thing on that morning. He tapped his falchion hilt. "What, this? Never go anywhere without one."

"But with so much bad blood between the various Towers, doesn't that invite, well, bad blood in the streets?"

"Bloodshed comes whether she's invited or no. Pushy entitled bitch, bloodshed."

I watched the leaders of another nearby Tower filing out and took care to lower my voice a little. Their color and cut of costume were essentially identical, although the badges were obviously different, marking them as men of the Elk Tower. "But isn't it more likely, with everyone armed all the time? And isn't the Emperor worried?"

Vendurro overheard and replied, "Good thing to be worried, when you're an emperor. Guessing the blades remind him to take care and not sit easy. And as to the likelihood," he thumbed a leather cord that was looped over the pommel and hilt of his sword. "Like to be inspired from tribes like Cap's over there, but we got the peace cords on. Now, they only slow you down a short bit if you got intent to draw and slaughter somebody, but someone with a cooler head will work some sense into you as you struggle to unknot the plaguing thing. Course, there's a way to tie the lash so it looks like the weapon is snug and secure, only it takes a quick flick to actually release the thing."

Mulldoos added, "Course, anyone sees you using a false knot on that string, especially if it's two or more someones to your one, well, you won't be worrying about tying anything anymore."

"Why is that?" I asked.

Mulldoos wiggled his fingers. "On account of you needing these to tie anything. Or hold a sword. Or a spoon. You see any poor bastard with a club hand and no fingers to speak of, it's a good bet he got caught using a false string."

Vendurro said, "I always wondered why Lloi's folk left her with the nubs at the bottom there. No better than no fingers at all."

"Crueler, truth be told," Mulldoos replied. "Taunts you into remembering the fingers you once had. Better to have nothing left at all."

"You thinking that's why they didn't chop them off in the entirety?"

"How should I know?" Mulldoos replied. "I'm not a plaguing pagan savage who wipes his ass with grass."

Vendurro nodded, and then asked, "Do they do that? Wipe their asses with grass?"

Mulldoos looked at the younger man, shook his head, and said, "You sure do ask some queer questions sometimes, boy."

We continued walking, most of Jackal Tower quiet. The other Towers walking before or behind, keeping a respectful distance in each case, were equally somber. Tense. You might have thought we were attending a funeral or an execution. Though I supposed it was possible we were, peace strings or no. The tale Braylar told about his father being murdered did nothing to quiet those fears.

Even with each Tower limited in the number of men going to the

Caucus, with so many filing out into the streets, it was still a sizable group heading through the city. Some chose to walk away from the Avenue and its massive wall, but most Tower Syldoon hugged the rim of the city, careful to allow plenty of distance between them.

As we walked, I moved to catch up to Hewspear and his long legs, wondering if his visit had gone any better than Vendurro's. I was almost reluctant to ask, but as ever, my need to know overrode other considerations.

"So," I said, "Did your grandson appreciate the flute you brought him?"

Hewspear looked down at me, his namesake spear left behind at the Tower, his flanged mace hanging on his hip. It also had a peace string, though knotted differently. "He did. Though I did not have much opportunity to see him enjoy it." He sounded melancholy enough that I instantly regretted prying. No wonder Vendurro and I got on fairly well—neither one of us seemed to know when to keep our mouths shut.

"His mother?" I asked, knowing the answer, but compelled by the inevitability of it all.

Hewspear nodded. "I had hoped. . . well, it doesn't much matter what I hoped. An old man's hopes don't matter a tremendous amount." Then he stood taller, and there was steel in his voice. "And yet. My grandchild is my last link to my son, and I won't have it severed by the likes of her."

That was unexpected, and although I suddenly felt like continuing this exchange could only end with me being saddened, disappointed, or horrified, I proceeded just the same. "What are you going to do?"

Hewspear kept his gaze ahead, steady, stern, suddenly not very grandfatherly at all. "She will allow me to see my blood, and not poison him against me, or she will find herself driven from the city, never to return, leaving behind her child, her sister, her mother, and all that she holds dear. She will decide her own fate. I'd hoped to be less severe with her, but I have few enough years left, and my patience is not what is once was."

After passing twenty or so of the prime Towers and all the barracks and granaries and stables between them, we left the wall and headed west, through residential districts, and then past Tanner's Lane, with its overpowering stench of urine, feces, and decaying flesh, and I saw several children out already carrying bags, looking for shit in the streets and alleys. While tanners were often relegated to the outskirts of the cities because of the terrible smell and filth, with the Towers girding the entirety of Sunwrack, the best they could do was position them in the poorest district. A few blocks later we were free of the stench.

Everything had looked so orderly from high up in Jackal Tower, but on the ground it was chaos. The moneychanger's lodge was full of people shouting and holding different currencies. Livestock was everywhere—oxen pulling cairns, goats with peculiar wavy horns, foraging pigs. Criers with staffs lined with bells marched among the Thurvacians, calling out something about this market or that bazaar. Girls and boys in simple shrifts carried trays and boxes of peaches, dates, and oranges to be had for pennies.

We crossed another plaza and round fountain, pigeons bursting up into the air at our approach and settling back to the ground after we passed. Some temporary tents and stalls sold merchandise, but the main attraction here was the halls where cloth and spices were sold, and the plaza was even more thick with colorful Thurvacians than pigeons, only they scattered more slowly.

Several streets later, we eventually emerged into a more open space where the buildings gave way, across a plaza from a massive structure larger than any castle or citadel. Straight ahead of us, up several stone steps, was the rounded frontage to an immense building that looked to be much longer on two sides. It was a dozen or more stories tall, the bottom level replete with hundreds of columns, the middle with arched spaces between still more columns, and the upper level with thinner columns still.

"What is this place?" I asked.

Hewspear answered, "This, my young scholar, is the Imperial Hippodrome. There are a few smaller hippodromes on the outskirts of Sunwrack, one of them Jackal, but none remotely approaching the size and grandeur of this one."

It was an extraordinary sight, I had to admit. There were two towering freestanding columns in the plaza in front of the Imperial Hippodrome that were impossible to miss, rising nearly as high as the hippodrome itself. As we got closer, I saw that both columns were carved with elaborate bas reliefs from top to bottom. Starting at the base and spiraling up, the frieze on each column told a different story of some military campaign, with incredibly detailed images of Syldoon warriors, some mounted and charging their way across a plain, others in tight infantry formation marching toward Anjurians in some epic battle, astoundingly ornate. There had to be thousands of figures on each one—soldiers primarily, but also Memoridons, sailors, engineers, builders, camp followers, and on and on.

The left column had a statue of a golden sun flaring at the top, while the one on the right had a golden statue of a leopard roaring.

When I asked about that, Braylar replied, "The statue on the left is dedicated to the imperial seat itself, with the sigil of the blazing sun; the one on the right is replaced each time a new emperor claims the throne, in this case bearing Cynead's emblem, as he hails from the Leopard Tower."

Imperial guards flanked the main entrance to the hippodrome, splendid in their alternating obsidian and gold enameled scale corselets and gleaming helms, crowned with the black horsehair plumes, each with the finely worked quiver and bow at their hips, long embattled shields at their sides, and spears with oddly spiraling spearheads on top.

The bas relief motif was continued on the columns supporting the hippodrome proper, though on a much smaller scale, with the carvings of each column depicting the animals or objects that correlated to the various Towers: cranes or eagles in flight, lions lounging, a boar charging out of the brush, a chariot thundering over the ground, horses rearing, a galleon cresting a wave, goats navigating a slim cliff on a mountain, griffins battling in midair.

We passed between the largest exterior columns and into the Imperial Hippodrome. It was open to the sky, though there was some kind of canvas cover at the top that extended out to provide some relief from the sun or rain for those seated in the top section. There was a vast oval field in the center, rich dark earth, nearly black, and on either end, several smaller rectangular sections, fenced off. But only smaller in comparison—they were still much larger than any list the Anjurians jousted in.

Vendurro saw me staring and laughed. "The middle there, that's where they hold the holiday races. Well, any old races they want, really. And mock pitched battles."

"And those other fenced off sections, on either end?"

"Training. Grappling. Archery. Drills."

Commander Darzaak led our small group up the stairs between the rows of benches. There looked to be roughly three-quarters of the Towers accounted for already. They were assembling in the same general area of the stadium, but leaving rows between each group. Some men glanced around suspiciously, a few from various Towers that had alliances of some sort exchanged greetings and small talk, but most simply ignored the fact that there were any other Towers in the immediate vicinity.

We chose a row further up from the field, with only a few Towers filing in behind us. The Emperor was nowhere to be seen yet. Even with the distance between them, and some Towers still entering, the hippodrome could have seated a hundred thousand spectators, so the hundreds of Syldoon were still dwarfed by the space.

After the last of the Tower Commanders and attendants were seated, I was surprised to see the Memoridons enter and move to the highest rows, sliding behind the assembly like silent shadows, witnesses but separate even from the Towers they served.

I was about to ask if that was strange when the broad wooden gates on the far end of the hippodrome opened inward. Four Imperial soldiers led the procession, leopard skin cloaks hanging from clasps on their lamellar cuirasses so they draped on the ground behind them. They bore large brass horns, so slender near the mouthpiece they looked like something floral and fragile, gently widening as they curled under the arm and back up over the shoulder until they ended in a broad bell. Four horn blasts silenced the Towers and announced the arrival of what could only be the Emperor.

Several men followed the hornblowers in, a pair each carrying huge wooden drums with skins so large they must have been sewn from the hides of several beasts. The horns kept blowing as the men set the drums up at an angle on wooden stands near the center of the hippodrome, directly in front of the assembled Towers.

The hornblowers took positions on the outside, the blasts coming until a bare-chested man stood behind each of the drums, and they ceased as the drummers began to play, booming their instruments until they were slick with sweat and then suddenly ceasing. The horns broke in again immediately with three quick bursts before stopping as well. The silence stretched on until I nearly whispered a question to Vendurro. But as I was leaning in to do so, it was suddenly broken.

Two chariot teams burst through the gate on the far end and raced in opposite directions. They passed each other once, wheels spinning so fast the spokes were a blur, dark earth churned up in their wakes, spitting long trails, the drivers hunkered low, reins in one hand, tall conical brass helms flashing, the long Imperial double standard whipping behind held aloft by a second man in the chariot.

As they continued another pass, I leaned over to Vendurro as they passed a second time. "Do the Syldoon still use chariots in battle?"

Mulldoos overheard and answered first. "Nah, ain't seen a battlefield in centuries. Pompous bastard likes his history and tradition though. Like a dog likes its balls."

Well. That clarified things.

After a third pass, the chariots slowed and came to rest on either side of the dais, the horse's sides pumping like bellows.

The curved horns blared again, and all eyes went back to the gate as the Emperor entered the hippodrome on a huge dappled stallion, a long white cloak draped from his shoulder covering the horse's hindquarters. On either side, he was flanked by a slave holding a long chain leading a leopard, a thick leather collar around the animal's neck. The large cats moved languidly.

The Emperor had dark hair, almost perfectly black, which made the single round patch of white on his crown stand out like alabaster. His face looked lined, but not excessively so, and he appeared a man of middle years, holding himself exactly as I imagined an emperor might: erect, confident, head high, at ease. The sort of man who felt in command of any situation and was likely right.

A long column of Imperial Syldoon followed him in, enough to deter any threat from the assembly. The soldiers were all armed identically, long shields with the crenellated tops and tapered points bearing the charges of leopard heads on one side of the field and sunbursts on the other. Each soldier bore the slightly twisted conical steel helms, and their mail hauberks were broken up in the front by several iron bands. Brass bazubands on their forearms, brass greaves covering their shins, long spears balanced on their shoulders with those spiral heads, and on their left hips, quivers with composite bows and arrows. And of course, the requisite long surokas.

The horns blew one last long, strong note together and the Emperor dismounted and strode up the small dais, his cloak trailing unceremoniously behind him in the black dirt. I was surprised he didn't have attendants carrying it. I expected the Emperor to slowly take the stairs, appreciating the moment, the attention. Instead, he ascended quickly—not rushed, but purposeful, as if he couldn't wait to stand before his people and deliver whatever message he had summoned them far and wide to hear.

The members of the various Towers were silent in anticipation. But it was the kind of silence that still spoke tension, frustration, discontent. Several groups did not appear overly fond of their Emperor, at least anywhere near us.

A herald stepped forward and began intoning, "All assembled at this Caucus, pay tribute to his illustrious Emperor Cynead, first of his name, Sovereign of the grand Empire, Lord Protector of Principalities, Premier Prince of—"

The Emperor put his hand on the herald's shoulder. "Bah. They know who I am, Isquinn. Spare us all, please." He projected loudly enough that everyone in attendance could hear—this wasn't meant for the herald's ears only.

Isquinn turned ten shades of red, but bowed and stepped back, leaving Cynead in the center of the dais alone.

The Emperor called out, voice clear, strong, powerful. "What you do not know, of course, is why you have been called here today. It's been some time since our last Caucus. Since I was sworn in, if I recall, or just thereabouts. So, it was high time we had another. Well, presuming we had something worth discussing. And as it happens, we do."

Though I had only just seen the man for the first time, I found myself captivated, despite the ill feelings bubbling everywhere around me.

Cynead continued. "As you all know, our Empire not only survives, but thrives, because every Tower Commander, every Tower soldier, embodies the same qualities—ambition, courage, cunning. And of course, the willingness to strike fast and hard, to make enemies in order to achieve ends. We battle each other endlessly for position, for power, for wealth. Of course, this is true of other kingdoms as well—the Anjurian barons squabble and stab each other in the back, the fieflords scheme with their brethren to unseat each other. But our culture not only allows for this kind of brutal and pragmatic maneuvering. . . it fosters it, encourages it. Demands it, even. That is the Syldoon way. It is what brought me to my throne, and every conniving and bloodthirsty emperor before me."

There were some mumbles and rumbles of disapproval, but Cynead raised his hand. "Oh, do not mistake me. I acknowledge some have come to power by exceptional guile and diplomacy, entreating rather than defeating. But no matter how an Emperor managed to secure the crown from his predecessor, you all must admit: very, very few have died of old age while occupying the throne. That simply is not our way."

Someone in one of the front rows shouted, "An Emperor holds the throne as long as he is able, no longer!"

I expected guards to rush forward and seize him for the outburst, or at least for Cynead to rebuke him. But the Emperor only smiled. "Exactly so. And still, even the strongest, most competent, and savvy of Emperors only sit the throne for a short time. The Syldoon way is to seize, to overthrow, to manipulate and orchestrate. They do not call this place Capital of Coups for no reason."

There were a few chuckles, and Cynead continued. "But therein lies our greatest problem as well. Not solely of our age, but of every age that has come before. Our strength is our greatest weakness. We are so busy constantly jockeying, bullying, trading, and making secret exchanges in the name of seizing power, that we are unable to achieve as much as we could. Our own system limits us."

Another Syldoon two rows down stood and called out, "We are the mightiest empire the world has ever seen! I'll take that kind of limitation!"

Several around us laughed and murmured agreement. Emperor Cynead handled the rebuttal with aplomb. "That is what we tell ourselves. But we have stagnated, my brothers and sisters."

One Syldoon a row behind me hissed and Mulldoos said, so loudly I was worried it would carry to the Emperor's ears, "Shit rhetoric!"

Always a way with words.

But Cynead maintained the smile and easy command as a few others hissed or openly booed. "When was the last time our borders moved outward? And don't tell me about the plague. No one conquers during a plague. But think back—when was the last time our neighbors trembled, fearing our advance, or paid tribute to keep us from storming into their lands and simply doing what we do best—seizing?"

Someone cried, "The Empire is large, vast. Bigger than any two kingdoms combined. The wealthiest as well. How else would you define might?"

"And that size, that vastness, was all achieved long before our lifetimes. In the last hundred years, we have done nothing save maintain our borders and trade routes, survive our various coups and assassination, and tread water. History does not remember stagnation. It remembers greatness, achievement, growth, power."

One Tower Commander stood long enough to say, "Growth or not, every kingdom the world over covets the kind of power we have."

"Do we measure ourselves by what other kingdoms think, or want?" the Emperor asked. "No. We are the Syldoon. And we deserve more than to simply clutch onto the lands our forefathers gave to us. We deserve far more than that. But our very nature prevents us from achieving it. I took the throne myself three years ago. Before that, Thumaar held it for longer than usual, but had the plague to contend with, so was lucky not to lose more than he did. Before him, every rule has lasted less than a handful of years. Not time enough to put serious plans in place, let alone carry them to fruition. Our rulers come and go, the power shifts, and our sons do not inherit it. Everything about the Syldoon is short-lived, finite, and limited. Even our greatness, such as it is. Unless we are brave enough to do what must be done to change. To grow, ourselves. To not only solidify what we have and who we are, but to extend our borders, our influence, our might. And that is why you were summoned here today."

Several Syldoon stood up, shouting one thing or another, impossible to figure out as they spoke over each other. I was surprised the Emperor didn't try to silence them, demand their acquiescence, but it seemed clear that the Syldoon handled things much differently than Anjurians. The Syldoon might have plotted against each other in the shadows, but here, there were no apparent repercussions for speaking plainly or giving voice to dissent.

Cynead waited the storm out, let them shout, and finally raised both hands. The hippodrome quieted again, and he said, "I will explain my plan to you. In time, and in detail. I have mapped out a way for us to all move forward, to achieve what we most need. But for today, I wanted to share one thing with you. I have discovered a way to save us from ourselves. To give us the time to build something, something that history will never forget.

"Our ambition is our greatest strength, as I said, but it all too often results in a dead or exiled emperor. And a new regime. And plans and counterplans from various Towers to undermine that one. And so on. It just won't do. While the kingdoms around us are not our models or inspiration, there is one thing that they have that we do not, that creates stability, allows for far-reaching enterprise. They have monarchs who rule for life."

There was booing and hissing from several quarters, longer and more pronounced than before.

Again, Cynead nodded as if he expected this, waited it out. And then he raised his voice. "Our culture, our rule, our very way of life rewards ambition and ruthlessness, ability and drive. But at the same time, our lack of stability prevents us from accomplishing all that we are able. Today, a new era begins. You see, today my rule is permanent."

One Tower Commander stood and yelled, "You presume too much! Three years on the throne! Three! Call a Caucus after you've had it a tenyear!"

There was some laughter and another ruddy-faced Commander stood. "Let's hear him out. What changes do you propose, Your Imperial Majesty?"

"Of course you want to hear him out, you halfwit lackey!" the first shouted.

Others stood and had their turn, those who supported the Emperor, and those who vehemently disagreed, though more often directing it toward the supporters than the Emperor himself. Still, I was amazed by the freedoms these once-slaves were afforded in expressing themselves. If they were in a kingdom assembly hall, some would have been branded traitors and clapped in irons.

I quickly figured out that hissing signified disagreement, whistling, consent.

Cynead raised his arms and held them aloft until the hippodrome fell silent again. "The Syldoon power has always been too equally dispersed. I'm not talking about our soldiers, you see, but the Memoridons. Every Tower, allotted their share. But until now, even I hadn't been able to bring more of them into the fold. It was impossible. But no more. Today, anything is possible."

And with that he clapped his hands once. And somewhere a gong sounded, or something like it, but muffled, as if it were behind several walls and far away. But there was no mistaking something ringing, reverberating, heavy, like brass or copper. I suddenly felt something strange, like a wind moving over us, though no breezed stirred. It was a hot gust that didn't shift a single hair or ripple the canvas shade above. Several other Syldoon had felt it as well, as they sought the source, eyes wide in surprise or narrowed in suspicion. But they felt it.

In every pocket of Tower men around the hippodrome, each Commander suddenly reacted in much the same way as if violently struck in the head by some unseen thing, some falling into their comrades, others off their benches, and a few standing and teetering long enough for one of their captains to catch them.

And then the Memoridons who had been sitting in the back rows were slowly walking down the aisle between the benches, toward the dark earth and hippodrome track below. Some cast glances at their stricken Tower Commanders as they passed them. But most of them were staring at Cynead, many with faces blanched or jaw muscles bulging, some with open fear.

Mulldoos saw Soffjian as she passed and said, "Knew that bitch couldn't be trusted. From the start."

She ignored him, all of us in the Jackal Tower, and kept going.

Skeelana looked over at me though, and gave a wan smile, and I felt my stomach wrench. No one else seemed to notice, and then she was facing forward and following Soffjian to the track below.

Hewspear was helping Commander Darzaak regain his seat, and asked. "He has done this thing, hasn't he? Not just here, but all of them?"

Commander Darzaak could only nod, the veins in his forehead thick and winding like gnarled roots, mouth clamped shut, face flushed.

Braylar looked at me and said, "Well. It seems he had a faster reader."

I wanted to object that had he trusted me earlier, I could have made much more headway, or that perhaps he should have gathered his research in a more timely fashion. Or not killed the previous potential translator. But I held my tongue on all counts.

Though it wouldn't have mattered if I hadn't—the hippodrome erupted just then. The majority of the Syldoon attending stood and began shouting, cursing, shaking their fists and pointing at the Emperor. One even started to unwind the peace string on his sword, but before he got very far his Tower Commander ordered him to stop and two of his Tower brothers grabbed him to be sure he did.

But the Syldoon raged in near unison, all but the Commanders themselves, many of whom were still regaining their wits and sitting dumbly or with their heads in their hands.

Cynead had just accomplished something no emperor before had done—he seized control of all the Memoridons in Sunwrack. If the displays of power by Soffjian and Skeelana were any indication, Cynead's scope was now unchecked. No amount of cursing would undo that, and anyone who dared draw steel would find themselves blasted into madness and death before they could take one step to use it. He had somehow managed to orchestrate the largest coup in Syldoon history without shedding a single drop of blood.

The Memoridons gathered around the dais, many looking confused or lost, glancing at each other uncertainly, back into the stands at their former Commanders, a few looking at the Emperor and looking away just as quickly. Soffjian, I noted, stared straight ahead, back rigid, eyes fixed on some section of stone directly in front of her.

With a nod from the Emperor, the hornblowers blasted out their notes, over and over until the Syldoon finally reined their rage in, quieting again, at least enough for Cynead to be heard. "I realize this comes as something of a shock. And I apologize for not delivering this news in easier fashion. But this is the way of things now. You lords assembled here command the entire might of the Syldoon armies. You are the body of the Empire. But I am its head. Someone said an Emperor commands only so long as strong enough to do so. True enough. And I assure you, I am now strong enough to command a very, very long time. Until dead, I'm afraid. Natural causes, of course."

One of the braver Tower Commanders stood and said, "Thief. Coward. You stole what was ours by right, Cynead. But if you think that makes you safe, you're mad."

"Oh, Commander Caruvik," Cynead said, smiling, "No one is truly safe. But some less so than others." He raised and dropped his arm and one of his Memoridons stepped forward, pointing at Caruvik, fingers splayed.

Commander Caruvik dropped to his knees, covering his ears, swatting at some invisible things assaulting his head, slammed his face on the bench. Most stepped away, but two of his captains moved forward and tried to help him back to his feet. But Caruvik started wailing, swinging his arms at them, knocking them back, and the wailing grew shrill, pitch rising, "Enough," Cynead commanded, and the Memoridon lowered her arm and stepped back into the fold.

Commander Caruvik stayed curled up like that, body jerking, but the spasms slowed down. Emperor Cynead called out, "Now then. You are the lords of the Empire. That hasn't changed. I would have you with me, have your support. However, what I will not have is rebellion, in word or action. The Age of Coups is over. Together, we will achieve things our forefathers never dreamed possible; we will grow this Empire to heights and greatness they never dared attempt. Together. Work with me, and your rewards will be boundless, and you will be remembered in history and song. But make no mistake at all: work against me, and I will crush you. Without thought, without remorse.

"Tomorrow is a new day. We will walk into it together, and I will apprise you of the specifics of my plans. But for today, I trust you to lead. Speak to your Towers, tell them of the new state of things, and prepare to move forward. That is all. Dismissed."

The Syldoon, angry, sullen, and teeth-gritting to a man, watched their Emperor climb down the dais and mount his horse, throwing the long cloak out of the way before it draped across the flanks of the beast. The hornblowers blew one final note, and then the imperial procession started making its way out of the stadium, Emperor first, leopard handlers second, the Memoridons a short distance after, and the soldiers, charioteers, and musicians lining up to take the rear.

Commander Darzaak looked at his captains, splotches of red around his prominent sideburns. "Well. That was unexpected. Come on. Got some planning of our own to do."

He started down the stairs with us filing in when we heard a voice from behind us. Sibilant, slithery. Oddly suggestive and sexual. We all turned and looked. A woman was standing there, her close-cropped fair hair even lighter in the sun, a leopard pin on the breast of her ash-gray jacket, a scarlet sash visible around her tunic underneath.

Braylar said, "Rusejenna. Looking severely lovely as ever, I see."

Rusejenna looked him up and down and replied, "Captain Killcoin. Looking. . . precisely as you always do. Your presence is required. Your men as well."

Commander Darzaak said, "Busy itinerary today, our Emperor. Where does he expect us?"

Rusejenna smiled, cold, edged with what I couldn't help suspecting was a hint of cruelty. "Oh, my mistake. I should have been more clear. Just you, Commander Darzaak, and your Captain Killcoin there and his cohorts. To the Circus. The rest of your captains and crew may go." She returned her gaze to Braylar. "And do try not to be late. One thing to keep an Emperor waiting when he is leagues and leagues away. Quite another when he can hear you dawdling."

"You and my sister have a great deal in common," Braylar replied. "The two of you will conspire like cats."

"So very droll. I am sure the Emperor will be endlessly amused." Then Rusejenna turned and left without waiting for a response.

It was difficult to tell if the other Jackal Tower captains were more irritated by the exclusion, or relieved.

One with thick purple lips and a weak chin said, "That haughty bitch. Acts as if sucking the Emperor's cock makes her special. Just makes her an expensive whore."

"And a powerful one," Braylar said. "And perceptive. Don't forget to add that your list, Belvick. Whatever else you say about Imperial Mems, know that there is a very good chance they will eventually hear you."

Belvick scowled at Braylar and managed a half-hearted harrumph. "I don't need etiquette lessons from the likes of you."

"No, just survival lessons. But suit yourself. Denigrate the Mems as much as you like. But wait until I am several streets over, yes?"

Belvick looked away and said something to another captain. But nothing else about Rusejenna, I noted. So perhaps he wasn't as large a fool as he seemed. Perhaps.

The other Jackal captains looked eager to get back to their Tower as quickly as possible.

Commander Darzaak might have been hiding his anger at being ordered about behind clenched teeth, but he always seemed to have them clamped tight, so it was difficult to tell for sure. "Guessing we're all about to get fucked in the ass by a big angry horse. Nothing for it but to put a bit in your mouth and take it. You heard the snow snake. Best get moving."

We walked away from the Imperial Hippodrome, continuing north while the rest of the small Jackal contingent walked south back toward their Tower. They didn't look back at us, and we didn't at them. Except for me, swiveling my head around looking at both like a simpleton.

Our small group moved down side streets away from the hippodrome and most of the traffic that clogged the main avenues in Sunwrack. Here and there we ran into some Thurvacians, and a few stray dogs, but otherwise the path we picked wasn't congested at all.

Mulldoos said, "Got to hand it to the cagey bastard. Really got a flair for the dramatic, he does."

"Indisputable," Braylar replied, marching forward.

Commander Darzaak was in the lead, keeping a fast pace despite short legs and being bowlegged, heading toward this encounter with far more stoicism than I could muster. I'd never been within one hundred yards of a king, and now I was not only about to be in an audience with an Emperor, but one who likely had very bad things planned for us. I couldn't stop myself from asking, voice lowered so not to arouse any anger from the Commander several steps ahead, "Do you think he, Cynead that is, suspects your affinity for Thumaar?"

Hewspear said, "Oh, you can be sure he is well aware of our affiliations. The Jackals supported Thumaar's own coup, and were staunch supporters during his entire reign. And I'm sure Cynead knows we would gladly welcome him back, if such an opportunity presented itself. What he might or might not suspect is that we are actively plotting to make it so."

"When Emperors seize power by force, don't they, I mean, wouldn't they—?"

"Destroy those factions supporting the previous ruler? Sometimes yes, sometimes no." Hewspear took a few more steps and added, "More often, they simply keep a vigilant eye on them."

"To prevent them from doing whatever it is you are doing to bring Thumaar back to power?"

He looked down at me, smiling, again a kindly grandfather. For the moment. "Just so, Arki."

"So he probably knows, then? Or strongly suspects?"

Before Hewspear could respond, Mulldoos turned around and said, "Shut your yaps. We're here."

We had stepped onto a broad avenue, and a little further down was a domed building that was gigantic, easily the largest construction in this district, with multiple smaller domes flanking a massive dome in the middle that was hundreds of feet high and brilliant in color, with numerous panels of stained glass. Much of the outside of the building was covered in scaffolding, and workers were lying or standing on platforms at several spots, though it was hard to tell what they were doing exactly, they were so high up.

The marble colonnaded entrance was bracketed by statues of what I assumed were Emperors or other noteworthy Tower Commanders, looking suitably somber, forbidding, and stately.

"What is this place?" I asked.

Vendurro said, "Great Circus, they call it. Name like that usually sets up a place to be real disappointing like, but I been there a time or two, and it's actually something to see."

We passed into the interior of the front hall that led to the domed sections further in. The grey and pink marble walls were broken up by large windows with latticed screens of mahogany, and stone benches between matching copper urns, and as we walked down the broad hall, I couldn't help but notice that the building was mostly empty, except for some dusty workers we passed.

I said, "I take it with the work being done, this place will be—"

"Deserted," the captain replied. "I expect that was no accident."

The hall ended and we entered what must have been one of the smaller domed rooms. The entirety of the inside of the domed ceiling was painted, and while some murals were cracked and badly in need of repair, they were still magnificent, and the apse at one end no less so, with spectacular mosaics and paintings, grottos with Syldoonian champions from ages past, mullioned windows with stained-glass depictions of battles, gardens, a profusion of animals, scholars, priests, merchant princes, and so much color it was dizzying. The entire room had an epic grandeur, speaking of conquest and artistry, rebellions and subtle line and contour, excess and so much exquisite detail it was stunning.

Another short hall and then we came to three wide arched openings. We stepped through, and even realizing we were entering the large central domed portion of the building, I still wasn't prepared for the immensity of the space. We passed towering bleachers, and my eyes were immediately drawn up. While the hippodrome was colossal, it was open to the air, whereas the dome was not. Well, mostly. At its highest point, several hundreds of feet up, there was a sizable circular section open to the sky, and several portions of the dome had panels of stained glass with the scenes and characters writ large enough to make out from so far below, where the entirety of the space was flooded with alternating color and shadow.

The floor changed from marble to parquet, alternating squares of dark and light wood, and it was only then I noticed that the interior wasn't completely deserted. A figure was sitting on a wooden chair in the middle of the floor, with three figures standing behind. I was also surprised to see that there were some acrobats practicing, two of them dangling in the air from what looked like two long ribbons suspended from some apparatus on the ceiling, though the acrobats were well out of earshot. And then I saw the Imperial Syldoon further back on all sides, in the shadows against the walls, backs to the endless murals and statues that rimmed the entire room.

Commander Darzaak slapped his meaty hands on his thighs. "Well, let's get this over with." He started for the center.

Braylar said, "I always enjoy a private audience. So very quaint and personal."

We followed the Commander across the floor toward the group, and though hardly shocking, it became clear that seated figure was Emperor Cynead, and the three standing were the Memoridons Rusejenna, Soffjian, and Skeelana.

The Emperor was leaning back in his chair, and he had given up the white (and no doubt filthy) cloak, but otherwise was dressed the same as he had been a short time ago in the hippodrome, in rich cloth, but nothing ostentatious. Even his plaque belt of alternating sunbursts and leopard heads was fairly subdued. You might have thought we were meeting a rich merchant and not the leader of the greatest empire in the world.

"Welcome, men of Jackal Tower. I do appreciate you meeting me on such short notice and," he gestured about the huge empty dome, "in such an unusual locale."

Commander Darzaak bowed slightly, though not so much as I would have expected. "Begging your pardon, Your Imperial Majesty, but I don't imagine we had much choice in the matter."

Cynead laughed, rich, unforced, the sound of a man clothed in more power than any one person should possess. "I must say, Commander Darzaak, it is such a wonderfully ironic pleasure to see one of the most cunning and duplicitous Towers led by a man so extraordinarily direct."

Darzaak bristled, his thick jaw clenched tight enough threaten his own teeth. "Again, begging your pardon, but surely you didn't summon us here simply to dart insults at us. I mean, you could have done that anywhere, and probably enjoyed it more with a big audience in the Citadel. So, seeing as how you value directness, maybe you'd like to engage in some. Why are we here?"

Cynead crossed his legs, leaned back further, tapped his chin twice and looked at Rusejenna, laughing again. "You see. I told you this wouldn't take all that long." He turned back to Darzaak. "You are correct, we are not in the Citadel for a reason. There are many ears, and here," he surveyed the Circus Dome, and I looked past him and the Memoridons, to the acrobats in the far distance. "It is only us. Perhaps one of the few places in this teeming city where that is the case."

The Emperor shifted and faced Braylar. "So then, in the interest of directness, let's begin with you, shall we, Captain Killcoin? Word on the wind is you have been quite the busy adventurer in Anjuria."

I expected Braylar, gifted liar that he was, to delay, distract, or downplay, but perhaps following his Commander's lead, he said, "I have indeed, Your Majesty. All in the name of Empire."

"Ahh, yes. But of course. The question remains though, whose Empire?"

The captain didn't falter in gaze or delivery. "Why, Lord Emperor, I do hope it was in the cause of every member of the Empire, great and small."

Emperor Cynead slapped his thigh. "Yes, see, this is the manner of directness I am more accustomed to. Sly and self-serving. But as much as I enjoy the dance, I will follow your good Commander's lead and mince no further. You were in Anjuria carrying out Thumaar's initiatives—" Commander Darzaak started to speak, but Cynead overrode him. "Do not dare interrupt your Emperor, especially only to beg pardon you shall not be granted. They *were* Thumaar's, there is no disputing that. At the time, I allowed you to, so they defaulted to mine, and I'm not especially concerned with ownership there, but with what else you were doing in the region."

Commander Darzaak waited to be sure he wasn't interrupting, and then said, "Captain Killcoin was there following orders. Which you endorsed."

"Yes, yes, to be sure." He looked over his shoulder. "And what else was the leal captain doing in the kingdom, Rusejenna?"

She grinned, vulpine. "Oh, he was trying to do what you were, Your Majesty, only slower and more clumsily."

Emperor Cynead smiled and nodded. "I suspected as much before. There were a few factions who were searching for the secret to mastering the Memoridons." He waited for protests or hot denial, but getting none, continued. "Oh, yes, I know of your little excursions to libraries and crypts and other dusty holds. That much has been confirmed. And while I sympathize with your covert efforts to research ways of controlling the Memoridons, obviously guilty of it myself, only more efficient, I am well within my rights to invoke the Fifth Man. You broke fealty by conducting the research without informing me, as it violates one of the most basic tenets, the Memoridon Doctrine, codified almost from our inception."

Darzaak started to speak but Cynead overrode him. "Yet there is more. Your man there, Commander Darzaak, broke into a tomb and looted a memory weapon out of our mystic past, but did not report it. That same man enlisted the aid of rogue witches in order to cure himself along the way, again in direct violation of the Doctrine. And when I recalled him from Anjuria, instead of opting to obey immediately, he and his little band chose instead to scurry across the kingdom on their own initiative. And it is known the Jackals have endured my reign, but never supported it."

Cynead nodded. "Yes, I would be well within my rights to invoke the Fifth Man. Other Emperors have done so for far less. The only reason I have not already is that today has been tumultuous. The Towers are surely going to have a rough adjustment to the loss of their Memoridons. I don't want to make the transition more burdensome by an alarming proclamation of the Fifth. But if it comes to it, it might serve as a good example just now. How we proceed will depend all on you. But thanks to a well-placed informant, I at least know what my tricky Towers have been up to."

Mulldoos glared at Soffjian. "Told you the bitch would betray us. Betrayed the whole lot of us."

Soffjian remained still, eyes locked forward, arms folded behind her back, jaw tight, that throbbing lightning bolt vein in her forehead the only telltale sign that she was fazed in the slightest.

Mulldoos laid his hand on his falchion, for all the good it would do, and seemed ready to stalk forward to his doom attempting to cut her down. "Always told him it was just a matter of time. Your kind can't be trusted further than I can spit, but you, less than that. Plaguing worst kind of horsecunt alive, backstabbing a brother."

Soffjian kept her gaze level, lightning pulsing, but didn't say a word.

Skeelana, however, had no such trouble. "You were right about the betrayal, just wrong about the bitch. Soffjian didn't know anything about it."

Mulldoos looked ready to spit on the parquet, Commander Darzaak little better, and Braylar was still looking at his sister curiously, as I took a step back, immediately thinking back to the kiss I shared with Skeelana in my room. Before I could stop myself, I blurted, "Why?"

I felt everyone's gaze, but ignored it, focusing on Skeelana who was looking at me with a sad smile. "The Emperor hadn't seized control of all the Memoridons yet. But still, you betrayed us, the Jackals, that is. Why?"

The Emperor allowed the question to hang there, and if the scrutiny made Skeelana squirm, she didn't show it. Instead, she shrugged her shoulders. "The Emperor demanded an audience with me a while back. And that's something you can't say no to, is it? He made it very clear that things were in motion, and soon every Memoridon would be his. I wasn't sure whether to believe him or not." She turned to Cynead. "No offense, Your Majesty."

"None taken." He smiled, arrogant, at ease, and delighting in having everything play out as he hoped.

Skeelana looked back to me, then the rest of the Jackal Syldoon. "I thought about telling you directly, Commander. And maybe I should have. But I gambled on the Emperor pulling off what he claimed. It just didn't make sense to throw my lot in with the losing side. So I investigated as he commanded, and reported back when we returned. Had he been wrong, I would have simply been a traitor to the Jackals. But if he was right, well, I would find a place of prominence among the Leopards and Sun Tower. And as it turned out," she swept her arm up and around at our little assembly, "it was a pretty smart gamble, as far as gambles go."

"Yes," Emperor Cynead said, "your diminutive Memoridon told me all I needed to know about your little treasure hunt. And while that alone doesn't prove you were plotting to use such knowledge directly against me if you happened to obtain it, it is certainly suggestive. And none of that was altogether surprising on your part, though I must admit, did nothing to warm my heart. That is the Syldoon way, to always be on the hunt for an advantage. After all, that is exactly why I was hoping to unearth such secrets myself."

The Emperor leaned forward, uncrossed his legs. "But no. What I was enthralled to learn about was that peculiar weapon," he pointed at Bloodsounder and leaned forward in his chair, eyes lighting up. "Yes, now that was entirely unexpected. I'd heard about such things, but assumed they were either myth to begin with, or if they ever existed, had rusted into oblivion. And yet Skeelana has confirmed that this is truly such a find. Now, a weapon that warns, that is tied into memory magic somehow, that could be of service to the Empire. . . yes, this *is* something very much worth exploring. Show me."

Everyone looked at Braylar, and he twitch-smiled, completely at odds with the murder in his eyes as he stared at Skeelana. Very slowly, the captain pulled Bloodsounder off his belt, held it out, chains draped over one hand, the haft in the other.

The Emperor looked at the weapon, several things flickering across his face—greed, lust, triumph, and possibly fear, or at least hesitation. "Yes, Skeelana mentioned the Deserter Gods. Oh, this is a fabulous find. Fabulous. Two or three times, my men in the field thought they had uncovered a weapon that might prove to be something the poets sang of, a piece of legend. Each time, I was skeptical, and each time, proven right. But now. . . simply fabulous." He beckoned Braylar. "Come closer. And show me the heads when you do."

The captain walked forward a few paces until the Emperor raised a hand, stopping him just short of striking distance. Still, all it would take was one step more. Perhaps it was having three Memoridons behind him, but Cynead didn't seem particularly worried. Rusejenna was the only one who tensed up, and while her arms were at her sides, I noticed the fingers were splayed already.

Braylar took the flail heads in hand, turned them over so the Emperor could see them better. Cynead slapped the armrest. "They are fearsome, for certain. I do hope if we ever see the Gods again, they have a friendlier cast." He moved forward, hardly on his seat at all, again apparently drawn to take the weapon, but holding himself back as well. "Skeelana says you are wracked with pain when separated for very long. Is that true?"

I gawked at her, remembering all the things I had revealed in confidence, assuming she was beholden to the Jackal Tower.

Braylar replied, "Though I wish it were a falsehood, there is no denying that."

"So," the Emperor said, "If you were to hand it to me, just now, would it grieve you?"

Braylar pulled the chains tight, laughing as Rusejenna took a step forward. "Put your hackles down," he said.

She stopped and replied with a tight smile, "Someday, I will dance to your tears, Killcoin."

"And I on your grave." Then he looked at Cynead again. "A little separation would not anguish me. I am happy to hand it over. But I should warn you, Lord Emperor, the bind, the curse, for a lack of a better word, that I am afflicted with. I do not know what will sever it. Nor what might cause it to attach to anyone else. I am hesitant to do anything that might potentially endanger your safety."

Cynead gave a crooked smile. "Oh, I am certain. Your vigilance is duly appreciated, Captain Killcoin. But no, until we have studied this weapon more, and the binding with you, I am in no hurry to handle it myself. Step back."

Braylar did as instructed, and Commander Darzaak said, "Studied, Your Majesty?"

The Emperor clapped once, loudly. "Yes, of course. It is a remarkable find, but as your captain astutely pointed out, a dangerous one as well. We would understand it, how it works, why it binds, uncover its secrets and how to make the most use of its power. This could be a great boon to the Empire. But that all requires study."

Darzaak, as ever, did not disguise his displeasure. "All of my captains are beyond competent—"

"Of course. Or you would not have promoted them. Unless you were myopic and obtuse. Which I know you are not. What of it?"

"Emperor Cynead, I—"

"Commander Darzaak," he mimicked Darzaak's tone. "Come to your point."

"Captain Killcoin can't relinquish the weapon. Not for long. As you know, and heard."

"And?"

Commander Darzaak said, "This study would require him then. I wouldn't willingly turn him over to be experimented on, Lord Emperor."

The Emperor slowly stood up, and after Hewspear he was the tallest person in the dome. "Your will in this matter is irrelevant, Commander. My Memoridons *will* study the weapon and its bond to your captain. You can be certain I do not want to see either destroyed or unduly damaged. But when it comes down to it, Bloodsounder is a prize beyond price, something straight out of misty legends—it is worth a thousand captains."

Just then one of the acrobats off to the side lost her grip on the long ribbon, fell fifteen feet to the floor. A man tried to catch her, but couldn't stop her from slamming into the parquet entirely. We all watched as two men helped her regain her feet, and while she could stand on one leg, the other was twisted badly or broken. They helped her toward an exit on the other side of the vast room, one of her arms over each of their shoulders.

Cynead sighed. "You see. We all risk something. They are an investment, with skills that are oh so difficult to replace. Sometimes there are simply accidents or losses. From high to low, we all risk something." He shook his head and turned his attention back to us. "I appreciate you coming on such short notice, men of Jackal Tower. And willingly. You are dismissed."

The Emperor started to step away from the chair when Captain Killcoin said, "Are we still speaking directly, Your Majesty? I admit, it is not a tongue I am overly accustomed to, but I would try it just once more today, by your leave."

Cynead looked both annoyed and intrigued, but nodded once.

Braylar replied, "What if I refuse? To willingly sacrifice myself on the altar of progress and knowledge? I confess, that prospect does fill me with more kinds of dread than I can articulate."

The Emperor's eyes narrowed. And while there was still a curl to his lips, it was as warm as a reptile's. "Oh, I do think you know. But in the interest of being direct and perfectly clear: you will be hung. I imagine that ought to sever the bond nicely."

Commander Darzaak stepped forward. "I'll be sure the Captain here makes his way when you call for him."

"See that you do. Oh, there is one other thing, Commander Darzaak. You will actually be the first to hear it. I planned on revealing the particulars later. But while I understand how having your Memoridons taken from you is no doubt seen as a crippling blow, it is not my intent to be a despot. They all are bound to me now, and answer directly to me or my own stable of Memoridons. But I know they will serve the Empire best by maintaining their day-to-day roles within the Towers. They will function exactly as they always have, yours to command, provided it does not run afoul of my orders or jeopardize the Empire in any way."

Commander Darzaak turned crimson. "Spies then."

Emperor Cynead smiled again, broad and superior and again nearly righteous in intensity. "Servants of the Empire, Commander. You are dismissed. Return to your Tower, Jackals."

We started marching out, the Commander in the lead, his captains and lieutenants following. I was in the rear, and stopped when I felt a hand on my shoulder.

I turned to see Skeelana looking at me, and I wrenched my shoulder free. She said, "You have every right to be angry, but it's about to get worse. I don't have to tell you this, but I feel I owe it to you. While the Syldoon cannot run without a Memoridon tracking them, you aren't exempt from that either. Not anymore."

"What? What are you talking about?"

She took several steps back, and again offered the melancholy smile that only made me angrier. "It was a lovely kiss though." Then she turned and headed off after the Emperor.

I stood there dumbstruck until I heard Vendurro hiss-shout, "Come on, Arki!" I hurried to catch up, feeling foolish and miserable.

By the time we left the hall at the entrance to the dome, I was close enough to catch Mulldoos saying, "Got to quit taking private meetings with powerful pricks. Just ain't working out for us at all."

Braylar replied, "You are not wrong, Lieutenant. In fact, I would recommend distancing yourself from me altogether, now that I have the Emperor's very unwanted attention."

Commander Darzaak shook his head as he led us to the Jackal Tower, bowlegged but still moving fast. "Wrong, Captain. Dead wrong, as it happens. Or might. The Jackals give up no one to the likes of Cynead. Not now, not ever."

After Hewspear cast a quick glance behind to be sure we weren't being followed, he added, "They have the right of it, Captain. We are in this together, to the last."

Vendurro said, "Aye, Cap. And sure as spit, where we go, the men go. Every last one of us. To the last. Ain't that right, Arki?"

I thought about what Skeelana had told me. Even if I hadn't thrown my lot in with the captain whole and full, there was no room for reservation or regret now. "I can only vouch for myself, and I am a poor shot, and no Syldoon, but yes, I am Captain Killcoin's man."

Braylar nodded twice, then asked, "What would you have me do, Commander?"

The Commander didn't answer right away, and we walked in silence down the Avenue of Towers. I wondered at all the heated conversations that must have been occurring in each massive Tower we passed as news of the Emperor's bloodless coup had spread to every corner of Sunwrack by now. It wouldn't be long before every Thurvacian and Syldoon knew something absolutely unprecedented had happened.

As we passed a large wagon pulled by oxen, Darzaak said, "That whoreson Cynead outfoxed us, for certain. Nothing to be done for that now. But he knows a lot more than I'm comfortable with. Only a matter of time before he uses one of our Memoridons—his Memoridons now, that plaguing cock—against us, roots out our alliance with Thumaar. And when that happens. . . "

Braylar finished, "The Fifth Man might have been the most generous threat we are likely to get."

"True enough. We've got less time than we thought, too. Would have been bad enough, him stealing all our Memoridons, but learning we were scuttling around in the shadows plotting the same thing ourselves? No, time is not our friend. We'll convene the captains. Immediately. I'd like to get word to Thumaar. Could be we don't even have time for that, especially with Whoreson Cynead keeping eyes on us."

A few steps later, Mulldoos said, "Going to sound bereft of sense, I know—"

"First admission of that sort you've ever made," Hewpsear said.

"Plaguing goatcock. But you're right, Commander. Cynead will figure out what we been up to. By torturing Cap here, most like, but could be he just has a memory witch snatch up me or Hew or some other poor bastard, plumb what we know, hang us all for traitors. No time and less. So maybe it's time we pull stakes and break camp. Move to the hills with Thumaar."

Hewspear asked, keeping his voice low, "Are you suggesting seceding? Moving the entirety of Jackal Tower out of Sunwrack?"

"I am, you wrinkled bastard, and you know it."

"You are right," Hewspear said. "That does sound bereft of sense. Entirely. The Emperor is suspicious and no fool. He will have eyes on us, and within us once the Captain's sister and her sisters are back in the fold, reporting every move to Cynead. We could not possibly move our troops without him detecting it and utterly destroying us before we even had half of them to the gates. And even if we somehow managed to get thousands of troops out of Sunwrack, we would be branded deserters, traitors, and enemies of the Empire."

Before Mulldoos could offer a surly rebuttal, Braylar said, "It is a mad plan. But there is one reason it could work. Emperor Cynead is exceedingly clever, but he is also exceptionally arrogant. He has just pulled off the greatest seizure of power in Syldoon history, and is basking in his triumph. While he was suspicious of us before due to our known allegiance to Thumaar, and is doubly, so now having learned of our own efforts to seize the Memoridons ourselves, he also is entirely too confident in his position."

"Meaning?" Commander Darzaak asked brusquely.

"Meaning, my lord, he could not truly conceive of anyone moving against him just now, not after he publicly stripped the Towers of what was inalienably ours for centuries. We might have an opportunity."

Hewspear nodded slowly, but said, "That is so, Captain. But it would be fraught with risk. We have thousands of troops in the middle of the most fortified city in the world, and our sovereign now has weapons on his side on a scale never before seen. If we failed to make it out, we would be obliterated."

Mulldoos replied, "Aye. And if we hold here, we're back to what the Commander said—time ain't doing us any favors just now. We stay, it's not a question of if Horsecunt Cynead figures us out, just when. Better to make a break before he's got the witches stuck in like leeches, reporting our every move. Too late then."

Hewspear started to respond when the Commander held up a hand. "Enough. We'll convene tonight, once we have some walls around us. And I'll hear you all out in full before settling on a course. But make no mistake—every path is slick with a precipice on either side. Only question is which is the widest."

We reached the Jackal Tower. The guards saluted their Commander as we started up the stairs on the outside, spiraling up, and they didn't give any obvious sign that they'd heard anything usual, so maybe the other captains had held their tongues.

But time was assuredly not any ally of ours.

As we ascended, Vendurro broke off first, followed by Hewspear and Mulldoos, and Commander Darzaak bid us farewell as he continued up to his solar.

Braylar closed the door to his room behind us. I avoided his gaze, still feeling guilty over allowing myself to confide in Skeelana, much less kiss her. But also strangely hurt and acutely disappointed.

The captain said, "The Commander will send for me soon. I will be gone some time. Possibly hours. Continue translating. Throughout the night if need be. I want to know if there is anything else in those texts beyond what you already discovered or Henlester confirmed, yes? Particulars about what Cynead has achieved, or even hints. Any reference to how it could be undone. Weapons like Bloodsounder. Any of it."

I sat down at the table. "Of course."

"Very good." He started toward his chamber but I called out, "Captain?"

I expected irritation, but instead he simply turned around and gave me a level look. "Archivist?"

"I. . . we are in some trouble here, aren't we?" I tried to keep any fear out of my voice. "What I mean is, everything that happened today, it—"

"Does not bode well for us, no. But we have a diminished but still formidable ally in the deposed Emperor, and confederates in some of the other Towers who questioned Cynead and his agenda. And that was before today. While the Emperor has appropriated something exceptional today, he did so at great cost—even staunch supporters are likely to chafe at having their own potency abruptly amputated." He gave what was likely intended to be a reassuring smile, though it was far too twitchy to accomplish that. "Do not despair, Arki. We are not lost. Yet." Then he winked and walked into his chamber, calling out over his shoulder. "Rouse me when it is time."

As ever, I was amazed and envious of his ability to rest when things were at their most turbulent. I had no interest in looking through those dusty tomes just then, but it was an order, not a request, and I hoped it would prove a distraction from thinking on precipices, betrayals, and vengeful mighty monarchs.

So I opened my writing case, unlocked the chest, and continued where I'd left off, doing my best to focus.

When the slave boy summoned Braylar an hour later, I hadn't made much progress, and certainly hadn't uncovered anything new. But after he left, it wasn't long before I encountered more absorbing information. And as the hours wore on and the tallow candle burned low, and my food came and grew cold, mostly untouched as I was so excited, I uncovered still more.

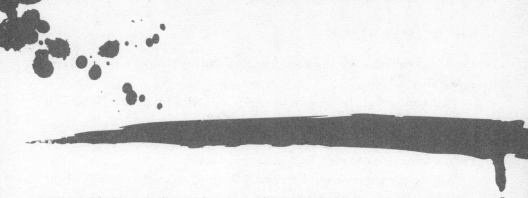

I was shaken awake, and not gently. Opening my eyes, disoriented, I found myself asleep on the table, a puddle of drool by my mouth, a page stuck to my lip. The other pages and inkwell were still in front of me, the quill still in my hand, fingers stained, muscles cramping, everything between my temples pounding.

Braylar rapped on the table, doing my head no favors as I slowly lifted it up. "Pack your things. We go."

"Go?" I asked, wiping off my mouth and looking out the window. It was the middle of the night, or at least not dawn yet. "Where? Why? What's happened?"

"I will explain as we move. Pack your things. Now. We won't be returning, so leave nothing behind."

I stood up, reeling, feeling almost drunk. Eating might have helped. I took a drink of warm water out of my cup. "Not returning? I don't—"

But the captain had gone into his chamber and either didn't hear me or was in no mood to answer. It was only when he came back out that I noticed he was in full armor from head to toe, the splinted vambraces, mail byrnie, lamellar cuirass, weapons belts. He had his helm with the aventail in the crook of his arm, and of course Bloodsounder at his side.

I was folding up my writing case and stopped. "I discovered something!"

"I do hope it was a sense of urgency."

"What? No. In the texts! I read throughout the night—"

"So I gathered."

"And there were three more references to Sentries, to weapons like Bloodsounder."

Braylar stopped by the door, turned and looked at me. "*Presumably* like Bloodsounder. We have no proof."

"No," I admitted. "But the Emperor didn't have any proof that whatever rites or rituals he discovered in his texts about syphoning control of the Memoridons worked either, but they did. And now he does. Have proof, that is."

He considered that briefly. "So then, out with it, quickly. What is it you think you've discovered?"

I started going through my notes, flipping over parchment and scanning, and he stopped me. "Quick. Ly. Summarize."

Putting the pages down, I replied, "Well, remember I mentioned the guardians disappeared from the temples, taking the weapons with them."

"I do. And I remember telling you they more likely died or got lost in a bog."

"Well, there are two accounts in here of guardians who returned. After crossing the Godveil."

I waited for that to sink in, elicit some kind of reaction. I might as well have been talking to his helm. "And this is proof of something how, exactly? Tales recorded by ale-addled priests or foolish boys. Nothing more."

"Perhaps. Always possible. But in one account, there were a dozen witnesses, notarized in the record, who watched the guardian, Frustwin, pass through, return for a time, but also cross back over. Only when he did, he took one of the underpriests with him."

Braylar did seem taken aback by that. If only slightly. "With him? How?"

"The sentry. The weapon. It was some kind of key, and it protected the guardian and the underpriest. They both passed through the Veil. Neither died."

He twitch-sneered. "According to the tale, which was likely found between bestiaries full of goblins and a tome of prophecies that failed to come true."

"According to the notarized tale that was sanctioned and included in formal temple records."

"And when he allegedly returned the first time in front of all these witnesses, is there a narrative of what he claims to have seen on the other side?"

I hedged. "There was. Though it was confusing. The temple guardian was overcome by fervor or fever or—"

"Unadulterated madness. Or the person who jotted down this episode was. Anything else?"

"You did ask me to look for references like this, Captain. I am simply recording what you ordered me to. And while it isn't conclusive of anything—"

"Anything. Else."

I sighed. "Yes, actually. There was another priest named Vortniss who must have come across Anroviak's writing, or Untwik's. And while he lacked the zeal and obsession with the subject, was actively skeptical in fact—"

"A healthy perspective."

"Vortniss was still gripped by what he discovered. And he continued hunting for any similar evidence of controlling memory witches. He made it sound like an academic exercise, or indulgence he allowed himself, but it was clear the more he compiled, the more invested he was. And while the memoir is incomplete, it sounds as if he was on the brink of creating something, building on what Untwik discovered, or maybe inspired by something else—there aren't enough details. But he mentions "frames" several times. And—"

"Plural?" Braylar narrowed his eyes. "Frames? You are certain?"

"Yes. Well, as certain as I can be. I would like to go through it more closely, and I would really like to find the remainder of that memoir."

"Now that is interesting." Braylar pulled the door open. "But we have a road to ride. Gather your satchel and case. Lock everything down tight. Syldoon will transport the chests to the wagon. Meet me in the stables. We leave."

And with that, he was gone. I continued packing up my things, shaking my head. Such a meager collection. Even journeyman craftsmen had more to carry on their backs than I did. It seemed whenever I began thinking I was going to settle down somewhere for a prolonged length of time, it was proven illusory faster each time. The idea of settling in Sunwrack as a complete outsider was daunting, and not an especially pleasant prospect, but I assumed that was going to be my life for the foreseeable future, at least until the captain and his crew were sent on campaign somewhere. I never imagined that would happen less than a tenday after arriving, and possibly permanently.

Now. . . leaving without changing clothes more than a few times, we were heading into a dark and uncertain future that surely didn't bode well.

When it came to the Syldoon, I simply needed to stop forming expectations at all. No matter what, they were destined to be thwarted.

⊕

I arrived in the extensive stables, expecting to see Braylar and his small retinue, but instead found what must have been close to one hundred Syldoon in armor with their horses saddled, grooms running everywhere, and several wagons harnessed to teams of horses. Wherever we were going, it was a lot of us.

Vendurro hunched down as he stepped out of the covered portion of a wagon, hailed me, and then sat on the bench in front.

As I walked over, I noticed there were only a few lanterns lit in the very back of the stables, and immediately thought about the eyes that might be on us right now. If we weren't doing anything illicit, we were at least being awfully secretive. Which seemed perfectly appropriate for the Jackal Tower.

And perfectly likely to get us all killed.

I climbed up and sat down next to Vendurro. He bit a boiled egg in half, offered me one with the shell still on it. Starving, I took it and started peeling. "What is going on here? The captain wasn't especially forthcoming."

"No," he replied, spewing bits of yolk. "Forthcoming ain't really Cap's thing."

"He only said we were leaving, and it sounded pretty final."

"Expect it would." Vendurro plopped the other half in his mouth.

"So it's true? We're leaving Sunwrack for good?"

"It ain't false." He managed not to spray any more egg at me.

I took a bite. Could do with some salt. Amazing that I could think about that when Jackal Tower could be crashing down around us at any moment. "So, what *is* happening? You are nearly as bad as the captain."

Vendurro laughed, dusted his hands off on his knees. "Captains convened last night. That knowing look on your face tells me you knew that already."

It was also amazing he could joke when our lives might again be hanging in the balance. He continued, "Commander Darzaak ordered Cap and a good chunk of his men out of Sunwrack."

I looked up and down the stables again, calculating. "How many?"

"Well, small portion, really. Couple hundred."

"That's *small?*"

"Ayyup. Cap commands a thousand in the Tower."

I had never asked, but it made sense, given how few captains Commander Darzaak had brought with him to the Caucus yesterday.

Vendurro winked. "Don't call the rank 'Captain of a Thousand' for nothing."

"But why is he, why are we, being sent off?"

"Protect Cap, for one. Keep Cynead from digging his claws in. And get word to Thumaar, for two. Commander figures Cap can do more good out there then being husked out here by Memoridons."

"But Emperor Cynead—"

"Will think he fled, instead of turning hisself over for experiments or whatnot. Commander's going to disavow Cap. Brand him deserter. Send a hunting party after us. Hopes to stall for time."

"What if Cynead blames the Commander, assumes he was complicit?"

Vendurro nodded a couple of times. "Ayyup. That's a possibility, sure as spit. Mulldoos was there, tried to light a fire under the notion we all ought to clear out now, before Cynead turns everything he got against us, wipes the Jackals out. Some support for that, but not enough."

That was a bold move, to be certain, maybe unheard of, but not without dangerous merit as well. "Why not?"

"Jackal Tower is eight thousand strong. Just Syldoon, not counting servants and slaves. Commander figures even if Cynead is all too sure of hisself just now, and not like to expect a whole Tower to break free, moving that many troops, supplies. . . Wouldn't make it halfway to the gates before the Imperial troops and Memoridons came out in force, routed us. Best bet is to sit tight, try to find a way to unravel what Cynead done, and hope Thumaar can make a play when we do."

I looked around at Braylar's men as they made the last of their preparations. I was accustomed to his retinue and smallish company, so this force did seem sizable. But against the Imperial forces out there in the city somewhere, only a pittance. "How many men does Cynead have in Sunwrack?" I asked, not wanting to know the answer at all.

Vendurro stopped, just about to throw another boiled egg in his mouth. "Hmmm. Fifty, maybe sixty thousand."

Yes, if Cynead got wind we were fleeing the city, we would be annihilated. Immediately. Utterly.

Captain Killcoin rode in front of our wagon, called out to the nearest men, "We head for the eastern gate. If we encounter any Leopards or city watch that bar our way, we ride over them. If we cannot for any reason, we break for the northern gate. One way or the other, we win free of Sunwrack today. We win free. I gave you all the option to stay or to ride with me, and yet to a man, here you are. You are all fools, to be certain, but I am honored to be in your company." That earned some chuckles and Braylar patted the quiver alongside his saddle. "It is a good day for cross-bows, Syldoon. A very good day." Then he smiled and pulled his helmet on, spreading the mail out on his shoulders and reaching underneath to buckle the helm tight.

Vendurro turned to me. "Best get in the back of the rig, Arki. Hope-fully, we won't get into any scrapes, but if we do, safer in there. Little, anyway. Stuff to take cover behind at least."

I pulled the flap back, saw the crossbow and quiver of bolts, leaned in and pulled them to me. Vendurro got the team moving as I spanned the crossbow, then slapped the folding devil's claw on the stock. "I may not be a crack shot, but if we get into any scrapes, I'll be right here, shooting in the general direction of the enemy."

He laughed, and that made my bravado feel a little less foolish. "Suit yourself. Though next time, we might need to kit you in a gambeson or boiled leather at least. That tunic's not like to stop any kind of anything."

Captain Killcoin and his two lieutenants led the way and we rolled out of the stables, with four dozen horsemen in front of us, some more wagons behind, and the remainder of the company following.

Dawn was nearly upon us, the clouds above the high outer wall of Sun-wrack long and thin and fissured with the first hints of peach and salmon and scarlet. The only thing that wrecked the beauty of it was the wafting manure from the stables and the fact that we could all die very soon.

Our convoy made its way down the Avenue of Towers for a few blocks, but turned down a narrow street, no doubt not trusting several of the Towers we might encounter along the way. The last time we rode out at dawn, it was to ambush Hornmen in Alespell. Now, we were hoping to move unmolested through a city three times that size and avoid ambush ourselves. It was difficult not to long for the bad but not horrific odds of hunting Hornmen, especially as we had no ripper or Memoridons now.

The clomping of horseshoes and rolling of steel-rimmed wagon wheels sounded obscenely loud in the silence of the nearly deserted streets. Here and there we came across some Thurvacians, three stumbling home from a whorehouse that was leaning so much it looked ready to topple itself; a pair carrying some wooden cages filled with chickens, feathers trailing behind; two beggars on the steps of a building, arguing about something in some dialect I had never heard before; a poacher who was dragging a dead bull crab by one claw and ran into an alley with it as we approached. There were merchants of all kinds opening shops as well, setting up small bazaars, and probably burglars skulking in the shadows, but most Thurvacians ignored us, accustomed to the military might that rode or walked through their city at all hours. My heart beat faster as twice we ran into a pair of town guards, but if they thought anything was amiss, they gave no sign.

We turned down another street, heading east again, toward the gate, and while it was still a ways off, I began to hope we might actually clear Sunwrack without incident. As we passed through a huge stone arch I felt something drip on me and looked up to see the aqueduct that crossed the street high above, and I was about to say something to Vendurro when I heard the commotion ahead. The horsemen with crossbows had them up, loosing them at something ahead of us. I found myself standing, holding on to the bench. Much further up the street, there was a line of Imperial foot soldiers, armed and armored like those in the hippodrome, with banded mail, long shields and spears, and the combined quivers and bowcases on their hips. The composite bows were all in hand now though, and the Imperial troops were shooting more quickly than Braylar's troops could manage, the arrows striking several horses and riders in the front ranks.

One arrow flew right over us, and Vendurro pulled me back on my seat and got the team moving fast. The riders immediately in front of us turned down a side street and we followed, and I lost sight of Braylar's men, who were holding off the Imperial infantry as we raced ahead, the horses galloping now, our wagon jumping and rocking on its springs as we picked up speed.

Ahead, I saw arrows flying down a cross street, and then a Jackal horseman came galloping round the corner, the rider with an arrow sticking through his upper arm. We slowed enough for him to report to Braylar, who then shouted an order back, relayed several times. There were more

Imperials marching in our direction down that street, and we couldn't afford to get flanked. We were to continue riding hard, at speed.

The company set off again, arrows flying as each horseman passed the side street, and I hazarded a look—another battalion of Imperial infantry were lined up, shooting at each of us as we crossed in front of them.

An arrow thunked into the wagon a few feet behind me and another tore through the canvas covering, and then the Imperials were gone. I realized that it happened so fast, I flinched after the side street was behind us. At least our horses hadn't been struck. Or us. I was closest, and armored in linen.

I turned to Vendurro. "Will we make it? To the gates? Will they be closed?"

His jaw was set as he hunched over, holding tight to the reins. "Can't say, can't say, and can't say."

We passed two more side streets and there were no more injured scouts or Imperials shooting at us. We were on horse and wagons and so far the Imperials were all on foot. Maybe we could outdistance any warning. Maybe we could still ride clear.

After another scout joined us, reporting something to Braylar, he led our convoy down the next side street, heading toward the eastern gate. And directly into a much larger group of Imperials a hundred yards ahead. There were several lines of infantry with bows and spears in a phalanx, and a dozen cavalry as well, one holding the double Sun and Leopard standard. There were also two Memoridons on horses in front of the soldiers. Both had scale corselets on, one with short blonde hair, the other with a crimson cloak, wielding a ranseur with what appeared to be a red tassel.

Rusejenna. Soffjian. We were doomed.

Braylar called a halt. Two scouts raced past us on either side of the wagon, one still bleeding around the arrow in his arm. They reported to Braylar and his lieutenants. The captain turned his horse in circles, looked back past the convoy and behind us. I craned and looked down the side of the wagon as well. They were still at least three or four hundred yards out, but there was a large battalion of Imperial footmen, and they were marching for us.

Vendurro was doing the same on the other side, then sat again and drove his fist into the bench. "Guessing that answers your questions, bookmaster. Not making it to the plaguing gate."

We might have been able to fight through men alone, despite bad odds—Braylar had survived worse before—but taking on two war Memoridons as well. . . ?

No. We were captured or dead men. Knowing Braylar, likely dead. I imagined the order for a mad charge at any moment.

The Imperials hadn't begun loosing arrows at us yet. Then Rusejenna rode her horse down the middle of the street toward us. Very deliberately. Clearly savoring the moment. She might not dance to the captain's tears, but she was obviously the victor, and in no hurry to see it end.

I expected Braylar to order one of his men to shoot at her, or do it himself, but perhaps he was unwilling to allow his entire company to be slaughtered, as no bolts flew. Instead, the captain, Hewspear, and Mulldoos rode out to parley, crossbows hanging from their saddles.

Rusejenna stopped, waiting for the three of them to approach. When they were fifteen paces away, she raised her hand and the Syldoon halted as well.

Vendurro slammed his hand into the wagon again. "Plague me. Didn't even make it to the plaguing gates. Can't believe Cap is giving hisself over. Better to die fighting then hung from. . . " He stopped, leaned forward. "Plague. Me."

Rusejenna was gesturing at the Imperial phalanx behind her when Soffjian spun her horse around and faced the lines of soldiers, arms outstretched. Even from so far away, I thought I saw the warping around her splayed hands, and before the Imperials could draw their bows she had used her memory magic on them. They were falling, staggering into each other, the lines breaking apart, as dozens of men were wracked by whatever unseen thing she'd done to them.

The captain and his lieutenants kicked their heels in, tried to close the distance to Rusejenna, drawing their weapons. But the Memoridon was already turning back to them, got her arms up. Hewspear dropped his slashing spear, fell over against his horse's neck as he rode past her and Mulldoos didn't even manage that, falling out of the saddle, hitting the ground hard, rolling once onto his stomach, hands on his helmet.

But Braylar was completely unaffected. Rusejenna pushed out at him with both arms, focused everything on him, but it did no good at all—whatever sorcery she worked on the lieutenants failed on him. And then he was on her, Bloodsounder whipping around, the flail heads arcing out, the Deserters taking off nearly half her head as he rode past. She dropped from the saddle, the last movement she would ever make.

The captain beckoned us on, and our convoy was moving forward again. I looked behind us, and the Imperials were marching, drawing their bows from their quivers, but they were on the edge of bow range and still moving closer. We started forward as the captain rode up to Hewspear, grabbed his horse's bridle, led him to our wagon, and ordered two Syldoon to get him inside. I looked back as they did—Hewspear was stunned and dazed, but could sit up, though barely, with his chin on his chest. Two more Syldoon got Mulldoos to his feet ahead of us, and while he walked drunkenly for a few steps, he was able to climb back into the saddle, cursing when they offered assistance, but still shaking his head and wobbling, and favoring one side of his body.

Down the street, Soffjian was gone but some of the Imperial Syldoon that hadn't been completely blinded or incapacitated were forming back up, and Braylar's company charged, loosing crossbows first and then drawing their other weapons. The Imperials didn't have the men or time to reform a phalanx, but they did their best at small impromptu shield walls here and there, their long spears angling out.

One Jackal Syldoon took a spear in the chest and was vaulted out of the saddle right into the overlapping shields, and another had his horse speared out from underneath him and went rolling across the stones, trampled under the Jackal horse behind him. But the other Jackals made it past the spear points, knocked men over, hooves smashing, swords and axes and maces bashing and cleaving the small pockets of Imperials out of the way.

When Vendurro drove our wagon through, we rolled over a body and I nearly flew from my seat. An Imperial on my side pivoted, shield up, the spear tip coming at me. It struck the bench right behind me and I trained my crossbow and loosed. The bolt struck him in the face, and he staggered back and fell as we raced past.

"Nice one!" Vendurro hit me in the arm. "Next time, try shooting the whoreson before he has a chance to stab you though. Reload."

I looked at him for a moment, then grabbed another bolt as we rounded a corner, nearly running down a Thurvacian carrying a wicker basket on his head.

"Out of the way, you dumb bastard! Jackals coming through!" Vendurro laughed, laughed like a madman, and I felt myself giggling as well.

And then the stunning dawn clouds were more visible everywhere as this street was wider, the buildings crowding less of the sky. And the immense wall and the eastern gates were before us. The captain slowed, arm raised, and our entire group followed his lead. There were far more civilians about now, their bright colored coats and long tunics everywhere, some leaving the city, others coming in, so the portcullises were up. And it was early still, so the path wouldn't be congested.

The eastern gate. The sun rising before us. Surely that was a good sign.

I glanced around the wagon and looked back—the Imperial infantry were nowhere to be seen. We had a chance.

Our company rode forward, Thurvacians turning to object as they were driven aside, until they saw not only Syldoon soldiers, but several covered in their own blood or someone else's.

We crossed the small plaza just before the gate, riding into the shadow of the wall. I glanced up at the wooden hoardings that lined the top of the high walls, and imagined rocks or boiling water dropping out of the trap doors above us. I started to look behind us again when Vendurro hit me in the arm. "Easy does it, Arki. And point that bolter downside, would you? You shoot a Syldoon in a gatehouse on accident, we ain't never seeing the other side."

I did as he ordered, watching as Braylar rode briskly up to the first gatehouse. He spoke to a guardsman, pointing back toward the middle of Sunwrack, then gesturing in the direction of the bridge, the other gatehouses.

The guard nodded, stepped back, sent another guard running to the next gatehouse on the bridge. Then he barked at some Thurvacians to get out of our way, and waved us through. Our company rode and rolled along through the next two gatehouses without any problem, despite the fact that the Jackals had clearly just been in combat of some kind. Perhaps given that it was the Capital of Coups, guards were used to bloodletting occurring by armed bands in Sunwrack, or maybe the guards were from a Tower affiliated with the Jackals.

No matter the cause, we were three quarters of the way across when we heard commotion behind us. I looked, despite Vendurro hitting me in the arm again, and saw the Imperial troops at the first gatehouse, the Sun and Leopard standard held aloft.

A few moments later, a horn sounded, and Braylar shouted, "Ride, you whoresons! Ride!"

We were off again, the wagon bouncing, rocking, and I nearly bit my tongue in half as we hit a divot in the stone bridge. Arrows started coming down from the gatehouse behind us as well as the final one in front. I looked up, saw Syldoon scrambling along the ramparts, shouting orders, and then heard a horrible grinding sound. The bridge was shifting underneath us, being winched away toward either tower, rolling away from the middle. The Jackals whipped their horses, and Vendurro snapped the reins on our team, and we plummeted forward, arrows raining down, two or three tearing into the back of the wagon. Syldoon were loosing crossbows up at both gatetowers, and I did the same, watching my bolt ricochet off the stone, but maybe keeping an archer from shooting another Jackal down.

I heard the portcullis winch free behind us after we rode through the last gate and made it to the solid ground surrounding Sunwrack. We kept riding down the road until we were out of bowshot. Braylar looked back at the bridge—while a good number of our company had escaped, more than a dozen Jackal soldiers were trapped, the bridge being rolled out from underneath their horse's hooves, arrows picking them off as they rode away from the opening in the middle, toward the portcullis on either side. Even well armored, there were simply too many arrows and nowhere to go. Horses were shot out from underneath them, and Jackals were cut down one by one, or fell into the chasm as the bridge rolled further into the gatetowers.

We were all watching, helpless to do anything, when I heard a muted whump and then a strange keening whistling sound. I looked everywhere before seeing the trebuchet missile flying down from high in the sky. The huge stone struck the earth twenty yards away and bounced several times in the distance. If it had been on target it would have destroyed the wagons, crushed men or horses into red sludge.

Mulldoos was still sitting oddly in the saddle, one shoulder more hunched than the other, body twisted somewhat, and when he pulled his helm off his head, I saw one eyelid drooping, and when he spoke it was through half his mouth, the other half almost paralyzed. "Best clear out, Cap." He might have said more until he realized how stricken he was.

Captain Killcoin looked around at our bruised, bloodied, and battered company, his face still obscured by mail. We'd lost at least two dozen men. Maybe more. Though I couldn't see the captain's expression, I could feel the fury as he called out, "We ride for Thumaar. We can lick our wounds when we are well away from here. Take a final look. If we ever set foot in Sunwrack again, it will be as conquerors."

He turned his horse around and rode off, and we followed into an indeterminate future, deserters from the Empire, very likely to be hunted by an Emperor who now commanded the mightiest armies and Memoridons the world had ever seen.

We rode hard for much of the day, stopping to feed and water the horses only briefly before moving off again. Even with the wagons slowing our pace, I still worried the beasts might come up lame or blown. Clearly, though, the Syldoon knew their horses better than I did and just how hard they could push them.

I left the bench frequently to check on Hewspear, but he was unresponsive each time, in the same position, chin on his chest, breath shallow, body stiff. He refused food and my attempts to give him water only ended with a wet beard. Whenever I returned to the front, Vendurro gave me a hopeful look, which soured as I shook my head.

Several times I found myself craning around the edge of the wagon and looking at what remained of our convoy, wondering if Imperial troops were thundering down the road after us, but scouts reported no immediate pursuit.

Vendurro hardly spoke at all during the ride, but my anxiety must have been palpable, because after seeing me look behind us for the tenth time, he said, "Got a few things working in our favor, bookmaster. Cynead must have figured those battalions and Memoridons would take us clean in Sunwrack, didn't have a hunting party ready to come after us. So we got a lead. That, and must have been survivors to report Soffjian turning on them, so they probably figure she's riding with us. Which she ain't, of course. But they don't know that."

"And she is a power to be reckoned with."

"Ayyup, going to be real careful on how they decide to try to run us to ground. Emperor's got soldiers and war Memoridons to throw at us, but got to figure he won't be rash about it neither. Even without Cap's sister, they got Memoridons who can track us, so no fire on their horses' tails. They might even figure we could lead them to Thumaar."

I sat back against the bench, took a deep breath that didn't relax me at all. "And the third thing?"

"Third?"

"You said 'a few things in our favor.'"

"So I did. Misspoke then. Just the two, really. Bought us a little time, is all. But still, better than being a corpse at the bottom of the Trench."

We lapsed into silence after that, Vendurro probably thinking about nothing except all the Jackals who fell to their deaths or were shot out of their saddles that morning, me trying to think of anything but them and failing most of the time, and when I did succeed, it was only to meditate on the false Skeelana, or the fact that we were all fugitives now, and likely doomed. It felt a mercy when we finally stopped for the night with the moon high and bright in the cloudless sky.

I offered to help Vendurro with the horses, but he seemed eager for a distraction and said he would take care of them on his own after he looked in on Hewspear.

After forcing cold food into my belly, I got down and stretched my legs, staying clear of the rest of the Syldoon. I only recognized a few soldiers here and there, and each time they were part of sullen, silent groups that were making camp for the night. Simply walking near them, I felt intrusive. I saw Mulldoos off to himself, cursing loudly as he struggled with his horse's harness, tripping and nearly falling, one eye full of murder, the other noticeably drooping. I moved away quickly, giving him an even wider berth than usual. Even as damaged as he was, he could easily kill me with one arm, and it would take nothing to provoke him now.

I was about to return to the wagon when I spotted a solitary figure out in a field, armor winking under the moon. Though I could sense the rage radiating even from a distance, I chose to cautiously approach. I stopped several feet behind him, suddenly wondering at the wisdom of seeking him out when the captain said, "I imagine the only way you would be disturbing me right now is if you translated the means of binding every Memoridon in Sunwrack to us, or striking the Emperor dead on the spot. Surely you would not risk my wrath with anything less momentous than that. Surely. So what marvels have you unveiled, Arki? Regale me. Astound me. I beg of you."

"I. . . that is—"

"No?" Braylar kept his back to me. "I thought not. Away with you then."

Perhaps I should have heeded his warning. But I suddenly had so many questions swirling I couldn't contain them all. "When Rusejenna tried to fell you and failed, you were immune, protected somehow, weren't you? By Bloodsounder?"

He finally turned and faced me, his left hand on the haft of the flail, face lost in shadow but eyes hot. "*That* is what you want to speak to me about? How I survived unscathed when so many of my men did not?"

I changed tack as quickly as I could. "You knew that we were going to be betrayed, didn't you? That's why you didn't want Skeelana or your sister to know about Bloodsounder, or the scrolls, or—"

"Of course I knew we would be betrayed."

"Before we left this morning, did Bloodsounder—?"

"Betrayal was inevitable, you fool. Because of who we are. Just as we hoped to betray Cynead and rethrone Thumaar. We are Syldoon. It is our nature." He glared at me, voice suddenly hoarse, anger and frustration and bile borne on each word. "And that is precisely why I would rather have died than hand over Bloodsounder or anything else we uncovered to the Emperor. I believed we might have had the key to Cynead's defeat in our hands. *That* is why I gave the order to let no Memoridon into my head. *That* is why I wanted to strike you and Mulldoos and the rest down for failing to heed me. The fact that it was that little bitch Skeelana and not my own blood is immaterial—betrayal was inevitable, if our secrets were known. And not simply my life in the balance, but those of my men."

The captain took two steps toward me, and I had to force myself not to step away, as he seemed barely able to check his fury. "Every single one of my men who died like a dog today fleeing their city, and those who will likely die tomorrow and the next. All of us, my Tower, my commander, on a precipice now, because you and my officers ignored my explicit orders and *saved* me in that forsaken plague village."

There was nothing I could say to that. I couldn't even stammer. Braylar shook his head, turned away again, and slowly released his grip on

Bloodsounder. "Back to the wagon with you, archivist. Disturb me again at your peril."

He stalked off into the darkness, leaving me with my thoughts, my fears, and my remorse. Sparing the Hornman in the grass, sparing the captain's own life in the village of the dead—each time, I considered them compassionate acts, simply the right thing to do. I never imagined they could lead to tragedy and greater loss, compounded death and devastation.

That was a drastic failure of imagination.

Acknowledgements

As always, there are too many people to acknowledge and not enough words.

First and foremost, I have to thank my lovely wife, Kris. She has been steadfast and endlessly encouraging as I pursue this dream, and I couldn't ask for a greater inspiration. Plus she puts up with Pollacky mood swings, Woody Allenesque worrying, and more Salyards shenanigans than any one person deserves. I would not be here without her.

My agent, Michael Harriot, has always been a terrific sounding board and insightful beta reader, supplying savvy advice and terrific guidance at every turn, and talking me off more than one ledge along the way.

The folks at Skyhorse/Night Shade Books have been infinitely patient, putting up with my countless questions and suggestions, with Jason Katzman and Lauren Bernstein deserving a special shout out for bearing the brunt of it. There are surely a number of folks operating behind the scenes who I don't know by name, but I wish I did because I'm grateful to all their hard work and effort in making this book a reality.

My editor, Jeremy Lassen, provided fantastic suggestions that helped make *Veil of the Deserters* stronger (and whatever fault lines remain are my fault alone).

Michael C. Hayes did a wonderful job on the cover art, taking all the notes and arms and armor pics I bombarded him with and transforming them into something dynamic and engaging. And speaking of artists, Will

McAusland endured a ridiculous amount of feedback from me and took my chicken scratch rough art and created a marvelous map as well.

And of course I'm indebted to every reader who picks up *Veil of the Deserters*. There are a billion books out there, so thank you for choosing this one. I hope it serves you well.